THE ANCIENT FUTURE:
THE DARK AGE

THE ANCIENT FUTURE • BOOK ONE

TRACI HARDING

Voyager

An imprint of HarperCollins*Publishers*

Voyager
An imprint of HarperCollins*Publishers*, Australia

First published in 1996
This edition published in 2006
by HarperCollins*Publishers* Australia Pty Limited
ABN 36 009 913 517
www.harpercollins.com.au

HarperCollins*Publishers*
25 Ryde Road, Pymble, Sydney, NSW 2073, Australia
31 View Road, Glenfield, Auckland 10, New Zealand
77–85 Fulham Palace Road, London, W6 8JB, United Kingdom
2 Bloor Street East, 20th floor, Toronto, Ontario M4W 1A8, Canada
10 East 53rd Street, New York NY 10022, USA

National Library of Australia Cataloguing-in-Publication data:

Harding, Traci.
   The ancient future — the dark age.
   ISBN 0 7322 8374 4.
   I. Title
A823.3

Cover illustration by David Harding
Cover design by Natalie Winter, HarperCollins Design Studio
Maps and castle plans by David Harding
Typeset in 11/13.5 Goudy by Helen Beard, ECJ Australia Pty Limited
Printed and bound in Australia by Griffin Press on 50gsm Bulky News

5 4 3 2 1   06 07 08 09

TO SUE
FOR SHARING THE DREAM
ALL THESE YEARS

CONTENTS

ACKNOWLEDGMENTS

What is a storyteller without the captive imagination of an audience? I would, therefore, like to thank all the girls and boys who have been following this adventure since its conception, especially Karen and Lisa, whose enthusiasm encouraged me, chapter by chapter, to finish this work.

I praise the universe for the unconditional love and faith of my husband, David. His creative genius, and many a late night in front of the computer, produced the fabulous cover artwork for this book. This could not have been closer to what I'd envisaged if he'd taken the picture straight out of my head; the ability to read my mind is only one of the many reasons I married him.

My gratitude also goes to my father, Terry Ludgate, for his creative stimuli and ongoing support.

I am deeply indebted to my three fairy godmothers, for weaving their magic to make this book a reality. The first being my earthly mother, Toni Ludgate, for her neverending belief in me. Lynny Rainbow, for helping me to find the right connections. And Selwa Anthony, my agent, a godsend, not only to me, but to the entire Australian literary world.

Most of all I would like to express my heartfelt thanks to my editor, Susan Moran, to whom I dedicate this work. She took a thousand-page nightmare from me — a dyslexic with no spelling sense — and turned it into a beautiful read of which I am most proud. I could not have written this without her.

CHARACTERS OF THE DARK AGE

Heroine	Tory Alexander
Prince of Gwynedd	Maelgwn – 'The Dragon'
High Merlin	Taliesin Pen Beirdd
King of Gwynedd	Caswallon
Queen of Gwynedd	Sorcha
Brother of King	Cadfer
Sister of King	Lady Gladys
Brother of Maelgwn	Prince Caradoc
King of Powys	Chiglas
Princess of Powys	Vanora
King of Dumnonia	Catulus
Ruler of Dyfed	Vortipor
King of Gwent	Aurelius Caninus
Ruler of Dalriada	Fergus MacErc
Ruler of Merica	Ossa

MAIDENS AND LADIES

Tory's maid	Katren
Mute from Aberffraw	Ione
Vanora's maid	Malvina
Maiden at Aberffraw	Cara
Maiden at Aberffraw	Alma
Head maid, Aberffraw	Drusilla
Head maid, Degannwy	Fenalla
Rhys' wife	Jenovefa
Cedric's wife	Mabel
Proprietor of whorehouse	Old Hetty
Chiglas' crone	Mahaud

KПiGHTS AПD ADViSERS

Maelgwn's Champion	Calin Brockwell
King's Champion	Tiernan
Maelgwn's messenger	Cadogan
Maelgwn's keeper of records	Madoc
Maelgwn's watchman	Vaugnan
Maelgwn's cook	Jeven
Red-headed knight	Cedric
King's accountant	Percival
Trainer of armies, Aberffraw	Gilmore
Maelgwn's adviser	Rhys
Maelgwn's knight	Angus
Maelgwn's squire and musician	Selwyn
Maelgwn's second squire	Tadgh
Vortipor's Champion	Queron
Brockwell's son	Bryce
Maelgwn's son	Rhun
Rhys' son	Gawain

Britain 519 AD

Alban
The Picts

Dalriada
The Scots

Mon

Cumbria

Northumbria

Gwynedd

Powys

Mercia
The Saxons

Dyfed

The
Kings Men
Stones

Gwent
is Coed

Danes

Dumnoia
Exter

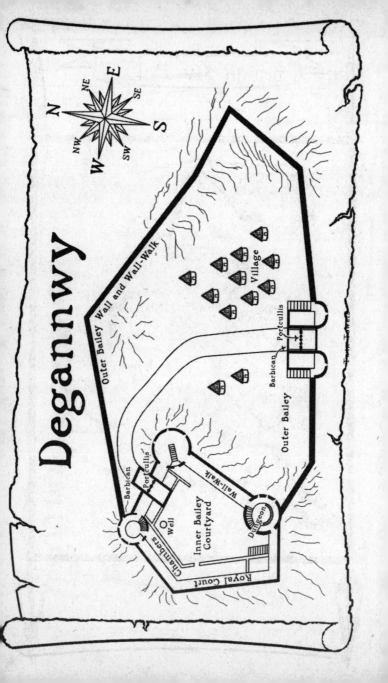

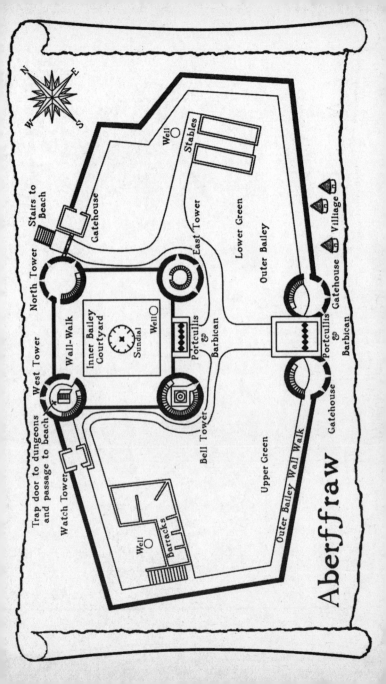

Aberffraw

PART ONE

TIME

I

THE STONES

As evening cast its shadow across the horizon, Tory secured the last nut and replaced the hubcap. She tilted back on her heels to admire her work when, out of the corner of her eye, she noticed that the back tyre was also losing air. 'Goddamn hire cars,' she cried, kicking the dying tyre with her steel-capped boot. 'I don't believe it!'

It was difficult to see how bad the puncture was as the old country road was poorly lit. Tory drew back her long hair and sighed, kissing goodbye to any chance of making it to her aunt's in Oxfordshire by dinner. Disheartened, she turned and lent on the car to mull over her problem.

The difference between a good situation and a bad one lay only in one's perception. The voice of her Sensei came into her thoughts.

It wasn't as if she was afraid to be in the countryside at night, for she was more than capable of protecting herself. Only a few months back she'd achieved her second Dan grade (black belt) in Tae-kwon-do. She'd also trained in kickboxing, a sport her brother, Brian, had encouraged her to pursue.

Brian had been Tory's driving force, her fiercest competitor and closest friend. Her recollection of the events that led to his death continued to plague her, though two years had passed since the tragedy.

On the final day of their first Dan grade competition, Brian and Tory had competed against strong opposition to secure the title in their respective weight classes. Brian had sustained a couple of bad strikes to the head, but the doctor who examined him afterwards gave him the all clear to go home. The next morning Tory found her brother dead. An autopsy determined the cause of death to be a subdural haematoma, which is swollen, bruised tissue that leads to a build up of pressure on the brain. The doctors compounded her family's distress by explaining that if this had been detected at the time of the injury, Brian might have been saved. Tory never competed again, and from then on she regarded the medical profession with considerable scepticism. Brian was gone and her family had to live with the knowledge that it didn't have to happen.

Tory's father Renford, a Welshman born and educated, was a professor of British history and language. He travelled the world lecturing at universities and was often called upon to investigate archeological finds.

Tory's mother, Helen, was a classical harpist of some merit, and was forever flying off to perform with one orchestra or another. These professional obligations sent her parents abroad soon after Brian's death. Tory had insisted on staying at home in Sydney as she wanted to finish her year at university. She spent most of her time on her own anyway, studying history, mythology, music, philosophy, metaphysics, and the like. Her father's knowledge of ancient languages had also ensured that Tory had a firm grasp of Brythanic (ancient Welsh) and Latin, in addition to the other languages she'd studied at university. Her parents had never pushed her into the workforce for they were well off and ardent students themselves.

Renford and Helen hated having to leave Tory on her own most of the year. So, out of fear that she would wind up a hermit, they suggested that a change of scenery might do her good. As her father's passion for his heritage had rubbed off on her over the years, Tory thought it high time she investigated Britain's historical sites for herself.

Tory glanced up at the encroaching night sky. She remembered seeing an inn on the corner as she'd turned off the highway, however that was quite a way back. She looked down the road in the other direction, but as there weren't any houses nearby, she considered the fence beside her.

The property was bordered by large trees, and as Tory approached them her heart began to pound in her chest. 'I don't believe it,' she uttered, as she saw a large circle of stones in the field beyond. She was tempted to investigate so she retrieved her backpack, shoulder bag and saxophone case, and locked up the car for the night.

The circle appeared to be at least a thirty metres in diameter, and Tory guessed there were about seventy stones. Some were much larger than others; the elements and humankind had taken their toll over the centuries of the circle's existence.

As she reached the perimeter of the circle a strong presence came over her and she stopped in her tracks. *How strange that I should find myself here tonight.* She was a little scared by this thought, for tonight was the summer solstice. When Tory recalled tales of Wiccan and Druidic practices traditionally held on this night a shiver ran over her.

She knelt down to retrieve her black leather jacket, the only possession of her brother's she had wanted to keep. Well known as Brian's lucky jacket, it was reinforced at the elbows and bore a large-winged Harley Davidson emblem on the back. It was also two sizes too large for her and very comfortable. As Tory felt the familiar safety of the jacket, she assured herself that it hadn't been fear that made her shiver, just the cool evening air.

She reached out to one of the taller stones and ran her fingers over its rough surface. She recalled stories of how these stones would go down to a brook to bathe at midnight on New Year's Eve ... *Or was it All Hallow's Eve?* It didn't matter, as for the Celts of old both days fell on the same date, October thirty-first, and were celebrated with a festival known as Samhain. Another story of how a witch had turned a king and his men to stone brought the name of the circle to mind, 'The King's Men, of course!' Tory turned to look out across the field behind her. Beyond she knew that there should be another small gathering of stones called 'The Whispering Knights', but they could not be seen from this distance. Across the road from the car, no doubt hidden by bushes, she would find the 'King Stone', set on a ridge looking to Long Crompton. This represented the king's wager with a witch that he could see the village from the ridge. It must have been bad weather because he obviously lost. The witch then turned all the knights to stone before turning herself into a tree. Well, at least I know where I am now, Tory thought.

Turning on her torch, Tory set about sorting through the clothes, books, sheet music and toiletries in her backpack in search of something to eat, rummaging amongst her CD Walkman and its speakers, her headphones, camera, spare film and batteries. It was a good thing Tory wasn't big on fashion as there was scarce room for any clothes. What she really felt like was a hamburger with fries and a Coke, yet all she managed to dig up was a half-eaten health slice, a bottle of water and a packet of unsalted cashews. It wasn't much but it was better than starving.

Tipping the last cashew out of the packet into her mouth, Tory stuffed her things back in her pack. She leant against a large rock and lit a joint that she'd rolled for the trip. 'Here I am getting high, at what some would consider a sacred site, on the night of the summer solstice, at . . .' She strained her eyes to check her watch, '. . . quarter to midnight.' Tory smiled, this was definitely not what she'd imagined she'd be doing this evening.

As she stood to face the circle again, she thought of all the celebrations that would be taking place tonight at the more public sacred sites like Glastonbury and Stonehenge. People would be performing old rites, dancing, singing and paying homage to the Goddess, that is, Mother Earth. Oddly enough, the atmosphere surrounding the stones no longer perturbed her. On the contrary, it seemed to welcome, even beckon her towards the centre. So she ventured into the middle, dragging her belongings along with her. 'Close enough.' Tory dropped her things where she stood and took off her boots. The potent energy of the place intrigued her, so she sat on the ground in the lotus position. The back of her hands rested gently on her knees and her thumb and middle finger met to form a circle, aiding the circulation of energy around her body. She closed her eyes and took three deep breaths, to achieve a relaxed, peaceful state.

Her attention was drawn to the sounds of little night creatures. She inhaled progressively deeper, focusing her thoughts on the hooting of an owl close by. Tory had become so engrossed with this sound that she did not notice the light around her growing steadily more intense. This often happened when she meditated; colours would emerge in her mind, intense colour at times, but never before had the light been so white for so long. She continued to breathe deeply, imagining that she was inhaling the brilliant white light throughout her body, and it filled her with a sense of strength and wellbeing.

The owl stopped hooting and Tory became aware of a faint humming, like the buzzing in your ears after a rock concert, only this was more melodic. It gradually increased in volume to the point where it bothered her and she was compelled to open her eyes.

The white light she thought she had imagined, truly surrounded her and appeared to be exuding from the ground within the circle. The mist rose towards the sky to form a large billowing cloud. From within the largest stone, a ball of blue light, no bigger than a coin, made its way towards her.

What is it? A fairy perhaps? She'd never actually seen one, so she couldn't dispel the possibility.

In her study of these stones, Tory recalled that scientists had documented sightings of this light phenomena. Some said it was caused by geological and electromagnetic factors, but the energy involved was so exotic that it was not yet understood. Others suggested that it could relate to consciousness itself, considering consciousness as a field effect; like actually seeing the equivalent of what the Chinese refer to as *Chi* energy.

The sound of laughter then began to filter through Tory's head and it sounded suspiciously male. This irked her and she looked around for its source. 'Is this some kind of elaborate hoax?' she asked.

The laughter rose again, only clearer now.

Tory drew herself up straight. 'Show yourself. I am not afraid.'

The light was still for a moment. Then in the blink of an eye it darted towards her, almost touching her forehead. Tory's limbs froze, and she began to feel faint as the light penetrated her skin.

2

TIME SHIFTS

Tory woke the next morning, bathed by the warmth of the sunshine. She squinted at the blue sky above, shielding her eyes from the glare, then stretched to relax the kinks in her body after sleeping on the hard earth.

The ball of light! She sat up so abruptly her head spun.

All her bags were accounted for, and as far as she could tell she hadn't been harmed in any way. 'Was that for real?' She rested her head in her hand, recalling the previous night.

Tory felt a gritty paint smeared on her brow and looked at her fingers that were smudged with blue. 'What the hell is this?' She pulled a small mirror from her backpack. Stamped on her brow was the image of a dragon. In Celtic mythology this symbol represented the guardian spirit of Ancient Britain. Why had she been marked with it? Tory decided that although it was rather cute, the dragon had to go. She began rummaging through her bag for a tissue when she remembered that they were in the glove compartment of the car. 'It's time I got moving anyway.'

It wasn't until Tory stood up that she realised there were a few things amiss. 'What's happened to the car?' She ran towards the road that was now nothing more than a dirt track. 'Where's the fence, and the road for that matter? What the hell's going on here?' She looked about her noticing that although the landscape was more or less the same, the landmarks had all changed. The trees not only differed in height and location but also in species, and there were many more of them.

'Stay calm,' she told herself. 'I'm sure there's a perfectly reasonable explanation.' But when Tory turned back towards her bags she was dumbstruck.

The stones, which had been crumbled and broken the day before, now stood over two metres tall and were fewer in number. The peace of the field enveloped her, there was no distant rumbling of traffic, no power-lines, planes, anything! Tory's mind went blank; she couldn't even begin to fathom the possibilities of what might have befallen her.

She became aware of a growing rumble. The ground beneath her began to vibrate before any sound reached her ears. In the distance she spied eight men on horseback, racing down across the open field towards her. She snapped out of her daze and pulled a cap from her bag to cover the mark on her forehead.

The men drew their horses to a halt outside the circle and were all, rather curiously, dressed in authentic suits of armour. I knew the Poms were old-fashioned, but this is ridiculous, she thought. 'Hey there, what's happening?' She waved in greeting as she walked casually towards the perimeter of the circle. Her greeting was not met with any reaction from the group, it was as if they hadn't understood a word she'd said.

'By the Goddess,' one of the knights exclaimed with playful delight. 'It be a woman.'

He wasn't speaking modern English, but what sounded like an obscure form of Welsh. Tory was able to discern this as Welsh and its ascendant Brythanic were like second languages to her. Her father's passion for the old tongues of his people was such that he persisted in using them most of the time.

Tory stopped some distance away from the men as they appeared a rather ominous bunch: unshaven and unwashed, their armour tainted with blood.

'What say thee, Majesty?' One of the younger men commented to the dark-haired man beside him. 'She be a feisty challenge, and I could use the exercise.' His request was met with much encouragement from his companions.

Tory didn't like his tone of voice, yet the word 'majesty' played on her mind. She turned to the one the young man had addressed thus; he did seem to possess a certain regal disposition that set him apart from the others. He sat quietly, observing Tory's attire with a very curious expression, before placing a hand on the young man's shoulder to advise him. 'This woman doth

13

employ a tongue and dress the like of none we have seen before. Caution Brockwell, a witch be said to haunt this place.'

'What!' Tory exclaimed.

'I am not afraid,' Brockwell said. 'If she be a witch, thou shalt have her head.'

The dark-haired man looked at Tory and, with some encouragement from the rest of the men, smiled to give Brockwell his consent.

The hair on the back of Tory's neck stood on end. She stepped away as Brockwell dismounted. *These guys are serious* . . . 'Now hold on,' Tory cried out. 'Could I speak to the man in charge for a moment, please?' She made her way towards them hoping to appease the situation.

'I would start running if I were thee.' Brockwell moved to intercept her.

'Brockwell, one moment,' the dark-haired man said, gravely. This woman bore a vague resemblance to his deceased mother, so he allowed her to voice her protest.

Tory nodded politely, grateful for the chance to reason with him. 'Why, may I ask, dost thou think me a witch?'

Brockwell began to answer but his superior held up a hand and replied, 'If thou art not a witch, then why dost thou appear so uncouth?'

'Uncouth!' she repeated. 'Ye all appear very strange to my eyes, I assure thee. Doth this mean that I should conclude that thou art involved in demonic practices and deserve to die? With no proof, no means to defend thyself.' Tory realised she was being a little over-dramatic, but she had him thinking. 'Be this thy concept of justice?'

Brockwell went for his sword. 'Who art thou to question a Prince of Gwynedd! I shall sever thy head from thy shoulders for such insolence.'

The Prince waved him to silence, but with a smile this time. 'Brockwell, I do believe I see her point.' He paused to consider her words. 'What dost thou suggest I do, give thee a weapon to slay one of my own men? This would seem rather absurd, would it not?' With this his men broke into laughter.

Tory held her tongue until they had finished. *They'll all be laughing on the other side of their faces by the time I'm finished with them.* 'May I suggest a solution that I consider to be fair?'

'Please,' the Prince implored her, rather intrigued by her manner.

'If thy friend here removes his sword and protective armour, I would like to fight him for safe passage.' Tory chose her words carefully. 'If thou art agreeable, I would consider that a good show.'

Again the Prince and his knights, including young Brockwell, fell about laughing. The Prince had to question this further. 'Am I to understand, that *thee* wishes to fight *Brockwell* with thy bare hands?'

Tory was not fazed and pretended to ignore their mocking good cheer. 'Why?' she asked, giving Brockwell the once over, 'dost thou not think him up to it?'

With this the Prince and his knights were beside themselves, however Brockwell's humour was dwindling. The Prince wiped a tear from his cheek as he caught his breath. 'I think it be only fair to warn thee, Brockwell be my champion, he hast never been defeated in game or battle.'

This announcement made Brockwell even more smug, and he stripped off his armour to reveal a sweaty, muscular body. His long dark hair, a mass of knotted curls, clung to his bare skin. He reminded Tory of her brother, as their eyes were the same piercing blue. He was no taller than her but looked to be twice her body weight in muscle alone. All the better, she concluded. It will slow him down.

'I am not worried,' Tory assured them.

'I can see that.' The Prince looked down at her, shaking his head. 'Still, I fear Brockwell will snap thy tiny frame like a twig.'

Tory found this comment rather charming and smiled as she reminded him, 'Only a moment ago thee gave Brockwell leave to violate me in whatever way he saw fit. Be there a difference?'

The Prince acknowledged this to be true, realising that he may have been a bit rash.

'She shall bewitch thee, Majesty. Speak to her no longer.' Brockwell stepped forward to draw the Prince's attention away from Tory. 'I am more than happy to rip her limb from limb with my bare hands.'

The Prince was now rather reluctant to give him leave, but his men would indeed think him bewitched if he did not. 'So be it.'

'*Safe* passage, remember.' Tory received a nod of confirmation from the Prince before she backed up to prepare herself. She took off her jacket and wrapped her hair quickly into a bun to prevent it from being pulled. *Where on earth am I?* Tory found some tape in her bag and bound her hands as she did for competition, managing the task within minutes. She decided she must find out who this prince claimed to be; if there was one thing she knew thoroughly it was British history.

She walked towards Brockwell and, after rolling up her sleeves, turned her cap around backwards so that she could see clearly. 'So, might I ask thy name before I meet my fate?' Tory said to the Prince.

'No Majesty. Do not answer.' Brockwell intervened, his fiery eyes fixed on Tory.

'I must also insist,' the eldest knight added.

The Prince was obliged to heed the advice of his men. 'Afterwards perhaps.'

'There will be no afterwards,' Brockwell assured him.

Tory pretended to be indifferent. 'Alright then, if that be the way of it.' She resumed her dry, confident tone of voice. 'I will just have to beat it out of thy boy here.'

Tory purposely turned her back on her opponent, walking slowly and confidently into the circle of stones to take her place. She could feel Brockwell's rage build to breaking point when she called him a boy, as this was obviously something he worked hard to disprove. Seconds later, and with a total disregard for chivalry, Brockwell came charging at her from behind. She stopped to time the impending impact and turned her body slightly to take the great weight of his body over her right shoulder.

He was mumbling something to the effect of, 'I will teach thee some respect . . .' before he'd even realised he was airborne.

Tory brought him crashing to the ground on his back. She went down on one knee and buried an elbow deep into his solar plexus before darting backwards to a safe distance.

It was clear that Brockwell had no idea what had happened. The other knights, who were laughing at Brockwell's misfortune, began teasing him from their mounts. 'Good show!' the Prince commented to Tory in encouragement, surprised that she was not dead already.

It didn't take Brockwell long to recover. He got back to his feet, and was seething with humiliation. 'I shall rip thy heart out and rape thee while thy body be still warm,' he taunted, stalking her.

Tory kept her humour. Brockwell was seeming more and more like her brother who had made worse threats over the years to frighten her into retreat. 'My, my, that be a vivid picture, still I do not think so somehow,' Tory replied. Brockwell lunged forward to grab her neck but she pulled his arms to either side of her, kneeing his stomach. This sent him stumbling backwards, and before he'd had a chance to recover, Tory spun a full 360 degrees to finish him off with a kick to the side of his head. Her adrenalin was pumping now and it felt good. She looked back to the Prince, who appeared rather wonderstruck. 'Champion indeed,' she said. 'What dost thou think, three points and I win?'

The Prince merely motioned behind her.

Tory turned to find Brockwell on his feet, blood oozing from the side of his face where her steel-capped boot had hit. With no time for her to fend off the blow, he punched her in exactly the same place, putting the full force of his body behind it. As she hit the ground it felt as if he had shattered her cheekbone. There is no pain, she told herself as she saw Brockwell approaching to finish her off.

'My dreams are filled with better than the likes of thee,' Brockwell spat in disgust, bending down to pull her to her feet.

Tory instinctively went into a tuck position. She grabbed hold of Brockwell's arms as he leant down, and used her feet to propel him over her and onto his back. She flipped herself onto her stomach, taking hold of Brockwell round the front of the neck to temporarily paralyse him by applying pressure to the vital points located there. She maintained a firm hold, pointing to the Prince with her free hand. 'Very soon he will be dead. Dost thou yield to spare this boy's life?'

Brockwell tried to shake loose of her grasp, his face red from the strain.

'I yield and pronounce thee victorious this day,' the Prince told her.

'And thy name?' Tory asked, as Brockwell began to squirm harder.

The eldest of the advisers whispered quietly to the Prince, 'Majesty, I beseech thee . . .'

'I swear I will kill him,' Tory yelled impatiently.

Little did she know that the life she held in her hand belonged not only to the Prince's Champion and best friend, but to his cousin who was a duke no less. The Prince was not about to let him die.

'I am Maelgwn, son of King Caswallon of Gwynedd,' he shouted. 'And if thee would kindly release my knight, I will be greatly indebted to thee.'

Tory let Brockwell go; it would take him at least a few minutes to recover. She got to her feet, her mind in motion. Maelgwn, a Welsh king, she recalled. Tory guessed him to be around the same age as herself. *Now then, when was he supposed to have been born? Around the late fifth century if memory serves.* 'So what year be this?' she asked. 'Around five twenty?'

The Prince, though surprised by the question, answered. 'Five nineteen, to be exact.'

Tory held her face where Brockwell had hit her. *Maelgwn, Maelgwn? Damn, what did they call him?* A cold chill ran down her spine as it dawned on her. 'Prince Maelgwn, Dragon of the Isle. I believe our meeting may have been intended.' Tory removed her cap to reveal the Dragon on her forehead. 'Recognise this?'

Upon seeing the mark there was a rumbling of discontent among the knights. The Prince, appearing a mite stunned himself, raised the shield from the side of his horse and turned it to face Tory; it bore the same Dragon.

Tory squealed with amazement. 'Dost thou know who put it there?' she asked.

'Nay, who?' the Prince mistook her meaning.

'Well, I am afraid I don't know,' she explained, mildly disappointed. Tory stopped mid-thought, feeling the cold steel of a sword at her throat; she could only assume Brockwell had recovered.

'No common woman possesses such skills, thou art in cahoots with demons.'

'I agree.' A heavyset, red-headed knight spoke up. 'Do it, Brockwell.'

'This doth not say much for thy word,' Tory squeezed out, looking to Maelgwn. She dared not move, to save cutting her own throat.

'Brockwell, withdraw thy sword,' Maelgwn ordered.

'But Majesty, hast she caused thee to take leave of thy senses. Did thee not see?'

'Calin!' Maelgwn's voice thundered, shocking Brockwell to silence. 'I ordered thee to yield!'

Tory was beginning to see why they called Maelgwn the Dragon. Brockwell reluctantly slid the sword away, making sure he nicked her neck in the process. She touched her throat to discover he'd drawn blood. 'Thee did that on purpose,' she accused him, angered by the scar it would leave.

'Aye.' He glared at her a moment, his wild blue eyes ablaze with hate and fear. He replaced his sword in its scabbard and moved to retrieve his armour.

'Majesty,' the eldest knight pointed behind them, where a single rider made haste towards the group.

'Now what?' Tory grumbled, nursing her wound.

'Cadogan,' the red-headed knight announced with good cheer, riding off to meet him halfway.

As the party seemed more interested in their comrade, Tory backed up quietly to collect her gear. Fairly confident that she knew where she was, she'd definitely decided that she wanted to be elsewhere. *Why me?* Tory slipped on her jacket and zipped it all the way up. *Because you always wanted to come here.* She hoisted on her backpack, looking over at the knights to see that the horseman had reached them.

A few torrid words passed between Cadogan and the others, before the Prince ordered them all to move out at once.

Something has got them worried. What would these men fear? Tory watched as the knights rode off ahead of the Prince who turned and rode towards her direction, his expression grave.

Brockwell, who had taken off after the others, pulled up when he noticed. 'Nay Majesty, please. She will only slow thee down.'

'I promised safe passage. I cannot leave her to Saxon mercy. Go with the others, I will catch thee up by nightfall.' Maelgwn was angry at his knight's incessant disrespect. He had his reasons for wanting to spare this girl and his decision would be questioned by none bar his father. 'Go!' He stressed the urgency.

The thundering sound of horses' hooves and wagons, perhaps hundreds of them, rose to a deafening roar as they approached from the hill behind them. Brockwell had to move now, or he would never make it round the ridge unseen.

'Saxons,' Tory whispered, knowing them to be one of the more barbaric tribes of the time.

'Climb on,' the Prince said. 'I shall take us around the other way, through the forest.'

Tory backed away; he was an important historical figure and she would not be responsible for getting him killed. 'Nay, thee will never outrun them with me . . .'

'Do not argue with me woman, get on,' the Prince snapped, short on patience and time.

The Saxon tribe emerged over the crest of the hill and a few of the riders bolted on ahead in pursuit of the Prince's party.

'They must have spotted Brockwell.' Tory took hold of the Prince's arm, and with one almighty heave Maelgwn lifted her, bags and all, onto the saddle behind him.

'Hold on,' he cautioned as he turned the horse around and headed off down the ridge towards the forest.

3

THE PACT

The Prince rode hard for well over an hour, but the forest had become so dense that he was forced to slow his steed down to a walking pace.

Tory wasn't too fond of horses and had found the ride a rather harrowing experience. Still, she was calm now, as she sat in silence, resting her head against her escort's back.

Her rest was interrupted as the horse came to an abrupt standstill. Tory opened her eyes and withdrew her arms from around the Prince. They had reached a stream, which was a welcome sight indeed for it had been a long time between drinks. The Prince threw a leg over the horse and slid off, turning to help Tory.

She could feel herself blushing; she'd never received this kind of treatment back home. Most of the guys Tory had hung out with were her brother's friends who'd never wasted any airs and graces on her. If they had, she probably would have found it patronising and decked them.

'I believe we have reached a safe distance,' he assured her, leading his horse to the stream.

When the Prince crouched down to take a drink, splashing his face and neck, Tory took off her cumbersome backpack and followed suit. The water relieved her aching cheek. Over the past few hours it had constantly reminded her of how cocky she'd been, and how stupid — turning her back on an opponent during a fight. The slice Brockwell had made on her neck stung like a paper cut, and became even more irritated when she washed it. Tory then let her hair loose and brushed out the knots, before tossing the brush back in her pack.

Only then did she notice that the Prince had taken a seat and was watching her with some amusement.

'Thou art so extraordinary,' Maelgwn said. 'By what name art thou known?'

'Tory Alexander,' she answered, feeling slightly embarrassed. 'Tory, to my friends.'

'And, where art thou from?'

This was a tricky question and she didn't want to pause too long to consider it, in case he thought she was concocting a lie. 'My home be far away, in a country known as Australia.'

The Prince seemed perplexed by her answer. 'Then how can it be that I, who consider myself to be fairly well learned, have no knowledge of this place? And how be it that thee speaks my tongue if thou art not from these parts?'

'Ah well, my country will not be discovered for another twelve hundred years. As for speaking thy tongue, my father teaches British history and language. He was born a Briton himself, or Welsh as they be known in my time.'

The Prince was taken aback a moment. 'Thou art from the future?'

'Indeed.' Tory looked him straight in the eye, hoping he wouldn't think her mad.

'What year doth thou claim to be from?' Maelgwn asked. 'The truth now,' he added firmly.

'I was born in the year nineteen sixty-six,' she began. 'Yesterday, for me, was the year nineteen ninety-three.'

The Prince rose in fury, his eyes wide with disbelief.

It was only now that Tory realised how tall he was. He stood at a little under two metres and towered over her. This was unusual for one of his race in this period in history, as most of the Britons were more akin to her height, as Brockwell was.

Tory held out her hand to calm him. 'I think I can prove it, if thee will just hear me out.'

Maelgwn was beginning to think his men were right about this girl; he didn't believe one word of her tale. Still, he was interested to see how far she'd go before he got the truth out of her. So he took a seat and beckoned to Tory to go ahead with her defence.

She smiled meekly and dived into her bag. *Thank you Mum, for giving me an instamatic.* Tory brought out the camera for his inspection, and the Prince reached for it.

26

'Careful,' Tory said, and he quickly withdrew his hands. This made her smile. 'It be harmless, I promise. Thee must just be careful not to drop it, as it be very fragile.' Tory offered it to him again.

Maelgwn looked over the camera, not game to touch it. 'Thee also appears fragile, yet thou hast quite a sting. Thou hast my leave to explain.'

'Okay.' Tory walked a few paces away and squatted down, looking at the Prince through the lens. 'This be a camera, it takes pictures.'

'It draws?'

'Sort of.' Tory glanced around to get a light reading. She didn't want to use the flash unless she had to, as no doubt it would startle him. 'It will be ready in just one moment.'

The Prince smiled, delighted at the thought. Just as Tory took the picture, however, he realised how preposterous it sounded and his stern expression returned.

'The smile looked better,' Tory informed him as the camera ejected the photograph. She gave it a couple of gentle blows then held it under her jacket to develop. 'Shan't be long, it has to sit in the dark for a moment.'

The very dubious Prince sat waiting with his arms folded. As she pulled the photo out to view, Tory broke into a huge smile. *My father would kill for this.*

'May I see?' Maelgwn's curiosity got the better of him.

'Only if thee promises I can keep it.'

A gentle smile graced his lips as he viewed the picture. 'Be this how I appear to thee? Thee must think me barbaric, like the Saxons.' He stroked his beard as if he'd only just noticed it was there.

'Not at all,' Tory smiled. 'I assure thee, I do not look my best either.' The Prince laughed and Tory felt the air of mistrust begin to lift.

'What else dost thou have in there? Show me more.'

Tory assembled her saxophone, an alto, and played a short, sultry piece that met with great approval from the Prince. Maelgwn loved the music of his court bards, and he found this high-pitched horn every bit as beautiful as the harp or pan flute.

Then, while Tory set up her CD Walkman and speakers, Maelgwn picked up one of the discs. He moved it to and fro, catching beams of sunlight which reflected a rainbow around the forest.

'Amazing, what does it do?'

'It plays music too.' Tory explained simply. 'Here.' She gestured to the disc in his hand.

Upon seeing the Prince's selection, a heavy metal album, she said, 'I don't think thou art quite ready for this just yet.' She flicked through her collection. 'I believe this may be more to thy taste.'

A soft piano piece began to fill the air, and the Prince stood astounded. 'By the Goddess! I have never heard the like.'

'It be piano,' Tory whispered, not wanting to break the mood she'd created.

The Prince closed his eyes and took a deep breath. 'It be the most beautiful music I have ever heard.'

The way he said this made Tory feel that this brief moment of pleasure was well needed. He wandered slowly around the small clearing, lost for a time in another world.

Could he possibly have something to do with my interest in this period of history? What if I never make it home? Will I again be born in the twentieth century to aimlessly search for information on the Dark Age, without a clue as to why?

Suddenly the Prince appeared disturbed, so Tory switched off the music. Now only the sounds of the forest could be heard. Maelgwn had drawn his sword and was watching the forest with caution. Tory remained low, even though she'd heard no sound out of the ordinary.

All was still a moment, then two bowmen emerged from the cover of the trees. There was little Maelgwn could do, his sword against two bows.

The pair yelled instructions in a Germanic tongue, and at a glance Tory guessed them to be outlaws. They were very fair haired and more primitive in appearance than any of the Britons she'd encountered thus far. These men were tall, but not as heavyset as Maelgwn's men.

The Prince dropped his sword as the bowmen ventured into the clearing. They circled him, gloating over their prize; they could see that he was a rich man. One stood back to cover their captive, while the more adventurous of the two approached Maelgwn to relieve him of his riches.

Tory took this as her cue and stood, letting loose a whistle to draw their attention.

It would seem the pair had been so focused on the Prince that they hadn't spotted Tory. The knave closest to the Prince was delighted at the discovery and stepped towards her.

Maelgwn had to smile at the two unsuspecting thieves. Tory noticed this and winked to assure him she had a plan.

The knave dropped his bow to take her in hand. He eyed her over, expressing his pleasure to his accomplice who sniggered in response.

Maelgwn took a step forward but the bowman interrupted any thoughts he may have had for her rescue.

As the man pulled Tory close to him, she could barely breathe for the stench of his body. *I'll die of suffocation.* He grasped her back with both hands and ground her against his groin; his legs were spread wide apart, as he was much taller than she. 'Perfect!' she whispered to her assailant and, gathering all the power she could muster, promptly kneed him in the groin. When the man keeled over she belted his face with her knee, so hard she broke his nose.

This distraction was all Maelgwn needed, and he reclaimed his sword to run the outlaw through. He turned to find the other knave out to settle the score with Tory. The Prince approached from behind and severed the man's head with one clean stroke of his blade.

Tory freaked as she watched the head roll across the ground; the man's body lay twitching where it fell. 'Art thou crazy!' she yelled, hysterical. 'I could have knocked him out or something, thee did not have to kill him.' She began to tremble from the shock and her stomach turned at the sight of so much blood.

Maelgwn didn't understand this at all. 'But he would have killed thee.'

She was going to be sick. 'I can take care of myself. What be wrong with you people?' She darted off into the bushes, leaving the Prince rather bemused.

By the time she'd returned the bodies had been dragged into the undergrowth. Maelgwn stood with the reins in his hand, ready to leave. Tory approached him, ashamed of her behaviour. 'I want to apologise, I did not mean . . .'

Maelgwn waved her to silence, tossing her an apple. 'If thou hast recovered, we should make haste to reach the others by nightfall.' He mounted his horse and smiled. 'Or Brockwell shall have the men believing thou hast turned me to stone.'

After clearing the forest, the terrain was more obliging and they travelled at a steady pace for the rest of the day.

The Prince slowed his horse to a stop on the crest of a hill. He spotted smoke from a camp fire and smiled, pleased that dinner would be well under way. 'Art thou hungry?' he asked Tory, who was dozing against his back.

She groaned in pleasure at the thought of food. 'I could eat a horse. No offence.' She patted the animal without moving her exhausted body.

'Well hopefully that shan't be necessary,' the Prince answered as they galloped down the hill.

The camp site was a hive of activity. A wild pig, slain by the warriors, was roasting over the fire. The

Prince's tent had been raised, and torches were lit around the encampment to discourage thieves. Most of the men had now settled by the fire, telling stories of their battles this day over much mead.

As the Prince rode into the camp, his men rushed to meet him. All except Brockwell, who appeared rather perturbed.

Madoc, the eldest amongst them, was the first to reach the Prince. 'Majesty, I shall never leave thy side again. I have been out of my mind with worry. What would I have told the King?'

Maelgwn dismounted in good cheer, the smell of pork filling his nostrils. He slapped his old companion on the back, assuring him. ''Twas no need to worry, Sir Madoc, I had Tory here to aid me.' Maelgwn turned to help her down, and no sooner had her feet hit the ground than Brockwell was in her face.

'Thou dost not belong here.'

Tory took a step back, holding her hand to her head. 'So the Saxons failed to catch thee, what a shame.'

Maelgwn intervened before the situation got out of hand. 'Brockwell, I swear this very day, I would have been murdered by thieves if not for the services of this gracious lady.' As Brockwell was about to protest, the Prince added staunchly, 'And I will not hear another word said against her.'

Brockwell glared at Tory a moment before withdrawing to the fire.

'So thou hast seen a bit of action, Sire?' a knight, roughly Maelgwn's age, inquired.

Tory noticed the man's steely blue eyes fixed on her. He was only of average build, but seemed a rather menacing character nevertheless.

The Prince took Tory by the arm and led her towards his tent. 'Cadogan, I have seen things this day I never before imagined.'

'Do tell, Majesty.' Cadogan smiled with open envy as he watched Tory disappear into the tent.

'Later,' the Prince said, closing the tent flap behind him.

Tory offloaded her bags and Maelgwn motioned her to a large fur on the ground.

'Rest, thou art safe here. I shall wake thee presently with food and drink.'

'Sounds marvellous,' Tory replied, crawling onto the thick fur rug.

Maelgwn freed himself from the confines of his armour, watching Tory while she rested. The candle beside her cast a light across the mark of the Dragon on her forehead and he studied it a moment. The Prince believed the story of Tory's origins, or at least he believed that she believed it. But if she was telling the truth, who had brought her back to this time and branded her with his mark? Was it sorcery or coincidence that she appeared so much like the late Queen of Gwynedd? There was only one man Maelgwn knew who had the knowledge and skill to carry out such a feat, but he had not seen the old wizard for over a decade.

Nevertheless, she was beautiful, the Prince concluded, when she was not conducting herself like a man. He made a mental note to inquire about her methods of fighting as he left to join his men outside.

Maelgwn gave Tory a nudge and she woke with a fright. 'Easy,' he said. 'Here, drink.' The Prince held out a horn full of liquid.

'I'm still here,' Tory grumbled as she sat up, rubbing her bruised cheek. 'No offence, but I had hoped it was just a bad dream.' She sighed and accepted his offering with thanks.

'I understand,' Maelgwn sympathised, watching her gulp down the mead.

Tory began to splutter and cough. 'Good grief!' She held her chest, trying to catch her breath. *What is it . . . 95 per cent proof?*

'Mead,' he said grinning, knowing full well it had quite a kick.

She stared at the warm brew. It reminded her of saki, only it was much sweeter, and on second taste she decided it was rather pleasant. The Prince handed her a large chunk of bread, crammed full of pork, which Tory accepted as if it were a jewel. 'Maelgwn, thou art a true legend, thank —' She clasped a hand to her mouth, realising she'd addressed the Prince by his first name.

Maelgwn just broke into laughter. 'Thou art most welcome.'

My, we are in good spirits, Tory observed. Maelgwn sat smiling, watching her eat. Tory found this rather offputting; it was as if he had something to say but couldn't come out with it. After a few minutes, she could stand it no more. 'So hast thou been speaking of me?'

'Aye.' He sounded perplexed. 'I told my men all I know and saw.'

'So?' Tory asked. 'What hast thou decided?'

'Well.' The Prince sat up straight. 'I would like thee to show my knights what thou hast shown me, so that they may decide for themselves.'

Tory considered his request and gave him a thumbs-up with her free hand.

Maelgwn presumed this meant yes, and so mimicked the gesture as he got to his feet. 'I will let them know, they will be most pleased.'

Left alone with her thoughts, Tory's heart sank as she cast her eyes around the tent. She had never before felt homesick, as she was well used to being separated from her parents. She had always taken it for granted that she would see them again. But now, who could say?

When Tory emerged from the tent with her bag of tricks, the Prince escorted her to the fire where the rest of the men had congregated.

Cadogan came forward to help Tory with her things. 'It would seem I have missed all the action this day,' he said, as he relieved her of the weighty backpack and looked to Maelgwn to be introduced.

'Tory, this be Sir Cadogan, my scout and messenger.'

Cadogan took up her free hand. 'At thy service.' He bowed forward to lightly kiss it.

Tory slid her hand away, wise to his type. 'Thanks, but no thanks,' she replied in the nicest possible way, reclaiming her backpack from him.

This brought a round of drunken laughter from the men. 'She be on to thy game, Cadogan,' called the red-headed knight with amusement.

Maelgwn was glad Tory wasn't so gullible as to fall for Cadogan's charms, and moved on with the rest of the introductions. 'This be Sir Madoc, who takes care of my ledgers. He be an old, dear friend of my father, the King.'

Madoc stood and bowed to her.

The Prince walked around the fire motioning to his men, who all nodded when introduced. 'Sir Angus, Sir Rhys, Sir Vaugnan, my watchman.'

'Never sleep,' Vaugnan said, flashing a grin.

'Sir Brockwell, thou hast already met.'

Brockwell fixed Tory with his usual glare, and she forced a sweet smile in return.

The Prince thought it best to move on quickly, motioning to the next in line. 'This be Jeven, my cook in wartime.'

Tory stepped forward and shook his hand. 'I am very pleased to meet thee, sir. Supper was delicious, I was absolutely famished,' she said to the young man who looked to be the youngest after Brockwell. He was of fair colouring and much smaller build than the other warriors.

Jeven blushed slightly at the attention she paid him. 'I am glad it was to thy liking, lady.'

Finally, the Prince introduced the large red-headed knight. Cedric stood up, quite serious for a change. 'I wish to thank thee for my Prince's safe return. I would have had thy throat cut this day —'

Tory shook her head, cutting him short. 'There be no need to apologise, sir. It was the least I could do after thy Prince spared me from the Saxons.'

He bowed, pleased that he'd said his piece. 'Thou art most gracious.'

The men were engrossed for hours, truly amazed by the evidence of Tory's claim that she had come from a future time zone. Maelgwn smiled as he watched her joke and drink with his knights as if she were one of them. She was expected to answer a thousand questions at once, and both she and the men were becoming more talkative as the mead took hold.

When the haunting tune from her CD faded, a quiet pause descended on the gathering. The Prince considered this an opportune time to bring up what had been on his mind most of the day. 'Tory?'

'Yes, sir,' she answered, still not sure how she should address him.

'Tell me of the way thee fights.'

This question seemed to strike a nerve in Brockwell, and his dark mood returned.

Tory tried not to notice and obliged the Prince with a full explanation. 'It be an old art of fighting known as Tae-kwon-do. The principle is that one's strength cannot be based on one's size. Each person has a great source of power within, which can be channelled through a perfect balance of mind, body and nature.' She placed her hands on her solar plexus.

'Ridiculous!' Brockwell interjected.

He was hushed to silence by the others, who were listening intently.

'But how did thee maim Brockwell with one hand?' the Prince asked.

'I wish I had seen this,' Cadogan mumbled, and was immediately reprimanded for interrupting.

Tory paused a moment to consider how she might best explain it. 'The brain sends messages around the body through a central nervous system, telling the body what thee wants it to do.' Tory looked to the knights who stared at her blankly. Maelgwn seemed to be following though, and nodded for her to continue.

'Within this system there art certain pressure points that when blocked, prevent any communication between the body and the brain. Thy opponent's limbs, therefore, tend to fail him, either temporary or permanently, depending upon thy intent.'

'Amazing,' Maelgwn concluded. 'Could I be taught this?'

'No Majesty, she lies.' Brockwell took a stand. 'She be trying to trick her way into thy favour. It be sorcery, I say.'

Tory rose to face the young knight. 'Thou art really starting to *bug me*. What dost thou want from me?' She threw her arms in the air. 'Dost thou want me to prove I could have killed thee today? Alright, I will.' She stormed off.

Brockwell was stunned by her outburst. 'She be not normal.'

'Indeed.' Maelgwn laughed at this, shaking his head. 'What on earth?' He watched Tory drag over a few large logs that had been cut for the fire, and beckoned for Sir Cedric to help her.

Tory had calmed down considerably and was courteous in her instruction to Cedric to place two logs parallel to each other, a third crossing them both. With this accomplished she smiled with satisfaction, and asked Brockwell to approach. When he didn't, Tory placed her hands on her hips and smugly said, 'Art thou afraid?'

'I do not fear the likes of thee,' Brockwell replied, as he stepped forward.

Maelgwn supressed a smile as he awaited her next move with growing interest.

'Question.' Tory put it to Brockwell. 'Could thee split this piece of wood in two, using only thy bare hand?'

Brockwell briefly examined the heavy log, seeing no purpose in the question. 'Nay. It would be impossible, even for the strongest man.'

'Be that so?' Tory asked. 'Watch and learn.' She knelt on one knee before the logs.

A hush came over the camp as Tory closed her eyes, breathing deeply to concentrate and centre herself. She joined her hands in prayer position, then tested her aim, bringing the side of her hand to rest on the middle of the target. *Focus*, her mind instructed as she raised her hand. With her eyes fixed on her point of contact, Tory let loose a mighty cry and brought her hand down towards the great hunk of timber. The inconceivable force behind the blow split the wood down the centre.

The knights were aghast for a second before they broke into a round of applause.

'Bravo,' cried Cadogan, giving her a standing ovation.

'Most impressive,' agreed Madoc.

Tory was oblivious to their adulation as she raised herself to face Brockwell, pointing to the splintered wood. 'That could have been thy skull.'

Brockwell stared at it blankly, knowing he would have trouble accomplishing the same feat with an axe. He approached Tory, taking hold of her hand to inspect it. 'Not even a scratch,' he informed the others.

At this moment, Tory felt his resolve changing. He seemed to take a softer stance, appearing weary and confused. On this note Tory thought it best to take her leave. 'Gentlemen,' she nodded.

'Tory,' Maelgwn called for her to wait for him. 'Where art thou going?' he asked as he reached her.

His gentle tone made her realise she had no idea. 'To sleep, I suppose. Where doth thou want me?'

The question brought a shy smile from them both, and Maelgwn waved towards to his tent.

'Where art *thou* going to sleep?' Tory pointed to the Prince, their grins even broader.

'In *my* tent,' he replied, walking off in that direction.

'I see.' She considered the option of sleeping outside with the rest of the drunken party but decided the odds for survival were far better inside. She turned to find Maelgwn already waiting with the flap held open for her.

'The men have not seen a good-looking woman since last winter,' he informed her, just in case she was still debating the option.

'That's a lot of hormones,' she commented as she reached him.

Whistles sounded from around the fire as Tory disappeared into the tent. Maelgwn motioned for them to quieten down but like any other young, single male, he was enjoying every minute of it.

The Prince followed her in and invited her to sit on the fur rug.

Surely I have been enough entertainment for one night. Tory was a little worried as this was obviously where he slept, but with a degree of hesitancy she sat down.

'Thee never answered my question.' Maelgwn removed his cape, spreading it on the ground to sit upon. 'Could thee teach me thy way of battle?'

'I doubt thee would have the time or patience. It be more than a way of battle, it be a way of life, a state of mind.' She prodded her backpack to find a soft spot to use as a pillow and leant back on it, too tired to discuss the matter further.

'Please Tory, I would like to try. I have good need of thee.'

His tone was so heartfelt that Tory sat up again.

'If thou hast nowhere else to go, come back with us to Mon. It would not seem so at a glance, but I am a wealthy man, thee would be well taken care of,' he told her quite definitely, considering that perhaps he could have put it another way.

'Art thou offering me a job?' Tory could hardly believe it, her first night in a new time zone and she'd already found employment.

'Aye, that be it!' He jumped to his feet, relieved that she'd found a way to describe exactly what he wanted from her. 'Thee could be my . . .' he clicked his fingers in search of a suitable title, '. . . adviser! Thee must know about a great many things I do not.'

'And personal trainer,' Tory added, holding up her hand for a high-five.

Maelgwn looked puzzled but crouched down, holding his hand up in the same fashion.

'Slap it,' she bade him, and Maelgwn obliged with good force. 'There you go.' Tory punched his shoulder in assurance as she lay down. 'Goodnight.'

Maelgwn sat pondering on his state of affairs, still fairly drunk and stimulated by the day's events. *The Dragon returns.* The thought came to him from nowhere, accompanied by a feeling of certainty that he hadn't felt since he was a boy of fifteen and had reclaimed his father's kingdom from his treacherous uncle. Whatever had guided him through that dire time was with him now. He wondered why the King had summoned him home, and what so many Saxons were doing this far west? There was indeed something afoot, *but what?*

Maelgwn lay down on his side to look at Tory, who was already asleep. 'I believe I was intended to meet thee, also.'

4

AN ARRANGED MARRIAGE

Come sunup, the camp was alive with activity as gear was packed on the horses. The knights had been campaigning for many months and were eager to begin the final leg of their journey home.

Cadogan entered the tent and went down on one knee to wake his lord. Yet he was distracted by Tory's shapely form lying to one side of the Prince, and lent over to view her more closely.

'What doth thou want, Cadogan?'

The knight was startled by Maelgwn's voice. 'We should go, Sire.'

The Prince sat up, a little woozy at first. 'We shan't be long,' he instructed, motioning his messenger to the door.

Cadogan dipped his head in response and quickly withdrew.

Maelgwn paused before waking Tory, observing how peaceful she looked — not harrowed or threatened as she had been most of the previous day. 'Tory.' He shook her gently. 'It be time to leave.' As Tory began to awake, Maelgwn started to strap on his armour.

'Oh God,' Tory moaned, trying to lift her head. 'I would never have imagined it possible for my body to ache this much.' She gasped and fell back onto the fur.

Maelgwn took hold of her around the waist and hoisted her up. 'Apologies for my means, but we seek to reach Castell Degannwy by evening, home to many of these men.' He helped Tory on with her backpack, placed her sax case in her hand, and turned her around. 'Thee understands, they art in a hurry.' He guided her outside.

Tory, still half asleep, saw Jeven rushing up to her, with an apple and a large piece of bread in his hands. 'For the ride,' he explained, handing them to her coyly.

Tory was touched by the gesture. 'Jeven, thou art an angel, I swear.'

Jeven blushed as he passed her a water bottle made of animal skin. He then bowed and quickly took his leave before any of the others noticed them together.

'So thou art coming with us?' Brockwell's voice boomed behind her.

Tory took her time turning around to face him. 'Thy Prince hast offered me a job,' she answered, not fazed by his tone.

Cadogan, who overheard her reply, laughed. 'I bet he did.'

Neither Tory nor Brockwell appreciated the remark, folding their arms as they glared at him. Maelgwn also caught the comment and approached Cadogan, gripping hold of his knight round the back of the neck. 'Doth thou have a problem, Sir Cadogan?'

Cadogan froze, realising his impiety. 'Nay, Majesty.' He closed his eyes, annoyed at himself, as the Prince released him.

'Pleased to hear it.' Maelgwn turned his attention from the troublemaker to address all his men. 'Let us make haste if we wish to reach Degannwy by nightfall.'

At his word, all made for their mounts. Tory took up her things, chasing after Brockwell. 'Wait.'

He turned around, annoyed.

'May I ask thee something?'

Brockwell's expression lightened a little, though he only nodded in response.

'Why doth my presence offend thee so?'

Brockwell, eager to get home, was growing impatient. 'In my experience, I have found it best to be wary of that which I deem unnatural. My only concern be for the welfare of my cousin.' He stared at her a second then took off towards his horse.

Tory was struck as she watched him, and once again she thought. My god, he's like Brian. The way he moved, his stance, even his manner was the same.

Maelgwn pulled his horse up alongside her. 'Ready?' He reached down to help her mount.

For most of the day they'd kept good time, as the terrain they covered was generally rolling green fields and light forest. But after six hours in the saddle the landscape was becoming more mountainous, and the knights decided to rest before commencing the final homeward stretch.

As Tory dismounted she could smell the sea, and she and the Prince climbed to the top of a hill where she looked out across the ocean. The wild, moist breeze swept through her hair, and she drew a deep breath, enjoying the magnificent view.

'If we follow the coast we shall reach the citadel by nightfall. The worst of the mountains lie further inland, we have come round them,' Maelgwn explained to her.

'I'm pleased to hear it,' Tory assured him wholeheartedly, rubbing her behind.

Maelgwn laughed at this. 'It will be over soon, I promise.'

As they turned to walk back, Tory had to ask. 'This citadel wouldn't happen to have a hot bath, perchance?'

'Of course,' Maelgwn declared. 'I shall have one drawn for thee as soon as we arrive.' Maelgwn took off his long cape and threw it around her shoulders.

'I am not cold.' Tory went to take it off.

'Please, I do not know what my people will make of thee dressed as thou art.'

So Tory agreed; it made good sense to keep the cloak on, and with the promise of a hot bath at Castell Degannwy, she was as eager as the men to get under way.

Four hours later the knights stopped on the crest of a great hill. From here one could see the citadel of

Degannwy, which was the official entrance to the kingdom of Gwynedd. This grand fort stood upon the largest of two craggy hillocks, and supported a flourishing little community that spread out around its high stone walls.

'Behold,' cried Madoc, pulling his horse alongside Tory and the Prince. 'The twin hills of the Gwynedd stronghold.' The old knight took a deep breath, obviously proud and happy to see his home.

'Well, what are we waiting for?' the Prince declared.

Tory clung on for dear life as the powerful black stallion took off down the hill as fast as it was able, with the knights following close behind.

To save being detained, the Prince's party raced through the outlying village. Cadogan had been sent on ahead to inform the King of his son's return, thus the knights found the portcullis already raised. A road led between the hillocks, through another large gateway, and into the courtyard within the walls of the citadel.

The Prince kept his promise to Tory, and as soon as they arrived had her whisked away to his chambers.

Fenalla, the frumpy head maid at King Caswallon's court, was under instruction to arrange a hot bath, a meal and mead. While this pleased Tory no end, it also suited the Prince; he needed his mysterious guest to be out of sight, at least until he'd decided exactly how much the court should know about her.

Without stopping to speak with the well-wishing servants, Maelgwn made haste to his father's quarters where the King would be residing this late in the day.

The Prince pushed open the huge oak doors of the King's library, which remained from the time of the Roman withdrawal. Cunedda, his great great grandfather, along with his eight sons, had come down from the Manau Guotodin (Firth of Forth) under instruction from Rome to restore order to the kingdom of Gwynedd and beyond. Cunedda had made this grand fortification his base and it had belonged to their family ever since.

'Percival.' Maelgwn sought the attention of a frail old man working alone in the room. He was sitting by the fire with quill in hand, recording figures on parchment. The old soul had been so caught up in his work that he hadn't heard the doors open. He looked up, not recognising Maelgwn at first.

'Prince Maelgwn? Be that the young heir of Gwynedd under all that hair?' Percival stood up, his old bones creaking. 'I mistook thee for a Saxon.' He laughed as Maelgwn approached and embraced him.

'It be good to see thee.' The Prince held him at arm's length for a moment then strolled around the room to take in the familiar surroundings. 'Where be my father?'

'Why he left for the court of Chiglas only yesterday,' Percival informed him, as if it were common knowledge.

'Chiglas! Why?'

'Why? The wedding, Sire.'

Maelgwn was set at ease, reaching for a jug of mead on the table by the fire. He filled a goblet for himself and Percival, taking a long swig. 'Ah, my father's mead, there be nothing like it. So tell me, who shall be wed?'

Percival suddenly went white. 'But, I thought thee knew, Sire?' He seemed to want to avoid the issue, making Maelgwn all the more curious.

'Knew what, Percival?' The Prince smiled, amused by his game. 'Who shall be wed?'

'It be thy own wedding, Sire. Hast the King not told thee?'

Maelgwn stood, enraged. 'What! Why?'

Percival humbled himself, afraid he was in trouble. 'It be not my place to say, Sire. The King said he would meet thee on Mon, presently.'

Maelgwn was so incensed that he began to pace to and fro like a caged beast. 'I will not marry the daughter of Chiglas.' He found this easy to say to Percival, but to his father — that was a different story. Still, it didn't seem fair to take out his frustrations on poor Percival, so Maelgwn left the room. 'Thee can tell my father, I am most displeased.' He slammed the doors behind him.

Maelgwn was storming through the hall in a fit of rage when he met Brockwell who was on his way to a feast to be held in their honour.

'Art thou coming to drink with us, cousin?' Brockwell took hold of him by the shoulder as they walked together.

'Maybe later, I have a lot on my mind at present.'

'Already?' Brockwell was amazed. 'But thee only just arrived.'

Fenalla carried out her duties in a huff, giving an occasional grunt in objection to Tory's appearance.

When Tory finally found herself alone, she dug out her CD player to listen to some music and relax. After undressing and wrapping herself in a towel she made for the bath, taking a goblet of mead with her.

The Prince's chambers were spectacular. She would never have imagined that a building as grand as this would exist in Britain during this time. Large stone stairs led up to the steaming pool of water that was over twice the size of a normal bath. It was distinctly Roman in design, and had a large open fire at the end to boil the huge pots of water it took to fill it.

'Well I must say, I am impressed.' Tory immersed herself in the luxurious bath and from there studied the rest of the room in the glow of candle and torch light. She admired the solid, raw furnishings, the thick curtains of Prussian blue, and the ornate tapestries that depicted the battles and daily life of Gwynedd. 'Yep, I could live here.' She smiled, indulging in the splendour of her surroundings.

As she rolled over to float on the water, she was startled by the sound of the door closing and quickly submerged herself once more.

An equally stunned page was turning circles upon discovering her, not knowing what to do. 'Forgive me, lady,' he stuttered out. 'I am Selwyn, the Prince's squire. I be just on my way to attend to my duties when I heard thy beautiful music.' His eyes looked everywhere but at her to seek its source.

'I am pleased to meet thee.' Tory reached for her towel but the door opened again before she could grab it.

Maelgwn and Brockwell entered, neither of them noticing Tory or Selwyn at first.

'But the men will be disappointed if thou dost not attend,' Brockwell argued.

Maelgwn spied his squire making himself scarce and removed his gunna, handing it to Selwyn. 'Please Calin, I just need some time to think.' The Prince seated himself, holding up his feet so that Selwyn could remove his boots. 'I will come down later, I promise.'

'Excuse me, but this was a private moment,' Tory interjected, a mite discomforted by her predicament.

All three men burst into laughter; Maelgwn had completely forgotten about his guest. 'Well, I have no objection.' His good mood returned as he noticed the soft music and reclined to enjoy it.

Brockwell, now clean and shaven, folded his arms and took a few steps towards Tory, smiling broadly. 'Well, well, well, what have we here?'

'I am warning thee, Brockwell . . .' Tory choked on her words, shocked to find her brother's face staring back at her; he even had the same dimple on his chin. She froze, wide eyed at the discovery.

'What be wrong?' The Prince stood.

Tory held up a hand motioning them to stay back. 'I am fine, please. I would just like to be able to dress without thy entire guard in here.'

'Of course. Brockwell, Selwyn, if thee would both excuse us.' As Maelgwn showed them to the door, he wondered what had frightened her.

Us! Tory grabbed her towel, managing to wrap herself up and take a seat on the bath before the Prince returned.

Maelgwn was rather surprised to find that this woman from the future was just as modest as any lady in his court. So he avoided looking directly at her, walking over to stoke up the fire. 'What scared thee just now?'

'Oh nothing.' She jumped up to pull on a sweat-shirt and pants as soon as his back was turned. 'Brockwell just appeared so different all cleaned up. More sort of . . . handsome.'

'I see,' the Prince said flatly, as if he either didn't like or believe her statement.

Tory made herself comfortable on some large cushions opposite Maelgwn and began to comb the knots out of her hair. The Prince didn't stir from his reflections for some time, his eyes lost in the open flame. Tory wondered what was on his mind as she watched him in silence.

'Tell me of thy home, Tory.' He sounded far away. 'Do people get what they want there?'

An odd question. She paused to think about it. 'Those who believe they can, do. Much the same as here, I expect.'

Maelgwn looked at her, his interest aroused.

'For although the civilised world be much larger in the future, it continues to be plagued by crime and war. And thanks to modern weaponry, some nations can destroy entire cities and their occupants without ever leaving home.'

'But thy people must have laws?'

Tory gave half a laugh. 'Indeed. But often it be the people who make the laws, who art the ones who break them — organised crime we call it. What the Saxons make a livelihood from here, slaughtering and looting, some do for fun where I come from. That be why I learnt self-defence,' she concluded with a sigh.

Maelgwn looked back to the fire. 'That be why I must learn it too.'

Tory woke the next day in a state of bliss. She was nestled in a pile of pillows in the middle of the Prince's huge four-poster bed, and she was covered by a light blanket of soft fur.

As she dozed, it dawned on her that she couldn't remember going to bed. *Did I really drink that much that I have forgotten, or did I fall asleep in front of the fire?* 'I've got to lay off that stuff.'

There was a knock on the door. 'Has to be his lordship,' Tory mused, sitting up.

Maelgwn entered, followed closely by Fenalla who was struggling with a large tray covered with the season's fruits, cheese, bread and a large pitcher of water.

'Dost thou ever sleep?' Tory asked, rubbing her eyes.

'Nay, miss too much.' The Prince waited for Fenalla to relieve herself of her load then closed the door behind her.

Tory stared at Maelgwn in amazement. His hair had been trimmed but still fell past his shoulders, and shone like moonlight on water, it was so dark and straight. His clear, ivory skin and his high cheekbones could be appreciated now that his face had been liberated from its hairy disguise. He wore thickly woven trousers and shirt and a gunna of dark brown that belted at the waist with black leather. His boots, made of the same black leather, were bound with laces round his leg up to the knee. A long, black woollen cape hung about his shoulders, partially covering a medallion of the Dragon that was made of black onyx and set in silver.

'So at last we meet, face to face,' said Tory.

Maelgwn flashed a cheeky grin. 'More becoming, I hope.' He strode over to pour two glasses of water.

Tory held her head. *Is he kidding me?* 'I have no objection,' she announced sarcastically, mimicking the same regal tone he'd used the night before.

This made the Prince laugh. 'Thy wit be clever. Thee must have slept well.' He handed her a goblet and took a seat on the bed.

'Very well, indeed.' Then her tone changed to a soft plea. 'Please, tell me we art staying here.'

'We shall leave as soon as thou art ready,' Maelgwn answered with regret. Seeing her disappointment he added, 'Though Degannwy be grand, I assure thee it be no comparison in beauty to my home at Aberffraw.'

'I shall look forward to it then.' She smiled and climbed out of bed, still dressed in her tracksuit. 'What should I wear?'

The Prince was stumped by the question. 'Doth thou own a dress at all?'

'I do have one dress with me, it might suit.' She sounded doubtful.

'Fine,' the Prince resolved, getting to his feet. 'I have one more thing to take care of, but I shall be back for thee presently. Please eat,' he added, disappearing out the door.

Tory's aches were considerably better this morning, and a glimpse in her hand mirror showed that her bruise was fading. She decided to leave her hair out as, judging from the little she'd observed of the maidens here, this seemed quite acceptable. Still, she wasn't sure about her dress. Made of black stretch cotton, it had long sleeves, a v-neck and flared to a full skirt that fell in waves to her ankles. If not for the snug fit of the bodice it might have been appropriate. She would have to wear her leather jacket over the top for, although her frame was tiny, Tory was fairly well endowed in the chest department and she was sure this would not go unnoticed. The dress looked a tad ridiculous with her long white socks pushed down around her ankles and her steel-capped boots. They were riding again today, however, and these were the most sensible footwear she had.

The Prince knocked and strode into the room without waiting for a response, slamming the door behind him. He came to an abrupt halt when he saw her. 'Heaven forbid,' he announced with a grin and a laugh.

'Thee could have waited.' Tory crossed her arms in front of her chest. She couldn't believe she was actually embarrassed, and blamed this on the fact that she had to wear a dress. She simply hated looking feminine, it always made her feel vulnerable. 'I am going to wear the jacket over the top,' she explained, reaching for it.

'No hurry,' Maelgwn assured her, doing his best to wipe the smile from his face.

Tory paid him no mind as she put on the jacket and zipped it all the way up.

'Art thou ready to leave?' she asked him.

'Aye,' Maelgwn said as he picked an apple from the platter. 'I have spoken to my men and we have decided it best to keep thee a secret for the time being.'

'How dost thou plan to do that?' Tory motioned to her outfit.

Maelgwn smiled, having thought this through. 'I shall tell whoever might dare inquire that we found thee wandering in the south. Thou art from a faraway land — Australia.' He recalled the pronunciation. 'In a shipwreck perhaps, thee lost thy memory and can only recall certain things.' He seemed quite pleased with himself when he'd finished explaining.

Brockwell knocked and entered, striding over to join them. 'We art ready to leave, Sire.' He looked at Tory with a smirk on his face. 'Art thou a woman today?' He referred to her dress.

Uncanny, he's every bit as annoying as my brother. 'I was a woman a day ago when I flattened thee,' Tory retorted, making for the door with her bags.

Brockwell chuckled, amused that he had struck a chord.

'Let us be off then,' Maelgwn resolved. He was pleased that Brockwell no longer appeared strongly opposed to Tory's presence. Now his mind was at ease, for Brockwell was his constant companion and Maelgwn had feared there would be a problem.

Only a small party would accompany the Prince to Aberffraw: Brockwell, Cadogan, Madoc, their squires, and Selwyn.

Tory was given her own horse to ride. 'I preferred being chauffeur driven,' she commented to Maelgwn as she made herself comfortable in the saddle.

Maelgwn caught her meaning. 'It will be an easy ride, I promise.'

It was a fine day, and only little puffs of cloud scattered the azure sky. As they moved out of the citadel into the village, they were escorted by a guard of a dozen soldiers that would accompany them as far as the Isle of Mon. They were to crew the boat that would tow a barge carrying the Prince's immediate escort across the Menai Strait from Bangor.

As the party made its way through the village, the Prince pointed out his father's refortification plans to Tory. For such a confused and barbaric period in history, she thought, the layout of Degannwy's little community was extremely organised. Tory had a huge urge to go shopping as they passed through the marketplace, but under the circumstances this was totally out of the question.

Crowds lined the road through the village, some people hung out their windows and doors. The locals called out their thanks and praise to the Prince and his men for their protection and good fortune over the seasons past. While Maelgwn and his family had been in power there hadn't been any serious threat to this town. The goodwill his people held for Maelgwn was obvious, as was the genuine regard he felt in return. The Prince and his knights shook hands with the men, and were hugged and kissed by the young women as they passed.

Once they'd cleared the merriment of the village the riders picked up their pace a little, heading into the outlying farmland of the common.

Tory watched the workers in the fields that lined their route. They appeared happy as they went about the chore of harvesting the yearly crop. As she was taking everything in, Tory had dropped back a little behind the others. It was then that a cry for help reached her ears.

She saw the door of a small farmhouse swing open and a young girl was propelled out into the yard, sobbing and screaming uncontrollably. An older man of unkempt appearance followed. He reached down, pulling the girl to her feet by her hair then brutally punching her back to the ground. The girl's next scream was loud enough to draw the attention of the entire party.

Tory jumped from her horse and yelled at the attacker. 'Oi!' she snarled, slogging him fair in the face. The unsuspecting man was sent hurtling back against the wall of the cottage. 'Pig! What right hast thee to strike this girl?' Tory demanded, outraged.

'Tory, no!' the Prince protested, turning his horse around.

The young girl staggered towards Tory, falling in a heap at her feet, blurting out her thanks between sobs. Tory watched the man stand up, and she prepared to strike again if the need arose.

By this time Brockwell and Maelgwn had arrived on the scene. Upon seeing them the man refrained from retaliating and bowed deeply to the Prince. 'She be my wife, Majesty,' he managed to blurt out. 'Married this very day.'

'And how dost such a poor example of manhood like thyself end up married to a beautiful young girl like this?' Tory asked, as she crouched down to see if the girl was alright; one side of her face was already a mass of bruises.

'It be completely legal,' he assured the Prince. 'She refuses to ...' The old man winked at Maelgwn and Brockwell, '... fulfil her wedding vows.' He laughed, sure that they'd understand. 'That not be justice. I paid good for her.'

The Prince closed his eyes, bringing his hand up to his forehead; he could feel a headache coming on.

'Thee bought her?' Tory stood to question the man, who nodded in response. 'He bought her!' She turned to the Prince, demanding an explanation.

''Tis quite common in the lower classes.'

'Aye,' Brockwell added. 'If she had been born at court, her father would have to pay this man to take her off his hands.'

Tory was pacing now, furious and shocked. 'And thee fails to see anything wrong with this?' She turned to Maelgwn, unable to believe the man whom she thought was sensitive condoned what was taking place.

'It be none of my affair,' Maelgwn told her calmly. 'Thee knows much about the future but little of our ways. This girl will die without this man to support her.'

'She would be better off, goddamn it!' Tory gave up, bending down to address the girl. 'What be thy name?'

59

Still shaken, the girl raised her tear-stained face. 'Katren, lady.'

'Dost thou love this man, Katren?'

The girl shook her head violently. 'Nay, I do not. I swear.' She clung to Tory's legs, bursting into tears once more.

'Get out of that,' her husband hissed, moving to drag her away.

'Do not even think about it, *slug*,' Tory warned, wound up like a coil and fit to burst.

Her tone was so harsh that the old bloke froze. 'But she be my wife!' he implored the Prince.

'How much did thee pay for her?' Tory interjected.

'Two head of cattle!' He made it sound a lot, grinning broadly when he realised where the conversation was heading.

Tory was so disgusted she had to laugh. She twisted a gold ring from her finger and showed it to the man. 'Will this cover it?'

He nodded vigorously, his face lighting up like a Christmas tree as he snatched the ring from her. 'Take her then, good riddance.' The man bowed to the Prince. 'Highness.' He staggered back inside the farmhouse, shutting the door behind him.

Poor Katren collapsed from relief. 'I be so indebted to thee, lady,' she mumbled through her tears.

Tory bent down to help her up. 'I would have done the same for anyone, and I be no lady.'

'Thou art right there,' Brockwell said.

Maelgwn was worried by all this; how was he going to keep Tory under control? Word got around fast here, and this kind of news would spread like wildfire. Lucky for him that none bar his men had witnessed the incident.

Tory led Katren to her horse, past Brockwell and Maelgwn. She looked at the Prince, holding her tongue to save angering him further.

Though the Prince was displeased, he did not have time to deal with her at present.

Brockwell could barely believe that Maelgwn said nothing. 'Great, what art thou going to do with her?' he asked Tory.

'Thee all have squires, well now so do I,' Tory told him, helping Katren onto her horse.

Brockwell looked back to Maelgwn.

'We will discuss it later.' The Prince's stern expression rested on Tory.

'Thee can count on it,' she replied, every bit as annoyed.

By early afternoon they'd met the barge at the Menai Strait, and the Prince was busy organising his men for the crossing.

Tory used this time to take Katren aside and clean her up. She found a shirt that the maid could wear over her dress to hide the rip that ran all the way down to her navel. The girl had hardly said a word except 'Thank thee,' or 'Thou art too kind.' She appeared to be in her mid teens and was only a tiny little thing. Tory thought her face almost angelic, despite her bruises. Her features were small and pointed and her large round eyes were icy blue. Once unknotted and brushed, Katren's hair fell to her waist in large ash-brown waves.

'Much better.' Tory sat back to view Katren, giving her a wink.

'Did thee mean it when thee said I could be thy maid?' Katren asked, timid as a mouse.

'No, thou dost not have to do that.'

'But I want to, lady.' Katren went down on her knees, pleading. 'It would be an honour, a dream come true!'

'Thee need only be my friend,' Tory assured her, but was forced to resign herself to having a maid when Katren's desperate expression didn't change. 'Alright, if that be what thee truly wants,' she announced, caught up in Katren's excitement.

'Oh thank thee, lady.' Katren bowed a few times, still on her knees.

Tory couldn't cope with this a second longer and placed her hands on the maiden's shoulders, pulling her up to look her straight in the eye. 'Listen to me, Katren. Unless thou art addressing royalty, never bow before anyone. From this day forth thou art thine own master.'

'But I may still be thy maid?' Katren asked before getting too excited.

'If his lordship agrees.' Tory held up her hand for a high-five. 'Now, hold up your hand.'

The Prince turned to see the two girls slap hands before hugging each other.

'It would seem they get along.' Brockwell chuckled, walking over to get them moving. 'Thee will have a whole harem soon.'

Maelgwn considered this statement to be not too far from the truth, as his intended bride was probably on her way to Mon by now.

Once they'd reached the isle, the soldiers returned with the barge to the mainland and only the royal party rode on to Aberffraw.

The island's terrain was flatter than the rest of Gwynedd, which made for an easy ride. They passed over miles of common, scattered with farms and cottages, before they finally arrived on the outskirts of the estate.

The Prince brought the party to a halt, and his knights and squires gathered around him to hear his instruction. Tory quietly advised Katren to hang back a little, as Maelgwn had not said a word to her since their run-in this morning.

The Prince looked to Cadogan. 'As soon as we arrive I want thee to take Tory straight to the northern caphouse.' This was one of the chambers to be found at the top of each of the house's four towers. 'Selwyn, thee will see to it that Katren finds the maids' sleeping quarters.' Selwyn nodded. 'Madoc, keep Gilmore distracted, and Brockwell . . .' Maelgwn looked to his champion, who was eagerly awaiting his task. 'I will need thee to help me with thy mother.'

Brockwell's mother, Lady Gladys, had charge of the household at Aberffraw, as she was sister to the King. The Prince's mother had been slain in the uprising of his uncle, and Lady Gladys had assumed the responsibility in her stead.

63

'I would like to speak to her of Tory before they meet,' the Prince explained.

Brockwell nodded, understanding this reasoning.

The royal house at Aberffraw was situated on the coast of Mon overlooking the ocean. High stone walls ran between its four towers and the inner bailey courtyard was located within the walls of the house. The outer bailey pathways led off in opposite directions to stables and to a great hall, which Tory presumed to be the army lodgings. Another large stone wall encompassed this huge area, its buildings and grounds, beyond which lay the village and the common.

The Prince and his company were met with a grand welcome from the locals as they made their way through the village. Tory noticed a beautiful woman sitting outside one of the cottages. The woman had drawn her attention because, unlike all the other women Tory had encountered thus far, she seemed quietly proud. She was obviously poor, judging from her dress, and her expression was one of deep malice. Tory noticed her spiteful glare resting on Cadogan as they passed.

When they reached the inner court of the grand Roman castle, Lady Gladys, along with a couple of young ladies in her care, and the servants of the house, were waiting to greet the Prince and his party. Sir Gilmore, the King's representative at Aberffraw who ran the estate and trained the men for their ever-expanding armies, was also in attendance with a small guard.

Madoc kept Sir Gilmore distracted, exchanging greetings during their long-awaited reunion; they had become firm friends during their many years of service to King Caswallon, but had not seen each other for some time.

The Prince and Brockwell tried to distract Lady Gladys while Cadogan went about the Prince's bidding. As overwhelmed as she was to see her boys safely home again, Lady Gladys didn't miss a trick. 'Where be Sir Cadogan taking that girl?' She gestured after him, waiting for one of them to offer an explanation.

'Shh!' the Prince and Brockwell urged her, not wanting to alert Sir Gilmore.

'I need to speak with thee at once,' Maelgwn whispered to her, stressing the urgency.

Unable to resist getting in on her boys' secret, Lady Gladys excused the three of them on the premise that they needed to discuss an urgent family matter.

Cadogan swung open the heavy timber door to the tower and beckoned for Tory to enter.

Said the spider to the fly. Tory strolled past him, not liking the way he leered at her. She entered the darkened tower to find a couple of stairs leading down to a stone bath and fireplace, and a high but narrow stone stairway spiralling up to the main chamber. 'I will be fine now, thank you Cadogan,' Tory assured him, reclaiming her bags and making her way up the stairs.

When she reached the top, Tory was taken aback. The round room contained a large bed, a fireplace, a desk, and a huge mirror that, although it was rather tarnished, would serve its purpose. Tapestries, archaic maps and even what appeared to be hand-drawn star charts adorned the walls. The rugs and furs that covered the stone floor would help fend off the cold, and there were candles and torches galore to light the large room at night. Tory imagined it would be quite bright and airy by day when the heavy wooden shutters were open.

Cadogan came up behind her, the sound of mischief in his voice. 'The Prince did not say that I should leave thee.' He took hold of her around the waist and lifted her off the ground.

Tory pushed him away, most annoyed. 'Watch thyself, Cadogan. Do not make me hurt thee,' she warned, sure that he couldn't be serious.

'Come on,' he urged, taking a step closer. 'Do not save it for the Prince.'

He was serious alright, the smug grin on his face said it all. Tory raised her hands to defend herself. 'Last warning.'

Lady Gladys led her son and the Prince to a small, cosy room, where they relaxed drinking mead while Maelgwn explained his woes to the two people he trusted most.

'I believe Caradoc hast somehow convinced our father that Gwynedd needs the support of Chiglas and his armies. This marriage be meant to unite our two kingdoms, but I do not trust it.' Maelgwn took a seat, perplexed. Caradoc, his younger brother, had kept the constant company of King Chiglas at his court in Powys since the uprising and subsequent death of their uncle Cadfer. He was power hungry and more fond of warring than pursuits of the mind, thus he and Maelgwn had never seen eye to eye.

It made Gladys' heart break to see the Prince so unhappy. 'Maelgwn.' She took hold of his hands. 'Thy father be no longer a young man, and thou art now of eight and twenty. Soon thee shall be king, and it be high time thee took a wife. Gwynedd must have an heir apart from thy brother.'

'But the daughter of Chiglas!' Brockwell cringed, disgusted by the whole idea. He was in sympathy with his cousin.

'I am sure she be lovely.' Gladys defended the good judgement of her brother, Caswallon. She then turned the conversation back to the matter that was of immediate concern to her. 'Who be the girl thou art hiding? And what hast she to do with all this?'

Maelgwn sat forward to explain. 'I know that her name be Tory Alexander, though unfortunately her origins are untraceable as she hast lost part of her memory. However ...' he lowered his voice, 'she possesses a fighting style superior to any I have ever seen. If this can be learnt and applied to our forces, it would give us a great advantage over the enemies of Gwynedd, whoever they may be.'

Gladys was intrigued by his story, but knew she was not getting all of it. 'Be she a sorceress, this girl?' Gladys could not understand a woman possessing such talents.

'Nay,' Brockwell assured his mother firmly, much to the Prince's surprise. 'I believe she be a good and honest person, just different.' Brockwell was at a loss to explain exactly how he felt about her.

The Prince told his aunt that the study of Tory's style of fighting was to be a special project of his own, and until he had fully investigated the matter, he wanted none outside the room to know of it. By some miracle, he managed to persuade her to help him keep Tory a secret. Lady Gladys was an intelligent woman and a good ally in any situation.

Maelgwn left Brockwell with his mother and made for the north tower to see how Tory was settling in. As he crossed the great foyer, he chanced to spy Cadogan limping away in the opposite direction. The sight urged Maelgwn to make haste to the caphouse to ensure that Tory was alright.

He found her safe and sound, unpacking her bags on the bed. She didn't appear to be in the best of moods, however.

'I have just about had it with the lot of thee.'

'Please, forgive me. 'Twas stupid to send Cadogan to accompany thee, I was not thinking.'

'I ask thee.' Tory unzipped her jacket and threw it off, too hot and bothered to put up with it any longer. 'What would a woman do if she could not defend herself here?'

Maelgwn took a step forward, hoping he wouldn't sound like he was condoning his knight's behaviour. 'Thee must understand, these men have no great learning. All they know is what they want or need.' Maelgwn struggled to keep his eyes from straying to her cleavage.

'Not thee, too!' Tory planted her hands on her hips and flaunted her figure. 'It be just a body for heaven's sake, get over it! It be not like thou hast never seen the female form before, I am sure.' She turned back to her unpacking, surprised that grown men would carry on so.

Maelgwn was quiet for a moment; he could not deny that Tory aroused in him more than just an interest in fighting techniques. As he gazed at her, he could quite clearly make out every muscle in her supple, young body through the strange black material that hugged her form like a second skin. 'Forgive me. I have not been in the company of a beautiful woman in as many months as my men.'

Tory felt a sudden twinge of remorse.

'Although most of them found solace at Degannwy,' Maelgwn added to lighten the mood.

That's why Brockwell was so chirpy this morning, Tory surmised. She felt guilty taking out her anger on Maelgwn when he'd been nothing but a perfect gentleman since they'd met. 'Nay, I am the one who should apologise.' She grabbed a sweat-shirt from the pile of clothes on the bed and threw it on. 'Back home we hardly wear any clothes half the year, it be too hot.'

'Sounds like a nice place.' The thought brought a smile to his face. 'Hast thou seen this?' He pointed to two large doors which he pulled open to reveal the wide walkways of the roof and a view of the ocean beyond.

'Oh my.' Tory stepped out onto the walkway, drawn by the picturesque seascape.

'I thought thee might like this tower, all my tutors have occupied it.' He looked at Tory and was spellbound. The sun shone through her long fair hair, shedding a golden halo around her. Who was this extraordinary woman? He couldn't help but feel that he'd known her before, though he realised this was impossible. Perhaps it was just that she bore a vague resemblance to his mother, Queen Sorcha, yet something inside told him there was more to his attraction than that.

Suddenly, remembering his place, Maelgwn snapped out of his daze. 'I thought thee could teach me here on the roof. There be plenty of room, and no one would disturb us.'

Tory was pleasantly surprised that the Prince considered her his tutor, though she hid her astonishment well. She looked around and nodded to confirm. 'I believe this will do just fine.'

5

THE NORTH
TOWER

The Prince arrived at the north tower at dawn the following day, eager to begin his training. The wooden shutters had been flung open, allowing the ocean breeze to waft through the room. As the sound of gentle music reached his ears, he followed it outside.

There on the roof's walkway between the inner bailey and the sea-wall, he found her. She was dressed in pure white clothes, resembling his own, that belted at the waist with a black tie. Her hair had been braided and the long plait fell to her waist. Tory appeared to be dancing in a style that strongly resembled the way she fought. She was beautiful to watch, for her graceful movements flowed in time with the music. As he didn't wish to disturb her, the Prince silently climbed onto the sea-wall to wait for her to finish.

Without opening her eyes or stopping her graceful movement, Tory said, 'This be known as kata.' Her voice was very calm, as if she were a million miles away. 'Kata be performed by every serious student of this art. It be through kata that one strives for perfection.' Tory continued her exercise, her balance and movement steady and precise. 'It be repetition in the form of fighting patterns that one carries out against an imaginary opponent. Kata, once mastered, will increase thy expertise and thy powers of concentration.'

Tory finished her exercise, bringing her hands together and bowing deeply to the Prince.

'That was wonderful, teach me.' He jumped off the sea-wall, eager to get started.

'Not today. We have much to do before thou art ready for kata.' Tory sat on the ground in the lotus position. 'This morning, I be going to teach thee meditation.' Tory beckoned for him to sit on the ground.

'What be meditation?' the Prince asked, following her instruction.

'It relieves one's body and mind of accumulated stress. Thee must set aside any emotional upsets or problems so thy concentration be not compromised. Only then can thee work to thy full potential. We will meditate before and after every workout.'

The Prince was intrigued by the way she explained things, it always made perfect sense.

'Now, close thine eyes. Let the music relax thee and just listen to my voice.'

Tory planned to start the Prince's real training in a few days' time. Meanwhile, she'd issued Maelgwn with a list and the designs of all the equipment she needed made. She was keeping the local leather craftsmen well occupied, having requested a punching bag, punching mitts, padded gear for the head and waist to be used when sparring, and padded landing mats to cover the hard stone ground. She made a space for a workout area, rearranging the room to utilise the large mirror that stood on the west wall, reflecting the sea through the windows opposite. She would use this to monitor the Prince's movements when they began kata.

Her equipment was delivered two days later by Brockwell and a few guards. This thrilled the Prince no end, as now the real training could commence. He watched while Tory directed the men to set up the equipment. Maelgwn was considering how Tory had been pushing him to the limits of his endurance these past two days. She'd justified this torture by explaining that she needed to know his limitations to determine what aspects of his technique required the most work. He had to admit he enjoyed the meditation though, and he'd never felt so exhilarated and at peace in all his life.

In making Tory's equipment, the Britons had used hides shorn very short. So once the men had laid the mats out on the floor, it looked like the room had been carpeted.

'What be this?' Brockwell referred to the punching bag as he hung it from a large hook and chain which was secured to a beam overhead.

Tory turned to answer his question and burst into laughter. The punching bag was made from cowhide, and it appeared as though she had a dead carcass hanging from her roof. 'I will show thee.'

At just under two metres long, the bag stopped just above the floor, so that it could be used to practise kicks at any height. She started with a few low, sweeping kicks and gradually built up to the stage where she was propelling herself round in the air and ploughing her foot into it.

Brockwell, Maelgwn and the guards were stunned by her aggression, speed and accuracy. 'Unbelievable,' Maelgwn mumbled in awe, motioning for Brockwell to get the other men out of there.

Tory grabbed the only pair of stockings she had, tying one end through a loop in the bottom of the punching bag, and the other loosely around a hook in the floor.

Brockwell returned after seeing the men out, and stood watching Tory demonstrate to the Prince how the bag would bounce back when struck. He observed with interest as she ducked and weaved her way around the bag, striking then darting out of the way. Tory was using more fist and open hand strikes now, and he was surprised by the amount of force she could summon up. He spied a punching mitt on the desk and picked it up. 'What be this?'

They're like kids in a toyshop, Tory thought. 'Put it on thy right hand, I will show thee.' She almost dared him. 'I think thee can take it.'

Brockwell smiled at the invitation, pulling the glove on firmly.

Tory showed him the correct height at which to hold his hand to fend off her attack, then took a few steps back.

Brockwell hesitated, watching her concentrating closely on the mitt. 'Thou art not going to do what thee did with the log?'

'Kind of . . .' Brockwell looked distressed. 'Just a joke.' She encouraged him to resume his position. 'The purpose of the mitt be to help thee localise thy target.' She spun round taking a step and kicked out from behind, driving her heel into the palm of his hand.

Brockwell grinned, impressed. 'Art thou married?' He suddenly saw in her his perfect mate.

Tory laughed. 'Nay, for some strange reason men find me threatening.' She grabbed a towel, having worked up a sweat. 'What about thee, Brockwell, doth thou have a lady fair?'

'Many.' He smiled with a glint in his eye.

She looked at Maelgwn who was reclining on her bed. 'What about thee, Maelgwn?' She'd been dying to ask this for days and now seemed like an inconspicuous time.

The Prince glanced at Brockwell, who was staring at him. 'Not yet.' Maelgwn edged his way round the question, looking back to Tory. 'Why? Art thou wanting a more recreational form of exercise?' He raised his eyebrows, flashing a cheeky grin. The Prince looked at Brockwell expecting to find him amused, but his expression was quite the opposite.

'In the twentieth century, no problem. Here?' Tory smiled. 'I would be hung.'

Brockwell burst into laughter, pleased that Maelgwn's lie failed to get him anywhere.

Tory picked up a book from the desk and opened it where she had marked her place. 'In the early sixth century, and I quote.' She held up a finger, presenting an argument she wanted them both to hear. '"Sexual irregularities were not sins punishable by the Church, but *offences*!"' She stressed the word, becoming dramatic, much to the amusement of the Prince and Brockwell who weren't really used to women talking openly about sex. '"Demanding compensation."' Tory raised her eyebrows. 'It then goes on to say that a failure to meet legal obligation would reduce even a king's thegn to slavery. See!' She closed the book and waved her finger about. 'I am wise to thee both.' She then turned to Maelgwn. 'So I am not looking for . . .' her tone became rather sultry, 'a more recreational form of exercise with anyone who dost not first place a ring on this finger.'

'Women!' Brockwell waved her off. 'Thou art all the same.'

'What book be this?' Maelgwn playfully reached for it, but Tory quickly pulled it away. 'Tory,' he demanded, firmly.

'No, I cannot let thee look at this. It contains information about thee that thee should not know. I should not have taken it out in the first place, sorry.'

'My death?' Maelgwn guessed, and Tory nodded her head slightly in response. 'My wedding?' he asked, not looking at her this time.

'It doth not really say, only that you had a queen, who was more fine and chaste than any other in the land.' Tory felt she could tell him that much. Then it dawned on her that there was no danger in letting him see it, as the book was written in modern English and only small passages were in the original language.

Maelgwn sat staring at the book, and Brockwell looked wary.

'It be written in my native tongue,' Tory explained, 'and I promise I will translate parts for thee later, but right now I need a bath.'

Maelgwn rose, his thoughts elsewhere. 'I will send Katren up.'

'I would like to thank thee,' Brockwell said. 'It hast been . . . different.' He joined the Prince and they walked down the stairs and out of sight.

Lady Gladys, Cara, and Alma, the two teenage girls in her care, were organising the servants with setting the table for supper. Lady Gladys noticed her boys as they passed through the banquet hall, and as she hadn't spied either one all day, she pursued them. She opened the door to the adjoining room to find her son raising a goblet to Maelgwn. 'Thou art absolutely right cousin, she be incredible.'

'Indeed?' Lady Gladys said with interest, closing the door behind her.

Brockwell nearly dropped his drink at the sound of his mother's voice, and the Prince stood to explain.

'I should like to meet this girl,' she announced. Maelgwn moved to object but she wouldn't hear a word of it. 'Maelgwn, I demand thee take me to the north tower, this instant!' She spoke forcefully, but without raising her voice. 'Unless I see with my own eyes what the pair of thee have been up to, I shall not be a part of this another day.'

Just as Tory had settled into her bath, sure that the day's events were over, there came a knock at the door.

'Tory,' Maelgwn called. 'I have brought someone to meet thee.'

'Now, Maelgwn?' Tory asked, looking at her towel across the room; Katren had gone to fetch supper and there was no one to pass it to her.

Lady Gladys looked at Maelgwn surprised. 'She refers to thee by thy first name, she be privileged.'

'Why dost thou never come to see me when I have my clothes *on*?' Tory sounded annoyed and in a fluster.

Maelgwn held his head, not liking the way this must sound to his aunt. 'Tory, it be my aunt waiting to see thee, Brockwell's mother and sister to the King. She can hear every word thou art saying.'

Oh shit. 'Come in.'

Maelgwn opened the door to find Tory dressed in a wrap that reached the floor, and he smiled at her in quiet approval. Her hair was in a bun to save getting it wet, so she looked quite presentable.

Lady Gladys gazed upon Tory in the soft candlelight. 'Thank you, Maelgwn, that will be all,' she instructed, shooing him out and shutting the door on him. She then turned to study Tory further. 'Well now, thou dost not look so different to my old eyes.' She smiled and reached out to lift Tory's chin higher, so that her face would catch the light. 'I can see now what keeps my boys so enchanted.'

'Enchanted?' Tory was struck almost speechless by this lovely woman. She was so refined in the way she spoke, the way she moved; her whole manner was most courteous and genteel.

'Indeed.' She let Tory go, looking to the stairway that lead to the caphouse. 'I have never known Maelgwn to be so . . . preoccupied.' She gestured up the stairs. 'May I?'

'Of course,' Tory insisted.

Maelgwn waited patiently outside; it seemed that his aunt had been in there for hours. What could they be discussing all this while, he wondered.

At last the door opened and Lady Gladys emerged. 'I will look forward to it, dear,' she said, closing the door behind her. Maelgwn approached at once. 'A lovely girl,' she commented as she passed him on the way back to her duties. 'I will help thee.'

Maelgwn went after her, still worried. 'Aunt.' He touched her arm lightly to draw her to a stop. 'Did thee speak to her of my wedding?'

He seemed ashamed to ask and she sighed, already aware that this was the main reason he had not wanted them to meet. 'Nay.' She appeared a mite disappointed in him, but the tone in her voice lifted as she said, 'Though I did mention that I had never seen thee so distracted by a woman.'

Maelgwn was shocked.

'It serves thyself right, Maelgwn. Besides, it be the truth. Thee can play thy games, dear boy, and I shall play my own.'

In the weeks that followed, Tory's life at Aberffraw began to fall nicely into place. She started her day with the Prince's training, which commenced at sunrise with meditation. Then came a stretch program which incorporated some yoga and breathing exercises to warm up and improve flexibility. Maelgwn's coordination was good from all his swordplay. His body, however, was so solid from wielding heavy swords and carrying iron armour, that stretching exercises were essential. They did a short abdominal program, more for Tory's benefit than the Prince's as his abdominal muscles were as strong as the stone walls that surrounded them. This was followed by a series of Tae-kwon-do movements, which were a faster version of kata. Once the Prince had mastered these to Tory's satisfaction, they would begin sparring and self-defence. At the end of each session, before their final meditation, Tory would teach the Prince a small section of a kata. He had begun to arrive early, to join her in her sunrise ritual of kata. He would execute the parts he'd learnt and try to follow those he hadn't. Tory was pleased that Maelgwn was so keen, and she found him to be an excellent student. Further meditation brought the workout to a close by early afternoon, approximately one o'clock on the sundial.

The Prince had come to look forward to this more than any other part of her tuition. These stories or meditations were unlike anything Maelgwn had heard from the court bards. Taliesin, a former tutor to the Prince, had schooled him in a similar thought process, but his lessons had been based on more shamanistic principles.

Lady Gladys usually arrived just as the meditation was coming to a close, and everyday she would join Tory for lunch. Lady Gladys had never invited the Prince to eat with them; he was excused to have lunch with his knights and to attend to his stately duties. Lady Gladys knew all about Tory's origins, even though neither had told Maelgwn. Tory could not have kept the truth from this woman, and she knew Maelgwn trusted his aunt, or he would not have introduced them.

Lady Gladys found little intelligent female conversation in the court, and so she looked forward to her discussions with Tory; her favourite topic being the future. Tory had become like an afternoon TV soapie to Lady Gladys, who laughed and delighted in her tales. This stately woman had lived through many an ordeal in her lifetime, so nothing much shocked her.

Katren had blossomed in the care of Drusilla, the head maid in the household at Aberffraw. Her bruises had faded, and so she began to wear her hair pulled back off her face and curled at the end in Roman fashion. She'd adjusted to life at the court with considerable ease and, unlike Tory, looked the part. As well as having charmed most of the household's staff with her large soulful eyes and soft smiles, Katren had also befriended Alma and Cara. She attended the two young maidens in the free time she found in the morning after bringing Tory and the Prince a small breakfast. Katren, born and bred on the common, seemed like rather a wild child to Cara and Alma, who were bored with their rigid life at court. The pair enjoyed the story of Katren's rescue from her 'disgusting pig of a husband'. She told them the gossip she'd overheard when serving lunch to Tory and Lady Gladys, and stories about the royal knights that she heard about the house. Katren's favourite knight was the young and handsome Sir Brockwell.

Needless to say, Tory had become almost an idol to Cara and Alma, who hadn't seen a trace of her since the day she'd arrived. Only Katren, Lady Gladys, Sir Brockwell and the Prince were allowed into the north tower or to enter any of the four towers that led to the open walkways of the roof. Guards had been posted on the walls of the outer bailey, so the roof was completely private and could not be seen by anyone.

Katren had refused to tell the girls what really went on in the tower. Yet after several days of persistent nagging, she cracked, making them swear they'd never tell another soul.

At first Tory didn't know what to do in the afternoons after lunch with Lady Gladys. She hadn't had any time to herself for so long that it seemed almost boring.

By the third afternoon of peace, Tory hung over the sea-wall staring at the water. It was a hot day and, frankly, all she wanted to do was to strip off her clothes and dive into the ocean. 'Damn, this was supposed to be a holiday.'

Growing more restless, she returned to the tower and changed into a black one-piece swimsuit and a pair of bicycle shorts. What the hell, Tory figured, as nobody came up there anyway. She settled down on her towel to catch a few rays.

Later that day, as Maelgwn was walking across the courtyard, he stopped to listen to a haunting tune that resonated down around the walls of the inner bailey.

'Maelgwn?' Lady Gladys came outside to join him. 'From whence comes that lovely music?'

'It be Tory. Listen.' Maelgwn was completely lost in it.

''Tis beautiful, darling . . . but surely it cannot be helpful to thy secret.' She smiled, making good sense as always.

Tory finished the piece to hear the unexpected sound of applause. She turned to find Selwyn, the prince's squire, standing in the doorway, his eyes lowered to the ground.

'Please forgive my insolence, lady. I mean no disrespect. It be just that I am a trained harpist and can fully appreciate a piece well played.'

'Thou art excused, Selwyn,' she assured him.

Selwyn was all of nineteen and gorgeous to look at, though he was of a smaller build than the other men. His fine, fair hair fell to his shoulders in a bob, his eyes were deep blue and his face was open and full of expression. Tory thought that in her day he would be considered quite trendy.

'Be thine instrument here at Aberffraw, perhaps we could play together?'

'Oh, lady . . .' Selwyn was filled with excitement, until he spied the Prince approaching.

'Whoops!' she said quietly, as she turned to discover his concern.

Maelgwn waved for Selwyn to take his leave. 'Thee knows thou art banned from here,' he scolded.

Selwyn, disappointed, did as the Prince bade.

'Hold on,' Tory called after him. 'Please, Majesty. Selwyn only wants to practise his music with me, and I've been so bored these past few afternoons that I'd be most grateful for the distraction.'

This was the first time Tory had ever called him Majesty, and Maelgwn rather liked it. 'Alright. But thee will have to practise inside the tower . . . for now.'

Tory threw her arms around his neck. 'Thank thee so much.' She let him go before bounding inside to get changed.

'My pleasure.' Maelgwn smiled after her, marvelling at her attire. He looked to his page, who seemed amused by it all. 'Well, off with thee then. Do not keep the lady waiting.'

'Thank thee, Majesty. I be greatly honoured this day.' Selwyn ran to fetch his harp.

From then on, Tory's days were filled. In the early evening she would take supper with Katren. The girl had begun to ask questions about the way Tory fought and why she meditated, so Tory proposed teaching her a few exercises for her own protection.

Cara and Alma got wind of this a few days later, and soon Tory found them in the tower, accompanied by Katren who introduced them to each other. Tory was extremely concerned as she considered their request, as the pair hardly looked the type for her tuition. Alma was fair and petite, with wide eyes the colour of acorns. Her hair was pulled back in a neat bun, which made her the very image of a little china doll. Cara was just as slender, though much taller. Her dark, copper brown hair fell in loose ringlets halfway down her back, and although her hazel eyes gave her a more fiery appearance, even she seemed too prim for the request they were making.

'Katren, thou promised not to tell anyone. The Prince will kill me if he finds I am corrupting the young maidens here,' Tory appealed to her, emphasising the sensitiveness of the situation.

'Doth not every woman have the right to defend herself?' Katren took the same stand Tory would adopt herself. 'Cara, Alma, and I have already thought of a good excuse to be here.'

'And what might that be?' Tory asked.

'Singing practice,' they announced in unison.

'We all have fine voices and I have heard thee sing, thy voice be as pretty as a bird,' Katren continued. 'I have spoken with Selwyn. He will tell Prince Maelgwn that he be accompanying us on the harp, but he will really be keeping watch by the door downstairs.'

'Please, lady.' Cara came forward. 'Thee cannot imagine how drab life hast been at court.'

Tory could relate to their dilemma. 'Alright. We will start tomorrow night.'

6

THE SECOND
PRINCE

After three weeks of training, the Prince had taken to the oriental fighting skills like a fish to water. He and Tory had recently begun sparring and had been delighting in toppling each other ever since.

Tory felt relaxed in the Prince's company, as she was not expected to humble herself before him as everyone else was. Maelgwn, on the other hand, was pleased to have one person in his world with whom he could be himself.

Taliesin had also been this way with him, and Tory made him feel as playful, cocky, and sure of himself as he had been in his youth. The Prince found himself sneaking up to Tory's room after the rest of the household had made for bed. She would read to him from her books or speak to him of the future, as he lay across the end of her bed. Some nights, they would talk for hours. He would have tried to seduce her weeks ago had he not known about his damn marriage.

Maelgwn was being particularly attentive to Tory this morning. He knew she was growing annoyed by his lack of concentration, but he just couldn't seem to focus. They were practising throws and holds. Maelgwn started the exercise to the side of Tory, bent over her with his arm across her back. But he became so interested in the view he had down her shirt that he showed little resistance to her counterattack.

Tory stood up, angered by his lack of discipline. 'Let's try it the other way around, shall we?'

Maelgwn grinned. 'I thought thee would never ask.'

This time his heart was in it. He twisted out from under her hold, and executing a sweeping kick to the back of her legs, flung her backwards to the ground. Maelgwn pinned her legs to the mat with his knees and stretched each of her arms above her head, maintaining a firm grasp of her wrists. He smiled down at her triumphant, raising his eyebrows as if to say, not bad hey?

'Much better!' Tory announced, pleased. 'I yield.' She waited for him to ease off, but he didn't. His dark eyes gazed at her and he held her fast.

'I have dreamt of thee,' he whispered, and their lips gently met.

A surge of adrenalin rushed through them. Maelgwn released her legs, sliding himself in between them. Tory didn't care about the repercussions of her actions now; she was tired of having to suppress how she felt about the Prince. She wrapped her legs around Maelgwn's powerful form and drew her body up to meet his in encouragement.

The expectant lovers didn't hear the door open and close downstairs. Brockwell came to a stop at the top of the staircase, rather perturbed by what he saw. 'Majesty.' He waited. 'Majesty!'

'What!' Maelgwn snapped, as Tory ducked out from beneath him.

'Thy father, King Caswallon, be here with thine *bride*,' Brockwell announced, with a blatant lack of diplomacy.

'Thine bride!' Tory looked at Maelgwn, who'd sprung to his feet in a fluster at the sound of his father's name. 'When were you planning to tell me exactly? Thee told me a barefaced lie and Brockwell be my witness.'

Brockwell gave Tory a fixed nod to confirm.

Maelgwn didn't know quite what to say; he had no excuse. The dream he'd had the night before must have caused him to take leave of his senses. 'Please Tory, I have no time to explain, I have to go.'

Tory ignored his plea and stormed outside.

Brockwell had to grin at Maelgwn's discomposure. 'He be waiting, Majesty.'

Maelgwn swung round to confront his champion. 'Why, Calin?'

'It not be right that thee should keep her hidden in this tower and use her ignorance to thine own advantage.'

Brockwell sounded as angered by his cousin's behaviour as Maelgwn was about his untimely betrayal.

'This be a change of heart . . . coming from one who wanted to slit her throat!'

'An *honest* mistake, Sire.' Brockwell suppressed his feelings and motioned the Prince to the stairs.

Maelgwn realised he was wrong, this predicament was of his own making. 'Forgive me, Calin. I do not know what hast got into me.' Maelgwn paused to gather his wits. 'I truly need thy assistance this day, as I am not sure that I shall come through it.'

'Go, change, and greet thy father.' Brockwell's tone softened upon sensing his cousin's despair. 'Thee will find him in the the west wing gallery and . . .' he gave Maelgwn fair warning, 'thy brother hast returned with him. In the meantime, I shall see if I can calm the she-devil on thy behalf.'

Maelgwn placed a hand on Brockwell's shoulder, 'I cannot thank thee enough. Thou art a true champion, Calin.'

Brockwell found Tory in her favourite spot, leaning on the sea-wall, looking out over the ocean.

She heard footsteps and even though her eyes were fixed on the blue horizon, she guessed it was Brockwell and not the Prince who'd come to pacify her. The gentle lull of the ocean and the warmth of the sunshine had calmed her, though she didn't look to him as she spoke. 'How long hast everyone known, Brockwell?'

The knight took a seat beside her, looking out in the opposite direction towards the village. 'Only Maelgwn, myself and Lady Gladys know. The Prince confided in us the night we arrived here. He was only told of it at Degannwy.' Brockwell noticed Tory's expression darken. 'But I do swear to thee, Maelgwn hast never even met the girl.'

Tory turned her large, green eyes his way. 'Hast thou met her?'

He smiled at the question. 'Aye, just then.'

'Be she beautiful?' Tory looked back to the ocean, not really wanting to know.

'Aye, I suppose, but I doubt she will be to Maelgwn's taste, no . . .'

Brockwell cut himself short, and Tory glanced over to catch him holding his hands cupped in front of his chest.

'Let's just say, thee need not fear comparison.'

She felt mildly appeased by his remark. 'Thou art a good friend to him, Calin.' Tory placed a hand on his shoulder in her first open show of affection toward him. She missed having Brian as a confidant and Brockwell was so like him. 'May I call thee Calin?'

Both sides of his mouth dropped to a mope as he considered the request. 'Well, it is my real name.'

'Is not Brockwell thy real name too?'

'Nay, Brockwell was my father's name. He was a fierce warrior, so they tell me. He died when I was very young.' Calin became melancholy a moment, then shrugged off his sadness. 'Sir Calin dost not sound very ominous. So when I was knighted, I asked to be dubbed in my father's name.'

'Well, you seem to do a fine job living up to his reputation. So then, *Calin*, allow me to ask thee, do you think I am making a contribution to the court at Aberffraw?'

Brockwell nodded, unsure as to where the conversation was heading.

'Then, should I not be allowed to be part of it?'

Brockwell jumped to his feet, alarmed. 'Thee could not, not as thou art!' he spluttered, glancing at her attire.

She grabbed his hand to implore him. 'Surely I can be dressed to appear like any other maiden here. Please Calin, or I shall surely go mad.'

What could he say? He agreed with her. He placed his hand on hers, his mind ticking over. 'If we give Maelgwn no warning then he cannot object. But there be much to consider here. Maelgwn's fears should not be taken lightly for he hast had good reason to keep thee a secret thus far.' He'd heard Maelgwn speak of his concerns about the safety of his father's kingdom on many occasions. Yet, perhaps they could use Tory's introduction to the court to their advantage, and dispel the rumours generated by her presence here at the same time.

'We shall need help,' he resolved.

Maelgwn took time readying himself; he was not looking forward to confronting his father, meeting this woman, or being united with his long lost brother. He tried briefly to meditate in the hope of becoming centred and calm, but without Tory to guide him it was useless.

'I need her on my side.' He scolded himself as he marched down the long hall, the doors to the gallery in his sights. 'I must make my peace with her before this day be over.'

As his hand came to rest on the handle of the large door, he could hear the murmurs of those who awaited him. He held his pendant of the Dragon and took a deep breath.

The Prince entered the gallery to find most of the knights in attendance, along with his father's officials and personal guard. The ladies of the house, with the exception of Lady Gladys, were standing by the tall, slender windows. Maelgwn spotted two ladies who were unfamiliar to him, one of whom he assumed was his bride to be. He spied his brother, Caradoc, in the corner, engrossed in conversation with Cadogan. I should have known they'd seek each other out, they always were as thick as thieves, he thought. This was a worry. Maelgwn had hoped to keep Tory a secret from Caradoc, so he summoned Madoc.

'Can I help thee, Majesty?'

Maelgwn urged him closer. 'Get Cadogan away from Caradoc, I do not trust them.'

Madoc quietly agreed.

'Send him on an errand of some description . . . I want him gone for at least a few days.'

Madoc nodded and went about his bidding.

'Maelgwn, my boy.' King Caswallon held out his hand to his son.

The Prince's expression was solemn as he went down on one knee before the King. 'Father.' He kissed the ring on his father's hand. 'I be comforted to see that thou hast returned to us in good health.'

At this the King laughed. 'I was in no danger, I assure thee. And I must say, thou art appearing exceedingly well thyself.'

But Maelgwn was not so convinced of his father's safety. 'I need to speak with thee at once. *Alone*.'

'Later. Percival hast already spoken to me of thy concern, but now I insist thee meet thy bride before thee raise an objection to her.'

It will not make any difference, Maelgwn thought, though he nodded in accordance with his father's wishes.

Tory studied her image in the mirror with reservation. She was dressed in an outfit that had once belonged to the late Queen, who had been small of frame like herself. The linen dress, or kirtle, was pale green and simple in design. It hung from her shoulders in soft waves and looked rather like a long nightshirt. Over it she wore a thickly woven tunic, or gunna, which had sleeves to the elbow, and fell to her knees. It was of a very deep green, almost emerald, which nicely complemented her eyes. Tory fastened the gunna in tight at the waist with her black leather belt. The women wore no undergarments at this time of year, but Tory wasn't too comfortable with that idea. She chose to wear her T-shirt, jeans and steel-capped boots underneath, which were well hidden by the dress.

'Goodness, I almost look like a lady.'

'What doth thou mean, *almost*?' Lady Gladys replied. She'd braided strands of hair from each side of Tory's face and fastened them in the centre at the back, leaving the rest of her hair loose. When she'd finished, she paused to view the result. 'Thee appears as refined as Queen Sorcha herself once did, bless her soul. Hast Maelgwn not told thee that thou bears a likeness to her?'

Tory didn't know if this was good news or not. 'He never mentioned it, no.'

'Maelgwn absolutely adored her, everyone did.' She paused briefly as the memories came flooding back, then sighed. 'If the King dost not take an instant liking to thee, I shall be very surprised.' Lady Gladys was struck by a thought. 'In fact, we had best couple thee with someone, save Caswallon or Caradoc do take a fancy to thee.'

Tory's eyes opened wide in horror as Lady Gladys concocted a strategy. A smile crossed her face as she made haste for the stairwell. 'Calin.'

'Lady Gladys, what art thou thinking?'

She turned back to Tory, taking up her hands in her own, 'Thee must trust me, little one.'

The Prince was having great difficulty engaging Vanora, his intended bride, in conversation. The girl was barely eighteen years of age, ten years younger than himself. Her hair, as dark as his own, fell in tight curls around her face and over her shoulders. She had a round yet delicate face and ivory skin, flushed rose red in her cheeks and mouth. She was taller than the other young maidens and her body was long and slim like a reed. The Princess, however beautiful, had eyes as cold and dark as ebony, and Maelgwn thought her a poor compensation for the bounty he'd forfeited that morning.

Lady Gladys entered the room, and the Prince excused himself politely then left to pursue his aunt who had taken a seat by the King. Over the rest of the conversations going on in the room, Maelgwn heard Lady Gladys inform the King that she wanted to introduce a special guest who was presently residing at the house.

The doors opened and Maelgwn turned to see Tory enter on Brockwell's arm. He felt his temperature begin to rise. *Have they gone mad?* He should have been furious but his heart leapt at the sight of Tory dressed thus, and he felt compelled to fall to his knees; she looked so much like his mother, the Queen. This resemblance didn't go unnoticed by the older members of the court, and their voices were hushed as Brockwell proudly led her to the King.

Caswallon was stunned as he stood to greet her. 'Sorcha,' he uttered under his breath.

Lady Gladys wore a cool smile of satisfaction as she rose to introduce her guest. 'Majesty, this be Tory Alexander, a traveller left stranded on British soil.'

Tory was nervous, aware that everyone in the room was watching her, and she didn't dare venture a look in Maelgwn's direction. Instead, she curtsied, her eyes lowered as she'd been instructed.

'Thy son saved her from Saxon cutthroats in the south-east,' Lady Gladys informed the King.

He extended his hand to Tory and she went down on one knee before him, kissing his ring.

'Arise, dear girl,' he instructed, drawing her up by the hand, completely enchanted. 'She be so pretty,

Maelgwn. Why did thee not tell me of this find?' Caswallon looked at Maelgwn who was at a loss for words. The King turned his gaze back to Tory, a million memories flooding his mind. 'Afraid I might snatch her up for myself, no doubt.'

Tory smiled at the King, who was tall like the Prince and no doubt very handsome in his younger days. 'Thee flatters me, Majesty.' Tory flirted ever so slightly.

Maelgwn became concerned by the way his father was looking at Tory, and also noticed his brother coming forward to eye her over. It was Brockwell, however, who stepped in to reclaim her.

'Thou art too late, Majesty. She be well spoken for.'

As Tory gave Brockwell an affectionate smile, Maelgwn's blood began to boil.

'Do sit down and tell me all about thyself.' The King motioned her to the seat beside him, choosing to ignore Brockwell's claim.

Tory spied Sir Gilmore studying her with a rather curious expression, as he came to stand behind the King. 'I have been recovering from my ordeal in the north tower, and have not yet had the opportunity to meet everyone.' Tory hoped this might explain why she hadn't met the man who ran the house in the King's absence. 'Thee must be Sir Gilmore.' Tory stood and held out her hand to him. 'I believe I have much to thank thee for.' The knight's brow was drawn in curiosity and so she explained, 'Art thou not the tutor in swordplay and battle to my saviour?' Tory motioned to Maelgwn, who couldn't help but smile at the way she so easily charmed everyone.

Sir Gilmore took up her hand and kissed it. 'Forgive

my staring, lady, but for a moment I thought thee the ghost of our dear departed Queen.'

Maelgwn relaxed slightly when he realised this was Gilmore's only concern.

''Tis a remarkable resemblance, I must say,' Lady Gladys commented, giving Tory a wink of approval; she was obviously enjoying herself immensely.

'How do we know thou art not a simple commoner? Any woman can look like a lady in the right dress.'

There was such evil in this voice, so deep and harsh, that Tory turned to view the speaker whom she assumed to be Prince Caradoc. He looked much like the other males of his family, but he was not as well groomed. His hair was very long with braids here and there, and he obviously took pride in being the black sheep.

'Prince Caradoc, I presume?' She tipped her head to him slightly. 'I have heard so much about thee.'

'I do not doubt it.' Caradoc looked to Maelgwn, who was watching him closely.

Tory sensed the malice between these two, and decided she'd have to discover the cause of their falling out.

'Tory possesses an instrument the like of none thou hast ever heard. It be simply beautiful, Majesty,' Lady Gladys announced, to break the feeling of ill will. 'We must have her play for us this evening.'

'Indeed, I shall look forward to it,' the King replied.

For the rest of the afternoon the King ignored the bickering of his sons, finding solace in the company of the women of the house.

Tory met Maelgwn's intended bride during the course of the afternoon, and strangely enough they took an instant dislike of each other. It was not only Princess Vanora's expression that made her appear so sombre; a menacing presence seemed to overshadow her whole demeanour. Tory considered it a pity that the Princess and Caradoc weren't betrothed, as they seemed well suited.

Later that evening everyone was treated to a feast in the banquet hall. As Brockwell's assumed lady, Tory was seated between him and Madoc; thankfully well away from Caradoc and Vanora.

A seemingly neverending stream of food was brought in and laid on the tables before them: meats, fruit, vegetables, bread, cheese, nuts and mead, which flowed freely throughout the evening.

Brockwell had been wonderful company, steadily drinking Tory under the table. Katren was in her element, pleased to be attending her lady in the court banquet hall. Tory made a point of properly introducing her to Brockwell, knowing that Katren had a soft spot for the knight.

'Calin, thee remembers Katren,' said Tory, directing his attention away from herself to the maid. Katren curtsied politely, hiding the admiration she felt as Brockwell eyed her with a look of approval.

'Well, well, well. Who would have thought thee would scrub up so nicely.' Brockwell sat back in his chair to view her better. 'A true rose.'

Though her heart was set aflutter, Katren didn't let her excitement get the better of her. 'May I say, Lord, that I am a great admirer of thee. Thy heroic deeds these past years be both numerous and notorious.'

'That thee may.' Brockwell watched her depart, thinking that she was as cheeky as her mistress. He took up his goblet. 'What shall we drink to this time?'

'To friends,' Tory replied.

'To lovers.'

'And enemies,' she cautioned. 'May we be granted the foresight to know the difference.' Tory clinked her goblet against his.

Brockwell could only smile; it seemed she had an answer for every advance.

Tory was quite tipsy when the time came for her to perform for the King. Selwyn, who was to accompany her, had collected her saxophone from her quarters. She took a short time to explain to King Caswallon how the instrument worked before taking up her place by the harp. The dulcet tones of the two instruments came together to create an atmosphere of bliss, keeping the audience spellbound throughout the performance. All bar the Prince, that is, whose enjoyment was disturbed by Caradoc who was sitting nearby.

'Thy little find appears mighty palatable from here,' Caradoc goaded, as he turned an evil eye to his brother. Though Maelgwn clearly disapproved of his connotation, he simply focused his attention on the players. Caradoc laughed at his brother's restraint, delighted to have found an obvious weakness.

When the music was finished, Tory and Selwyn were overwhelmed with applause. Selwyn held Tory's hand as they took a bow and his face beamed with satisfaction.

The hour was late and the moon was full, thus the knights enticed young maidens to stroll in the moonlight. Maelgwn had been urged by his father to accompany Vanora, and for the first time in her life Tory felt a twinge of jealousy. She looked at Brockwell who was slouched in his chair quietly watching her observe everyone else. 'Well, I am history thanks to thee.' She slapped his knee. 'And so I should retire.'

'I shall escort thee, then,' Brockwell offered in a drunken but friendly manner, getting to his feet.

'Good, because I be totally lost.' They both laughed. Once Tory had stood up, Brockwell locked her arm firmly around his own and they bid the royal party goodnight.

As soon as Tory reached the privacy of her quarters, she stripped down to her T-shirt and jeans and flopped back onto the bed. With all the mead she'd consumed, however, the room began to spin and she was impelled to sit straight back up. She opened her eyes as she regained her composure, and was startled to find Brockwell staring down at her. 'Damn thee, Calin, thee scared me!' Tory scolded. 'I thought thee had gone to bed.'

'But I am not tired yet.'

Brockwell slumped onto the bed beside her in an intoxicated state, and Tory couldn't fail to notice how amiable was his mood. 'Now Calin, thou hast had much to drink . . .' she began her good-sense lecture, getting up off the bed and opening the doors to let some fresh air into the room. 'And despite how fond I am of thee, I will have to inflict real pain if thou art up to mischief.'

Brockwell, completely ignoring her caution, slowly approached Tory to trace a finger along the fading scar he'd left on her neck. 'I deeply regret that I ever caused thee pain, Tory. This scar be a thorn in my side. Each time I see it, I am reminded of my rash and brutal judgement of thee.'

This resolve was most unexpected and Tory lowered her defences. 'Please, do not feel guilty, I bear thee no malice. On the contrary . . .' She took a step away, feeling uncomfortably intimate with him. 'Thou hast been the best friend I could have asked for this day.' Tory was in need of some air, and moved to the walkway outside.

Brockwell followed her into the moonlight, more than a little confused. 'Then why dost thou keep such a distance between us? Doth thou find me so undesirable?'

She reached out and gently touched the face that was so familiar to her. 'No, thou art very handsome.'

Brockwell took hold of her arms, anxious to know her mind. 'Art thou in love with Maelgwn?'

Tory's head was swimming. 'It hast got nothing to do with him. I . . .' Brockwell startled her with a kiss filled with passion. After all the mead she'd consumed, Calin's attentions were hard to resist and she seemed to be involuntarily returning his advances. But, as angry as she was at Maelgwn for his deceit, Tory could not bring herself to betray him like this. 'Calin. I am sorry, but I cannot do this.'

'But it was going so well?'

'Please, come inside, I have something to show thee.'

Tory produced a photo of herself and Brian from her wallet and handed it to Brockwell. The picture had been taken at the competition the day before Brian died; they had been so proud of each other's win and it reflected in their faces.

Brockwell went quiet, glancing up from the picture to his own image in the mirror. 'Was he thy lover?' he asked.

'He was my brother,' Tory answered, trying to hide the pain of his loss. 'He died a couple of years ago.'

'Thee must miss him.'

Tory nodded her head in confirmation, and the tears began to roll down her face. 'Every day.'

Brockwell stood to embrace her; he'd never been too good at consoling weeping women. 'So thou art telling me I remind thee of thy dead brother,' he surmised. 'Well, no wonder thou art not swooning at my advances.'

Tory gave half a laugh. 'I am so sorry, Calin. Under different circumstances I would be swooning, truly . . . well I was really,' she admitted, embarrassed.

'I should leave thee to thy dreams then.'

'Calin.'

He looked back to her from the stairwell.

'I do love thee.'

'Now thee tells me,' he rolled his eyes, throwing his arms in the air. 'Women!'

Tory felt a warm comfort come over her as the door downstairs closed. It was the feeling one gets upon finding a new friend or, in this case, a very old one.

It seemed she'd only been asleep for a minute when Maelgwn came bursting through the doors from the wall-walk. 'Tory! Thou art here?' He peered through the darkness to her bed, sounding surprised for some reason.

'Well where did thee think I would be at this hour?'

'So, 'tis not thee with Brockwell in his room,' he said, breathing a sigh of relief.

'Brockwell hast a woman in his room?' Now Tory was the one who sounded disturbed.

'Aye.' Maelgwn wondered why this should bother her.

'Typical.' Tory thumped herself in the head for being so stupid. 'And may I say how nice it was of thee to think that I would take to Calin's bed, in any case . . . I mean, what kind of a girl dost thou take me for?'

'Well what am I to think when I see him carrying a woman into his room, and thou hast been the only one flirting with him this day.'

'Flirting! I was covering thy royal butt. Perhaps thee would have preferred that I told thy father and thy bride of our encounter this morning?'

The Prince was not listening. 'Why art thou so annoyed with Calin? Was he here with thee this night?'

'That be my own affair.' Tory's head was absolutely splitting, and she didn't have the patience to give him a detailed account at present.

'He touched thee?'

As Maelgwn suddenly sounded quite hurt, Tory slowly shook her head. 'We were both the better for drink, but nothing came of it. So, my pleasures art still very much my own. Happy now? Goodnight.'

Maelgwn couldn't blame her for being angry. He thought it best to let her be for tonight, to save aggravating the situation further. 'Goodnight,' he whispered, closing the doors quietly behind him.

'Lady, lady, please wake up.'

Tory stirred slowly, her head still heavy. A vague recollection of being wrapped up in Calin's arms made her groan, and she held her hands over her eyes in an attempt to dispel the horror.

'Lady, I am so sorry to wake thee like this, but I fear something dreadful hast happened.'

Tory noticed Katren was sobbing. 'What distresses thee so?'

'Sir Brockwell approached me last night as I finished my duties . . .'

'Katren, it was thee in Calin's room last night?'

'Nay, lady! I would never shame thee in such a manner. But when I declined, Sir Brockwell took Vanora's maid, Malvina, in my stead. I fear I have passed up the only chance I shall ever have.' She collapsed onto the bed and burst into tears once again.

'Katren, look at me. Brockwell drank so much last night that I doubt he will remember a thing this day, and I'm quite sure he hast kicked Malvina out by now.' This brought a smile to Katren's face. 'Thou hast done the right thing, believe me. For if thou wishes to catch Calin for keeps . . .' Tory paused for confirmation and Katren nodded eagerly, wanting to hear more, '. . . thee must ignore his every advance. Brush him off as if thee did not care for him at all.'

'But then Sir Brockwell will find himself another woman who be more obliging, like last night.'

'He will keep coming back to thee, though. Want to know why?' Tory prompted, and Katren nodded her head. 'Because, although Sir Brockwell be used to getting what he wants, if there be no conquest, there be no glory. Understand?'

Katren smiled. 'Aye, I see the sense of it.'

Tory glanced at the stairwell to find that Maelgwn had taken a seat, and was listening intently to every word they said. She leaned closer to Katren, wondering how long he'd been there. 'The way I fight seems to excite these men, and we shall use this to thy advantage when the time be right.' Katren giggled as Tory sat back and gave her a wink.

'Oh thank thee, lady, thou art too good to me.' Katren rose, pulling herself together. 'I shall be about my duty and get thee fed.'

The maid turned bright red on discovering the Prince. She curtsied to him then left as quickly as she was able.

Maelgwn's mind was set at ease by what he'd heard, and he admitted that Tory was quite correct in her analysis of his cousin. Her words gave him hope that she might be using the same strategy on him. For surely if Tory was advising another woman on Calin's entrapment, she could hold no true interest in him herself. 'Art thou still angry at me?'

He strolled over to take a seat on the bed, while Tory silently debated the issue in her mind. 'When thee said yesterday that thou had dreamt of me, what did thee mean?' she asked.

He found the question an amusing one. 'I assure thee, if enlightened thee would never speak to me again.' Some of it had been rather erotic so he wasn't lying, yet in his experience the Prince knew it to be much more than a dream; it was a prophesy. He'd had these waking dreams when the Dragon first came to him, and they would stay with him for days, tormenting and guiding him to do things he wouldn't normally consider.

'I see.' Tory found it hard to keep a smile from her face.

The door downstairs slammed open, startling them both.

'Majesty, thee will never guess who be here?' Brockwell reached the top of the stairs, short of breath.

'Taliesin,' answered Maelgwn, calmly.

'How did thee know?' Brockwell stared at his friend amazed, before racing back downstairs; he was still a bit embarrassed by his behaviour the night before and wasn't yet ready to face the repercussions.

Tory's eyes had parted wide. 'Taliesin! The Taliesin? Maelgwn, thou dost know him?' she clutched Maelgwn's shoulder, excited. If only part of what the history books said of him was true, this renowned magician might know of a way to get her home. 'Why of course you do!' Tory hit herself as she recalled reading something to that effect.

'Aye. He was my tutor and occupied this very tower. My mother held him in very high regard.'

The star charts on the wall are his! She viewed her tower in a different light now. 'Be he as powerful and all knowing as they say? Be he truly immortal and a shaman? He could help me get home, could he not?'

Maelgwn just laughed in response to the interrogation, fully suspecting Taliesin of having everything to do with her being there in the first place. 'Thou shalt have to ask him thyself.' He rose, eager to greet his old friend. 'I will bring him to meet thee.'

'Can I not come down?'

'I believe a more private meeting be in order. I will not be long.'

Maelgwn hadn't seen his old mentor in over ten years, and he remembered that they didn't part on the best of terms at the time. Still, Taliesin's indignation about the puerile resolutions Maelgwn made as a boy hadn't stopped the old man from arriving when he was needed most.

Brockwell strode alongside the Prince, his conscience plaguing him. 'I believe I owe thee an apology.'

Maelgwn was unsure of what he meant and had to stop and think about it for a moment. 'If thou art referring to Tory, I would say she be the one to whom thee should apologise. I cannot very well blame thee,' he replied to Brockwell, who appeared surprised that the Prince was taking it so well.

'She told thee, then?'

'Nay, she did not. She knows about Malvina. I saw thee taking a woman to thy bed last night, and presuming it was Tory . . .' The Prince shrugged.

Brockwell was horrified. 'What must she think of me now?' He wondered if perhaps the Prince had told her on purpose.

'I am sorry, Calin, but thee made thy own bed, so to speak.'

As the Prince didn't have time to train with her this morning, Tory had decided to jog a few laps around the open wall-walk instead. After a few simple stretching exercises, she set off around the path.

By her fourth lap she had settled into a good rhythm when, to her horror, the door to the west tower opened and Prince Caradoc led the Princess Vanora onto the walkway.

Tory didn't slow down, but nodded in greeting as she approached. 'Good morning, Highnesses.'

As she passed them, dressed only in her tracksuit and joggers, Caradoc's smirk broadened. Vanora just stared in cryptic disapproval.

'Wait downstairs,' Caradoc urged her.

Vanora stood defiant. 'Why?'

'Just do it,' he hissed back. Caradoc watched the Princess leave and waited for Tory to make her way back around to him.

Oh shit, Tory thought, noticing that Caradoc was alone. She put her head down and picked up speed to get past him.

Caradoc leaned against the sea-wall to admire Tory's form, and allowed her to pass before demanding, 'Halt right there!'

As she came to a standstill, Caradoc strolled up to her. 'What dost thou think thou art doing?'

Tory was not in the mood to be reckoned with. 'I think thou art intelligent enough to work it out.'

Caradoc smiled as he reached his hand round the back of her neck and gripped her tightly. 'How sharp be thy tongue for one of the weaker sex.' He observed her closely, considering the pleasure to be had in breaking such spirit.

His laugh was unnerving, and he pulled her toward him, forcing his tongue into her mouth. Tory clenched her fists; this bastard really knew how to push her buttons.

'Thy tongue be lush,' he told her. 'It would be a shame to have to bite it out.'

'And miss the pleasure of my conversation?' She smiled, not in the least bit fazed.

Caradoc lifted a hand to strike her but the sound of his name stopped him. He backed off, letting her go.

Tory breathed a sigh of relief as Brockwell strode up and stood between them. 'If thou hast a gripe with my lady, thee will take it up with me.'

Tory noticed that Brockwell didn't show Caradoc the same respect he did Maelgwn.

Caradoc held his disdainful air. 'Nay, I have no gripe,' he assured the knight as if he had never been angered. 'But I would suggest thee teach thy woman some manners, before she lands thee in serious trouble.'

Tory watched Caradoc leave, looking forward to a time when she could kick his chauvinistic butt back to whence it came.

'Art thou alright?' Brockwell turned to her, pleased she'd had the sense to refrain from defending herself.

'Aye, that be two I owe thee, Calin.' Tory smiled briefly. 'I did fancy smashing his royal worship right between the eyes ... 'twas a good thing thee came along.'

'Dost thou not think me volatile after my wanton conduct last night?'

'Who thee chooses to bed be thine own business. But Malvina, Calin?' She gave him a distasteful look. 'I find that insulting.'

'Thee did not have to wake up to her.' Brockwell held his head that ached with a vengeance. 'I honestly swear, I remember naught of it.'

Tory felt sorry for him; men were so stupid sometimes. 'Doth thy head ail thee?'

'Aye, almost as bad as my conscience.'

Tory flung an arm over his shoulder. 'Come to my tower, I have something that will fix thee right up.'

7

THE MAGICIAN

Maelgwn entered the library to find the old wizard standing in front of the long windows, savouring the sun's rays. 'Should I be glad to see thee, High Merlin, or hast thou come to vex me?' Maelgwn poured himself a well-needed drink and filled a goblet for his guest.

'Thou art one of my most notable students, Maelgwn. Thee should know the answer to that. Hast thou not been expecting me?'

Maelgwn's fears were set to rest, he knew his old confidant could never truly despise him. 'Dost thou know what lies ahead for Gwynedd?' The Prince held out a goblet in offering, observing the aging face of his mentor. Taliesin's body, though twisted and old, was still strong, and he never seemed to lack vigour.

The Merlin turned his eyes of palest violet to the Prince. Under his long silver moustache and beard

Taliesin smiled as he accepted the drink. 'This situation be of thine own making. A monk indeed.' He chuckled at the thought. 'No wonder thy father be so eager to see thee wed.'

'That much I know,' Maelgwn replied impatiently. 'Be that why thou hast sent Tory and have plagued me with visions of her?'

'The dreams be thine own.' Taliesin cocked an eye. 'Quite enlightening, were they not?'

'What am I to do with her? She be driving me to distraction.'

'Thee and every other male in this household.' Taliesin closed his eyes as he sensed a disturbance on the roof above them. 'Even as we speak thy brother be up to mischief.'

'Caradoc be with Tory?' Maelgwn didn't wait for an answer.

'Halt, all be well. Brockwell hast found them.'

'Art thou sure?'

'Pardon?' said Taliesin, insulted.

'My apologies, I should have known better than to ask. Now, what of my question?'

'Well, I would marry Tory if I were thee.'

'Of course! Why didn't I think of that?' Maelgwn gave up. 'Thou art no help.'

'Chiglas still despises thee for the loss of his ally, even though he claims otherwise,' Taliesin informed him. 'Understand, Maelgwn, thy father feared losing thee to a monastery and his kingdom to Chiglas, that be why he sought this arrangement. But thine instinct serves thee well and thy own plans art quite sound.'

Maelgwn was taking him more seriously now. 'What should I do, confront my father?'

Taliesin waved off the idea. 'He be not of the mind to listen at present. And in any case, there will prove to be no need.'

'So what should I do then?'

'Thou art not a child any more.' Taliesin became serious. 'And soon thee will be king.'

Maelgwn was unnerved by the comment.

'Stop worrying about thy father's plans and instigate thine own.' The magician began to fade before Maelgwn's eyes. 'The fate of Gwynedd be again in our hands, Dragon.'

'Wait! Damn it.' Maelgwn reached for him but the Merlin was gone. 'Thou art always disappearing before I am done with thee.'

There was an urgent hammering on the door and Lady Gladys entered with haste. 'Maelgwn, thou art here, praise the Goddess.' She raised her eyes to the roof and took hold of his arm. 'Thy father hast taken ill, thee must come at once.'

Tory waited impatiently for Maelgwn to come with the famous Taliesin, but with every passing hour she grew less hopeful of their meeting.

Selwyn had arrived for practice, as he did every afternoon around three, and upon finding Tory engrossed in a book, he'd quietly seated himself and begun to play.

Tory hummed along with his tune as she read up on her expected guest. She had amongst her things a book that told of the Mabinogion, a volume of the ancient writings of the Britons. These were not quite fiction nor mythology, more folk tales with some history thrown in. The writings were deemed by historians to be amongst the few sources of information on the Dark Ages in Wales, as most of the great scholars and writers had retreated to Rome more than a century before. This left only the bards and the romantic poets to record the everyday life and events of the time. Tory was delighted to find a whole chapter on the writings of Taliesin. As she read a couple of passages jumped out at her — the first was a direct address that the bard had supposedly made to Maelgwn.

> *Primary chief poet*
> *Am I to Elffin.*
> *And my native country*
> *Is the place of the Summer Stars.*
>
> *John the Divine*
> *Called me Merlin,*
> *But all future kings*
> *Shall call me Taliesin.*

This long poem went on to tell how Taliesin had been present at the birth and crucifixion of Christ, with Noah on his ark, and with Moses at the River Jordan. It claimed he'd carried the banner for Alexander, and went on to name just about every significant hero and event known to humanity at this time. It also told of how Taliesin knew the names of each star and was able to instruct the whole universe. He referred to himself as 'a wonder whose origin was not known', as one of 'the Old Ones' who were the guardians of cosmic time.

The other passage from the book captured her interest on a more personal note.

> He who would seek the muse, he who would seek
> To marry himself to any kind of sovereignty,
> Must take the descent down to the earth's centre,
> To face his utmost fears and his most secret
> anxieties.

It seemed quite possible that Taliesin would be able to give her an explanation for her predicament.

Selwyn had moved on to a new piece, which struck Tory and she was suddenly overcome with the urge to cry. A small sigh slipped from her lips, and Selwyn stopped playing.

'Something ails thee, lady?'

'It reminds me of a piece my mother used to play,' Tory answered, overcome with a longing for home. 'She be a harpist too.'

'Be she a great master like thyself, lady?' Selwyn hoped he wouldn't upset her further by asking.

'Oh,' Tory waved him off. 'Far better than I could ever dream to be. My mother plays alongside many famous musicians. She hast been invited to play in huge, grand concert halls all over the world, and thousands upon thousands of people gather to listen to their beautiful music.'

Selwyn's eyes opened wide in awe. 'Thee must be honoured to have such a heritage, music be thy birthright.'

'Although I have her love of music, Selwyn, I do not have her dedication. It is her whole life. Music consumes her completely.'

Tory sounded a little perturbed by this, and there was silence in the caphouse for a time.

'I was not born of a bard,' Selwyn began his story. 'I do not know who my parents were. I have no birthright to music, only a pure and loyal love of it. So it be grand that thou hast come to share thy inheritance with me. Truth be known, lady, I had never before been asked to play at court. That be a privilege reserved for high court bards, not a humble squire like myself. I owe thee more than I could ever repay.' Selwyn paused, placing the harp aside. 'I know thee must miss thy home, but I assure thee, thou art well loved here. Many of us hope that one day thou shalt consider Gwynedd thy home.'

'Oh Selwyn, that be a lovely thing to say.' Tory brushed a tear from her face. 'Truly.' She went over to the young page and gave him a huge hug, which he quite innocently returned. 'I am happy to know I could be of assistance to thee in thy quest.'

Selwyn couldn't recall the last time someone had held him thus, and it was more than welcome. 'I swear thou art too good for this world, lady.'

Katren arrived later than usual with their supper. She climbed the caphouse stairs with haste to find Tory engrossed in kata. 'Lady please, I be sorry to bother thee, but hast thou not heard, the King hast taken ill.'

'Good grief, will he be alright?' No wonder Maelgwn hadn't made it back to see her today.

'He be stable now, but I do not think his ailments come from natural causes.'

'Dost thou know something of medicine, Katren?'

'Nay lady, I do not. I am a simple farmer's daughter. But from what Lady Gladys hast told me, the King be suffering from the same ailment that inflicts cattle who have been eating hemlock.'

'Hemlock! Art thou quite sure?' Tory knew the plant could be deadly if one ingested it in large quantities.

'As sure as I be standing before thee. I have already told Lady Gladys of the remedy, which only be flour mixed with water to absorb the poison.' Katren was obviously proud to have had a hand in saving the King's life. 'Lady Gladys did kiss my cheek and bless the day thee brought me into the service of this house.'

'Good for thee.'

The maid glanced around to make sure they were alone, then added in a whisper, 'We suspect that witch Vanora and her maid, but to send her and Caradoc back to Powys without proof of treason would surely insult Chiglas and bring his wrath upon us . . . and that not be the all of it.' Katren paused to catch her breath. 'Sir Cadogan arrived with an urgent message from Castell Degannwy, and the men have been locked in council ever since.'

'How be the Prince faring?'

'Lady Gladys said he hast the Dragon in him this day. I do not know if this be good or bad.' Katren put her arm around Tory to reassure her. 'Try not to worry, lady. Thy prince be the bravest and most feared in all Britain. He hast seen much worse than this. Allow me to draw thee a hot bath, then he will *surely* come to tell thee all about it.'

Tory laughed. It was true, Maelgwn did seem to have a sixth sense when it came to her bath time. She resigned herself to the fact that there was nothing she could do, at least not until she knew all the facts. Still, deep down she had the most terrible feeling. Why had Caradoc waited until now to poison his father? Surely he would have been a much easier target in Powys.

The meeting adjourned a few hours before dawn. Maelgwn was tempted to drop off to sleep where he sat, but with the thought of Tory he had to see her. His father's entire kingdom was under threat, yet his main concern was for her.

As he entered the north tower, Maelgwn heard sounds of a struggle and a harrowed scream, so he made haste up the stairs. He found Tory alone, embroiled in a nightmare. 'Wake up, thou art dreaming.' He took hold of her shoulders and sat beside her.

Tory sat up with a start, flinging her arms around his neck. 'Thou art safe,' she cried into his shirt, not really awake. 'I saw thee under siege.' She pulled away, the tears and perspiration trickling down her face as she struggled to recall the rest.

''Twas just a bad dream, I expect,' Maelgwn took her in his arms, seeking comfort in the embrace himself.

'I am so sorry about thy father, Maelgwn. How goes his recovery?' She gently pulled away from him.

'My father be a fighter and be holding on.' As Maelgwn brushed the hair out of her eyes, he was alarmed to find the mark of the Dragon upon her forehead. He promptly covered his surprise and took up her hands. 'I have had word from Degannwy that they be under Saxon attack. At present there be no serious threat, but I must leave at dawn to see to the citadel's defence in the King's stead.'

Tory gripped his hands tightly; her dream was beginning to make sense. 'Be Caradoc going with thee?'

'Nay, I am afraid not. With my absence and the King's failing health, he has managed to secure a station here. But,' Maelgwn jumped in before Tory had the chance to panic. 'The King's guards suspect, as do I, Caradoc's involvement in our father's affliction. They shall keep a close eye on him and his men in my absence.'

'Thee will not make it past the Menai, that be what I dreamt. They had thee surrounded on both banks.' The tears returned to her eyes and she tightened her grip on him. 'I saw myself fight thy brother.'

'Nay. I would not leave thee here with Caradoc.'

'So thou art taking me to Degannwy then.'

'Nay!' Maelgwn was mortified. 'I would not take thee into battle.'

Tory pushed him away, insulted. 'Goddamn it! Stop treating me like a defenceless female. I be one of the best warriors thou hast.'

Maelgwn stood up, and Tory suddenly felt what most referred to as the Dragon in him. 'It hast nothing to do with whether thou art a woman, Tory. I cannot *afford* to lose thee. Our plans for an army that could conquer Chiglas and the Saxons would come to naught.'

Tory bowed her head in understanding, so Maelgwn softened his tone. 'I have left instructions with Brockwell, he awaits thee beyond the stables.'

'Nay, thee must take Brockwell to Degannwy for thine own protection.'

'I trust no one else.'

'Katren could ride with me,' Tory pleaded, at her wit's end. 'Please Maelgwn. I felt this dream. It was *real*. Like the dream thee had about us. I did not say so before, but I have had it too.'

Maelgwn shook his head, very doubtful that this was the case.

'I saw myself crowned as queen and the two of us making love in a forest,' Tory blurted out before she had the chance to feel embarrassed.

Maelgwn was forced to a smile by the truth of it. 'Tory, I value thy concern, but I have many knights around me and I am weary of arguing this day. I have thought this through well, so please, dress and take thy things. Katren awaits thee downstairs and will take thee to Brockwell.' He turned to leave. 'If all goes to plan, I shall meet thee back here in a few days.'

A terrible feeling was still brewing inside her. 'Wait!' She sprang to her feet, and gripping hold of his shirt she drew him into a kiss. 'I love thee, Maelgwn. There, I've said it.'

Though Maelgwn was stunned he didn't allow her to retreat, he pulled her closer. 'Art thou quite sure about this?'

'I am,' she stated, very matter-of-factly. 'How do you feel about it?'

Maelgwn kissed her with fervour. 'Perhaps thee should consider wedding me then,' he suggested, then left, not waiting to catch her reaction.

It took a minute for his words to register and she nearly fell over when they did. Still, with none to share her excitement, Tory resolved to a smile. 'A British prince, father would definitely approve.'

Katren led Tory through the house, across the inner bailey and into the darkness of the outer bailey. She couldn't help but envy Tory, riding off with Sir Brockwell, but said little of it. She was just thankful to be in the thick of the action.

At the rendezvous point, Brockwell had the horses ready.

'Why Calin, fancy meeting thee here?' Tory secured her baggage to the horse that Brockwell was leading and moved to mount it.

'Nay. Thee shall ride up here with me,' Brockwell told her firmly.

Tory gave him a look of apprehension.

'It will be much safer for both of us,' he explained. 'I have seen thee ride and quite honestly, it be a worry.'

Tory corked Brockwell in the leg for the insult. 'Thanks very much. Still, I see thy point.' She swung herself up into the saddle behind him. 'Take good care, Katren. Remember what thou hast learnt.'

'I will, lady.'

'Thou hast done much for the House of Gwynedd this day.' Brockwell took up Katren's hand and kissed it. 'And I, for one, thank thee for thy part.'

The maiden seemed to be floating off the ground as she watched them ride into the shadowy morning mist. 'Aye, he be mine.'

Maelgwn met his men at dawn to ride to Degannwy, and was not surprised to find his brother waiting to witness his departure.

'If thee just gave ransom to the Saxons, they would not vex thee so,' Caradoc advised his brother.

'If our father had wished it, would thee have come to the defence of the citadel in the name of Cunedda and the House of Gwynedd?'

Caradoc noticed the Dragon in his brother this morning, but he was not frightened by that superstitious nonsense any more. Without the old wizard, Maelgwn had no more mystical power than he did. He knew Maelgwn and the bard had not spoken in some time, having argued over his brother's desire to study under the priests of Rome. The Prince had wanted to take the vows of a monk to spend his life in study. Though Caradoc thought the notion sickening, it certainly would have spared him all this trouble. 'I serve Chiglas, who be a great great grandson of Cunedda, as indeed am I. When Degannwy be truly mine, I shall defend it.'

The heat of Maelgwn's hatred was burning him up. 'I assure thee, Caradoc, that day will never come.' He reared his horse and made for the outer bailey portcullis.

Caradoc smiled. *That day hast come.*

Brockwell would have known his way to Llyn Cerrig Bach blindfolded. As they descended into the valley, towards the blue tranquillity of its lake, the landscape became extremely pretty and Brockwell slowed his horse to a more leisurely pace.

'Where hast thou brought me, Calin? 'Tis most enchanting.' As Tory breathed in the scented air, she became aware of a pulsing that seemed to permeate everything around her.

'This was the last stronghold of the Druids against the Romans some four hundred years ago. The temple ruins be hidden in the forest yonder.'

'Taliesin?'

'I am not at liberty to say.'

'I know I am right, tell me, Calin.' She stuck her hands underneath his breastplate to tickle it out of him.

Brockwell, who was extremely ticklish, jumped right off the horse. 'Do not do that, I hate it.'

'Thou art not getting back on this horse until thou hast answered me,' Tory informed him, holding him at bay with her foot.

Brockwell folded his arms, amused. 'Thee and what army art going to stop me?'

'Thou art so gullible,' Tory shoved him backwards and took off with the horses.

Brockwell raced after her, but was not quite fast enough to grab hold of the horse trailing behind. 'Tory, stop!'

She just giggled, safe in the knowledge she could get away with it. 'I shall see thee there.'

Tory found the ruins on her own. The forest path suddenly parted wide to reveal huge stone pillars, ten times her height. The surrounding trees, so old and hardy, had overgrown what remained of the temple, and vines climbed everything in view. The place held the same mysterious allure as had the stones.

'Taliesin?' Tory dared to utter as she dismounted. She was beginning to wish she hadn't made sport of Calin as she became aware of someone whispering close by, although she couldn't discern the source.

She was staring at the ominous old temple, thinking how much her father would appreciate it, when it dawned on her that she had a camera. She could photograph it for him. In the back of her mind, Tory still held the hope that she would see her father again and was confident that Taliesin held the key to her dilemma.

After taking the shot, Tory decided to make a few adjustments to her attire. She had worn the Queen's clothing to leave the castle, but saw no need for it any longer. She folded the long under dress, and crammed it into her backpack. The green gunna she belted at the waist over her jeans and shirt. If not fashionable, it was at least practical.

The whispering startled her again. Tory was hesitant as she reached down to retrieve the photo, and was alarmed when she found a couple of dark, blurry spots in the otherwise clear exposure. Cold shivers enfolded her in waves, and Tory felt a hand come to rest on her shoulder. She swung round with full force, setting her stalker off balance.

'Tory!' Brockwell protested.

Tory leapt at him with a big hug. 'Calin, don't ever let me do that again.'

'The spirits gave thee a scare, did they?'

Tory pushed him away. 'Thee could have warned me.'

Brockwell just chuckled. 'Now who be gullible?' But his humour vanished when he noted the dark patch on her forehead. 'Thy Dragon hast returned.'

'What?' Tory rummaged for her hand-mirror and checked the mark in its reflection. 'The dream . . .' She paused to recall how real it had been. 'Maelgwn must have seen this, how could he not? And yet he sent me away, anyway, damn it.'

'I think we should proceed,' Brockwell said, and strode off to the entrance of the temple.

As Tory entered the ancient stone structure, the magnitude of her trip through time really hit home. The roof, if there ever was one, was long gone; you just looked straight up into the green canopy of the forest. The stone floor, like everything else, was slowly being engulfed by vines. Yet the carved images of the naked female form which adorned the inner pillars surrounding the large stone altar had been liberated from the undergrowth. This temple must have been a beautiful sanctuary once, she thought. It seemed a crying shame that war had destroyed it. Tory took a few more photographs, as by the twentieth century nothing would remain of it at all.

Brockwell was admiring one of the naked women. At the age of seven, he'd thought himself in paradise when he and Maelgwn had ripped away the vines to discover the shapely carvings. 'Thee can see why I liked it here.'

'Calin, thou art incorrigible,' Tory rolled her eyes and moved to inspect the altar. 'So where be this Taliesin?'

'Good question.' Brockwell headed for the huge altar and jumped up on it to look round.

Tory threw her gear up to Brockwell and stepped back a moment, encouraging him to smile. He didn't, but Tory took the photo anyway, stuffing it and the camera back in her bag.

Brockwell grabbed hold of her belt and hoisted her up with one hand. 'Thee weighs like a feather,' he said with disgust; it was beyond his comprehension how she could possess the strength she did.

'Just imagine what thee could do with what I know,' she replied.

Brockwell gazed round the ruins, acting as if he wasn't interested. He was a little uncertain about his next move. 'Taliesin!' he cried out into the eerie silence. 'I seek thee in the name of the Dragon, and request that thee show thyself.' After a few moments, he wasn't as confident of finding the bard. 'I have Tory Alexander in my care.' The temple at once became brighter, even though the sun was still hidden by the trees above.

Tory chanced to look down at a cross engraved in the stone under their feet, and found it had begun to glow. The light gradually extended outwards, engulfing the whole altar, and a white mist exuded from the core. 'Calin, hast this ever happened before?'

Brockwell pulled Tory close, afraid she would become lost in the haze. 'Nay, never.'

That figures. She looked around, but the mist and light were so intense that she could no longer see the temple or the trees.

The ride to the Menai Strait was swift, and so far they'd seen no sign of trouble. In fact, the place seemed almost too quiet. Maelgwn paid heed to Tory's warning about crossing the strait and sent scouts down both sides of the waterway.

He boarded the barge, accompanied by Cadogan, Madoc, and his second battalion. A storm was approaching from the mountains in the south. Their party would make the citadel before it reached them, and Maelgwn was relieved to note that his attackers would not be so fortunate.

Upon reaching the mainland, the Prince received news from Degannwy that the Saxons had withdrawn and were regrouping with reinforcements in the mountains. He could hardly believe his ears; the Saxons didn't usually band together.

As a race they weren't that organised or loyal. They had too many leaders who were all far too greedy and power hungry to co-operate with each other. *Unless, of course, someone has rallied them together?* Maelgwn recalled his brother's sly remark about paying off the Saxons. How could his father have led them into this? Did he not suspect Caradoc and Chiglas were up to no good? Maelgwn had asked the King this very question, but the old man was delirious in his weakened state. He'd just smiled and told Maelgwn that this was all for the best, and that in the end he would not think him such a foolish old man. The Prince, losing patience with his father, sought the whereabouts of the King's closest friend and champion, Sir Tiernan. Unfortunately, the knight had been sent on a diplomatic errand. The Prince could only hope that Sir Tiernan's absence meant that his father had suspected Caradoc of having malicious intent, as the rest of the King's staff seemed to think this arrangement with Chiglas was legitimate. They had seen for themselves the armies he was building in Powys and thought the King's plan to unite the kingdoms wise. At least Tory was safe from his brother's grasp for the moment. It worried him that she had seen herself fighting Caradoc. Perhaps his decision to send her away would save her from any such horror.

'Shall I send word for more troops from Aberffraw, Majesty?' Madoc half advised, half inquired.

As Cadogan stood right beside them, following every word, Maelgwn merely shook his head, and walked off to be alone with his thoughts. If he suspected correctly, this was exactly what his brother wanted him to do. For if Caradoc had poisoned their father and was conspiring with the Saxons, he must be planning a simultaneous assault. Maelgwn figured that as the Saxons besieged Degannwy, his brother might be planning to bring Chiglas' forces over the mountains. A large force could easily be hidden further down the Menai Strait to await a dawn attack on the island. Caradoc wants Aberffraw, Maelgwn surmised. Why else would he have gone to such pains arranging this marriage, if not so that he could conveniently be present when all this came to pass. Caradoc knows the main route that our armies take to Degannwy. He also knows better than anyone the way through the mountains of Gwynedd between here and Powys.

As a boy, Caradoc had taken to the mountains to live wild for months on end in the company of their uncle Cadfer. Cadfer dabbled in black magic, and calling upon the darkest aspects of nature, he conjured up the dead spirit of a wretched witch, who helped him devise a means to steal his brother's kingdom. Years later, Cadfer did rule as King in Gwynedd for a short time. He seized power from Caswallon and imprisoned him. Cadfer, who had lusted after Queen Sorcha for many years, reportedly raped and murdered her. Though another account claimed Sorcha had cut her own throat to save her dignity. The Queen swore, with her dying breath, that upon her passing she would become even more powerful and her wrath would fall on all those who opposed Gwynedd.

Maelgwn had arrived on the scene with Taliesin and Tiernan, but an hour too late to save her. The Prince, ardent for revenge and only fifteen years old, killed his uncle with a sword that had been sharpened on the Whetstone Tudwal Tydglyd — one of thirteen Treasures of Britain that Taliesin had collected in his travels. Maelgwn believed that his brother, but ten years of age at the time, was fully aware of their uncle's intent. Cadfer had probably named Caradoc as his heir, as Chiglas had, with none but bastard sons of his own and a daughter.

'I must keep Mon well guarded,' Maelgwn resolved. 'Yet, what if this proves to be nothing but a coincidence? To remove troops from Degannwy, which be under threat, to meet an army that may not exist would be ridiculous.'

The best he could do was send out scouts and wait for news.

Tory and Brockwell felt light-headed and experienced an eerie sensation of travelling, yet as far as they could tell they hadn't moved at all. When the thick mist cleared, however, they found they were no longer standing in the temple, but under their feet was the same intricately carved cross.

'Well beam me up Scotty, dost thou believe this?' Tory exclaimed as she ventured into an enormous room that was similar in style and size to a cathedral. But it had no windows and was entirely candle-lit. While the foundation of the structure seemed to be of the same period as the temple they'd been in only minutes before, the architraves reflected a distinct Romanesque style. The room was oblong in shape with double colonnades, rounded archways, and an apse to one end. This building plan was not employed in Britain until around the twelfth century. Tory was amazed by the rare exhibits that lined the walls and covered the floor. Some of the furnishings, decoration and artwork must date back to before recorded time, and there were prime examples of work from cultures throughout the ages.

At the opposite end of the room to the apse were a set of large mahogany doors, covered with panels of deep red padded leather fastened into place with flat silver studs. As Tory was admiring them the doors unexpectedly opened. She waited with bated breath for their host to emerge from the shadows. Brockwell, who was by nature more cautious, took a stand in front of Tory.

'Brockwell.' Tory tapped his shoulder. 'May I ask what thou art doing?'

'I am responsible for thy safety. Maelgwn would have my throat cut if any harm was to befall thee.' Why couldn't she just be a woman and stop confusing the issue?

Tory was ready to argue with him when a voice even more enchanting than Maelgwn's stopped her.

'Down, Calin. It be only I, Taliesin Pen Beirdd.'

'Taliesin, old man,' Brockwell answered relieved. Then he moved to greet the aging Merlin.

Tory was a little confused by Brockwell's words, as the man she saw before her appeared no older than about thirty-five. Of a medium build, Taliesin had fair skin that seemed full of vigour and not old at all. His hair, as white as snow, sat high on his shining brow and was pulled back tight off his face, falling in a ponytail to halfway down his back. The Merlin's long, thin, oriental-style moustache and beard were as fair as his hair. He was attired in a flowing purple robe that accentuated the colour of his large, soulful eyes, which were the most amazing shade of mauve-grey.

'I would be a foolish man indeed to threaten the lady in thy care.'

Brockwell nodded in response to his words.

'She be one of the greatest female warriors I have ever had the pleasure to witness in action . . . no offence intended,' Taliesin continued. 'We are, of course, all one and the same.' He graciously bowed to kiss her hand.

This man was potent. Tory could feel the energy he generated flowing from his fingertips. She had never voluntarily knelt before anyone in her life, yet, bowing her head to rest on his hands, she fell on one knee before him. 'I am most honoured, High Merlin, that thou hast summoned me back.' Tory realised she was not speaking with her own voice. She looked up to the magician's face; it was so familiar yet she couldn't place it.

Taliesin patted her hand. 'I have been watching and waiting for thee a long time, Sorcha. Or would thee prefer I call thee Tory?'

'Sorcha!' Tory and Brockwell cried in unison.

'Alright then, Sorcha.' He mistook their meaning on purpose. He let Tory go so he could lead them from the room.

'Wait.' Tory nursed her head, feeling giddy as she got back to her feet. 'Would thee mind telling me what be happening to me?'

'We have many urgent matters to discuss, lady, but first let me treat thee both to something to eat. Thee should rest before attempting to fathom the enormity of our situation.'

'No,' Tory protested, not about to be moved. 'Why did thee call me Sorcha?'

'That was thy name in a previous incarnation, when I had the honour to be thy close acquaintance and adviser.' Taliesin approached her so she could look him straight in the eye. 'Following thy needless death, I waited a long time for thee to incarnate again, and who should accompany thee into life but the finest warrior thou shalt ever train.' Taliesin motioned to Brockwell. 'Who in turn, did drive thee to be the great warrior thou art this day.'

'So Brockwell is Brian?' she asked, to ensure she was following him correctly. She didn't realise she'd broken into modern English until Taliesin answered her thus.

'That is correct.'

Tory clapped her hands together, excited. 'You speak English, this is great! So you're telling me that I was Maelgwn's mother?' Tory held her head again. *Does this change things?*

'Once,' Taliesin clarified. He wanted to ease her fears and spoke again in a tongue Brockwell could understand. 'Genetics art not really a factor here, though Maelgwn hast got so much of Sorcha in him that the attraction was, in a way, inevitable. A monk indeed!' Taliesin took pleasure in his little ploy to lead the Prince away from his monastic retreat for good. 'Maelgwn and thyself have loved each other dearly, many times, as brother, lover, son . . . and so the world turns. It will always be thus, forwards and backwards through time. All of us shall be drawn back together. Doth this not explain why Brockwell be so attracted to thee, and the other way round? For you recognise each other as kindred spirits, a bond that extends far beyond the boundaries of physical attraction.'

This was true enough. Even that first night in camp, when Brockwell had vexed her so, Tory could not bring herself to dislike him. As far as being physically attracted to the knight, she had always considered her brother to be good-looking. Had she not been his sister, she felt she would surely have fallen for his charms.

'So,' Taliesin summed up, 'I have merely bent the rules a little to bring thee back to us and believe me when I say, we need thee now.'

Tory had question after question running through her head.

Taliesin felt this and decided he'd said more than enough for the moment. 'Please, will thou not come and take advantage of my hospitality? I advise thee to indulge while thee can.'

Tory looked to Brockwell who had turned as white as a ghost. 'I think that be a good idea.'

8

THE STORMS
OF GWYNEDD

The Saxons observed the approach of the Prince's party from their vantage point in the mountains; all was going to plan. They weren't instructed to ambush, although they could have massacred the Dragon's party with the number of men they'd rallied together. Still, Maelgwn was notorious for escaping such ploys and might make it back to Aberffraw before Chiglas' troops had finished the crossing. Caradoc had insisted that they first allow his brother safe passage to the citadel in order to barricade him in. If they managed to take Degannwy, all the better. By that time, Caradoc would have claimed the Isle of Mon and the mountains, which in his mind belonged to him anyway. Once Mon was secured, Caradoc would concentrate all his forces on the citadel at Degannwy. He would slay Maelgwn to avenge Cadfer's sorcerous death, and proclaim himself King of Gwynedd. Upon Chiglas' death, he would marry Vanora to become King of Powys and wherever else he pleased with the armies he'd inherit.

Maelgwn beat the storm to arrive at Degannwy earlier than expected. He was pleased to find his old consort of men still together and in surprisingly good spirits, considering the circumstances. After they'd exchanged pleasantries, the knights congratulated their Prince on his engagement to the Princess Vanora. They presumed he would welcome the arrangement as it would eventually make him King of two kingdoms, so they were confused by the Prince's obvious lack of enthusiasm. He merely thanked them politely, not wanting to comment further.

Cedric changed the subject, informing the Prince that the Saxon savages were proving no threat to Gwynedd. He joked about their poor form and gross lack of numbers.

It was about this time that Maelgwn noticed that Cadogan was not present at their reunion, so he sent Madoc to find him. The Prince hated the fact that he mistrusted one of his knights, but there was too much at stake to ignore the danger. With any luck his fears would prove unjustified.

During the hour the Prince spent consulting with his advisers, scores of Saxon thugs had joined forces, preparing to converge on the citadel. Maelgwn silently observed the multitudes from the court window. The

Saxons could never have organised such a force without higher supervision, he decided.

The Prince and his knights had been battling Saxons all their soldiering lives, and in all that time not one of them could recall seeing so many of these disgusting barbarians in one place.

Maelgwn ordered every available man to the outer bailey wall. He knew now that he must return to Mon as soon as possible, although he would have a huge battle ahead of him before he could even leave the citadel.

His advisers and knights left the room to see to the fort's defence as Madoc entered, his expression grave. 'Majesty, the scout thee sent down the Menai toward Caernarvon hast not returned. Apparently when Cadogan learnt of this he left the citadel, without thy leave, to investigate.'

Maelgwn looked back to the impending confrontation out the window. *Did he know?*

As Cadogan trained the younger scouts, it was not unusual for him to go chasing one of them to check on their whereabouts. Yet how convenient that this chore should leave him absent from the imminent onslaught.

The storm clouds began to rumble, black as night. Drums pounded in the distance and a loud cry sounded from the Saxon ranks. As they charged the outer walls of the citadel, a deafening thunderclap was heard and the rain came bucketing down.

'Madoc, old friend, I fear I should not have left Caradoc inside Aberffraw.'

'Sir Gilmore will not allow any harm to befall thy home, Sire.'

Maelgwn turned back to Madoc, praying he was right. 'May the Spirits of the Otherworld be with us this day.'

'The great Houses have always accompanied thee into battle, Dragon,' Madoc said as he headed for the door, full of confidence. 'This day shall prove no different.'

Taliesin led them down a wide torch-lit hallway, beautifully carpeted with long red rugs. Tory had never seen a wider or wilder array of armour and battledress than that which lined the corridor. Even Brockwell was turning circles in wonder as he viewed the life-size figures so strangely clad. It seemed that the Merlin's entire abode was one big museum that appeared to go on and on forever.

Their host finally stopped, opening one of the doors that led into a cosy dining hall. The fire was lit and their meals were already laid out on the table. For Brockwell, a quarter of a pig had been roasted to perfection, with bread, fruit, and mead to accompany it. Tory's prayers were finally answered when she spied a hamburger with fries and a Coke.

'I wouldn't go wandering off alone, as my home be a labyrinth of deception. I designed it that way so in the incredible impossibility of someone discovering it, they could never actually find their way out,' Taliesin explained, impressed with his own ingenuity.

'Surely they would find thee sooner or later?' Brockwell asked, not really understanding what a labyrinth was.

Taliesin, sensing his scepticism and aware that Calin was often too adventurous for his own good, continued. 'There be over a thousand rooms contained herein, and only I know what lies behind every door. I tend to keep some fairly unearthly and somewhat eccentric company at times, and I have a few animal acquaintances.'

'What, like pets?' Tory asked, not comfortable with the idea.

'Nay, of course not. Most art perfectly free to come and go as they choose. For shamanistic studies I prefer the more unusual and rare creatures, but unfortunately these tend to get a bit violent around strangers.'

'Such as?' Brockwell inquired, before biting a huge chunk of meat off the bone.

'Well, several dragons, one of which I keep for Maelgwn.' The bard thought he'd tell the story for Tory's benefit. 'Some time ago, as a test of courage, Maelgwn sought to slay the dragon that had been menacing King Catulus' kingdom for years. The King had offered a great reward to the warrior who could rid him of this beast. In the end, however, Maelgwn, who was not much more than a boy at the time, felt sorry for the dragon. Thus he befriended the creature and coaxed it back here.'

Tory's face filled with delight at the story, though Brockwell seemed rather perplexed. 'I thought he did slay it, that be what he boasted to me.'

'Maelgwn rid Dumnonia of the horror that was plaguing them and thus earnt the respect and support of King Catulus. That was all that mattered at the time. The beast be far happier here with none to torment it.'

'Dragons art not so fierce,' Brockwell claimed, sounding in no way dissuaded by the Merlin's caution. 'Dost thou not have any creature more formidable than that?'

'Hast thou ever laid eyes on a griffin, Calin?' the Merlin asked, smiling.

The knight shrunk away, discouraged. 'I am happy to be wherever thou doth see fit to put me,' he said.

Tory pushed her plate aside. 'A million thanks,' she bowed her head to her host. 'Best burger I ever had.'

'Thou art most welcome,' assured Taliesin, graciously. 'Now, if thou art both done I would suggest some rest before nightfall.'

Tory was about to ask why, but Taliesin held up his index finger to show he was not prepared to discuss the matter at this time.

'Follow me,' the Merlin instructed politely as he walked towards the door.

His guests looked at each other a moment and shrugged, resolving that the Merlin knew best.

Brockwell began to realise what a labyrinth was, as from the hall stairs led off in all directions. The battledress that stood between every doorway became more and more bizarre as they moved deeper into the maze. Taliesin eventually came to a standstill and gestured towards a doorway, 'Brockwell . . .'

'Nay, I must stay with Tory. Maelgwn made me swear an oath.'

Taliesin just smiled at him. 'Surely thee can trust an old man like myself with the Prince's lady? I am a proven ally, after all.'

Brockwell did not favour the bard's suggestion that Tory already belonged to the Prince. Maelgwn was bound to wed Vanora, and Tory would never succumb to the role of mistress to a married man. Brockwell, therefore, felt sure he could help Tory over her brother fixation.

Taliesin, aware of Brockwell's thoughts, swung open the door to reveal a sizeable room decorated according to sixth-century taste, and fit for a king. In it were five scantily-clad young maidens, who were eager to tend to Calin's every whim.

Brockwell looked at Tory, suddenly feeling obliged to resign himself to the Merlin's wishes. 'Rest well.' He patted her shoulder and cheerfully entered his abode.

Tory was about to protest, unsure of whether it was his fickle nature or the ease by which he was distracted from his duty that bothered her most. But the Merlin just guided her back, closing the door. 'Brockwell has much ahead of him this night. Is it not right that he should be allowed to indulge a little beforehand?'

'Something has happened then.' Tory panicked. 'It's Caradoc, isn't it? Is Maelgwn in danger?'

'Indulge me one moment longer.' He took her hand and immediately Tory felt her anxiety melt away. 'I must show you something that will no doubt be of interest.'

He guided her towards a pair of large doors at the end of the corridor. Taliesin held his hand out before him and the doors parted wide to reveal a technological phenomenon within.

The large, space-age room contained a series of hexagons that rose out of the floor, and lining the walls was enough computer hardware to run NASA. 'This is far beyond even my time,' Tory gasped as she perused the control centre. 'What are the applications?'

'Good question,' Taliesin replied, pleased to see the same direct manner he'd come to expect from Sorcha.

He walked past the first of the hexagons which measured over seven metres round, making it much larger than any of the others. Its base was covered in chips of black onyx and large glass screens extended to the roof. Then he took his place behind a smaller hexagon that housed a control panel. 'Do you know much of satellite communication, Tory?'

The hexagon before her lit up like a television monitor, showing an aerial view of Castell Degannwy and its surroundings. Tory experienced the sensation of soaring over the citadel, which could barely be seen through the storm.

'How does it happen that a sixth-century Merlin possesses technology dating far beyond even the twentieth century?'

'Beyond the year three thousand, satellites are so small that they can no longer be seen by the naked eye and are operated by remote control.' Taliesin still hadn't answered her question, but before Tory could point this out, he continued with a sigh.

'I have travelled through time witnessing the Earth's disasters, discovering its wonders, and collecting its treasures. I have returned here to try and restore its balance and right the wrongs where I can. This is my quest. I am, as you might say, everlasting, and assume whatever form I see fit.' He smiled. 'That is why

Brockwell refers to me as old man, because to him I appear thus. Neither he nor Maelgwn would have listened to a word I'd said if I'd appeared the young man you see.'

Taliesin passed his hand over a smoky crystal ball that was embedded in the centre of the panel. The soft hum of the machinery dropped in pitch, as the ball changed in colour from purple to red. The image on the screens of the hexagon became stationary and appeared to fall flat before rising to display a detailed holographic image of the citadel at Degannwy, which one could view from all angles.

Fantastic! Tory walked around the hexagon, observing the miniature world of the fortress below. The storm clouds sat a bit above eye level behind the glass screens. 'What's happening?' She became alarmed when she realised the little figures scaling the citadel walls were Saxons. 'This is what Maelgwn considers no serious threat, yet they are being overrun!' Tory looked on in horror, wondering where the Prince was placed in the uproar. 'He made the wrong decision, didn't he?'

'No, he made a decision. There is no right or wrong when it comes to war, only what we make of it. I had hoped your dream would keep Maelgwn on the isle. By ignoring the mark of the folk, he has made matters worse, but by no means hopeless. Destiny will run its own course. We can only watch out for the interests of Gwynedd and try to prevent any disasters.'

'You know who has been doing this?' Tory pointed to the fresh mark of the Dragon on her forehead. 'Who are these folk, *exactly*?'

'Why the Tylwyth Teg, of course. The etheric beings, who co-inhabit this planet with us.'

'Fairies,' Tory frowned, sure she'd misunderstood him.

'Whatever,' he confirmed with a shrug. 'The occupants of the Otherworld are ever mindful of the events of the Middle Kingdoms. It is through their grace and guidance that we can see beyond the present, or travel through space and time. The prophetic dreams and the mark of the Dragon were a means by which the folk could warn Maelgwn. But alas, the Prince has spent too many years away from the native faith. The Otherworld to him seems nothing more than a childhood fantasy, I'm sure. It was all those years he spent studying the rigid material logic of the scholars from Rome that did it.' The Merlin shook his head. 'He should have known better.'

Dumbfounded by his retort, Tory thought it best to get back to the problem at hand. 'But there must be something we can do to help him?'

'Well, where do you think such a storm came from at this time of year? In good time you shall have your chance to help. There is no point running to his assistance now, however.'

Tory looked at Taliesin, horrified that the fortress had already fallen.

'Do not fear, all is well. Look into the screen opposite mine.' Taliesin waved his hand over the control. The tone of the instruments rose as before, and the holograph flipped back up to a two-dimensional picture.

The angle of the citadel, featured on each of the hexagon's six screens, progressively changed as Tory walked slowly around it. This gave her the option of viewing the situation from every possible direction. On the screen to which the Merlin referred was a view looking out from the citadel into the distance. She saw many other armies approaching, which didn't appear to be Saxons. 'My god, Taliesin!' Tory was overwhelmed by the multitudes. 'I hope they're on our side.'

The Saxon onslaught had been relentless, despite the pelting rain that hindered them in their repeated attempts to scale the wall and raise the portcullis. The Prince took a more active part in this battle than he usually did and was surprised to find that, without even thinking, he used his newly acquired fighting skills. This, combined with his hatred for his brother and his desire to speed back to Aberffraw, was making him a fearsome adversary this day. After many hours of this the opposition were beginning to avoid him, and Maelgwn had to keep chasing up on his opponents. Six of the Saxon thugs tried to launch a simultaneous attack but it did not serve them well. The Prince cut four of them down with ease before the remaining two turned and fled. He laughed triumphantly, scanning the area to see where he could best be of aid. To his horror, he saw the outer portcullis being raised and ran to prevent it.

'Cedric!' Maelgwn spotted his knight and, slaying the Saxon Cedric was battling, recruited his services to help him lower the portcullis. 'We have to stop them, or Degannwy will be lost.'

'As be thy wish, Majesty,' growled the huge, brawny warrior, charging off to cut a path to the outer-bailey wall.

The fighting was thickest around the barbican that housed the heavy iron grille gate, making it difficult to tell who held the upper hand. With Cedric covering his back, Maelgwn fought his way to the gatekeeper's station. The bodies of men from both sides were strewn along their path, as the battle for control of the gate's winch had been intense. Maelgwn killed a Saxon who was racing for the tower also, then burst through the door of the mind to slay the soldier guarding the winch.

'Nay Majesty,' the gatekeeper pleaded for his life, weary from fending off the enemy to secure the gate. 'We must open it. See,' he pointed to the scene unfolding beyond the citadel walls.

Sir Tiernan, accompanied by King Catulus and the other noblemen of the south, had already dispersed the enemy outside and were awaiting entry.

'In that case,' Maelgwn placed his sword in its scabbard, and took hold of the huge iron winch, 'allow me to give thee a hand.'

Within minutes the portcullis was raised and, as their allies entered the outer bailey, a victory cry was heard from the ranks of the Britons.

'Good show,' the Prince congratulated the gatekeeper. Then, taking hold of the gates' heavy iron chain, he slid down it to greet his fellow nobles.

'Got a tad quiet down our way. I wondered where all the lanky bastards had got to,' King Catulus cried out in jest to the exhausted Prince.

'We gathered thee might need a hand,' Tiernan added.

So Caswallon suspected after all, the Prince realised. At this moment Maelgwn had to admit his father was indeed not the crazy old man he had thought. 'I tell thee all, most assuredly, thy timely presence be most welcome.' He bowed to them. 'I fear the battle may be only beginning, however, for I expect we will find an even greater threat waiting near Caernarvon.'

Though Tiernan suspected Maelgwn's fears were justified, he dismounted to advise. 'Let us speak inside the citadel, out of this dreaded rain. I am sure we have much to discuss before charging off anywhere.'

By nightfall, Maelgwn had conveyed the whole sordid tale to Tiernan, holding nothing back. The Prince found it hard to break the news about the King's affliction, but Tiernan took it better than expected.

Although Tiernan was only thirty-seven years of age, he was more of a father figure to the Prince than the King had ever been. As Maelgwn's war chief and right-hand man during the uprising of his Uncle Cadfer, the Prince trusted him completely and felt at ease to speak his mind.

When the subject of Tory arose, Tiernan couldn't help but notice how Maelgwn's spirits lifted. 'I never thought I would see the day the Dragon would fall,' commented Tiernan, appearing grave as he swished the mead around in his goblet.

'Fall!' The Prince looked at him. 'I have no intention of being defeated.'

'In love,' Tiernan explained with a chuckle.

Even at his age, this ruggedly handsome knight was still a bachelor and openly confessed to being an incurable romantic. Tiernan claimed to enjoy the company of ladies far too much to ever tie himself down to only one.

Maelgwn grinned with embarrassment, refilling his goblet. 'Oh, that. Aye well, if love keeps thee awake at night, plaguing thy sleep with visions and cold sweats, then I dare say thou art right.'

The Prince's view amused Tiernan. 'Did thee say she fights, this girl?' He appeared sceptical.

Maelgwn looked at him earnestly. 'Thee could not imagine the power of her technique, not in thy wildest dreams.' Maelgwn held up a finger as if struck by a thought, and retrieved a piece of wood from the pile near the fireplace. After removing his boots, he instructed Tiernan to hold the chunk of wood out in front of him. The Prince focused on the object, then kicked out and split the wooden target with the side of his bare foot. This proved impressive enough to capture Tiernan's interest.

'By the Goddess!'

'At first I thought it impossible myself! Yet in only a month she hast taken me this far. This be nothing compared to what Tory can do, and I foresee no limit to how far we could take this skill.'

'Dost thy father know?'

'Nay, he fell sick so suddenly that now he be too delirious to comprehend it.'

Tiernan slapped Maelgwn's shoulder in excitement. 'The men said thee fought like a demon today, now I see why!'

At last the Prince truly felt his plan was plausible; if Tiernan was excited it had to be sound. This led him to wonder, and he asked, 'Must I still wed Vanora?'

Tiernan had to laugh at the Prince, who appeared so terribly harrowed by the thought. 'Nay, that was never truly intended. 'Twas just a means to an end.'

Maelgwn collapsed back into his seat, relieved beyond all comprehension.

'After the slaying of Cadfer we suspected Chiglas and Caradoc would retaliate. It was only a matter of time before they felt Powys was in a position to do so. So thy father was compelled to agree with Chiglas' proposal, and we led everyone to believe thy marriage was legitimate so that none would suspect us of biding our time to arrange a counterattack strategy. We should rest overnight and make for Aberffraw before dawn tomorrow.'

'Nay!' Maelgwn stood in protest. 'We must cross tonight.'

'Please Majesty, see reason. Chiglas' troops will not be able to cross the strait in this frightful weather, and it be far too risky for Gwynedd's heir to be crossing in darkness. I am afraid I must insist.'

'They will manage, as will I. Caradoc will not suspect the Saxon defeat here to have been so swift, and we must take advantage of his ignorance.' A knock on the door silenced him. 'Enter.'

It was Sir Madoc. 'I hope I am not disturbing thee.'

'Nay Madoc, close the door. We could use thy wisdom a moment. Our young Prince hast got it in his head to cross the Menai this night.'

'Nay! Certainly not!' Madoc was horrified. 'Thee will surely perish in the storm.'

'Nonsense!' Maelgwn was angered by their childish treatment of him. 'I can swim that strait four times over, and I shall be departing this night escort or no.'

After allowing her to witness Maelgwn's triumph, Taliesin flatly refused to answer any more questions until after Tory had some rest. He showed her to a room that was almost an exact replica of her own at home, en suite included. It contained all the twentieth-century mod cons that she'd been secretly missing this past month.

'When you leave take whatever you desire. I know the adjustment to sixth-century life can't have been easy.' Taliesin sympathised with his awestruck guest. 'You'll find shampoo and the like in the bathroom. I guessed you would probably be low on supplies by now.'

Tory discovered that the toiletries were the same brands she normally bought. It spooked her that this celestial entity, a stranger to her but a few hours before, could know her so intimately. He'd thought of everything from toothpaste to tampons. There was a solar recharger of double A batteries, the size that her CD Walkman took, and there were new clothes, her style and size, in the wardrobe. All her books were there for her reference. Her two other saxophones, a tenor and a soprano, sat in the corner where she had left them at home. The only apparent difference was that there were no windows. 'I don't know what to say,' she told him quietly, feeling both delighted and surprised.

'Then best say nothing. This has been quite an adventure, even for a woman of Sorcha's courage and strength, and it is far from over yet.'

There was one question in her million that Tory had to ask. She approached the kindly bard so he might see how much it meant to her. 'I have to contact my parents, Taliesin. Can you get me back home?'

'Not till summer solstice, I'm afraid.' He seemed, in a way, to be bothered by the notion. 'I have no machine for time travel. I brought you here the old way, by channelling the universal energies that abide at particular sites on this planet at certain times of the astrological year. The calculations for such an enterprise, as you can imagine, are enormous! These days, however, I have my computers to assist me with the chore. Now that is all. Time to rest.' The magician held the palm of his hand to the Dragon on Tory's forehead, and caught her up in his arms as she fell unconscious.

'My, how I have missed thee.' Taliesin laid her down on the bed, then took a seat to observe her at peace. 'So many fine adventures we have had, you and I. And so many more await us yet.'

Though Tory's sleep was deep, she woke with a start feeling ill at ease. Taliesin sat opposite her on a lounge. He smiled, seeming content to wait for her to get her wits together.

'What has happened, Taliesin?'

He rose to calm her. 'We are one step ahead, fear not. Bathe, dress, eat . . . there is no rush.' He waved to the food that had been laid out. 'I shall return for you thereupon.' He gave a slight bow and headed for the door. 'I have need to rally Brockwell, and that could take some doing.'

Tory did as instructed, sensing as she bathed that her encounter with Caradoc, which she'd been dreading these past few days, was soon to take place. She didn't understand how she knew this, as she'd never shown any evidence of psychic skill. Who was this Sorcha? Could it have something to do with her, she wondered. Tory didn't really dig the idea of someone else looming in her mind. *Still, if Sorcha is really just an extension of myself, a part of me I have long forgotten, a whole wealth of information may be lying dormant in my subconscious.*

Tory picked at the food as she dressed. She found a new white shirt and pulled out her old Levis from her luggage. Over the lot she wore the dark green gunna. As she laced up her steel-capped boots Tory felt prepared for just about anything. She pulled her hair back into a tight bun and inspected herself in the mirror. The Dragon on her forehead held her gaze. She hadn't attempted to remove it, for, in this time of war, she was proud to bear the Prince's mark.

Taliesin and Brockwell arrived just as Tory was ready to go.

'Holy Mother!' Brockwell strolled in, checking everything out. 'Look at this place.' The bathroom in particular seemed to interest him and he walked inside. 'What be this?'

'Not now, Calin,' Taliesin scolded him, then turned to address Tory, employing a very different tone of voice. 'You appear much refreshed. Are you ready?'

Tory, unsure, nodded anyway. *Ready for what?*

'Caradoc hast made his move.'

Taliesin's statement was so direct that it startled Tory, and the very mention of Caradoc's name sent shivers down her spine.

'What doth thou mean?' Brockwell grumbled loudly, still blissfully unaware that there was any major threat to Gwynedd.

'Come,' Taliesin turned to guide them, his voice conveying the gravity of the situation.

As they made haste to the control room, Taliesin brought them up to date with their state of affairs. 'Maelgwn hast left Degannwy, and be on his way back to Aberffraw.'

'The Menai?' Tory caught Taliesin up.

'Nay, he hast yet to cross it.' Taliesin was well aware of her fears. 'Caradoc's timing be indeed inconvenient. I fear Maelgwn will not make it home in time to stop him. That leaves *us* to prevent a siege at Aberffraw.'

'Have I missed something?' Brockwell was stunned by the news.

Taliesin paid him no mind, holding his hand out before him and parting the doors to the control room.

Brockwell stopped and took a step backwards. 'This be too strange.'

Tory turned to him, feeling pressed for time. 'Calin, thou art a child at times, would thee like me to hold thy hand?' she teased.

He shook his head slowly, bemused by all of Taliesin's paraphernalia. 'Hast thou no fear at all?'

'Fear exists in the mind alone.' She coaxed him closer.

'I will remember thee said that,' Taliesin replied.

But Tory remained focused on Calin, fed up with his silly superstitions. 'Maelgwn, King Caswallon, and quite possibly the rest of thy kin, art in grave danger, so get over it, soldier!'

Taliesin had taken up his position behind the panel. Tory approached, stepping up behind him. 'Okay, let's have it.'

The Merlin passed his hand over the crystal ball and the huge hexagon rotated the equivalent of one screen. It lit up to display the scene inside the main dining hall at Aberffraw, in a two-dimensional form.

The entire family and staff were seated at the tables, still dressed in their bed clothes and closely guarded by Caradoc's men.

'How can this be?' Brockwell thundered. 'Where art our armies?'

'Those soldiers who have not been ambushed, sleep on unaware. That be thy task, Brockwell. Chiglas' forces art on the island but have not yet reached Aberffraw. Some have split from the main group to intercept any reinforcements that may try to cross from Degannwy.'

Maelgwn! Tory's heart sank. 'Then my vision was true.'

'Aye. Now, I could take thee to his aid, or I can send thee to theirs,' he motioned to the hopeless situation on the screen. 'I ask thee to bear in mind that there were no outcomes in thy dream.'

Tory viewed the scene with growing concern. Caradoc had entered, demanding Lady Gladys accompany him at once. 'Why must it be like this? Why didn't we do something sooner?' Tory was torn when she saw Katren in the room with the others. Caradoc harassed the maid briefly before he departed; Tory guessed he was inquiring after her whereabouts.

'I could do naught until Caradoc proved himself treasonous,' Taliesin explained with regret. 'The key here be prudence, Tory. This be the kind of decision that could be required of thee at any time if thou art seriously considering the role of Maelgwn's Queen.'

'What?' For Brockwell, this day was just one shock after another.

So, this is a test, Tory surmised to herself, recalling the words of Taliesin's ancient riddle. *He who would seek to marry himself to sovereignty, must face his utmost fears and his most secret anxieties.*

Taliesin took hold of Tory. 'Listen to yourself, deep down you know where you will be of greater assistance to Maelgwn this night.'

She pulled away from him, reluctant to admit even to herself that she knew the truth behind his words. 'Thou art saying I should confront Caradoc. But he will see the way I fight and the surprise strategy for Gwynedd's forces will be lost. So tell me Taliesin, how can I possibly win?'

'I shall face Caradoc,' Brockwell intervened. 'Maelgwn would not hear of Tory being exposed to such danger.'

Taliesin shook his head slowly. 'Thee cannot be in two places at once, Calin. Thee must contend with Chiglas' forces. Tory cannot rally the armies to battle, and my role in this affair can only be implemented from here. However,' the Merlin held up a finger in promise, one step ahead as usual, 'thou hast no need to worry about Tory, as she will be wearing this.' He walked over to the wall and motioned to the only spot along it that was not occupied by computer hardware.

Tory folded her arms, annoyed that he would jest at a time like this. The same thoughts were running through Brockwell's mind until the Merlin revealed a majestic suit of armour from thin air, and in his hands was a woollen cape that he'd turned inside out.

'This be the Mantle of Gwydion, son of Don.' He walked towards Tory with his prize. 'It renders the wearer invisible, when worn the right way round.'

Tory was speechless as he handed it to her. 'This was truly his?' She felt an affinity with it at once, hugging it to her breast.

'Aye. I have also employed it often.'

'I have heard of this,' Brockwell said, just as fascinated by the legend. 'It be one of thirteen such treasures.'

'True,' Taliesin confirmed. 'Now listen to me carefully, we have not got much time.'

As it was a moonless night visibility on the strait was non-existent, though the pelting rain had eased somewhat. Maelgwn deeply regretted dragging his troops through another ordeal so soon. He'd wanted to set forth for Aberffraw alone, feeling he would have a better chance of going undetected. But Sir Tiernan, superior in years and wisdom, pulled rank on the Prince, insisting they take a more cautious approach.

Thus, in the midnight hour of this stormy night, Maelgwn found himself trying to organise a whole army of men across the torrid strait. I could be there by now, he thought.

'We shall take one of the long boats, there be less risk of incident,' Madoc advised.

'Whatever thee thinks best.' Maelgwn tried not to sound short with the knight; he was only doing his duty in wanting to protect him.

'Saxons!' A cry rang out from one of the distant guard posts. The warning was repeated down through the ranks as the men hurried to board their transport.

'Make haste,' Tiernan urged the Prince, as the sounds of battle reached their ears.

Tiernan, Madoc and a band of soldiers guided the Prince swiftly to the vessel. They cast off into the stormy waters and made for the banks of Mon.

As the boats carrying Gwynedd's soldiers caught up with them, the rain started to pour down. Blinded by the water in his eyes, Maelgwn could see naught of how his men fared back onshore. Yet he could hear their death cries, and was startled when a similar commotion was heard out in front.

The soldiers ahead of the Prince raised the alarm to an impending ambush.

Maelgwn peered into the darkness, shielding his face from the water. He spied a multitude of small craft closing rapidly in on them from Mon. From what he could discern from their appearance, these men were Britons. Chiglas' troops, no doubt. So Tory was right, he was sorry to concede. The safe crossing of the Menai had momentarily put his mind to rest in regard to her warning. *I should have known*.

The Prince rose, sword in hand, ready to face the latest onslaught, when Tiernan yanked away the armour from his body.

'Into the water,' he commanded over the rising din, pushing the Prince overboard before he could argue.

Madoc helped Tiernan out of his heavy battledress. 'May the Goddess protect and guide thee both, Sir.'

Tiernan turned to Madoc, hoping he would fare well himself. 'Fear not, Madoc old friend, we shall overcome.' Tiernan followed Maelgwn into the stormy waters of the strait.

Madoc turned to view the approaching troops. He quietly appealed to the Spirits of the Otherworld, as he always did before battle, for safe passage for his Prince, his comrades and himself. But Madoc, no longer a young man, could see little chance of his own escape this time. 'Long live Gwynedd!'

Maelgwn heard the cry and the clash of steel as he rose for air. His heart went out to Madoc and regretted that he'd been unable to stay and fight.

He and Tiernan managed to bypass the action unobserved, as they had both been raised near the sea and were strong swimmers. They agreed it was best to let the current carry them down-river towards Caernarvon before attempting to go ashore since

Chiglas' forces had spread themselves across the lower part of the island.

As he was tossed by waves and showered with rain, Maelgwn found it difficult to accept Tory's theory that pain was all in the mind. After what seemed an eternity at the mercy of the strait, Maelgwn, exhausted and freezing cold, dragged himself onto land.

Tiernan collapsed beside him, catching his breath. 'I hope she be worth it, this girl.'

Maelgwn's head shot up. 'My father's life and house art also at stake here.'

'I know,' Tiernan said as he got to his feet. 'But in my experience, only a woman will drive a man to such extremes.'

'Tory warned me not to leave Aberffraw and of the dangers of crossing the Menai,' Maelgwn confessed. 'I fear for her, as she has seen herself engaged in battle with Caradoc. And although I sent her away in Brockwell's protection, I hesitate to doubt her visions when she hast been proven right about everything else.'

'Well then,' Tiernan said as he helped Maelgwn to his feet, 'we had best steal ourselves a couple of horses and see to the rescue of thy future Queen.'

9

DEATH OF
A KING

Katren sat quietly in the dining hall with the
rest of the servants, cursing over and over that
she hadn't been born a man. She longed to run
her captors through and save Lady Gladys from
whatever Caradoc intended. The maid couldn't bear
the thought of any harm befalling the kindly woman.
Lady Gladys had become like a mother to her, as
indeed she was to all of the younger folk of the house
without family of their own. What could Caradoc
want with his aging aunt anyway? With most of the
army officials still off fighting Saxons at Degannwy,
Katren fretted for the household. Sir Gilmore had
been badly wounded when he'd refused to surrender
to Caradoc's treasonous intent. She feared for the
knight's life, but could do naught but witness the

bound man bleed, as a dozen hefty guards watched over them.

These warriors from Powys didn't appear to have a compassionate soul amongst them and even with as much gall as she had, Katren was not game to risk aggravating them. Where were Prince Maelgwn, Sir Brockwell and her lady? Could Caradoc have been telling the truth when he boasted that Maelgwn suspected naught, and that by this time tomorrow he, Caradoc, would proclaim himself King of Gwynedd. Yet King Caswallon was still very much alive, thanks to her, and Caradoc would never get past the King's personal guard.

Katren's imagination ran wild a moment, her eyes opening wide. *By the Goddess! That be why Caradoc hast taken Lady Gladys as a hostage, to get past the guard? Oooh, if only I had trained under my mistress a while longer* . . . Her head awhirl with theories and girlish dreams of chivalry, Katren stared into the firelight. *Sir Brockwell shall save us. The Prince's champion would never allow Gwynedd to fall into the hands of such scum.*

Her gaze wandered up over the mantel, coming to rest upon the weapon of Cunedda the Great. It was a double-ended iron sword and was comparative in length to a grown horse. One wielded it with two hands from the centre, defending oneself against an attacker's blows with a long iron rod between the two deadly blades. Katren sat staring at the weapon, wishing she knew how to use it, when before her very eyes it vanished. Startled, she quickly looked about the room to see if anyone else had noticed. She then turned back to the wall above the mantel to confirm that it was definitely no longer there. Katren had but seconds to ponder what could have become of it when, like a vision from her dreams, Brockwell came bursting through the doors. In one hand he held a beautiful sword that bore a white hilt; its blade appeared to be of solid flame. With the other he dragged along one of Chiglas' soldiers. Katren trembled as her hero let the slain villain drop to the floor.

'Come forward, if thee dare, and taste Dyrnwyn — the sword of Rhydderch. Which one of thee wishes to die first?' Brockwell challenged. 'What, no takers?' He winked at the ladies, who all appeared more than relieved to see him. As he held in his hand one of the Thirteen Treasures of Britain, Brockwell fancied himself to be invincible and lashed out with confidence at his closest opponent.

Caradoc's troops towered over him, yet this young swordsman more than equalled their skill and daring. Katren realised that Tory was right in saying that power came from will and had nothing to do with size. *Real desire within the heart hast magic power.* She recalled the phrase Tory had quoted, feeling that Sir Brockwell was living proof of this. The knight jumped up on the tables to continue his assault with the further advantage of added height. The remaining guards closed in to attack. Katren believed her love would surely die, when, one by one, his attackers were ambushed by an invisible enemy, which violently slashed out and pounded them into submission.

'The Dragon returns,' Brockwell taunted, exploiting the old legend. The guards resolved to flee the room but their attempt was thwarted, as whoever approached the doorway died.

From the violent action of the surprise attack, Katren knew immediately that Tory was behind it; she now had a very good idea of where Cunedda's weapon had disappeared to. Not one to waste time, Katren ran to the side of Lord Gilmore and unbound him. If she didn't clean and bind his wounds soon they would surely become gangrenous. That was, of course, if he didn't die from the loss of blood first.

Driven to fits of frenzy, the enemy warriors were sitting ducks, losing their will even to try to compete with the invisible onslaught, or the fiery blade. The last two remaining soldiers, seeing their fate splattered around them, fell to their knees and begged for mercy.

Brockwell, keeping a close eye on them, instructed Selwyn to help blindfold and bind the pair. When this had been accomplished, the knight pressed a button on the side of his sword's hilt and the fiery blade vanished.

Tory came out from under her magical cape to congratulate him. 'Brockwell, thou art a true master. High-five!'

Brockwell, familiar with Tory's gesture, responded with enthusiasm, yet he held her hand firm. 'Thou art the master, Tory Alexander. I was wrong about thy ways.'

His deep blue eyes nearly drowned her and it was clear that Calin was experiencing some strong emotions. 'Thee must go,' Tory instructed. 'I shall see to thy mother and thy King's safety.'

Katren, having tended Lord Gilmore as best she could, stood to watch Brockwell depart. She tried not to envy the way he eyed her mistress. One day soon he shall long for me, she vowed, I shall train much harder. To Katren's great surprise, Brockwell approached her before leaving.

'How fares Sir Gilmore?' he placed a hand on Katren's arm, looking towards his mentor with concern.

'I think it not be as bad as it looks, but he will need proper attention before long.' She was elated by his brief touch.

'Calin, go now!' Tory urged, growing impatient.

He bowed to the ladies, serving them one of his grins. 'I shall see thee all at breakfast.'

Katren was quietly dismayed to note that most of the younger maidens sighed as they watched the knight slip quietly from the room.

What a ham. Tory rolled her eyes, turning her attention to phase two of their plan. 'Alma, see to Lord Gilmore. Selwyn, watch those two and if they move, kill them.'

Selwyn jumped to his duty, taking up a sword from one of the dead. Tory realised she felt no remorse for the men she'd slaughtered, nor did she fear facing Caradoc. She turned to Katren, taking up her hand. 'Katren, I need thee to guide me to the King's chambers.'

The inflection in Tory's voice implied that her request could be dangerous, but Katren's heart leapt at the chance of some action. 'It would give me the greatest pleasure, lady.'

Tory smiled, giving her a hug. 'I have much to tell thee once we have rid Gwynedd of this menace. So let us be done with it. Cara, bolt the door behind us and answer to no one but Katren or myself, understand?' The young girl nodded in confirmation as she sprang to her feet.

With a dagger resting at the throat of Lady Gladys, Caradoc had easily persuaded the royal guard to throw down their weapons. He had locked the men in the adjacent room and four of his soldiers were now stationed at the door to the King's chamber. Caradoc instructed them to inform anyone from Gwynedd who wished to enter that he held Lady Gladys and the King inside, and would kill them both upon sighting opposition.

Tory and Katren watched the entrance to the King's chamber from a doorway down the hall. The four guards were backed well up against the doors and Tory had no chance of slipping between them undetected.

'Art thou ready, Katren?' Tory whispered, eager to be done with the task.

'Aye lady,' she replied, taking up a jug of mead and goblets.

Tory placed her hands on Katren's shoulders. 'Remember, be meek, and as soon as they art distracted make for the dining hall as fast as thou art able.' Katren gave a firm nod. 'And most importantly . . .' Tory paused to stress, but Katren already knew the punch line and said it with her. '. . . no fear.' They smiled at their resolve. Tory resumed her invisible cover and followed Katren up the hall.

The guards were immediately up in arms upon sighting a resident of the castle, so Katren stopped some distance from them. She gave a small curtsey, keeping her eyes lowered to the ground. 'Mead?' she announced, so timidly the men barely heard her.

'Good show,' the most tolerant of them said, beckoning her to approach.

Tory turned the door handle and slipped inside the King's chamber unnoticed.

Those in the room were staring straight at the doorway, and for a moment Tory was horrified that her magic cloak had failed her. Caradoc held Lady Gladys while Vanora stood at the King's bedside, swishing some liquid around in a goblet.

'It be nothing,' Caradoc resolved, motioning to Vanora. 'Get on with it, and make sure to kill him this time.'

'Caradoc, I beseech thee . . .' Lady Gladys begged, 'he be thy father, thy King.'

Caradoc roughly cast her aside. 'He be neither. If I had my way, Caswallon would die by the sword.' Caradoc approached the bed to gloat upon his ailing relative.

'What would thy people think?' Vanora scoffed sarcastically at his impetuous nature. 'Besides, father was very specific, best not anger him, save . . .'

'Just do it,' Caradoc hissed, intolerant of these stupid precautions. He wanted to thrust his sword into someone, namely Maelgwn.

The goblet Vanora had been preparing for the King flew abruptly out of her hand, and Caradoc drew his sword.

'Woman, thou art trying my patience!'

'It was not me, there be someone else in here,' Vanora snapped, unnerved as her bottles of poison went crashing to the floor. Then she screeched as she was violently thrown across the room.

'Bitch!' Tory felt a wave of numbness come over her, and she started speaking in a voice much harsher and more mature than her own. 'Caradoc, thou art a festering thorn in my side.' She moved around as silent as the air itself, so that the mortified Prince could not follow the direction of her voice. 'Taliesin was right. I should have slaughtered thee at birth.'

'Sorcha?' He sounded wary.

'Did thou really think I would allow my noble husband and his only beloved son to be ruined in such a manner?' Tory lashed out with her boot to his stomach, followed by a knee to the face that sent him rocketing backwards.

Lady Gladys was speechless, she would have known Sorcha's voice anywhere. The Great Sorceress had returned to seek vengeance as promised.

Caradoc, his noise bloodied, was foaming at the mouth. 'Guards!' he yelled, striking out with his sword but hitting nothing.

Tory managed to score a nice gash across Caradoc's upper leg before turning to face the guards. As the first two entered she thrust the twin sword forward, and the warrior's heads were sliced from their shoulders. The third was severely beaten about before colliding with a wall. Tory turned to address the fourth guard, only to find him mysteriously absent. *Where is the son-of-a-bitch? Oh shit, Katren.*

Tory didn't have the time to chase him as Caradoc was heading for the King. *Oh no you don't.* Under Sorcha's wilful control, Tory moved to intervene. She slashed a long incision across Caradoc's back from his shoulder to his hip. 'Since thou art so fond of pain and fear, I thought thee should become more intimate with it.' She booted him away from the bed and stood to guard Caswallon. 'The Dragon wants words with thee, Caradoc.' Her voice was colder than his glare. 'So let us await his arrival, without thee forcing me to send thee to thy maker.'

Caradoc lashed out at where he suspected her to be. 'Cadfer's dagger did not cut deep enough, Mother. Show thyself, witch and let me finish the job my father started. I know thee for the vulgar adulteress thou art, taking to the bed of thy husband's brother! Deny that I be the living proof of it.'

Lady Gladys could barely believe her ears; how was it that she had never gotten wind of this scandal? She waited, breathless, for Sorcha to reject his foul claim.

Tory served Caradoc a slight slice to his neck, having crept up on him from behind. She could keep him occupied like this for hours, if that's what he chose. 'True, thou art nothing but the bastard son of a treacherous leech,' Sorcha vexed him back, not bothered at all that he knew about his illegitimacy. 'But get thy facts straight, boy. I cut my own throat. I did not give Cadfer the chance to take my pleasures from me a second time.' Tory felt shivers as she was caught up in the memory of Sorcha's last hours; she had died in this very room.

Vanora had slithered her way round the chamber during the scuffle, and now held a dagger at Lady Gladys' throat. 'Show thyself crone, or lose another member of thy family.'

Caradoc smiled at Vanora. 'I do adore thee at times.'

'I know.' Her black eyes were void of any emotion. 'Finish the King thine own way.'

Lightning tore through the storm clouds and the thunder boomed so loudly that Maelgwn thought it would burst his eardrums. The relentless rain made it impossible to see a thing; they could run straight into the enemy ranks and not realise. Still, Tiernan seemed to know where he was going and Maelgwn followed blindly, glad that Tory had got his physical fitness up to scratch.

Maelgwn gave a thought for his horse, Aristotle, named after the scholar whose teachings the Prince respected greatly. He regretted that the magnificent animal had probably drowned or been stolen during the dreadful crossing.

Fortunately, the wind was to their backs and seemed to be spurring them along. Maelgwn felt himself settling into a good rhythm as they cleared the thicker forest that boarded the shore of the Menai. But as they entered the more open expanse of land, Tiernan came to an abrupt stop.

'Troops?' the Prince leaned forward to catch his breath.

A great flash of lightning lit up the area and Tiernan clapped his hands together, letting loose a laugh. 'Behold, our own stampede.'

Maelgwn followed Tiernan to inspect a group of horses. Aristotle grazed with about a dozen other horses that must have followed the black stallion from the barge. The animal looked up to watch the Prince approach, and shook its head as if to ask what had taken him so long.

'I must say,' Tiernan said, climbing onto his horse. 'The Gods certainly seem to favour thee.'

'Let us hope.' The Prince sprang to his mount, wasting no time in getting the pack moving.

Exhilarated, Maelgwn hugged close to Aristotle as they rode quickly towards Aberffraw. He let loose a war cry, inspired by the furious power he felt in the charge of these beasts; a whole army couldn't stop them now.

Brockwell moved silently through the darkness as his troops spread out to scour the land. He was enjoying stalking the enemy on foot as they were on familiar ground and under the cover of rain. Caradoc had only brought, at most, forty men with him when he'd accompanied the King to Aberffraw, and Brockwell had sent small parties back to pick them off, leaving a few legions to guard the house from the outer bailey.

As he crept through the long undergrowth, Calin sought the strength and guidance of Gwyn ap Nudd, the Night Hunter. This Underworld King held the right of passage through darker realms, and always caught his prey before the light of dawn.

They found the exhausted troops from Powys further inland, lying in wait for a dawn attack. Brockwell's legions managed to catch them off guard, as they had expected to be the surprise this day. The sword of Rhydderch was not affected by the pouring rain, and as Brockwell blazed his way through his foe lightning began to shoot from the sky to slay them also. Gwynedd's troops, inspired by the spectacle and freshly rested, fought vigorously against the enemy and finally had them on the run.

The sound of horses' hooves thundering through the darkness toward them sent Brockwell rushing to investigate. Sword retracted, he climbed the nearest tree and without thought for his own safety he made ready to jump.

Bodies of the dead and dying were trampled under hoof as the pack of charging horses came bursting through the front line. Maelgwn wondered how Gwynedd was faring, as soldiers from both sides hurried out of the path of the stampede. As he hunched lower, heading into the forest, Maelgwn heard Brockwell's familiar war cry. The knight came flying out of the tree overhead to land on a horse nearby. 'Brockwell!' Maelgwn cried, astonished.

The knight, clearly having the time of his life, was ecstatic to find Maelgwn behind the brilliant ploy. 'Maelgwn! Excellent!' he yelled his approval loud enough to be heard over the noise of the horses, thunder and battle.

'What art thou doing here, where be Tory?' Maelgwn shouted.

'Later,' replied Brockwell, pushing his horse harder to catch up with Sir Tiernan. Calin slapped his greatest rival on the back.

Tiernan smiled. 'Where did thee come from?' This kid never ceased to amaze him. Brockwell was totally fearless, much like himself ten years ago.

'I be everywhere, old man,' Brockwell teased King Caswallon's champion, as he often did, taking off ahead of him.

With the sword of Rhydderch held high, Brockwell rode towards the outer-bailey wall, its flaming blade a signal to raise the portcullis. The entire stampede ran inside the huge stone walls of the outer bailey. Brockwell, Tiernan and the Prince continued on to deal with Caradoc.

'Where be Tory?' Maelgwn demanded from Brockwell, beating him to a dismount. Brockwell hesitated but a second to reply before the Prince proceeded to shake it out of him. 'Calin, answer me!'

'She went to save thy father.'

'Damn it!' Maelgwn was gone before Brockwell was given a chance to explain.

Tiernan, who could sympathise with the young knight's position, gave him a slap of encouragement to get him back on track. 'Thou hast done well this day,' he assured Brockwell, who obviously felt he'd failed in his duty to his Prince. 'But it be far from over yet.'

Tiernan turned a corner in time to see Maelgwn enter the King's chamber. Brockwell, who followed behind him, was distracted from their course by a scream coming from his own bedchamber. He burst through the door to discover Katren trying to wriggle free from beneath a huge warrior twice her size. The man was having some trouble trying to hold her still to rip open her gown. Katren was kicking violently, despite how hard she was struck for her struggle.

Brockwell ran his glowing blade across the barbarian's butt, which certainly served to raise him in a hurry. He grinned at the awestruck villain as he ran him through, and watched with satisfaction as his foe slid off his blade to the floor.

Her virtue still intact, Katren pulled together her tattered clothes.

Brockwell, not good at handling such delicate situations, thought best to make light of it. 'What on Earth keeps possessing men to rip thy clothes from thy body and bruise thy lovely face, Katren?' He held out a hand to help her from the bed.

Katren declined his help, a little upset but stable. 'I be fine, Sir Brockwell, really, and I do thank thee. But there be nothing but a torn dress to cry over here. Please, the King be more important, thee should make haste to him.'

Brockwell was stunned by her resolve as he backed up to the door; most women would have been hysterical after such a violent attack. Katren was truly one of Tory's ilk. 'Thou art right.' He opened the door to leave. 'Besides, I quite fancy thee there.'

Having been dragged into the room under force, Katren didn't understand his meaning at first. But when she realised she was in Sir Brockwell's room, she smiled, exalted, and collapsed back onto his bed in a state of bliss.

With only a split second to decide between the life of the already comatose King and Lady Gladys, it was the latter Tory chose to save from harm. Her invisible blade left its imprint on Vanora's jugular, and the Princess released her captive when Tory threatened to cut her throat.

'Caradoc,' Sorcha's voice loudly hissed in caution, hoping to dissuade him from hurting the King. 'I care not for thy whore.'

Lady Gladys, not unaccustomed to harassment, retrieved the dagger from Vanora and threatened her with it. 'Foolish child, thou art dealing with forces whose power be way beyond thy feeble skills and understanding.'

Caradoc paused only a moment to consider his priorities, and unfortunately he did not care for his lover as much as Tory had hoped. Even though she near flew to the King's aid, Tory was not fast enough to stop Caradoc from running Caswallon through. 'Damn thee to hell!' She booted him away with all the might she could muster, so he couldn't repeat the offence.

'He be mine,' Maelgwn's voice resounded throughout the chamber.

With the King's blood dripping from his sword, Caradoc raised himself. 'At last — thou art next, monk.' Caradoc lunged at his brother with his blade.

The Prince effortlessly blocked Caradoc's sword with his own. 'Thy Saxon thugs have fled in fear, Chiglas' armies art massacred,' Maelgwn informed him, looking as if he'd been to hell and back. 'Now thee will pay along with thy vomitus scum.' He lashed out with a powerful kick that thrust his brother clear out of the room.

Caradoc's free-wheeling form nearly collided with Tiernan, who was about to enter. Maelgwn was upon his brother, not giving him the chance to rise. He dug his boot into Caradoc a couple of times before dragging the traitor to his feet.

'Ah, brotherly love,' Tiernan said, amused.

Maelgwn ripped the sword from his overwhelmed foe and cast his own aside, experiencing far more satisfaction in a bare-handed assault. 'What be wrong, dear brother?' The Prince referred to Caradoc's astounded expression. 'I do not fight like a monk now, do I?' Maelgwn belted him with kicks and blows, all the way down the hall.

Brockwell came racing down the corridor to assist, but Tiernan stopped him and stood back to observe the Prince's new and intriguing form of hand-to-hand combat. Though Tiernan found the skills very much to his liking, he left Maelgwn to his fun to seek out the welfare of his King.

Upon entering the chamber, Sir Tiernan rushed to the bed where the King lay in a pool of his own blood. By some miracle, Caswallon was still coherent and aware of the goings on around him.

'Did we win?' The King's eyes could no longer focus, yet he knew the one who gripped his hand to be his champion and dear friend.

Tiernan kept the tears from his voice. He saw that the King was fading from life as they spoke. 'Aye Majesty, thy son hast done thee proud this day, against unbelievable odds. I dare say, Gwynedd will not be troubled for a long time to come.'

'Chiglas lives.' The King strained to convey his warning, coughing blood. 'Guard Maelgwn, guide him . . .' There was so much he wanted to tell his son, but now it was too late; the effort was far too great for his failing lungs.

Tiernan begged him to hush, hoping Maelgwn would arrive at his father's bedside in time.

Brockwell, having liberated the imprisoned castle guards from the room across the hall, ordered them to take Vanora out of his sight before he killed her. He embraced his harrowed mother then quickly spun around, calling out with concern, 'Tory, how dost thou fare?'

Tory, who was right beside him, lifted the mantle from her shoulders. 'Thee will not be rid of me so easily.'

He grasped hold of her, relieved to find her unharmed. 'I never wish to be rid of thee.'

He regarded her with that same alarming glint in his eye, which did not escape the attention of his mother. As Katren humbly approached the doorway, Tory broke away from Brockwell and rushed to embrace her friend. 'Katren, art thou alright?' She held the girl at arm's length to check her over. 'I was so worried when I came up a guard short in battle.'

Katren smiled meekly, glancing to Calin. 'Sir Brockwell came to my aid in time to preserve my honour.' She blushed slightly, recalling his last words to her.

Tory followed Katren's coy look to catch Calin's bashful reaction. How appropriate, she considered. I can see that I'll not have to worry about Calin's admiring glances for much longer. With Tory's mind set partly at ease, Sorcha resumed wilful control and guided Tory to the bedside of the King.

Tiernan was startled by Tory's touch, and his eyes opened wide in amazement as he looked at her.

'I shall take it from here,' the young woman told him calmly in Sorcha's voice. So close in image to his Queen was she, that he fell on one knee before her. In his mind, Sorcha was still the only woman Tiernan considered worth dying for. In fact, the knight had willed death upon himself when he hadn't been there to prevent her from being slain.

'The prophecy,' he uttered, head bowed low to the ground in homage to her presence.

'Aye.' She bent down, lifting his face to look at him. 'My devout Sir Tiernan, and we bless thee for thy part.'

Tiernan, exulted to have met with the touch of a Goddess, backed away to give the couple some space.

Lady Gladys drew Katren under one arm for comfort as they witnessed the King's passing. Though Katren didn't understand much of what was happening, she felt moved to be so intimate with the royal family.

Tory took a seat on the King's bed, and in the room so dimly lit she glowed with angelic grace. As she took up Caswallon's hand in her own, his eyes opened wide at her touch.

'Sorcha,' he said, a smile of peaceful delight lighting his wrinkled old face. He stared not directly at Tory but at a space just above her head, and it was plain to all present that the King was addressing his dear wife.

'Indeed Caswallon, I have come for thee at last,' she assured him, resting a hand on his cheek. 'It be time to leave this rare and gracious woman to the care of our fair son. It be his time now, my love, and like his father before him, he will be a formidable king. Come,' she beckoned with a soft smile.

Caswallon reached up, and to those who bore witness to the scene it appeared that the King simply went to her. As his earthly vessel collapsed back onto the bed, the King's expression was one of peace and contentment.

Sir Brockwell was moved to tears by the sad occurrence, and waited a few minutes before he approached to comfort Tory in the wake of the ordeal. To his surprise, however, she hushed him away.

Tory continued to stare into the King's lifeless face, as if listening to him speak. She gestured now and then to acknowledge the words that none in the room, apart from herself, could hear. When she finally sat back, Tory looked up at the ceiling and took in a deep breath. 'He hast gone,' she announced, her head bowing low in silent respect.

'Long live King Maelgwn,' Tiernan said softly, overcome by what he'd seen. The others repeated this with conviction.

Maelgwn, dropping the bound and beaten body of Caradoc in the doorway, drew the attention of all present. Tory would have run to him at once, but she suddenly felt as if she would faint.

The Prince's face was filled with remorse having heard the announcement, and it was Lady Gladys who came forward to console him. 'Thy mother came for him, Maelgwn. 'Twas lovely.'

'Aye. 'Twas her.' Tiernan braced the Prince's shoulder firmly. 'He died a very proud and happy man.'

Maelgwn gently loosened himself from them and approached the bed where Tory sat with her hand in his father's, tears rolling down her cheeks. The Prince had only to look into his father's face to see that the end had been peaceful.

As he crouched down to address her, Tory reached out with trembling hands to touch his face. She battled to hold herself together, and she had to force out every word. 'He left thee a message.' She so badly wanted to convey it, but her body gave in and she collapsed unconscious into Maelgwn's awaiting arms.

Distant voices filled Tory's dreams and she stirred from her slumber a few hours later.

'As I told thee, 'twas just the exhaustion of channelling. She'll be as right as rain, now.'

Tory opened her eyes upon recognising the Merlin's distinguished tone, and sat up. 'Taliesin, thou art here!'

'Easy does it,' he advised with a smile. 'I be the bearer of grand news.'

Even Taliesin's calming aura was not enough to allay her at once, and she took a strong hold of his hand. 'We won?'

'Indeed we did.'

'But I failed the test, I did not save the King.'

Taliesin laughed away her anxieties. 'Dear lady, that was not the purpose of thy quest. Why, even as we speak, the folk of Gwynedd are singing your praises and throughout the land you are being hailed as a warrior Goddess.'

Tory grinned modestly. 'That's ludicrous!'

Nay, it be all important if you truly love Maelgwn, Taliesin thought, and although he did not say it out loud, Tory heard every word, clear as a bell. She frowned in question. 'More about that later,' he said. 'Meanwhile, there be an exhausted young man who hast been patiently awaiting a word with thee.'

Taliesin stood, bowing to Maelgwn as he came forth out of the shadows. 'I shall leave thee to talk. Talk, mind,' the Merlin cautioned the Prince. 'It would be wise not to anger those who bestowed such a beauteous paragon upon thee.'

The Prince was deeply grateful for all his mentor's support this day, but it seemed that the bard never ceased his lecturing. 'Taliesin, old friend, I understand the behaviour I am required by privilege to uphold. Thou hast prepared me well for what lies ahead, and may rest easy that I shall not jeopardise the future of Gwynedd.'

'The land shall unite and prosper upon thy crowning, Maelgwn.' Taliesin admired his work in the form of the young King to be. 'I will leave thee and shall speak with thee both in the courtroom at thy leisure.' The Merlin headed back downstairs to tend to the many affairs of state that needed his attention.

Maelgwn opened wide the caphouse doors to behold a glorious sunrise. The clouds had departed, along with their enemy, and a rainbow now sparkled over the land.

'My court advisers and bards tell me that thou hast been brought back from the future by the spirits of the Otherworld, to guide and protect . . .' Tory rolled her eyes and made ready to object, but Maelgwn raised a hand to prevent it. 'Please, hear me out. I have pondered these words too many days now, and I shall surely go mad if thou dost not allow me to speak them.' The Prince beckoned for her to join him as he stepped outside.

The inflection of his voice, so anxious and heartfelt, had Tory fascinated. 'Maelgwn? I am sorry. I promise I am listening now . . . to guide and protect . . .'

Maelgwn smiled, as he began to walk with her. 'I need thee to understand why the people here in Gwynedd, who mainly be of the old faith, consider thee a Goddess. To them, the days of such extraordinary feats executed by a female be long past with the days of Gaul. Even then a woman would have had to earn the right to carry such a title. A good thing too, or I could never ask of thee what I will.'

'Which be?'

'I am afraid this will seem sudden, but my circumstances leave me pressed for time.'

'Maelgwn, it be me, Tory. Thou art my dearest friend, thee can ask me anything.'

The Prince took hold of Tory's right hand and, confronting his fear head on, went down on one knee before her. 'If I am found worthy to hold the office of King, would thee, Tory Alexander, do me the great honour of becoming my wife and Queen.' Maelgwn couldn't believe that the words had left his lips, and he listened to his heart beat as he awaited her reply.

Tory, though stunned, didn't want to keep the Prince in suspense and went down on her knees to speak to him. 'I am the one who be honoured, Maelgwn, believe me. But thou art a prince, dost thou not have to wed a princess?'

Maelgwn was forced to smile; she obviously hadn't even mildly comprehended what he'd been trying all this while to explain. 'I think a Goddess will suffice.'

'Oh!' Tory was enlightened. *That's what Taliesin was trying to tell me.* She was quiet for a moment, considering the proposal seriously.

Maelgwn watched her closely, and to his dismay Tory's expression became one of growing concern. For as much as Tory wanted to say yes, there were two very important points that she needed to discuss. 'Hast thou thought this well through?'

'Aye, I have.' He was alarmed by her reaction.

She stood and took a few steps away so he could view her clearly. 'Look at me, Maelgwn. I am not like the women thou art accustomed to, and I have no intention of changing the way I am, or what I hold true and just, to suit anyone else's ideals. I will not.'

'But I do not want thee to change,' Maelgwn insisted, standing also.

'Wait, thee must hear me out. Please Maelgwn, this be very important as it bothers me greatly.'

The Prince was silenced and took a seat on the sea-wall to listen to her.

'If I was to rule here at thy side then the two of us would represent the law of the land, would we not?' she began.

'Aye, that we would.'

'Then, I can only respond thus. Unless certain laws were enforced throughout the kingdom for the protection of women and children, then to my deepest regret I would have to decline thy lovely proposal. For how can I be expected to represent that which I cannot condone?' Tory's expression was serious and she prayed Maelgwn would not take offence to her terms, or think her too insubordinate for saying so.

Already she employs Sorcha's foresight and strong will. Heaven help me! 'I know my kingdom and people be far from perfect, but together we could change that.' He slid off the wall and took hold of her. 'I have come to realise these few days past that I do love thee beyond my life. I am prepared to do whatever I must to be one with thee, Tory.'

'I can certainly appreciate that,' Tory said, sharing his sense of urgency as he bent down to kiss her. 'But, there be one last thing.'

Maelgwn let her go, feeling a mite exasperated by her resistance. 'Ask away.'

'Maelgwn, do not be mad with me. If thou hast missed me these past few days, please believe I missed thee tenfold.' As he appeared to calm a little, she continued, 'However, try as we might to forget, the simple fact remains that I am not supposed to be here. This doth not worry me greatly, but somewhere in the twentieth century, the two people I care about most art beside themselves with worry.'

The Prince nodded slightly. 'I could not keep thee from thy kin, Tory. I understand.'

'I do not want to go back there, silly,' she teased. 'I just want to visit and let them know I be safe and well. Taliesin said it may be possible next summer solstice.'

Maelgwn reacted to the news like a man possessed. 'But that not be for near a year,' he cried, lifting her into the air.

'Aye,' she laughed, revelling in his joy.

'And would thee promise to return to me?'

'Nay.' She toyed with him, trying to hide her smile as he brought her back to the ground.

'Nay?'

Tory slid both arms around his neck. 'I never wish to leave thee again. Thee must come. My parents would want to meet my husband.'

Maelgwn's expression melted to a smile, and with all the formalities out of the way, he finally induced her to a kiss.

PART TWO

SPACE

10
INAUGURATION

All his life, Maelgwn had dreaded taking on the huge responsibility of his father's office. Yet with Tory at his side, the thought was not so daunting. He smiled at her as she walked with him. His inauguration was all that stood between himself and his idea of paradise. *I be deserving of my father's position, so I must not doubt my own ability. This vision of the Goddess be my rightful claim, no matter what the spirits may ask as proof of my worthiness.*

As they stopped outside the Great Hall the Prince whispered, 'This could be a little overwhelming, my subjects tend to get rather excited by the news of a wedding.'

Tory smiled, every bit as nervous as she was thrilled by their impending announcement. She had no idea what to expect, knowing little about local ceremony. 'Well, I am ready if thou art.'

The Prince hugged her, proud of the way she was taking this all in her stride. He'd been allowed a lifetime to become accustomed to the idea of leadership, whereas Tory had only been given a few days. 'Right.' He moved to open the doors.

'Wait.' Tory pulled him back for a kiss of encouragement.

The pair, preoccupied for the moment, didn't heed the doors in front of them parting wide. When the eyes of all at court beheld their Prince and his lady in a strong embrace, the whistles and applause were almost deafening.

Maelgwn and Tory burst into laughter, embarrassed.

'I think we've been found out,' she said in jest.

'Indeed.' The Prince turned to address the rowdy gathering and somehow managed to quieten them. 'I be very pleased to inform ye all, my family, dear friends, loyal knights and ladies . . .' He was forced to pause when his men again raised riot to confirm their allegiance. Flattered by their enthusiasm, Maelgwn shouted over the din, '. . . that upon my inauguration, Tory Alexander will do me the great honour of becoming my wedded wife and Queen to all Gwynedd.'

Taliesin was overjoyed as the cries of the rejoicing crowd filled the huge room. But as he rose to address them, silence fell over the court.

'As messenger of the Otherworld,' he began, 'I decree that the initiate, Maelgwn of Gwynedd, shall face inauguration five days hence. Should he be found worthy and succeed in the task set for him by his forefathers, he shall wed with the Goddess seven days thereafter. This be the will of the Great Houses, Don and Llyr.'

'So be it!' the crowd responded in unison, giving a cheer.

Lady Gladys was beside herself with tears, and near drowned the couple with her joy as she embraced them. 'In the whole of creation, thee could not have found thyself a fairer match.' She kissed Maelgwn's cheek then turned to Tory. 'May I be the first to welcome thee, child, to the clan of Cunedda the Great. I cannot express how overjoyed I be to accept thee as my kindred.'

Tory was moved to tears as they embraced. 'I thank thee Lady Gladys, for everything. I shall do my very best to live up to thy high ancestral name.'

'Dear girl.' Lady Gladys had to chuckle. 'I hold no fear of that.'

When silence descended, Tory and Lady Gladys turned to find that Maelgwn had raised his hands.

'Good people. Much hast happened this night, and although Gwynedd will deeply mourn the death of my father Caswallon, he shall be remembered always as a great King among Britons.'

Tory considered his words, knowing to the contrary; Caswallon would only be remembered as father to King Maelgwn of Gwynedd. It was Maelgwn who would be revered as the Great King among Britons.

'My divine mother, Queen Sorcha, manifested to tend the King in his passing. So I assure all thee who grieve, that the King be a far happier soul now that he hast joined his beloved wife. Together may they at last find their peace eternal.' Maelgwn bowed his head in remembrance, as did everyone in the room.

After a moment of silence, the Prince slapped his hands together and moved on to a brighter subject. 'However, as my father was a man renowned for honouring occasion, I feel sure Caswallon would not have seen his subjects so solemn on a day as auspicious as this! Sorcha's dying prophesy of retribution hast been fulfilled. The Might of Gwynedd hast triumphed over the treasonous House of Chiglas, *and* their hired Saxon thugs!'

A cry of victory was raised.

'I have never seen him so spirited,' Lady Gladys whispered to Tory.

'And with my imminent wedding to celebrate, I invite all to join me in a feast, just as my father would have had it.'

A second cry sounded. Weekends were not heard of in this age, so a feast was as good as a holiday.

'Caswallon be dead!' Tiernan cried, which incited the rest of the gathering to respond: 'Long live King Maelgwn!'

The ladies of the house flew into action with the announcement of the festivities, and Maelgwn left to attend the pressing affairs of State.

Tory wandered down the grand halls of the castle, when it dawned on her that, through her participation in Gwynedd's victory she'd not only won the right to marry her love, but she had obtained her liberty as well. This prompted her to chance something that she'd been longing to attempt since first setting foot on Aberffraw.

The gateway to the stairs leading to the beach was located below her tower room. There was no access to the beach from the castle, however. One had to exit through the inner portcullis into the outer-bailey grounds then walk round the east tower.

Tory followed a cobbled pathway through the outer gardens that led down the outside of the northern wing; the gateway she sought was just ahead. Maelgwn had given her his medallion of the Dragon, which served the same function as a backstage pass might in the twentieth century. She flashed it at the gatehouse guards and was granted access to wherever she pleased.

As the iron grille was lowered behind her, Tory paused to breathe deeply the sea air and feel the sunshine on her face. The beach was completely deserted as everyone was at the celebrations; the peace and isolation of the moment filled her with joy.

Tory hurried down the old sandstone stairs, then pulled off her boots. She burrowed her toes deep into the sand and sighed with delight at the memories of home. With her jeans rolled up to her knees, Tory shrieked as she felt the icy water rush against her bare skin and she splashed her way along the shore break, basking in the release of her new-found freedom.

When she returned from a brisk jog, Tory met Brockwell seated on the stairs that led from the beach to the bailey wall. She smiled, pleased to see him. 'Hey Bro.'

'Stop calling me that,' he shot back at her as he stood up. 'I am not thy brother yet.'

Uh-oh! Tory took a step backwards. She was a little confused by his sudden change of heart. 'It could be short for Brockwell. I meant no offence by . . .'

'Why art thou wedding Maelgwn when thee told me thee did not love him?'

I see. 'What I said was that Maelgwn had nothing to do with why I wouldn't sleep with thee, or dost thy memory of that night escape thee completely?' She made her way past him, not wanting a confrontation; Brockwell had, no doubt, been drinking for hours.

'So now thee will be Queen,' he called after her in spite.

Adrenalin shot through her body, and had it been anyone but Calin Tory would have lashed out. Instead she paused and took a deep breath. 'If thou art seeking to hurt, thou hast succeeded.' She did not turn back to look at him but continued her climb.

'Nay, don't go.' His tone softened dramatically and although Tory was hesitant, his plea managed to sway her. 'I did not intend to attack thee, truly.'

As Tory's eyes met his, she became more sympathetic. 'Oh Calin, what am I going to do with thee?'

'Be thee aware . . .' he informed her, taking her in his arms, '. . . that it be customary for a young knight like myself to take an older woman as a mistress? I do truly worship . . .'

Tory panicked. 'Calin, please. Dost Maelgwn's friendship and trust mean nothing to thee?'

'Honour be more important than life,' he assured her. 'Still, thou art fairer than even honour and I will fight to the death for thy favours, if need be.'

This angered her; she would not be the cause of dispute between the Prince and his champion. 'Over my dead body, Calin. Just listen to thyself! Hast thou never heard the tale of Lancelot and Guinevere?'

'Nay,' Brockwell shrugged. 'Was it a tale of love?'

'Aye,' Tory thought it rather odd that the knight should have no knowledge of the Arthurian saga; perhaps the historians were right in saying that this King had never existed. 'And 'twas a tragic love story at that. When Queen Guinevere fell in love with Sir Lancelot, King Arthur and his kingdom were lost. She became a nun, and the gallant Sir Lancelot went mad.

'Even if thou wast not the very image of Brian, which thou art, I love Maelgwn. Surely it shows?'

'Aye, all too well.' He clenched his jaw, as he looked away to the ocean.

'My whole life was just a meaningless stream of information until I met him, Calin.'

Brockwell wasn't too thrilled by her reckoning but the tenderness in her voice urged him to take a seat and hear her out.

'And now I have a purpose. I *can* make a difference here. I realise,' she said, only now becoming aware of her situation as she spoke, 'that everything I have ever studied — the fighting, the history, the language — was not all for naught. It hast all been in preparation to wed him.'

'I follow,' he replied softly.

'Calin, I am sorry.' She came to sit beside him. 'But I would just be another in a long line for thee, and there art so many beautiful maidens here that —'

'Nay, there be none to compare, not here, not anywhere.'

'Then I shall have to find and train one to keep thee out of mischief.'

''Tis not possible.'

'Of course it be possible, dost thou think I was born with these skills?' She nudged him, as she would Brian when he was being stupid.

'How long would it take?' he asked and Tory was forced to laugh.

'Let us discuss it over lunch.' She slapped his knee. 'I need a drink.'

By mid-afternoon, Sir Cedric, Sir Rhys, Sir Angus, and their legions had arrived at the castle bearing the headless body of Sir Madoc. They had made the sad discovery during their passage to Aberffraw, finding the old knight washed up on the Mon side of the Menai Strait.

Some of the native clans, like Chiglas, still followed the savage practice aptly known as 'the taking of heads'. They believed that the head was the temple of the soul, and by decapitation it would be forever trapped there. The severed remains of their fallen enemy were then nailed to the front of their houses, as proof of their prowess.

The knights brought the news to Maelgwn, who was still in conference with his court. The Prince grieved Madoc's death even more than his father's, feeling directly responsible. Sir Madoc had been one of Caswallon's finest knights and Gwynedd would miss him dearly. Maelgwn could only hope that Sir Gilmore would pull through, as he would require the guidance of his father's old colleagues in the years ahead.

Cedric reported that the troops at Degannwy had carried out a dawn raid on the enemy in the strait and mountains, to prevent any risk of a force regrouping for a third attack. 'By sundown,' he predicted, 'there will not be one enemy soldier left in Gwynedd, dead or alive.'

Except Caradoc. Maelgwn slouched back in his chair, unsure what should become of him. The Prince had resolved to send Vanora and her maid, complete with a letter of warning, back to her father in Powys. Chiglas may choose to pay ransom for Caradoc's release, and if his offer was substantial and befitting his grievous crime, Maelgwn would consider it. This was the procedure that the Prince knew he must follow to avoid further blood feuding. Had the shoe been on the other foot, Caradoc probably would have disregarded diplomacy and had the King's murderer and his accomplice slain. But such an action would cast the kingdoms of the Britons into another decade of war, and they had enough to worry about just keeping the Saxons at bay. So, while Chiglas was making up his mind, the Prince decided he would have the traitor taken off the island and away from his peacetime haven and training ground. Perhaps to Degannwy, where Caradoc could spend the winter pondering his misadventures in a dark, squalid dungeon.

'Our thorough search hast failed to find any trace of Sir Cadogan, and it be highly unusual for either Chiglas or the Saxons to take prisoners with so many of their own wounded,' Sir Rhys informed the Prince.

A couple of years younger than the Prince and a distant cousin, Rhys was lord of his own lands on the island and a married man. His first child was expected before the end of the fall. Like Maelgwn, Sir Rhys was quite a scholar and therefore was the obvious choice to appoint to Madoc's position as the keeper of the King's personal records and accounts. Rhys' new position would not become official until Maelgwn's crowning, though he'd already assumed the responsibilities of the office.

'What art thou implying, sir? Cadogan be no deserter,' Cedric demanded of Rhys, annoyed that one so young was to be appointed to such a high station.

Sir Cedric was not a well-educated man; he'd been knighted for his battle skills more than his intelligence. He knew that he was unqualified for the academic appointment, but at times like this his lack of education frustrated him; these kids thought they knew everything!

'Calm, Sir Cedric, we art implying naught,' Maelgwn said, detecting the spite in his knight's voice. 'We are merely examining all the possibilities.'

'Please excuse me for saying so, Majesty, but I know Cadogan better than anyone,' Cedric persisted. 'True, he may have been a friend to Caradoc once, many of us were. Yet I would stake my life that he be still loyal to the House of Gwynedd.' The large, red-headed knight turned towards Rhys. 'And treachery be not a possibility worth wasting our Majesty's time on.'

Rhys was not intimidated by Cedric's harsh tone. 'I am as confident of his allegiance as thou art, Cedric, and if it be the truth then Sir Cadogan hast nothing to fear. However, with circumstances unfolding as they art, only a fool would not consider —'

Cedric stood ready to draw his sword in challenge. 'Thou art the fool, boy!' he growled, spurring Rhys to his feet.

'Enough!' Maelgwn thundered, spared from lecturing the pair by a knock on the door. 'Come in.' He sat back preparing for more bad news, but to his surprise it was Tory and Brockwell who entered. 'Tory.' Maelgwn rose to meet them, delighted by the interruption.

All the knights and advisers seated at the table sprang from their chairs to kneel before her, aware of her status as a Goddess. Brockwell fell on one knee ashamed, for he'd not considered the Otherworld proclamation when he'd propositioned her earlier.

'Gentlemen please!' Tory insisted, quite embarrassed. 'We have all fought hard this day, so please rise.'

They all did as she asked, except Brockwell. 'I owe thee an apology, great lady.'

'Brockwell?' Tory was alarmed that he sounded so distant. She knew to what he referred, and wanted him to drop the subject immediately. 'Stop being so ridiculous.'

'Nay,' he resisted, making his remorse felt. 'I have near shamed the House of Gwynedd with my own selfish desires and damned love of drink. I do swear, I shall never touch another drop if thou can forgive my ignorance.'

'Calin, thy roguish ways be a growing concern,' Maelgwn said, most displeased.

'Your Majesty, please,' Tory spoke up. 'Thou hast been quick to jump to conclusions before. Brockwell's offence was neither his fault nor as grievous as he claims.'

'Aye Majesty, it was,' Brockwell said, making matters worse for himself. 'The lady doth not understand the all of it.'

Sir Tiernan had turned white at Calin's confession; this was Sorcha and himself all over again. 'Time to join the festivities downstairs.' He motioned the other men to leave.

'Tory, I bid thee leave us also,' Maelgwn instructed her softly, his dark eyes fixed on Brockwell.

'Nay, Maelgwn, please listen to me —'

'Why must thee defend him so?'

Those leaving the room froze at the sound of the Dragon's roar.

'Majesty.' Tory was deeply hurt by his inference. She was radiating a mystical quality, much like the Dragon in Maelgwn's nature, only she projected a sense of love and calm. 'As I wanted to tell thee, and Taliesin will confirm this, Calin be my brother.'

'Not till four and ten hundred years from now,' Brockwell added in an attempt to clarify things.

'What?' Maelgwn was a little confused; Tory had never mentioned that she had a brother.

'That be why I was so shocked in thy bath that first night at Degannwy,' she reminded him, pretending to be unaware that she'd said anything even mildly humorous, while those around them suppressed their chuckles. 'Dost thou not remember?'

'Aye, I do.' Maelgwn was forced to better spirits and continued before she could embarrass him further. 'Perhaps thou had best send Taliesin up to join us.'

Tory approached the Prince, of the mind to charm him. 'But it was Taliesin who sent me to thee. King Catulus hast arrived, and the High Merlin suggests that thee join thy people. After all, the celebration be in our honour, surely this can wait.'

Maelgwn found it very hard to resist her, but he also realised that, as an outsider, this was beyond her understanding. 'My request be still the same. I trust thee can entertain our guest, King Catulus, until I can join thee.'

Tory propped herself up onto her toes to whisper in his ear.

'But King Catulus be an old man! Be there no one in whose company thou art safe?' Maelgwn said, in a playful manner.

'Thy lady shall be safe with me, Majesty.' Rhys stepped forward and offered Tory his arm.

'Of course, Sir Rhys will accompany thee. This shall not take long, I promise.'

Tory looked back at Brockwell. She knew Calin was not very good at explaining himself, and he was liable to land himself in more strife.

'No harm shall befall him, I promise,' Maelgwn assured her as Rhys escorted her out the door.

In amongst the merrymaking in the courtyard, Tory awaited the outcome of the Prince's meeting with

Brockwell. She was gradually going insane with worry, so she decided to seek out Lady Gladys to confide in her.

As mistress of the house and Brockwell's mother, Lady Gladys was most interested to discover what had been taking place with Brockwell.

'If I do not see my son wed soon, I know he shall be the death of me,' she told Tory in confidence. 'Do not get me wrong child, I am overjoyed that thou hast found in Calin thy lost kin, yet I fear thy pure intentions art easily misread by him. I think it fortunate that this hast all come to light now, as Taliesin can deal with it accordingly.'

'But thy son did naught to offend,' Tory stressed.

Lady Gladys was rather surprised by her words, believing it to be quite the contrary. 'Tory dear, thou hast been hailed a Goddess. Only a king by way of initiation be worthy to lay claim to thy privileges and not insult the powers that brought thee to us.'

'What?' Tory was suddenly alarmed. 'Art thou telling me I have to wait until Maelgwn and I are wed before we . . .'

'Spirits preserve us!' Lady Gladys grabbed hold of Tory's hands, quickly guiding her to a quiet corner. 'Doth thou know much of our beliefs, child?'

'Some, I'm not too sure I understand them all,' she admitted, eager to learn.

Lady Gladys took a deep breath. 'A Queen, to us, personifies the land and its prosperity henceforth, so if thou art virtuous, happy, and appear to flourish with the King . . .'

'So will the land,' Tory stated to acknowledge that she was following.

'The new monarch, in this case Maelgwn, gains his right to rule over the land by way of union with the Goddess in wedlock, thus linking him with the Otherworld. Only this shall bring the sanction and glory of the Great Houses upon his reign, Tory. And thou hast already witnessed the great might of their wrath when angered.'

Tory became a mite confused as she pondered, the Gods, or Taliesin? Is there any difference between the two?

'And surely thee would not want to risk an illegitimate heir with Caradoc still breathing,' Lady Gladys said.

'We have not even considered children yet.' Tory sounded none too thrilled by the suggestion, she liked her body just the shape it was.

Lady Gladys shook her head, astounded. 'But thy wedding will only be deemed legitimate upon the birth of a male heir to the throne.'

'I did not realise.' Tory was mortified, and she became a little nauseous at the idea of childbirth in the sixth century. *No happy gas!*

'My dear child.' Lady Gladys embraced her. 'I can see we shall have to sit down and have a long chat about a great many things. But for now, thee must swear to me that thee will withhold thy pleasures from Maelgwn until the appointed time, which be only twelve days hence.'

'Aye.' Tory tried to smile. 'I swear to thee.'

Lady Gladys, nevertheless, feared this was not enough to prevent Tory and Maelgwn's overwhelming attraction for each other from getting the better of them too soon. Thus she made the pending Queen repeat an oath after her, then said, 'Thou hast sworn by the elements and art bound by life itself to comply.'

This request was obviously very important to the stately woman and Tory felt bound to do her will. 'I would not bring shame upon thy home, Lady Gladys. In my time sexual attitudes art very lax, so I hope thou will not look too poorly on my eagerness to bed the Prince.'

Tory realised she should be more careful with what she said from now on, at least until she got a grip on the customs and beliefs of the people in this era.

'I hardly think so, I was young and in love once.' Lady Gladys smiled.

When at last Taliesin, Maelgwn, and Tiernan entered the courtyard, Tory panicked as Brockwell was not with them. She decided it best not to approach the Prince at once, he was surrounded by his colleagues and she didn't have any desire to get caught up in formalities again. It would be better to wait for him to seek her out, or else he would surely become jealous of her concern for Calin. Tory opted to take a wander amongst the real folk of Gwynedd and so made her way towards the outer bailey.

'My lady Tory.'

Tory turned to find Katren bounding towards her.

'Or should I say, my Queen,' Katren giggled, bowing deeply, before overwhelming Tory with a hug.

'Congratulations! I am so happy for thee — and me, to be maid to the Queen, a Goddess, what an honour!'

'Please, don't remind me.' This marriage was shaping up to be much more complicated than she'd first imagined. 'Dost thou know if I am allowed a bridesmaid?'

'Thou art,' Katren grinned from ear to ear.

'Well then, for the next two weeks, as I know naught of what preparations art appropriate, thee, as my bridesmaid . . .'

Katren began to squeal softly, the excitement getting too much for her.

'. . . will have to advise and educate me. I am in great need of a friend right now, Katren.'

Tory's lack of sleep was beginning to catch up on her, and Katren sensed this. 'Then as thy friend, I must recommend that thee take a long hot bath then go straight to bed.'

Tory nodded in agreement, but she caught sight of a disturbance that had erupted outside the courtyard walls.

'Nay, Lady thee should not . . .' Katren tried to stop her, but Tory was already halfway there.

A crowd had gathered to watch a very drunk soldier teasing one of the village women with a dead fowl. Tory thought it a game until he punched the woman hard in the stomach for biting him. 'Come and get it, wanton witch. What be wrong, hast thou changed thy mind?' he sneered.

'Enough!' Tory stepped into the circle. 'Tell me the name of thy superior, soldier?'

The soldier just laughed at Tory. 'Who wants to know?'

'Look sharp, thou art addressing the future Queen of Gwynedd.' Tiernan came to stand beside her.

'The War Goddess,' the soldier said, falling to his knees.

Upon hearing this the whole crowd went to kneel, however Tory demanded very loudly, 'All rise!'

Tory looked to his game, recognising the woman involved from her first day in Aberffraw. As their party had passed through the village, this woman had been viewing Cadogan with some resentment, if memory served her. 'Who doth that belong to?' Tory asked, pointing to the fowl.

Before the distraught soldier could answer the woman in question sprang to her feet. She tore the bird's carcass from the man's hand, punching him straight between the eyes. The crazed woman then took off through the crowd with her prize, howling and chattering like a lunatic.

'Wait!' Tory leapt over the soldier to go after her.

Tiernan sprang into action, grabbing hold of Tory's arm. 'Thee will not catch her now.'

'Did thou see that? Incredible!' Tory could hardly believe it. 'Who be this woman, I have need to speak with her.'

'Nay, great lady, thee could have nothing to say to this woman. For she be mute, mad and nothing more than a whore.'

Tory resented the distaste reflected in the knight's tone. 'Gee, Tiernan, I wonder why?' she said sarcastically, as she turned and headed back to the castle in a huff.

'She hast got a lot on her mind. I am sure she meant thee no offence, sir,' Katren curtsied to Tiernan, before turning to go after her mistress.

Tory, meanwhile, had done an about-face and walked back down to them. 'I apologise to thee, Sir Tiernan, it hast been one hell of a day. Tell me, what hast become of Calin?'

Katren's eyes opened wide with the mention of her beloved, and she listened intently.

'I believe the Prince will wish to discuss that with thee. Understand, it be not my place.'

'Come on, Tiernan. There art so many seeking Maelgwn's council at present that I should be lucky to speak with him this side of a week from now.'

But still Tiernan refrained.

As she was clearly getting nowhere, Tory changed her line of questioning. 'Where be Calin then, I shall ask him myself?'

'Nay, thee cannot. He hast been forbidden to look upon or speak to thee until such time as thou art wed to thy King.'

What hast happened? Katren wondered, dying to ask.

'What! I don't believe it!' Tory cried. 'This be too much! Who decreed it?'

'Fate.'

Tory swung round to confront Taliesin.

'Calm thyself.'

'I am not a child, and I do not require cautioning from you,' she said, then controlled her emotions at once. 'What else hast thou *decreed* about my life that I should know, High Merlin?'

Taliesin stepped forward to touch her, but Tory backed up to avoid his contact. 'Oh no. Nobody controls me, but me.'

'I think we should talk,' Taliesin suggested, sensing her confusion and frustration.

'I think we should. And I should like to see the Prince, if that not be too much to ask.' Tory left them and made for her tower.

Maelgwn and the High Merlin later found Tory on the open walkway.

'I want in on this conspiracy,' she demanded. 'Thou art both making decisions concerning me without my knowledge!'

Taliesin stepped forward, ever so meekly. 'Tory, thou art hysterical.'

'Do not think for a second that I do not know thy game, Taliesin,' Tory said. 'If thee wishes to see the native faith strengthened throughout this land, then so be it, but surely thee must realise that setting me up as an idol in the eyes of these people can only be detrimental to my mission here. Dost thou want it to seem humanly impossible to master my fighting skills?'

'Thee needs to be more of an ideal, to which others can aspire,' Taliesin replied, seeing her point.

'Aye. People have to believe they can achieve all that I have *and more*, through their own desire and willpower. Not by worshipping me! That be where the human race keeps failing. People keep turning to all

206

these religions, when all they really need, be to love, know and believe in themselves.'

Taliesin raised his eyebrows. 'I agree, in principle. But these art a simple people, Tory. Myths and legends be how they learn the ethics and beliefs that thou dost hold so dear. I shall give thee some material to read on the subject, thou shalt be surprised at how much of it thee will agree with,' the Merlin told her.

'That be not my only beef with thee, High Merlin. I have a list.'

'Thou art already beginning to sound like a Queen.' He folded his arms and leant against the sea-wall.

'Thee must know I have the situation with Calin under control.'

Taliesin nodded to confirm this.

'So why art thou punishing him when thee said thyself that he could not help but feel as he dost?'

Taliesin rubbed his forehead, frustrated at having to explain his actions, which were in the best interest of all involved. 'I know it doth not appear so at present, but I assure thee that this will be for the best. Can thou not trust me as thou hast so many times before?'

'Look, Taliesin, thee could be the devil himself for all I know. Why should I believe one word of what thou hast told me?'

Taliesin found Tory attractive when she was riled up. 'My dear lady, Brockwell nominated his own punishment.'

'No!'

'Yes,' Maelgwn finally spoke up. 'He declined to be my champion and my first man at the inauguration and the wedding.'

'This be all my fault.' Tory was unnerved by the revelation. 'Maelgwn, please, let me talk to him, this be so ludicrous, he did not do anything.'

'Tory, thou art exhausted, could we not discuss this on the morrow? Thee will surely have more patience by then.' Saying this, Maelgwn dared to sweep her up into his arms and take her to the bed himself.

Tory hated herself for not being able to resist his bidding. 'Thee should talk. When was the last time thee slept?'

'If my brain was still working, I could tell thee.' He carried her into the caphouse and collapsed onto the bed with her.

As they lay there a moment, their minds awhirl in the silence, another question that had been plaguing Tory suddenly sprang to mind. 'What be this inauguration all about?'

Maelgwn kissed her to avoid another inquiry. 'Tomorrow,' he vowed as he rose to leave. 'I shall see thee at sunrise as usual.' He closed the door and joined Taliesin outside.

Tory gazed around the caphouse, realising that all her belongings that Taliesin had acquired for her had been placed in her room.

'Excellent.' Tory picked up a few history books to do a little research. She turned to a chapter on the inauguration of kings, in the hope of gaining some enlightenment.

Come sunrise, Maelgwn hasten to the rooftop to join Tory for kata, but he didn't find her on the sea-wall as usual. After an extensive search, the Prince leant on the wall, his gaze falling to the beach below. There, along with a few early morning fishermen, he spied Tory seated on the sand in the lotus position.

Tory noticed that the Prince was approaching, but did not break from her meditation until he'd sat down beside her. 'I did some reading last night and I have to tell thee, this inauguration ritual hast got me worried.' She turned her large green eyes towards him. 'I did not go through all I did for Gwynedd, Maelgwn. I did it for thee. And now I discover that thy men will probably kill thee on some male bonding weekend before we art even wed.'

Maelgwn was amused by her misconception. 'Thee need not fear. Inauguration be a test of the spirit. The task I am requested to perform be usually of a political nature, rather than a show of strength. Besides, I am the heir to the throne, dost thou really think my men would see me killed, when they have dedicated their lives to keeping me alive?'

Tory saw the sense of this, yet her frown did not waver. 'Doth this ritual in any way involve thee having sex with another woman, fertility rites, that sort of thing?'

Maelgwn couldn't help but laugh, as he was stunned by her directness. 'Well I . . . I do not think so,' he answered, as he'd resolved to play naive.

Tory folded her arms, waiting, showing that she needed more assurance than this.

'My father was the last King of Gwynedd to face this initiation, so I have never witnessed it myself. However, I have survived a similar ritual —'

'The Dragon, right?'

'Aye.' He seemed surprised that she knew. 'And I did not have to perform any such rite then.'

This was not the entire truth; following this quest, Maelgwn had returned to Dumnonia to celebrate the dragon's departure with the overjoyed King Catulus. It was the feast of Beltaine, and the young Prince had lost his virginity to a willing young maiden by the bonfires.

'Thou art the Goddess who awaits me at the end of my quest, and the Great Houses have stated such.'

'That be good news, indeed,' Tory warned, and within seconds had him pinned to the ground. 'Because if thee should ever sleep with another woman, I would make thee wish that thou *had* wed Vanora.'

The thought of Vanora made him shiver. 'Nay, thee and I shall lovers die,' he said with zeal, and when she still didn't release him he added, 'I swear to thee.'

'Not good enough.' Tory was in the mood to play. 'Swear by the elements for me.'

Maelgwn laughed again. 'Where art thou getting all this from?'

Tory let him go, and knelt up. 'Lady Gladys made me swear by them.'

The Prince sat up, pulling Tory towards him. 'And what did thee swear to exactly?'

Tory wrapped her arms around his neck and straddled her legs to take a seat in his lap. 'That until we art wed, I shall withhold my favours from thee.'

Maelgwn's expression grew more mischievous. 'And thou art doing a fine job of it, too,' he said.

Tory was enjoying the opportunity to arouse him a little. We deserve it, she thought to herself as the Prince caressed her neck with his lips. 'How would thee define favours exactly?' Tory asked him.

'Um . . .' He could barely think for the distraction of her body. 'I would say that as long as I keep my clothes on, we art safe.' Tory went to hit him, so Maelgwn wrestled her into a more manageable position beneath him; he noted in the process that Tiernan was heading down the stairs towards them. 'Could I come and see thee later tonight, perhaps?'

'I think that would be highly dangerous.'

'I shall behave, I swear.'

Tory procrastinated over the answer for so long that Tiernan had reached them before she'd had the chance to reply. Maelgwn climbed off and gave Tory a hand to her feet, explaining their position to his knight. 'Training.'

'I can hardly wait to get started.' Tiernan grinned and bowed to them. 'I am sorry to disturb thee both, but I bear grave news.'

'Not more,' Maelgwn said, his mood darkening. 'What hast happened now, another death?'

Tiernan gave a slight nod.

'Please Goddess, not Sir Gilmore?'

'I am very sorry, Majesty.' Tiernan felt for the young leader, it was a cruel stroke of fate indeed to lose another trusted adviser so soon.

Tory looked at Maelgwn, who appeared as if he might explode. She quietly wrapped her arms about him tightly. The Prince, after a moment of resistance, crumpled into her embrace and she felt he would have burst into tears had Sir Tiernan not been present.

The King's cremation ceremony was held the next day in the traditional burial grounds just outside the town limits. The Prince tried to dissuade Tory from attending the funeral as she was not of the faith, and he feared she would only find the ritual gruelling. But Tory was determined to learn more about the culture and knew that Calin would be in attendance. She so desperately wanted to speak to him, or absolve him, or whatever the hell it was she had to do to have his friendship back.

She'd shown Maelgwn the photo of her brother and tried to explain to him how much Brian had meant to her. The Prince began to understand her strange predicament, and so had apologised for his jealousy and for ever doubting her love. This had not been her main concern, however. Tory wanted the Prince to make amends with Calin, or at least to try. After she explained that she would sooner leave than come between two friends of such long standing, Maelgwn agreed he would see to the matter before he left for his inauguration two days hence.

Calin stood not far from Tory, yet not once throughout the ceremony did his eyes turn in her direction. His head remained bowed low in mourning and his expression was solemn.

The punishment is rather severe for nothing more than a proposition, Tory thought. If I had been any other woman he could have raped me and been deemed a hero. This was part of their way too, she supposed. And,

212

as this did not seem the right time or place to attempt a reconciliation, she resolved to let the matter rest.

The overcast sky enhanced the darkness of the occasion. As the King's body was set to flame, Taliesin recited:

> I saw death approaching
> down the corridor of time,
> where it has loitered since my birth,
> waiting to accompany my spirit back
> through the ethers to the Otherworld.
>
> With the touch of the divine,
> I see the sum total of my life, my deeds,
> all I have done, that which I leave undone
> and shall accomplish upon my returning.
>
> I mourn my loved ones among the living,
> whom I will watch over and protect
> from my place at the side of the Goddess,
> until such time as we are united in the Otherworld,
> or in the next earthly life.

Once the day of the burial had passed, the sorrow which had overshadowed the house lifted, and all began to look forward to the great celebration that lay ahead. For the next few days Tory resumed her normal routine: training with Maelgwn in the morning, lunch with Lady Gladys, music with Selwyn in the afternoon, and more training with the maidens in the evening after supper.

The Prince hadn't spoken again about coming to see her at night; perhaps he had also decided it was too risky. Still, Tory needed to see him before he embarked on his adventure. So on the day before his departure, she requested that he join her in the north tower that night. 'To talk,' she said, to stress the innocent intent.

It was some ungoldly hour when Maelgwn quietly made his way across the open wall-walk to Tory's tower, carrying a large basket.

He found Tory dozing on her bed. After whispering an apology for his tardiness, Maelgwn tipped up the basket and showered her with fresh flowers. He then tossed it aside and climbed onto the bed next to her.

Tory sat up, enchanted with his gift. 'Maelgwn, how lovely.'

He ran his hand down her bare arm and, taking hold of it, gently urged her to lie back next to him. 'Aye, now what did thee wish to discuss?'

Maelgwn's lips enveloped her own, and before Tory could stop him, he was on top of her. His attentive kisses slowly moved down her neck, as his hands slipped the straps of her singlet from her shoulders. She felt a twinge of guilt as Lady Gladys' voice resounded through her brain. *Thou hast sworn by the elements and art bound by life itself to comply.*

'Maelgwn, I am required to take offence if thee continues along thy current course of action,' Tory said, but she made it clear by her playful tone that she was reluctant to do so.

His kisses had reached her breastbone and he gazed up at her, smitten as a schoolboy. 'Thee would not deny me but a small taste of thy pleasures to see me through my quest?'

Tory smiled, yet one of them had to be responsible. 'I am afraid I must insist.'

'But it be tradition to bed one's intended wife a week or so before one weds her.'

Tory laughed, 'I do not believe thee for a second, Maelgwn. How gullible dost thou think I am?'

'It be true: Thus a man be assured his betrothed will not back out on him for fear she hast fallen with child.'

Tory sprang up at the suggestion and grabbed her wrap from the end of the bed to cover herself. 'Thou hast no need to worry about that. Thy mother warned me that if thou had any of thy father in thee, keeping thee at bay would not be easy.'

'Thou hast spoken with Sorcha?' The Prince sat up, intrigued by her words.

'Aye, thee might say that. I hear her whispering little messages sometimes, in my head. And thy father has spoken to me also, the day he died. That be why I asked thee here.' Tory took hold of his hand. 'He left thee a message. Caswallon said that the two of thee had not been very close since thy mother's death. Thee claimed, according to thy father, that the only time he had ever trusted thee was when he had been chained in prison with no other choice.'

Maelgwn raised an eyebrow, recalling the incident of which she spoke. 'I did.'

'He confessed that he had never thanked thee or Taliesin for freeing him from Cadfer's imprisonment, or for the salvation of his kingdom. This was his deepest regret in passing, Maelgwn, for he knew he owed thee much. He was terribly distraught following Sorcha's death, and he did not consider how thee might be faring without her. He believed the reason thee hid in a monastery for so many years, was to escape his remorse and narrow-mindedness.'

Maelgwn looked rather surprised. 'My father said that?'

'Aye. He realised he had been a fool for not listening to thee more often, and he was pleased that he had trusted thee to contend with Chiglas' attack. His last words came in the form of a prophecy, I suppose: *When Maelgwn be crowned King of all Gwynedd, the land shall unite and prosper. Goddess blessed, he will be hailed as one of the greatest leaders among Britons.*' Maelgwn appeared doubtful as he pondered her words, so Tory added as verification, 'The history books say the same.'

His eyes met hers. 'Thou art aware of everything that shall befall me, art thou not?' He changed the subject, not wanting to dwell on his father after the events of the past couple of days.

'Some things.'

'Doth thou know if we will have an heir?' His siren mood returned and he was all hands.

She smiled, placing her fingers on the pressure points at the top of his arms to paralyse them. 'Do I have to ask thee to leave?'

The pain forced him to control himself. 'Forgive me, thou wast going to say?'

Tory, in all honesty, was a bit perturbed by the question; this heir business obviously meant a lot to Maelgwn so she felt she should put his fears to rest.

'Aye, his name be Rhun. He grows to be a fierce warrior and a rather notorious womaniser, so they say.'

This made Maelgwn tremendously happy. 'I can hardly wait to return to thee so that our life together may begin. I do miss thee already.' He leant towards her.

'Maelgwn, art thou up there?' Lady Gladys' voice echoed up the stairwell.

'Damn that woman,' Maelgwn whispered under his breath, and Tory's chuckle gave them away. 'I had best go.' He kissed her quickly.

'Maelgwn!' His aunt called again in warning.

II

THE QUEST

The Prince's party left at noon the following day. Tory was present to see them off, as were most of the household. Brockwell seemed to be having no trouble ignoring her, so she returned the favour.

As additional penance, Brockwell was to remain at the house to attend to the training of the men. Sir Cedric had been appointed to Sir Gilmore's old position as trainer, and Sir Percival, Caswallon's accounts' keeper, would be arriving from Degannwy to resume the administrative work of the court. With Gilmore's death, Percival was the last of King Caswallon's advisers, and Maelgwn needed him close at hand. The Prince also considered that Aberffraw was a much cosier environment for the aging scholar.

All knights and lords of high rank in Gwynedd were to accompany the Prince to Llyn Cerrig Bach for the ritual. The only outsider permitted was King Catulus. Over the years, those of the Roman faith had discouraged him from maintaining the old ways and beliefs of his people. Yet since the King had met Maelgwn all those years ago, he'd become rather fond of him. Catulus was inspired by the ancient mysteries in which his young friend believed, and so he was thrilled to be along for the ride.

Brockwell's decision to stay behind can't have been easy, Tory considered as she glanced in his direction. A king's inauguration was a rare and esteemed affair for the male members of the court, and it was a great honour to have earned the right to attend.

Tory kissed Maelgwn goodbye, knowing that he would come back to her triumphant and unharmed. 'I shall see thee at the altar then.'

'Thee may be sure of that.' He left in fine spirits to join his men, who were all mounted and eager to depart. The knights raised a riot, spurred on by the cheers of the crowd, as the Prince led them charging off through the open portcullis.

Once the party had left, the gathering of well-wishers dispersed and Tory turned to Katren. 'Ready?' Katren gave a firm nod. 'Lead the way.'

Katren had been moved out of the servants' quarters and into a room with Cara and Alma in the main wing. Her participation in Gwynedd's victory led her to be deemed a lady by royal decree, and she was therefore eligible to pursue a knight's affections. Together with Tory and Lady Gladys, she had been devising Calin's entrapment, and he'd become the major topic over lunch. The three women agreed that Katren and the other girls would go into intensive training this week while the knights were away. If Brockwell wanted a challenge, then that was exactly what they would give him.

Katren and Tory strolled slowly across the great lawn of the sunny outer bailey, observing the training taking place there and remarking on the more skilful or handsome of the soldiers. Brockwell was not far off, overseeing a large group of men being put through their paces. He spied the women walking towards the outer-bailey portcullis, and moved at once to inquire as to their intent. After all, he was in charge, and their safety was his responsibility. Though he was forbidden to speak with Tory, he could ask Katren. *Lady Katren in fact.* Brockwell considered that she'd done rather well for herself. 'Lady Katren, where art thou going this day?'

'Why Sir Brockwell, we art —'

'Nay Katren. Why should we answer to one who hast chosen freely to ignore me,' Tory said as she stormed off ahead.

Katren's soft blue eyes looked up at Brockwell full of sympathy. 'She misses thy company, sir, that be all. We art only going to see the tradesmen in the village about a wedding gift for the Prince.' She smiled but did not linger to chat.

But again the knight stopped her, 'Lady Katren, I need to ask thee a great favour. I know I am in disgrace and thou hast no —'

'There be no disgrace in the truth, sir ... if thou dost not mind me saying so.' Brockwell's eyes were so intense as they heeded her that Katren began to blush. 'I would be honoured to help thee, what doth thou require of me?'

Tory wandered round the marketplace meeting the local merchants while waiting for Katren. She asked directions to the workshop of a wood carver and a gold-smith, as she had a commission for them to carry out. The men were most helpful, and very proud to be entrusted with the creation of the wedding gift for their future monarch.

Instead of exchanging rings, as is done in modern ceremony, the Britons exchanged gifts. Tory, knowing Maelgwn to be a great thinker, decided to have a chess set crafted for him; after all, chess became known in later centuries as the game of kings. Tory supplied the gold and silver for the pieces, courtesy of Lady Gladys, and selected oak and white willow for the board. She paid the craftsmen handsomely for the many hours they would have to put in to finish the gift in time, and they both set to work immediately, carefully following the drawings she'd given them.

Katren had caught Tory up by this time, and the pair ambled back through the centre of the village. As they walked, Tory noticed that they'd attracted a few children on the way. The throng of excited youngsters trailed along behind them, interested to know what a Goddess was really like. When Katren became aware of the curious group she initiated a game of chase, so Tory stood aside to watch and ponder their plight. It would take little effort to educate these youngsters, she thought.

'Be Prince Maelgwn going to slay another dragon, Lady Goddess?' A young boy, maybe five years old, had plucked up the courage to approach her.

Tory, rather amused by his title for her, was stunned when she looked down at him. This boy was the very image of Calin, the piercing blue eyes, dark curls, dimple, and all. 'The Prince never killed the dragon, he befriended it. Nothing can be learnt from death and destruction.'

'I am going to be a knight,' the young boy told her with zeal, despite the mocking laughter of the other children.

'His mamma was nothin' but a whore!' one of the older boys sneered.

Tory, seeing the boy's embarrassment, went down on one knee to address him. 'And what be thy name, soldier?'

'Brockwell.'

His answer nearly knocked her over.

One of the older girls ran forward and clasped a hand over the boy's mouth. 'It be jest, his mamma claimed Sir Brockwell was his father, and when she died in birthing old Hetty nicknamed him thus. But he be really known as Bryce, lady.'

Katren also found the resemblance rather striking, and was filled with sympathy for the boy. 'Hast thee no kin?'

'Nay.' The girl held Bryce firm. 'He be kept by old Hetty and her whores.'

Katren and Tory looked at each other, unable to resist investigating this further.

Bryce led them to a small village just outside the marketplace, that consisted of six or seven little round huts. Tory spied the town's presumed mad woman outside one hut, but she didn't appear so crazed now. She was steadily chopping her way through a large pile of wood, wielding the axe with the same force as any adult male. When she noticed them, she brought the axe to rest in a large stump and folded her arms. She had the build any female gladiator would envy. Her expression was perfectly blank.

'Who be this woman, Bryce?' Tory asked, before they were within earshot.

'She be Ione, she hast no tongue and cannot speak, but I understand her,' he told Tory. 'She would not hurt thee, only bad men make her mad.'

'I see. Would thee introduce us? I have need to speak with her.' Bryce nodded, eager to please.

'Careful,' Katren warned, casting an eye over the strong figure of the woman.

Tory shrugged, not in the least bit worried as she followed Bryce.

Ione bowed her head ever so slightly as they approached, before making a few gestures with her hands for Bryce's benefit. It was a simple form of sign language, and Bryce chuckled at what she had to say.

'No offence, but she thinks thou art rather small to be a great warrior.'

'Of course.' Tory could see her view. So, to the delight of the children, Tory decided to do her wood-splitting exercise, which left the little audience gaping in awe. The children begged her to do it again and when she would not, the rowdy flock ran home to tell their parents what they'd seen.

After Ione had inspected Tory's hand, and found not a mark on it, she bowed low to the ground, urging Bryce down beside her.

'Please rise,' Tory urged. 'The Goddess be within us all, Ione. If thou art willing, I would very much like to instruct thee in my ways. Be there someone I must speak to about this?'

'Me.'

Tory turned to find an old woman watching them from the doorway of the closest hut.

Old Hetty was the owner of the huts, though she'd never intended the village to become a brothel. After her husband died, she'd taken in female boarders who had nowhere else to stay, and the rest was history. She did seem to be a caring soul and was very businesslike. She sat Tory and Katren down with a cup of wicked mead, as she mulled over Tory's proposition.

'I believe that with the proper training, Ione could be as fierce a warrior as any man, and of just as much service to Gwynedd. I would pay thee for her time, of course, and Ione for her efforts.' Tory believed this to be a fair deal.

'Ione hast already taught herself to wield a sword, did thee know that?' the old woman asked to establish her girl's value.

'Nay I did not,' Tory admitted, 'but still . . .'

'All well and good, but who shall attend to my heavy chores? Ione be the man around here.'

'I will allocate a soldier to thee, upon Ione's arrival

for training every day, to carry out these chores in her absence. If thou hast any complaints, just let me know.'

'I shall, never fear about that.' Hetty seemed pleased with the deal, though she did a good job of hiding it.

As the old woman stood to leave, Tory thought to ask, 'One more thing, about Bryce. Be his claim to the name Brockwell true?'

Old Hetty appeared surprised that Tory chose to bring up the subject. She resumed her seat, pouring another round of mead. 'There art many soldiers at Aberffraw, yet few with such distinctive features as Calin Brockwell, Duke of Penmon. Bryce's mother, a young girl of six and ten, did claim to have sought out Sir Brockwell on Beltaine that year. When she found herself with child she believed that it was of the Goddess and would be born, exactly nine moon cycles later, on the twelfth day of Luis.'

This didn't make sense to Tory at first, but then she recalled there were thirteen months in the old calendar.

'And did she give birth then?' Katren asked, intrigued.

'Aye, and she died that day also. The poor little mite was so small the effort killed her.'

Tory and Katren looked at each other in horror, both of a small frame themselves.

'That be why it dost not surprise me that, as a Goddess, thou hast come to seek out Bryce,' Hetty said. 'And I do not mind telling thee, ladies, I fear for the child's welfare when I have passed on. Most of the girls here have children of their own to worry about, and

Bryce be just another hungry mouth to feed. So, if ye have some intent for him, I pray thee, speak it.'

Tory was stunned, this woman was more straight-forward than she was. She'd been thinking more along the lines of education than adoption.

'Oh aye, Tory, I would help thee,' Katren said, this miniature of Calin had already stolen her heart.

'Now hold on one second, I have to think this through,' Tory replied. Even if he wasn't Brockwell's son, which she very much doubted, he was bright, eager, unwanted, and training him would be a good indication of how the children here might take to her skills. 'If Bryce agrees, I shall make provision for him at the castle.'

Katren sprang from her chair and wrapped her arms around Tory. 'Thou art too good to me.'

'Yeah, yeah.' Tory patted her arm, wondering how Calin and Lady Gladys would react when they saw him, not to mention the Prince.

Hetty smiled. 'Thou hast brought me great relief, lady. Both the souls I hold most precious have been provided for in one day. Let us celebrate.' She topped up their glasses for a toast to seal the deal. 'To the Great Mother.'

'To the Goddess,' they replied.

The outer bailey was in near darkness by the time Tory and Katren returned with the child. Tory had spent many hours with Hetty discussing the problems of women in their society, and she felt angry at the male population for their irresponsibility. She would begin work on new laws regarding this immediately, so that they would be ready to present to court before her crowning. As Maelgwn was not here to advise her, Tory felt sure Lady Gladys would be sympathetic to her cause.

Brockwell approached the women with haste, having had guards out looking for them half the day. 'Lady Katren, where hast thou been . . . and where did he come from?' he asked, sounding most annoyed that Tory was picking up strays again.

'Be that Sir Brockwell?' the boy asked, taking a long look at the famous knight.

'Hush now,' Katren said, leaving Tory to contend with Brockwell.

'Bryce came from a night of lust by the fires of Beltaine some six years past,' Tory stated, taunting Calin. 'A young girl of old Hetty's keeping. Am I ringing any bells yet?'

Although he looked as guilty as sin, Brockwell said naught.

'Look, forget that, just say something to me. Thou art breaking my heart with this damn penance.' Tory was frustrated by his silence. 'At least explain!' But no matter what she said, Calin would neither answer, nor look at her. 'Oh, what's the use?' She threw her arms in the air and made her way to the inner bailey.

When Maelgwn arrived at Llyn Cerrig Bach, Taliesin led him to a small room. The chamber was designed for meditation and reflection, as it could be blackened and silenced completely. Here the Prince was to fast in a state of trance for two days and two nights, taking only

227

water during that time. This was the shaman's way of getting in touch with a part of one's inner self that was wiser, stronger and balanced.

Alone now, Maelgwn was enfolded by the darkness and he lost all concept of time; was his period of reflection nearly over or just beginning?

These trance states of fasting and isolation had been a part of Maelgwn's childhood tuition, and he had found them similar to Tory's meditation. The discipline brought about a greater level of consciousness by enabling him to access other realms of awareness. Taliesin had taught him, as a young boy, that all mystical paths can only be experienced when one can suspend normal awareness and rational thought. An empty mind allows an alternative level of transpersonal experience.

As part of the traditional inauguration, the Prince was given a mild hallucinatory drink. Taliesin explained it to be, 'An inspiring drink, aged over five brewing cauldrons.' This brew of kings was intended for the main part of the ceremony, when the Prince would emerge from his reflections to face the Otherworld spirits who would name his quest and final judgement.

Only a few select descendants of Cunedda had undergone such an inauguration and amongst the number was Ambrosius. Ambrosius Aurelianus was descended from a warrior's son granted charge of land around Gwent Is Coed, where Aurelius Caninus now ruled. This lineage had since turned to the Roman faith, however, thus improving its trade relations with the main continent. The other ruler in Prydyn at this time was Vortipor, in Dyfed. Of Scottic (Irish) blood, Vortipor had been born in Britain and at one time had secured the support of Rome to seize his kingdom. Known as the Usurper of Dyfed, Vortipor also carried the title of 'Protector' and his dynasty was known as the Desi clan. He was of the native faith by birth, but he hadn't descended from the same great liturgy of kings as had Maelgwn. The Prince's predecessors, while inhabiting and ruling Prydyn, had created its Otherworld legends. No doubt the Desi had brought with them from Scotia (Ireland) their own legends and names for their Otherworld ancestors and deities. Chiglas in Powys, although of the native faith and a great great grandson of Cunedda, maintained no real spiritual understanding of the ways of his ancient forefathers. He knew the legends and teachings as well as any British king, yet he observed the festivals and rites of his people mainly for the sake of celebrations. His bards were foolish men who had failed to give him any real evidence of Otherworld support.

'There art three main prerequisites thee must have to be a king,' the Prince recalled Taliesin saying to him. 'The ability to rise above inevitable setbacks. To adjust the views thee may hold true in the light of new evidence. And most important of all, one must adhere firmly to that which one knows deep inside to be right and just, for true wisdom and awareness come from the realisation that one knows very little, compared with all there be to learn and know.'

And wisdom be not synonymous with knowledge, Maelgwn resolved.

The Prince became comfortably numb as the hours passed, yet every now and then he was sure he felt something stroke against his skin. Maelgwn remained motionless and without fear, for no one could have found him without the High Merlin's consent. Through the darkness, he heard soft humming voices, whispering and chattering; the same sweet, high-pitched sound that the Prince knew to be synonymous with the Tylwyth Teg or fairy folk.

Maelgwn hadn't considered their interest in him, even though it was common knowledge that the fairy folk inhabited Gwynedd in vast numbers. This partly explained his dynasty's great wealth, which came primarily from the livestock and abundant crops harvested each year from the farmlands of Gwynedd. Of course, the fairy folk be eager to see me resume the old ways, Maelgwn realised, so as to ensure they art not driven from here, as they have been from other kingdoms in Britain. Knowing this, the Prince didn't object to them painting his skin for the initiation. It was, no doubt, for luck and part of the sacred tradition of his forefathers.

The ladies and Bryce had completed their second full day of training and Tory's two newest students were already showing great promise. Dedication and willpower were essential for mastering these techniques, and Ione and Bryce had both in abundance.

Lady Gladys was besotted with Bryce, seeing in him her long-since grown babe. Here stood her own dear grandson. Whether Calin cared to admit to the infidelity or not was of no consequence to her, the Brockwell traits were unquestionable. As the child's grandmother, Lady Gladys had the legal right to claim Bryce, in her husband's name, as her own. If Calin chose not to recognise the boy, she would. Thus Bryce became Calin's brother and was granted his rightful title of Earl.

Tory stood in the doorway and watched as a storm cut its way across the heavens. The brilliant spectacle had been menacing the night sky for hours — booming thunder threatened to bring rain, yet not one drop fell. The locals said this was because it was the night of judgement for the initiate, and the performance of the ancient rites was evoking the spirits. Rain would mean that the Prince had been denied any right to his claim of king. If the storm cleared without a drop, he'd been found worthy by his forefathers and had set out upon the task they'd given him, which he was required to complete by the wedding date.

'Why did we not elope?' Tory wondered out loud, not noticing Drusilla who had come to collect her dinner tray.

Drusilla, the head maid at Aberffraw, had assumed Katren's duties in the wake of her new appointment. She'd once been handmaiden to Queen Sorcha, and it pleased her to be in the service of the Goddess again as she missed the Queen terribly. 'Do try not to worry about His Majesty, lady. He will return in time, thee will see.'

'I hold every confidence that he will.' Tory smiled briefly before turning back to watch the stormy scene outside.

'Lady Goddess.'

Tory looked around to find Bryce standing at the top of the stairwell. 'My dear Earl of Penmon, what drives thee from thy bed at this hour?' She received her answer as he was startled by a clap of thunder and ran to grasp hold of her around the legs.

'The spirits art angry.'

'Nay,' Tory laughed, as the child's simple fears took her mind off her own. 'I have it on good authority that as long as it doth not rain, the Prince still holds their favour.' She crouched down to him and took up his hands in her own. 'Thee must not fear nature's forces if thou art to become a brave knight like Sir Brockwell. If thee can see the beauty of the storm, admire and draw upon its power, then it be not such a fearful thing.'

Tory stood, raising her arms high into the air, and while the thunder pounded out its fury she cried, 'I am not afraid of thee.' She looked down at Bryce, who was staring back at her in wonder. 'Can thee do that?'

Bryce thought a moment. Then, with a deciding nod, he turned to face the storm and waited for the thunder.

Katren appeared at the top of the stairwell, just in time to catch the child's proclamation. To Tory's surprise, Brockwell was with her.

'I am not afraid of thee,' Bryce yelled at the storm with conviction. He repeated the statement over, more confident each time as his fear left him. 'I shall be a brave knight,' he told Tory, his head high in triumph.

She knelt and held up her hand for a high-five. 'Aye,' she said as he slapped her palm as hard as he could. 'Thou art truly legend material, Bryce, but thee must get some sleep as thou hast much work ahead of thee yet.'

He bowed deeply and did an about-face like a soldier, to find Katren and Calin. 'Sir Brockwell!' He was overcome by the presence of his hero and bowed low.

Katren, seeing Brockwell at a loss for what to say to the child, intervened. 'Off to bed with thee now, we have important matters to discuss.'

As she led Bryce to the stairwell the boy looked back at Calin, a little disappointed not to have been introduced.

Brockwell just shrugged his shoulders at the child being hauled away. 'Women will be telling thee what to do thy whole life . . . may as well get used to it.'

'I already am.' Bryce smiled, pleased to have been acknowledged, and left them for his bed without further objection.

Tory stood, looking at Brockwell. 'To what do I owe this unexpected pleasure?' she asked, adopting a more aggravated tone.

Katren came forward to explain, although she seemed disinclined to do so. 'Sir Brockwell would like to speak with thee, but as he be forbidden, he hast asked that I act as a mediator. Regrettably, I promised him I would do this but only if it be pleasing to thee.'

'Fine, whatever works. I just want to know why thou art doing this to me?' Tory aimed her frustration directly at Brockwell.

Katren looked at Calin, who was finding the situation extremely difficult.

'Ask her if she be aware that any grandson to a King of Gwynedd, such as I, hast the right to lay claim to her throne?'

Katren's eyes opened wide at his words, as she was not aware of this. Tory spoke first, 'What art thou saying, that thou hast —'

'The right, by law, to challenge the Prince for thy hand. And I very nearly did,' Brockwell declared, turning to Katren as if it were Tory he was addressing. 'The sight of thee did drive me to such distraction, that I actually considered betraying my oath to Gwynedd to have thee. Maelgwn hast since spoken of thy love for each other, and I realise now that I would be wrong to pursue thee further. So please understand why I must stay away.'

Brockwell's confession was driving Katren insane. She wanted to throw her arms around him to comfort him, yet his affection was directed at Tory. 'Excuse me, I am so sorry.' Katren had to leave before she fell to pieces.

'Lady Katren, please.' Brockwell watched her disappear downstairs.

'It would seem we've lost our mediator,' Tory sighed. 'Never mind, there be a few things I have been wanting to say myself, if it be pleasing to thee?'

Brockwell took a seat, folding his arms as he nodded to let Tory know he was prepared to listen. This made Tory smile, as Brian used to behave this way when he didn't want to hear her out.

'The blame for our situation hast fallen on the wrong shoulders, Calin. If I had not made the mistake of treating thee as my brother, this would never have happened. Perhaps I should have continued to vex thee, life seemed much easier when we hated each other.' Brockwell smiled in agreement. 'Understand that Brian was my other half, and thou dost look and act so much like him.' Tears welled in her eyes and her voice faltered. 'He seemed infallible, I never dreamt I might lose him . . . and when he died, a huge part of me died with him.' Tory drew a deep breath. 'How could he just die without warning like that? I miss him so much.' Tory turned away and, with a sniffle, brushed the tears from her face. 'Perhaps thou art right to stay away from me, Calin. I will obviously keep misleading thee, as it would seem I cannot help it.'

As Katren returned, Brockwell rushed over to resume her services. 'Please Katren, tell the Lady Tory that I do look forward to our time together in the twentieth century, and tell her I promise to try not to die next time round.'

Tory smiled at his words, though poor Katren hadn't a clue what he was raving about.

'But for the time being,' he continued. 'I would consider it a great honour if the future Queen were to continue to regard me as her kin.'

'Doth he mean it, Katren?'

Brockwell looked Katren straight in the eye, and gave a firm nod.

'I think so,' Katren replied.

'Then may I ask thee a favour, Calin?' Tory turned to him.

'Aye, anything!' he besought her, or rather Katren.

'As my only living relative at this time, would thee stand in for my father at my wedding? If I am asking too much please say so.'

'Nay, it would be a fine thing, I agree.'

'Only we may have to blindfold him. His oath did say he could not look upon thee till after thou hast wed,' Katren pointed out.

'Then so be it,' Brockwell insisted. 'I shall be honoured, all the same.'

The Prince gradually became aware of the presence of light in the room, so he gathered that his isolation was drawing to a close. The fairy folk had left him ages ago, and as he slowly stretched his limbs he viewed the detailed artwork of deep blue with which they had covered his body. The Prince considered he looked rather like one of the Northern Pictish warriors before a battle, but even the Picts' body paint was not as ornate as this.

The folk had depicted beasts from the legends of the Old Ones. On the Prince's chest was the head of a lion, representing the greatest of the Otherworld deities — Gwydion, 'Lion of Greatest Course'. The God of Science, Music, and Light, Gwydion represented the old truths as they were brought to the isles from across the water; thus it was he who set the task that would be required of the initiate. Serpents wound around the back of Maelgwn's hands, around his arms and over his shoulders; these creatures had long been associated with wisdom and magic. The Prince looked in a mirror to follow the tails, finding they crossed to form a crow with its wings spread wide in flight. The crow was synonymous with the Goddess of Life and Death. Below it was the head of the stag, its antlers reaching up to the bird. This beast represented the male companion, protector or masculine side of the Goddess, like Pan. When Maelgwn brushed the hair from his forehead he viewed his own affiliate, the Dragon.

'*Dost thou know who put it there?*'

The memory of Tory revealing the mark to him the first day they'd met, sprang to mind. Maelgwn smiled, wondering if she would think him mad when he told her that the fairy folk were responsible for branding her with his mark.

Taliesin was proud and delighted when he beheld the folk's handiwork. 'The Tylwyth Teg have not left a blessing on an initiate for a very long time. This be a splendid sign for thee indeed, but I must say, not entirely unexpected.' Taliesin felt he did owe himself some credit. 'After thy time away I feared they might reject thee. Still, as they have marked thee as one of their Chosen Ones and a Lord of Beasts, thy success be as good as assured.'

The Prince again looked at his reflection, viewing the folk's gift to him in a new light. 'The land shall unite and prosper.' The Prince uttered the words he'd heard so often since his father's passing.

'Aye, that be the prophecy, follow me.'

Night had fallen in the valley, and large torches encircled the clearing outside the Temple of the Goddess. Great bolts of lightning and turbulent winds played across the skies, yet naught but a warm breeze could be felt in the glen below. Maelgwn, dressed only in trousers, emerged from the ruins to the sound of pounding drums. Taliesin brought the Prince before his men who were seated around a fire where a large cauldron simmered.

The cauldron belonged to Taliesin's mother, Keridwen, the Goddess of Inspiration, hence her cauldron was renowned for the same. Of the Triple Goddess, Keridwen was the Crone or Wise Woman. As the dispenser of the old truths, it was she who would announce Gwydion's quest to the initiate. Her cauldron contained the elixir of kings. The men present, having painted their bodies in the old tradition, all had a sip from its contents in turn, but only the Prince was permitted to drink his fill of the brew.

Maelgwn sat before the cauldron, with his back to the temple ruins. He felt detached from his physical form now; it was as though, with the slightest provocation, his mind, thoughts and feelings would float away. He drank yet another cup of the dreamy brew, and this sensation intensified with the beating of the drums.

I am the one who heartens the soul,
to the glory of the spirits.
On behalf of us all,
I am the bard, trained through time to treat the great
mysteries.

Taliesin's words rang out through the din and he came to stand behind his student. His role this night was both master of ceremonies and record keeper. When Maelgwn went into a trance and left them to journey through the Otherworld, it was the Merlin's task to note the Prince's account of what took place there.

> *And I am the silent proficient,*
> *who addresses the bards of the land:*
> *it is mine to animate the hero;*
> *to persuade the unadvised;*
> *to awaken the silent beholder —*
> *the bold illuminator of Kings!*

The storm crashed and flashed with fury. Maelgwn's eyes, which had been lulled closed, suddenly opened wide, and the drums stopped. 'The Dragon returns,' he told them all, and the breeze rose to a wind with his words.

Far away, the ancients' bell began to chime, its tones so pleasing to the ear. From the most distant heights behind the temple, the storm clouds gathered and billowed down over the mountain peak. The thick white mist whirled its way towards the gathering, engulfing everything in its path.

Taliesin smiled like a man returning home as the haze came over them. The scent of a thousand flowers wafted through it, tranquilising the senses with its potency. Out of the silence of the forest, a choir slowly raised a mesmerising chant. The men knew the voices which graced their ears to be those of the Tylwyth Teg, come to lay blessing on the future King.

'The gateway to the Otherworld hast opened for the initiate,' Taliesin announced. 'May he be pleasing to the Goddess and succeed in gracing this land with her wisdom and blessing. Summon forth the beast who shall guard the gateway for thee and allow thy spirit to enter and travel the Otherworld unharmed.'

Maelgwn closed his eyes in concentration, the bells and chants filling his soul with a sense of divine power. From this source that lay seething deep inside, he silently besought his spirit guide which dwelt beyond the open gateway to come forth to his aid.

After a moment, a great thud vibrated across the earth, and then another and another. Tall trees were heard to topple and the rumble of the pounding became more intense as the beast approached. King Catulus, knowing all too well the echo of a dragon's steps, raised his horrified eyes. The trees behind the temple shook as the red glowing eyes of the huge beast emerged from the dark mists.

Sir Tiernan watched defenceless as the giant beast came round the ruins. It reared up onto its hind legs and slowly edged its way forward. The knight wondered what he would do if the dragon was malicious. But it came to rest, without incident, directly behind the Prince, who didn't even bat an eyelid.

The dragon spread wide its huge wings and released a mighty screech, the flame of its breath spewing into the atmosphere way above the heads of the mystified knights. None had ever expected to see the like of such phenomena, and those who remembered Caswallon's inauguration knew this to be an extraordinary occurrence. This wasn't any mortal beast that the young Prince had summoned forth. This was a creature of the Otherworld, a pet of the great Goddess Keridwen herself.

Taliesin, quill in hand, set ink to parchment to record what would become known as 'The Legend of Maelgwn, King of Gwynedd, Dragon of the Isle'.

The Prince's eyes opened and he began to convey his tale, 'I stand outside my body now, and see myself as I address this gathering. The forest that surrounds us be alive with colour and light, so bright it be blinding to my eyes . . .'

The Prince's spirit left his physical form to the telling, to get on with his quest. Amidst the electrifying colour created by the fairy folk, the temple appeared resurrected to its original form and glory. As he approached the temple steps, Maelgwn spied a white-hooded figure who awaited him there.

Sorcha drew back the hood and held out her hands to him in greeting. 'My beloved Maelgwn, how I have looked forward to this moment.'

'Mother.' Maelgwn knelt before her and kissed both her hands, before resting his forehead against them. 'How I have missed thee.'

'Arise dear child, I have come to show thee the way to the Goddess, where thou art expected. Come.' She took hold of his hand and led him to the altar where a blinding white light began to stream from the Celtic cross engraved upon it. The heavy stone tablet slid aside, revealing a staircase.

Deeper and deeper into the earth his mother led him. When at last they emerged from the side of a mountain, they beheld a kingdom so perfect and beautiful that it could only ever exist in the Land of Fairy.

'Do not drink or eat while thou art here, lest thee may never return to thy bride,' Sorcha cautioned.

The Prince nodded, heeding his mother's advice. As he stepped forward to make his way to the castle gates, Maelgwn found they were standing in front of two of the largest doors he had ever seen. These parted wide to grant admittance to a great feast that was in progress. Maelgwn entered at Sorcha's side, doing his best not to gape at the frivolities taking place around them. As they approached the main table, his mother kissed him and left to resume her seat by Caswallon.

Three women were seated at the main table, one dressed in white, one in red, and the other in black. When they rose to address the Prince, the entire room silenced in attention. Maelgwn stopped and bowed deeply.

These three comprised the face of the triple Goddess. Branwen, in white, was the maiden, the teacher of truth and the guardian of righteousness. Her skin was fair with a slightly golden hue, her long hair as dark and straight as Maelgwn's own. The maiden's eyes were black as night, and her slender form and beauty did not escape the Prince's attention. The warrior Goddess in red was Rhiannon who had charge of justice and the airing of truth. Her colouring, build and appearance were very similar to Sorcha or Tory, but her hair fell in fiery red waves. The enchantress or wise woman in black was, of course, Keridwen. Although young of face, her hair was as silvery as her son's and her eyes of soft green-grey were the colour of the ocean after a storm. Her build was tiny, like that of the Tylwyth

Teg, and she exhibited the same pixie-like features and huge slanted eyes they did.

Maelgwn had stopped in front of the Crone, who eyed him over with decided interest. 'We bid thee welcome, young Prince. The folk have marked thee as Chosen, we see. And Taliesin claims thou art his most promising initiate ever. We have considered this in naming thy quest, Maelgwn of Gwynedd.'

The maiden Branwen passed straight through the table before her to approach the Prince. 'Dragon of the Island, we call upon thee to defend the Chair and the Cauldron of Keridwen, lest thine people will not always be free to honour the Goddess.' The beautiful maid offered him encouragement as she moved gracefully round him, gently running her fingertips over his bare skin. 'Our pleasures await thee upon thy return . . . Our milk, our dew, our acorns, shall be thy reward.'

Rhiannon, the warrior Goddess, approached Maelgwn, cluching a bunch of grapes in one hand. She clasped him firmly round the back of the neck, her eyes looking deep into his soul, and her words mesmerised him. 'We have considered what could befall us. Trouble already menaces the lands to the East and Powys.' She popped a grape into his mouth, and in his enchanted state, Maelgwn very nearly ate it. When the Prince spat out the forbidden fruit, Rhiannon was quite impressed. 'Thou art not easily distracted, Dragon. Good, very good.'

The women withdrew to the side of Keridwen, where they merged to become one being that glowed green and spoke with the voices of all three.

Maelgwn, overawed, fell on one knee before Don, the divine mother.

'We must unite Prydyn against Powys and the invaders, my people must become as one race. Only then shall the Goddess be preserved in our great land. Maelgwn of Gwynedd, thou art destined for this duty and thus we find thee worthy to hold the office of thy forefathers. Dost thou accept this as thy quest in the name of the Goddess?'

'Aye, I do.'

'Then stand and face thy task.'

As the Prince did as he was instructed, the three women again separated and Keridwen alone addressed him.

'Gwydion hast decreed that thee must go as thou art to Castell Dwyran in Dyfed, for there thou shalt find Vortipor of the Desi Clan. Then on to the court of Aurelius Caninus in Gwent Is Coed, where thee will find the King at his residence in Caerleon. Thou art to warn these men of the alliance between Powys and the invaders, and must invite both kings to thy wedding celebrations. King Catulus of Dumnonia be required to attend also. Upon the fourth and last day of the feasting, I shall address all these leaders. If my dragon consents, take him to speed thy journey, for he shall mark thee as our messenger. If these kings consider themselves of my flock, they shall be urged to comply, lest they risk our disfavour on their kingdoms. Thy words Dragon, be my own. For this be the will of the Great Houses of Don and Llyr.'

* * *

'So be it,' the men all cried.

Maelgwn blinked to find himself returned to his seat before the cauldron. He stood and faced the dragon. 'What say thee, Rufus?' (the dragon's chosen name). 'Would thou consider braving the Middle Kingdoms again to aid me in my quest?'

One might consider it, if one may be permitted to make a small request in return, the dragon bethought the Prince as it gazed down upon him.

'What be thy request, old friend?' the Prince asked before agreeing; he'd played with this dragon before and they didn't always see eye to eye.

If Chiglas fails to buy thy bastard brother back, thee must give him to me. As one hates the little mongrel, and imagines he would make a very tasty appetiser.

'Well I cannot blame thee really, although I would not fancy eating him myself,' the Prince said, still considering the beast's request. If Caradoc's own people didn't want him back, Maelgwn certainly didn't hold any love for him. 'Alright, if a fair price be not set by the spring, Caradoc shall be thine.'

The dragon seemed to smile as it lowered its claw to give the Prince a hand up to sit between its large shoulder blades and wings. Without further ado, the beast screeched, raised its huge body and flew off into a hazy dawn sky. The mist had settled over the land, where it would stay until the Prince returned from his quest, triumphant.

Tory was summoned from her training by Lady Gladys, who announced the arrival of Taliesin Pen Beirdd. Thus she left Katren to continue the lesson and accompanied Lady Gladys to greet him, relieved by his visit. In addition to wanting to inquire after Maelgwn, Tory had been pondering her harsh words to Taliesin on the day of their victory, and felt she owed him an apology.

Taliesin had been right about the teachings of the Old Ones, they were much closer to her beliefs than the more orthodox religions to which she was accustomed. There was no life and death for these people, just differing states of consciousness on the path to the soul's perfection. This was basically what she believed, and Taliesin had, of course, known this all along.

Tory entered the library to find the Merlin gazing out the window.

'There is no need to apologise, dear lady, you were perfectly right. I should consult you and Maelgwn before deciding the course of matters that concern yourselves and Gwynedd,' he announced, already understanding her mind.

'Taliesin!' She smiled, feeling a twinge of annoyance. 'Will you please let me speak my mind before jumping in with a resolve. You're always two conversations ahead of me.' Tory noticed she was becoming flustered again and calmed down. 'Here I was coming to apologise for being angry with you and you've made me angry again.'

'So sorry, please run through the formalities if you feel you must.'

'I give up, why bother?' Tory concluded, eager to find how Maelgwn fared.

Taliesin almost answered but conforming to her wishes, waited for Tory to ask.

'How is Maelgwn? I know he must have embarked on his quest by now as the storm has cleared. You know his quest, do you think him capable of completing it in time for our wedding?'

'My dear child, all goes splendidly. You are the bride who shall be Queen, rejoice and indulge yourself. You have naught to worry about but your wedding preparations. I assure you that the celebrations shall go ahead as planned.'

Taliesin and Tory had lunch served in the library. The Merlin told her most of the story of Maelgwn's journey into the Otherworld and of his quest, omitting only the details that the Prince would wish to discuss with her himself.

'Fairies, shamanism, astral travelling, what else is he into that I don't know about?' She was only just beginning to realise how extraordinary the man she was to marry, truly was.

Over mead they spoke of a great many things, but as a bride, naturally her first concern was the dress.

'Dresses,' Taliesin corrected her, explaining that the celebrations would span the period of four days.

'Four days! That's what I call a party.'

'The first day you shall wear a dress of white, representing the maid and first aspect of the triple Goddess. After the Prince hast been crowned in the presence of his men, you will be brought forth to exchange gifts with him. There will be a great feast and the Prince will lay claim to you this night.'

'There is a God,' Tory remarked in jest. 'Do go on, I am listening.'

'After your union with the Prince you shall wear red, the colour of the warrior. This day is for tournament, the quest for the Queen's Champion amongst other competitions.'

Tory wasn't too sure how she felt about that. What do I need a champion for, she wondered. Still, she'd never seen a tournament, it could be interesting.

'And no, you can't compete.' Taliesin knocked that question on the head before she'd even thought of it.

Tory rolled her eyes as if to imply it had never entered her mind. 'The third day?' she prompted.

'Black. The colour of the enchantress, the wise woman and third face of the Goddess. This shall be your first day in court with your advisers and officials. A perfect time, if I may say so, to present your proposals concerning the women of this land.'

'You truly know everything, don't you?' Tory looked at him surprised. 'But I thought, in all fairness to the Prince that, as this proposal was a condition of our wedding, I should really present it to him on day one.'

'Why? Maelgwn will agree, I do! And I shall be present to support your cause. After all, is it not in the best interest of the Goddess? A bit more respect for women would certainly not go astray around here.'

Again he surprised her. *Remarkable*.

'Thank you.' He gave a smile. 'Now, where was I? Ah yes, the fourth and final day — a dress of green, the colour of the land, the triple Goddess and Mother Earth. This day you shall be crowned Queen before holding conference with all the Kings of Britain, bar Chiglas of course.'

'What! What am I supposed to say to them?'

'When the time comes, you will know, trust me.'

'Trust you! Taliesin, that's a lot of faith. I don't want to look foolish —'

'Tory please, I can't discuss it with you as the Prince wishes to first. But you will be well briefed, I promise.'

'Okay, I'm sorry. I'll try to relax,' Tory resolved, feeling it wasn't going to be easy. 'One more thing. Where are these dresses coming from? I hope I'm not expected to make them, I'm hopeless on a sewing machine.' Taliesin laughed and Tory caught on to his amusement. 'Needle and thread, you know what I mean. I'm hopeless!'

Taliesin didn't appear too worried about it, gesturing over her shoulder. 'With many thanks from the Goddess and her folk.'

Five beautiful garments suddenly materialised behind her.

'Oh my stars,' Tory gasped as she rose to her feet. She circled the garments, thinking them too beautiful to touch, let alone wear.

The fifth dress was of white with a sash of green, red and black that draped over the right shoulder and fell in a long train behind. Taliesin explained this was for her bridesmaid, and Tory knew Katren would simply die when she saw it.

'Thank you Taliesin, they are exquisite.'

The Prince was near frozen by the time the dragon landed in the courtyard of Castell Dwyran, in Dyfed. Needless to say, the court's soldiers were quite alarmed and would have attacked the great beast if Maelgwn hadn't emerged from its shoulders to prevent them.

'I am Maelgwn, Prince of Gwynedd, and this be the pet of the Goddess Keridwen. I am unarmed and bring a message from the Goddess for Vortipor, the Protector of Dyfed. Will he grant me audience or doth he wish to bring the wrath of our Otherworld forefathers upon himself and his kingdom?'

The Prince was soon led to Vortipor's private chambers, with the assurance that the beast of the Goddess would not be harmed. Maelgwn found his Roman-appointed counterpart reclining by a fire with a couple of maidens tending his every whim. When the Prince had been formally announced, he bowed deeply to his adversary before stating his business. 'I have but two questions to put to thee, Vortipor of Dyfed. Dost thou still hold true and honour the ways of the Goddess in thy Kingdom? And dost thou hold any allegiance to Chiglas, King of Powys, or the barbarian invaders that raid our land?'

Vortipor gave a hearty laugh, brushing away the attentions of the women. 'My dear Prince of Gwynedd, do slow down. I can hardly follow a word thou art saying.' The ruler sat up to address the Prince, who appeared even younger than himself. 'It be so rare that we art honoured by a legend, do sit for a moment and have some wine. It be imported from Italy, compliments of King Aurelius Caninus of Gwent Is Coed, and be truly a treat.'

Maelgwn was relieved that the two leaders knew each other, and Vortipor appeared quite a civilised fellow. Although shorter than Maelgwn, Vortipor appeared of sturdy build and a warrior to be reckoned with.

'Thy hospitality be most generous, sir, but I regret that I must decline. I am to be wed in a few days, and must complete this errand for the Goddess before then. So, if thee could answer my questions, I shall be on my way. I still have Aurelius Caninus to see before I may return to my bride.'

Again Vortipor laughed but with greater understanding. 'Now I see what drives thee so. Could I not offer thee some relief, perhaps?' He motioned to the two lovely young maidens in his company, who appeared more than eager to oblige.

'Thy women be truly tempting, but I must again decline, as only my due bounty shall bring me any solace, I am afraid.'

'If thou insists on being so damned official.' Vortipor clapped his hands and the maidens left the room. 'Thy bride must be quite a prize. Come and seat thyself, friend. I shan't keep thee from her any longer than necessary.'

Their talks began over lunch and finished over dinner. Sharing the same age, the same beliefs, education and ideas, made it very easy for the two to agree on most subjects. Maelgwn informed Vortipor of the attack on Degannwy, of Chiglas' growing forces and of Powys' alliance with the invading savages.

Vortipor found the information fair cause for concern. He could count on little support from Rome, should such a situation arise in Dyfed, as they had plenty of battles of their own to contend with. Thus he had good reason to unite with other kingdoms against Chiglas, and was delighted to agree to attend Maelgwn's wedding and the gathering, called in the name of the Goddess.

'Allow me on the morrow to accompany thee to the court of Aurelius Caninus,' Vortipor suggested. 'Not that any harm might befall thee, mind. It be more that the King, no longer a young man, could keep thee detained for days with his damned procrastinating. I have been dealing with him for years, he trusts me and tends to follow my advice.'

So they sat drinking wine by the fire in Vortipor's private chambers until well into the wee hours.

At dawn the Prince woke his new companion, eager to get on the move. Vortipor, somewhat amazed by Maelgwn's powers of recuperation, dragged himself from his peaceful slumber, not wanting to miss out on the adventure. Times had been quite blissful in the Kingdom of Dyfed since the Desi had assumed power. Till now, Vortipor had only to send troops to the aid of Gwent Is Coed to hold back the encroaching Danish and Saxon raiders. Chiglas in Powys, however, was a threat that was much closer to home. If he'd indeed made a pact with the barbarian bastards, they could pass right through Powys and ravage Dyfed directly.

The allies entered the courtyard of the huge fortress to find Rufus peacefully curled up asleep. The locals all gasped in awe at the dragon as they went about their daily business, trying to avoid the huge obstruction.

Vortipor stopped in his tracks and roared with laughter. 'When my men told me thee had arrived on a dragon, I thought them exaggerating. Thou art a truly wondrous soul, Maelgwn of Gwynedd.'

The dragon opened one eye to observe the Prince. *Like I have nothing to do with it, I suppose.*

'Ah Rufus.' The Prince ignored its comment. 'This be Vortipor, the Protector of Dyfed.'

The dragon turned his one open eye to view the man as he stepped forward and politely bowed. *A big brawny Scottic man, yum, yum!*

'Now that be enough of that,' the Prince insisted, and Vortipor took a step backwards, wondering what the dragon had bethought his affiliate. 'I believe Vortipor will be of great assistance to our quest. Would thee mind if he accompanied us to Gwent Is Coed?'

Depends. What does he have to offer one in the way of breakfast?

Maelgwn turned to Vortipor, a mite embarrassed by his travelling companion's hideous taste in cuisine. 'I hate to ask, but dost thou have any grievous criminals lying about that thee might want to be rid of? It would seem Rufus here be a bit hungry, and thou art appearing a bit too appetising to merely transport.'

'I see, well we can't have our Otherworld friend going hungry now, can we?' He addressed the dragon directly, 'Would a couple of fat thieves do? Unfortunately most of our more grievous offenders have grown rather thin, and would not be very appetising, I'm afraid.'

One finds this acceptable.

The Prince gave his friend the nod and Vortipor clapped his hands together. 'Splendid! I shall have them brought to thee at once.'

Rufus threw down breakfast in seconds flat, and was then more than happy to make haste with the Prince and his new ally to Caerleon.

Vortipor was so exhilarated by his first experience of flight that he gave the Prince a sterling introduction and recommendation to Aurelius. He ranted and raved about their journey, the Prince's great quest, and his invitation from the Goddess.

At first, the old King appeared rather caught up in the excitement of his younger colleague. But when it came down to Aurelius agreeing with Vortipor, his procrastinating began.

Known as 'the dog', King Caninus reminded Maelgwn of an old hound that had lost the scent and couldn't decide which way to go. The Prince was quietly driven insane by the King's unwarranted fears and delays, as he impatiently watched the day slip into night. He thanked the Goddess for Vortipor, if not for him they may well have been stuck there for months.

By the end of supper the King had agreed to attend the wedding and hear what the Goddess had to say. Maelgwn was satisfied to have accomplished this much, and on the morrow he would return to his men at Llyn Cerrig Bach. There he would celebrate with them, as he had a day to spare, before he would, at last, wed his lady.

12

UNION

The mist vanished from the land the day before the set wedding date, and Tory was advised that the Prince had most surely returned from his quest, successful. She waited all day and late into the evening for his arrival, but fell asleep while finishing off her proposal for the court, to be delivered three days hence. Not that they were allowed to see each other before the wedding; this superstition existed even then. A good thing too the way Tory saw it, as her hair was wrapped in long tight rags which were not very flattering.

She awoke the morning of her wedding to find Katren at her side, waiting to serve her breakfast. Fresh flowers covered the bed and Tory cringed. 'Please tell me that Maelgwn did not see me like this?'

'Nay,' Katren giggled. 'The flowers be from thy Prince, though. He asked that I deliver them to thee, and instructed me to give thee this.' Katren passed Tory a note, which she opened and read:

> We strangely met,
> like not so many,
> yet still my love
> be true as any.
> In the Old One's choice,
> my soul does rejoice.
> And no gift could express
> the love for thee I do possess.
> So love him in thy heart,
> whose forever joy thou art.
> And our love will know no end,
> my dear and sweetest friend.

After reading it to herself, and taking delight in the lovely verse, Tory read the note out loud to Katren, knowing she would well appreciate it.

'If only every man were so true and could express himself so beautifully, every woman would know thy joy this day, Tory.'

'Every woman in Gwynedd shall by the time we finish with the men here. Mark my words Katren, thou shalt know this joy and in the not too distant future.'

'Be that a prophecy, Goddess?'

'It be a promise, provided of course that thee can stick to our plan. I know how persuasive Calin can be, it will not be easy to resist him, especially when thou wilt be wearing that dress!'

'If thee can do it, I can do it. Anyway, no one shall even notice me for the beauty of my lovely mistress.'

They had the good part of a day to prepare as Maelgwn's crowning, which none of the women bar Lady Gladys were permitted to attend, would run well into the noon hours. They also had every woman in the household waiting to assist them, so there wasn't really any need to rush.

Rhys, Tiernan, Selwyn, and Taliesin were all present to attend the Prince as he prepared for his crowning and union with the Goddess. This was fortunate for Maelgwn, as he had a mild case of the premarital jitters. His support team did their best to calm him, filling him with mead and assurances while they near drowned him in a hot bath.

Selwyn was having a fine time trying to scrub away the fairy folk's artwork from his Majesty's torso and arms, whilst Rhys poured the drinks for everyone and pointed out the advantages of wedlock. Tiernan was no help, as a confirmed bachelor he was constantly contradicting Rhys with his point of view.

Rhys turned to Tiernan. 'Thou shalt die a very lonely and bitter old man, sir. And if thee insists on being a hindrance, thee can leave.'

The Prince panicked. 'Where be my gift from the folk for Tory?'

'I have it,' Taliesin answered. For the wedding, Maelgwn was fitted out in a shirt of the purest white linen, and his trousers, gunna and long cape were pitch black, like his belt and boots. Taliesin placed the medallion of the Dragon over the Prince's head, and it sat on his chest as the perfect finish to a majestic outfit.

Lady Gladys knocked and entered, followed by Cara and Alma who were carrying large baskets of freshly cut flowers and vines. The three women were dressed to the nines in new creations of their own, that they had been working on since the announcement of the wedding. Lady Gladys' dress was of dark green, in honour of the Goddess, and it had been created to enhance her favourite pieces of the family jewels. The earrings, bracelets, necklace, and tiara of gold were set with emeralds and diamonds, and had been a wedding gift to her grandmother from the folk.

'My dear boy,' Lady Gladys took up Maelgwn's hands, standing back to view him. 'Be he not the most handsome man in all Brittany?' she asked the girls who would have become rather coy at the question only months ago. Since their frequent association with Tory, however, Cara, the older and gamer of the two, was more than happy to step forward and voice her opinion.

'Aye Lady Gladys, it be a sad day for the womenfolk of Gwynedd.'

'Indeed,' Alma nodded in complete agreement.

It was seldom Maelgwn blushed, but feeling the heat rising in his face, he bowed to them. 'Thou art too kind, ladies. And may I say that thou art all the very picture of the Goddess this day.'

'Here, here.' Tiernan held up his goblet in agreement.

Lady Gladys beamed with pride as Maelgwn kissed her hand. 'Well, enough chatter, it be high time we got thee crowned and out of here, so that these ladies can prepare the chamber for thy wedding this night.'

This brought a round of whistles from the men present, embarrassing the poor Prince yet again.

'A definite advantage of wedlock,' Rhys commented with cheer, looking at Tiernan.

'I cannot argue there, my friend,' the bachelor was pleased to admit.

Katren gazed into the mirror with disbelief; she didn't recognise herself. 'Thy talents be truly endless. I never imagined I could appear thus.'

Although she seldom bothered with them herself, Tory carried a few cosmetics when she travelled and certainly knew how to use the array of colours to their best advantage. 'My mother was vain to a fault, being in the public eye all the time,' she explained. 'I'd learnt how to do a complete make-up by the time I was ten.'

The white dress of the maiden made Tory feel and look every bit the feminine Goddess. Its neck draped across her shoulders in soft folds, as was the Roman fashion. The silky fabric drew in tight to fit her tiny waist, dropping to a V-shape at her hips. The skirt then fell in gentle waves to the floor and to a long train. The sleeves were transparent and flared wide from the elbow, with the underside dropping by her side almost to the floor.

Tory's mass of long golden ringlets had been smoothed back tight to her crown. Combs, laced with tiny white flowers, held in place a shimmering veil, so sheer and delicate that it appeared almost as if it were not there at all.

As the bell of the south tower tolled to inform all of the King's crowning, Lady Gladys arrived to fetch the pair. She held out her hands, glowing with happiness as the girls approached her. 'I swear thou art more breathtaking than even Sorcha. Thee and Maelgwn art a most handsome match, indeed,' she told Tory as they all linked hands. Her eyes turned to Katren. 'And I foresee a double victory for us this day. We art counting on thee, child.'

'Fear not, Lady Gladys,' Katren said with confidence. 'I will not fail thee in this.'

Tory walked through the courtyard arm-in-arm with Lady Gladys, listening carefully to her last minute words of wisdom. The balmy aroma of her beautiful bouquet of white flowers, thankfully seemed to be calming her nerves.

Katren moved quickly ahead of them to meet Brockwell, who was the only member of the household who still remained outside the Great Hall. He was wearing a blindfold, having decided he wouldn't be able to resist the temptation to look upon Tory this day.

'My dear Sir Brockwell, I was joking when I said thee would have to be blindfolded. It appears more like thou art going to an execution,' Katren said.

'Be she here yet?' he asked, catching a most beautiful scent in the air.

'Nay, I have been sent ahead to prepare thee,' she informed him, reaching up to untie the blindfold.

'Nay, lady please. I shall surely fail.' He took hold of her hands to stop her, noticing how tiny they were in his own.

'Trust me. I shall make it very easy for thee.'

When the cover was lifted from his eyes, Calin beheld the face of an angel gazing back at him and he returned her smile, completely enchanted.

'I will be in front of thee all the way, so thou hast only to keep thy eyes fixed firmly on me,' Katren whispered.

Brockwell was still a little dazed by this vision and wondered how a maiden of such beauty could have escaped his attention this long. 'That will not be difficult Katren, thou art the very image of beauty. How could even the Goddess compare?' He took up her hand and lightly kissed it. *Here be the one I shall have the Goddess train to my liking.*

For once Katren was not overcome by his flattery, but rather amused by it. 'Hast thou not discovered that the Goddess be in us all, Calin. I am sorry, I meant —'

'Nay please, call me Calin.'

'As thee wishes.' Katren's slip of the tongue had been quite purposeful. She turned to see Tory approaching. 'Here she comes. Now remember, just concentrate on me and all will be well.'

'Be that a promise, Katren?'

Though she was amused by his sultry tone, she chose not to comment and turned to face the doors before them.

Tory stopped beside Brockwell, placing her hand on top of his. 'I truly thank thee for doing this, Calin, and my father thanks thee also.'

The huge doors of court parted wide and as Katren led them down the long aisle, Calin's eyes were glued to her slender, shapely form. 'It gives me the greatest of pleasure, I assure thee.'

The guests and members of the royal household stood for the exchange of vows. Selwyn was honoured to be playing harp alongside twenty-five visiting bards of prestige from all across Brittany. The holy men had come forth to raise song in celebration of this great occasion.

Maelgwn was entranced as he beheld his bride. The King felt a hand come to rest on his shoulder and Tiernan, his best man, whispered his mind, 'I do believe that in this case, even I would wed in thy place.'

'Not a chance.'

Just as Tory and Brockwell had almost reached Maelgwn, she brought him to a standstill and turned to face him. 'Look at me, Sir Brockwell, Duke of Penmon.'

Taliesin, who was conducting the ceremony from an indiscernible pulpit in mid-air, nodded to Calin to comply.

Given his leave, Brockwell turned his eyes to Tory. Although she was more beautiful than he'd ever seen her, he was surprised to find that she no longer stirred in him the same desire that he'd felt for her only weeks before.

'I release thee from the punishments of thy own design and declare that, if so desired, thee may compete on the morrow for the title of my champion.'

'I thank thee, great lady. I have seen the error of my ways, which shall be much improved from this day forth,' Brockwell pledged solemnly as he bowed to her. 'On behalf of thy father, allow me now to present thee to thy King.' When Tory's hand was placed on Maelgwn's, the couple saw no one else. Taliesin led them through their vows, very similar in intent to those still made today. In place of rings, a ribbon was tied to Tory's right wrist and Maelgwn's left. These ribbons were then wrapped around and over their hands as they were joined in wedlock.

'Those whom the Goddess hast joined, let no man put asunder.' Taliesin rested his hands on both their heads, serving Brockwell a look of caution. 'For this union be the will of the Great Houses Don and Llyr.'

'So be it!' the gathering responded with great merriment.

'By the power invested in me, I pronounce thee husband and wife. Thee may kiss thy bride, Majesty.'

Maelgwn raised Tory's veil. As he leant down to kiss her, the gathering was thrown into riot, for this kiss marked the beginning of the four days of feasting, sport, music, conference and merrymaking.

The guests were guided into the banquet hall, while the wedding party remained present to witness the signing of the marriage document for the archives. Tory asked Taliesin to take a photo of the wedding party for her parents, a subtle hint to the bard in reminder of the matter they had yet to discuss in detail.

By the time the King and his bride joined the rest of their guests in the huge dining room, the feasting and music were well under way. Maelgwn and Tory took their places in the middle of the main table. Brockwell and Katren beside Tory, Lady Gladys and Tiernan to Maelgwn's other side. Their guests, in order of precedence, were now allowed to approach the couple to congratulate and present them with gifts.

King Catulus was the first to address the newlyweds. The elderly warrior was obviously still reeling with exaltation for his young friend following the events he'd witnessed at the initiation. After expressing his honour and great delight in their invitation, he presented the couple with two large goblets of gold, set with rubies and intricately engraved with Celtic motifs.

This gift was to the great delight of the old King of Gwent Is Coed, Aurelius Caninus. He bestowed on the couple five whole barrels of the imported wine that he so cherished and for which he was famous. His daughter brought forth a decanter and filled Catulus' golden goblets with a sample for the recipients' approval. Maelgwn toasted his bride before entwining his arm in her own to drink. There were cheers from the court and all present did likewise with whoever of the opposite sex was closest.

When Vortipor came forward, the King rose to introduce his new and respected colleague to Tory. Maelgwn explained briefly how much assistance the Protector of Dyfed had been to him in his quest, thus speeding his return to her. Tory stood to express her gratitude, and their new ally took up her hand and kissed it.

'The very least I could do for the Goddess. I understand thy king's sense of urgency to return to thee, for thou art truly the paragon he described.' Vortipor then turned back to Maelgwn. 'I am an envious man indeed, Dragon.' He clicked his fingers and his squire came forward bearing a gift in a long wooden box. 'Such a jewel be well worth protecting, sir, and when thee mentioned that thee still wielded a sword of iron, I knew at once the perfect gift.' Vortipor opened the box and lifted a gleaming sword in its scabbard from the case. He then drew the sword to display it. 'Welcome to the age of steel, my friend. After all, we can't have a legend wielding any less than the best now, can we?' He replaced the sword in its sheath and launched it in Maelgwn's direction. 'Compliments of Rome,' he bowed in conclusion.

Maelgwn was exulted by the man's gesture, for to give a fellow ruler such a fine weapon was a true token of one's goodwill and allegiance.

The other lords and ladies of Gwynedd came forth to bestow their gifts and be introduced to their new Queen. When all had been seen in turn, it came time for Tory and the Prince to exchange gifts.

Maelgwn summoned Taliesin forth. He carried a cushion of red, on top of which was a fine silver necklet. It featured a dainty pendant, no bigger than Tory's middle fingernail, with the same black onyx dragon that Maelgwn wore. The King lifted it and spoke in a whisper as he placed it around her neck. 'This be the work of the folk. I shall explain its enchantment and place it where it be truly intended, later.'

Tory raised her eyebrows at the suggestion. 'I can hardly wait,' she kissed him. 'I love it.'

On cue, Bryce carefully made his way toward the King, the gift of the Goddess that he carried in his hands was hidden by a cloth of royal blue.

'I thank thee, Bryce,' Tory said. 'Majesty, may I introduce the young Earl of Penmon.' Bryce bowed deeply to the King, dumbfounded by the honour.

Maelgwn could barely believe his eyes; this was Calin, just as he remembered him from childhood. The King didn't have to think too hard to figure out where he'd come from. 'Arise dear cousin, I am pleased thou hast found thy way home to thy kindred.' He ruffled the boy's hair. 'And what have we here?' He cocked an eye at Tory as he raised the cover and observed the beautiful set before him. 'Magnificent! A game of sorts?'

'Aye. A game of wits and strategy known as chess.'

As Maelgwn hugged her tightly, Taliesin came forward rubbing his hands together. 'Splendid, so who fancies a game?'

Sir Rhys approached the royal table and politely interrupted the merriment. He bowed before announcing quietly to the King, 'Chiglas hast sent thee a wedding gift, Majesty, and frankly thou art not going to like it.'

Tory's eyes narrowed at his words. 'Cadogan,' she concluded without a doubt.

'Aye,' Rhys nodded, his tone as suspicious as her own. 'Chiglas wants to offer him in exchange for Caradoc's release. Shall I show the messenger in, or have him wait for thee in thy room of court?'

Maelgwn looked at Tory, confused. Should he rejoice at Cadogan's deliverance, or lock him up for fear of treachery?

'Do not trust it,' Tory cautioned.

Maelgwn, still unsure, turned to Taliesin for advice, but the High Merlin only shrugged. 'Thou art well aware that I am not permitted to advise thee in such matters. In thy place, however, I would surely heed my wife, for she be thy intuition, Majesty.'

Tory held a hand to her heart. 'I feel I am right about this.'

Though he was still far from convinced, Maelgwn said, 'Take Cadogan to his chamber where he may bathe, eat, and recover. See that both he and the messenger are confined to separate quarters until two days hence, when we shall consider the matter at court. Place a guard to ensure my wishes art adhered to, and tell Cadogan I shall see him on the morrow.'

Rhys bowed and went about his bidding at once.

'I hope thou art right, Tory. Cadogan hast served me well in the past.'

Tory was not about to let Chiglas spoil the day. 'My dear husband, if Cadogan hast truly been held prisoner these two weeks past then he shall need to rest. And besides, this be our wedding day, dost thou not have more pressing matters to attend to this night?'

Maelgwn grinned. 'Of course, I quite forgot myself for a moment. Please, tell me of thy wondrous game.'

Tory presented him with a book of instructions and moves that she had written, with a little help from Taliesin, in the King's own tongue.

'Thy penmanship be truly outstanding,' Maelgwn noted, and he invited Tory to a game. This was to the great entertainment of the menfolk, who all gathered around with their mead trying to get the gist of the rules.

Following a scintillating match of wits, Tory found herself in checkmate and so took the opportunity to leave. It was high time she made for her husband's chambers to ready herself for her wedding night.

'How long?' Maelgwn whispered, wearing a lurid grin.

'Katren will fetch thee.' She kissed him, before bidding all a good night.

The whistles and cheers of encouragement that arose from the men as she accompanied Katren, Alma, and Cara from the room could only compare to a grand final football match. As bold as she was, Tory nevertheless found this embarrassing and was glad when they reached the hallway.

The girls quickly ushered Tory to Maelgwn's chambers, but she came to a stop in the doorway, taken aback by the sight and perfume of so many flowers. Ivy spiralled up the posts of the huge bed, and was intertwined with roses, jasmine and lily of the valley. Posies of flowers filled the candle-lit room, and a small feast was set out on a table by the fire. Tory had never seen Maelgwn's room at Aberffraw and considered it a fair exchange for her tower. All her things had been brought to her new quarters, which were not as large and grand as Maelgwn's room at Degannwy but more snug and intimate. Her love had grown up in this room, and thus she felt an immediate affinity with it.

'Say something!' Katren prompted.

'It be simply beautiful, ladies.'

'Jasmine be for joy and lily of the valley be for thy happiness,' Alma explained with delight.

'White roses represent spiritual love.' Cara raised her hands to prayer position.

'Red be for passion and the ivy . . . be for devotion,' Katren finished in a dramatic fashion, before she broke into a giggle.

'What be this?' Tory asked, lifting off the bed a perfectly plain, long, white silk slip.

My wedding gift to the King.

Tory heard Taliesin's voice in her mind.

Let us just say, I know what he fancies.

Aye, Tory thought, decidedly. Maelgwn will love it.

Maelgwn was aware of Katren the second she entered the room, as was Sir Brockwell. Despite being in the midst of a game of chess, the King didn't wait for Katren to reach him before he stood to take his leave. 'My greatest apologies to thee, Vortipor, but I am afraid duty calls.' Maelgwn grinned broadly as he bowed to his guests.

'I shall not detain thee when such fair game awaits thee elsewhere. Nominate a replacement that I can massacre in thy stead,' Vortipor requested with cheery confidence, before adding as an afterthought, 'Not the magician!'

Maelgwn looked about at those who had been following the game. 'Sir Rhys, doth thou feel confident to complete my victory?'

'Aye Majesty, blindfolded.'

With this settled, Maelgwn made haste to his chambers. He passed Alma and Cara in the hall, who were en route back to the festivities.

'Sleep well, Majesty,' Alma said.

'But I doubt it,' Cara emphasised as they both hurried on.

Tory was kneeling down in the middle of Maelgwn's bed when he entered. Her long golden ringlets, freed from the combs, fell softly about her bare shoulders and down her back. The white silk of the slip caught the candlelight, and she furnished Maelgwn with an alluring smile. 'More becoming, I hope?'

He recalled the conversation they'd had on her first morning at Degannwy. 'I have no objection.' He gloated upon her loveliness as he removed the black gunna and cast it across the room. 'So long ago, yet I desired thee even then. I must confess, I did battle with my conscience when I found thee asleep by the fire that night.'

'So that be how I got to bed.' Tory smiled in recollection; it had all been a bit hazy at the time.

'Aye.' He threw aside his boots. 'I showed great restraint, I must say. Thou wast rather the worse for mead as I recall, and somewhat keen to oblige.'

This was news to Tory, still she didn't care about that. 'I shall always be keen to oblige thee.' She watched as Maelgwn removed his shirt, exposing the smooth muscular torso that she hadn't even been granted a glimpse of till now.

'In that case . . .' Maelgwn crawled onto the bed to take a seat before her. He'd dreamt of their union many times, yet now that it had arrived he no longer felt in any hurry. 'I promise I shall never leave thee wanting.' He held a hand to her cheek and gently guided her lips towards his own.

For a warrior of such size, Maelgwn's caresses were very tender. His hands almost quivered as they slid from her neck down over the thin film of silk that concealed her naked body.

A wave of awareness beset Tory, and every part of her tingled as her skin became alerted to his touch.

Maelgwn's hands slipped to her waist, his kisses finding their way towards her cleavage. Ever so gently, he raised her to a kneeling position and paused to look at her.

'I almost forgot.' He smiled as he lifted the thin straps of the slip from her shoulders. As he let them go, he delighted in the sight of the garment slipping down over her body. His fingertips glided over her soft, smooth skin, from her knees, over her thighs, and up behind her neck to remove his wedding gift. 'This,' he began, but he was distracted by the desire to kiss her and did so several times; the sensation of her naked body pressed hard against his own was far too compelling. 'This,' he tried again, 'is very special, and it belongs . . .' His eyes lowered and he gently kissed each of her breasts before kissing the space just below her navel. 'Here.' He hung the charm in its place. 'It shall protect thee, and Gwynedd's heir from harm.' He kissed the pendant.

Tory reached down, running her fingers through his long silky hair and held him close a moment. 'I do love thee, Maelgwn of Gwynedd.' She thought of the intent of his gift sweet, though its purpose was a bit of a worry.

'And I thee, Tory Alexander.' He overwhelmed her with affection as they sank back onto his bed.

The desire she'd been suppressing for so long finally found its release, as the tears of sweet relief trickled down her cheeks. She closed her eyes and lay back in a state of rapture, savouring the sensation of her husband exploring her pleasures for the first time.

Rhys had gone on to victory over Vortipor on the chessboard, and King Catulus of Dumnonia now matched wits with the old King of Gwent Is Coed. In his drunken state — one that now prevailed over the whole court — Catulus was furnishing old King Caninus and Vortipor with a detailed account of the new King of Gwynedd's colourful history.

Taliesin was pleased to expand on the stories, feeling that his every word drew the allies closer together. Rome had many problems and was far away. Its priests here numbered but few and could be easily suppressed before they forced the native people into submission. Catulus seemed more than eager to return to the old ways in Dumnonia. King Caninus, although truly amazed by it all, had been raised in the Church of Rome and admitted to hold little understanding of the great mysteries of the land of his birth. He was, however, curious to learn, as Maelgwn's great ancestry was also his own.

Lady Gladys was in her element, seated by two kings who were roughly the same age as herself. She lent her wisdom to advise on the game and the great legends, as she remembered them. The aging widow was constantly flattered and propositioned by the noble pair, and she basked in the attention.

Tiernan, Angus, Rhys and his wife Jenovefa, who was heavy with child, were seated by the fire. The knights were entertaining Cara and Alma with mead and adventurous tales of battle. Selwyn accompanied their stories with his harp to intensify the mood.

Brockwell looked on, discontented. He hadn't had a drink all night in a gallant attempt to stay out of trouble, but his sobriety only served to make Katren's virtuous curves seem all the more attractive to him. To add to his woes, he hadn't been given a chance to say more than two words to her since the wedding. Now that he thought about it, she hadn't returned to the dining room in quite some time . . .

As Brockwell made his way to the kitchens, he conceded that he was quite pleased with the way things had turned out. His King and Tory were most likely in the throes of marital bliss, and if Katren was in the mood to show him some favour, all would be rather grand this night.

The huge kitchens of the house were a hive of activity, as they would be for the next three days. Brockwell found Katren sponging Bryce's face clean, preparing the exhausted youngster for bed.

'Sir Brockwell.' Bryce became excited and Katren turned with a smile to greet him.

'Bryce, thou art my brother now, thus thee must call me Calin.' He lifted the boy from the bench and relieved him of the tedious task of being bathed.

'Wow! Will thou teach me to be a great knight like thou art, Calin?'

'Aye. And in years to come, thee shall grow to be the King's Champion.'

'Thou art going to win on the morrow, I know it.' Bryce placed a small hand on Brockwell's shoulder in support.

'I shall certainly pursue the title to the best of my ability, and thou art coming to watch, of course.'

'Aye, I have never been to a tournament before,' Bryce exclaimed, jumping up and down, unable to contain himself.

'Then thee had best get to bed where thee should have been ages ago, or thou shalt surely sleep in and miss all the action,' Katren teased, taking up his hand.

'Nay.' Bryce withdrew his hand from hers. 'My brother will take me.' Bryce looked at Brockwell, who shrugged at Katren as he tossed the boy over his shoulder.

'Do not go anywhere, I will be back,' he advised her over Bryce's squeals of delight.

Upon his return, Katren was fussing about preparing trays of food.

'Katren!' Calin took hold of her hands. 'Leave this to the servants, thou art a lady now and the last place thee belongs be in a kitchen. Come with me for a stroll through the grounds instead.' He raised his brow in anticipation.

'Some fresh air and exercise before bed would be good,' she supposed, wrapping the long train of her dress about her shoulders and accompanying Calin outside. 'Thou hast done very well this day, Calin.' Katren made polite conversation as her escort had gone rather quiet. 'Thy lady love married another, and still thou hast not touched a drop of mead all day.'

He turned to her, somewhat alarmed, sorry now that Katren even knew of his feelings for her mistress, as she would think his sudden change of heart just a ploy to seduce her. 'I am overjoyed for my King and sister. I feel no need to drown my sorrows, believe me.'

Although well pleased to hear this, Katren didn't show it. She maintained an expression of interested concern as they resumed their stroll.

'I have not indulged, as I wished to see if my wanton thoughts were provoked by drink alone.'

'And were they?'

'It would seem not.' He turned to face her again, his expression torrid.

Here it comes. Katren prepared herself. *Stay in control.*

'I know this confession will sound volatile, Katren, but I have seen no one but thee this day. Thy beauty be a revelation to me.'

To her great relief, she was not set swooning. Katren felt she held a kind of power over him, and she had the royal consent to use it. 'How awful for thee, Calin, for I fear that I can only bring thee more torment.'

A submission or flat denial he had expected, but this response was not anticipated. 'Nay Katren please, thou hast not pledged thy love to another?'

'Nay.' She was pleased with his dismay and began to spin her tale. 'Though I have sworn an oath of celibacy.'

'Katren! To whom?'

'To the Goddess, of course.'

'Tory,' Calin spitefully concluded.

'Nay, the Goddess herself. I have no husband and no deep desire to keep or obey one. Thus, I have spoken with Taliesin, and he feels I would make a fine priestess.' Calin was completely taken aback, and Katren played on this. 'Be it not truly wonderful? *Me*, a priestess of the Honey Isle.'

Brockwell sat down on a long garden bench, disheartened.

Katren let her excitement wane a little. 'What be the matter?' She took a seat beside him.

'I thought thee, I mean, I felt sure . . .' He was tongue-tied a moment.

'That I was attracted to thee?'

'Aye!' he acknowledged.

'Calin, I was.'

'Was?'

'Indeed.' She stood to finish her address. 'But any woman who believes herself capable of keeping thee faithful to her and her alone, be truly fooling herself, and I am no fool. Thou art a free spirit and that be fine, most men art by nature.' She smiled, very sincere in her intent. 'The kind of love I seek, I fear I shall be hard pressed to find. So, that be why I have chosen to devote all my time to pursuing the greater mysteries of this land and leave the lesser ones to other women who wish to be subjected to the frustrations of seeking and holding a husband. I have been there once, Calin, it be not for me.'

'Thee listens to Tory too much.'

'Calin, please give me my due. I had thee figured all by myself.' She remained very cool, which frustrated him all the more.

'How do women do that? Feel that way for someone and just walk away?' Brockwell rose, angered that all

276

wasn't going to plan. What was wrong with him lately? Was he losing his charm, or were the women becoming more difficult?

'Not how do women do it, Calin, but why? Women do not have the choice.' As Calin appeared sceptical and bored by the answer, Katren continued. 'Ask Bryce's mother, the price she paid for her choice was dear. But thee had a good time, right?'

'She sought me out.'

He obviously thought this justified his part in the incident, which served to anger Katren all the more. 'She was just a child.'

'So was I!'

'And thou still art.'

'What can I do about it now, Katren, I beseech thee?'

Katren glared at him. 'Grow up,' she suggested, and left.

Much to the new King's amazement, he had overslept. He snuggled closer to his wife, deciding that married life was going to do him the world of good. He could have snoozed blissfully on all day, and probably would have if Lady Gladys hadn't woken them politely with breakfast. She informed them that it was fast approaching noon, when the tournament was hailed to begin.

It was the red dress of the warrior that Tory proudly paraded this day. Of a similar cut to the first, this garment was made from a heavier fabric that did not shimmer like the silk of the maiden's gown. Its sleeves came in tight at the wrists and it had a high neck. The dress sat well in her opinion, but it was the accessories that excited her most. Made of fine chain mail, the belt hung in a V-shape following the waistline. The neck piece had a wide band that fastened tight around her throat, then spread out over her shoulders. The two matching rings that slid onto the middle finger of each hand, featured the same fancy chain mail, running in a V from the ring to a band that fastened about her wrists. Tory truly adored this outfit, it felt powerful to wear and made her look every bit the proud warrior.

The guests were feasting in the sunshine and making ready for the tournament in the inner bailey. The crowd sounded with fine force as the King and Tory entered the courtyard, clinging to each other to endure the jests from the men in regard to their tardiness.

'Majesty, how grand that thee could join us,' Rhys said, in very good spirits. 'Dost thou wish to compete for Gwynedd this day? Vortipor of Dyfed hast suggested that instead of single competition, we should have teams that art allowed five men-at-arms.'

Rhys spoke of the general competitions that were held as entertainment prior to the main event — the battle for the title of the Queen's Champion. The heats for the Queen's event would continue until only four warriors remained. These final competitors would do battle before the guests in the marquee, in the final three duels of the day. The runner up, if still alive, became the King's Champion, as the Queen was supposed to require the greater protection. This competition was for the locals only, though the other games gave the visiting legions a chance to be involved in the festivities. It was left to Tory to nominate the mode of battle for her title. The games that preceded this event were swordplay, archery and, of course, jousting.

'Very tempting indeed,' Maelgwn smiled, rather keen on the idea until Tory raised an objection.

'Hold on, I would still like thee in one piece tonight.'

'Never fear, Goddess,' Vortipor came forth, claiming her hand for a kiss. 'I shall leave all the important parts intact.'

'My dear Vortipor, how gracious, but it be thy own safety that concerns me. For if thou was to harm my husband in any way, I would have to beat thee most grievously — hardly the way I wish to treat such an honoured guest.'

Vortipor laughed, delighted by her wit.

'My good man, she be quite serious.' Maelgwn told him. 'My people have not hailed Tory as the War Goddess without good reason. Besides, I have been looking forward to a day of leisure with my fair wife. Sir Cedric shall fight in my stead.'

Maelgwn was the first interesting challenge Vortipor had come across in quite some time, both mentally and physically, and there was no way he was going to give up so easily. 'Come my friend, humour me. We art going to keep points, so the challenge be nothing more than a game. It will not be any fun if thou dost not compete.'

Maelgwn's men voiced their agreement with Vortipor.

'What, outrageous! Maelgwn must compete!' Catulus protested as the news reached him. 'I have a wager on thee boy, thee cannot let me down.'

Maelgwn laughed at the King. 'Surely thou hast thine own representatives, Catulus?'

'Aye, but I know too well how the Otherworld favours thee, thou hast never lost. Thus I put my gold on Gwynedd,' he chuckled, turning to appeal to the bride. 'Thee will have a whole lifetime to be together, lady. Could we not steal Maelgwn for the afternoon?'

'Alright, if he wishes. But be warned, gentlemen, I shall hold every one of thee responsible if any dire harm befalls my King.'

'Understood, lady, thou art most gracious.' Vortipor bowed to them both. 'May the best team win.'

Maelgwn greeted the rest of his guests, before accompanying Tory to a large marquee, that opened onto the view of the battlefield. Chairs, rugs, cushions and refreshments had been placed in the shade of the tent for the honoured guests and family. Selwyn strummed a blissful tune on his harp, creating a very pleasant ambience. Similar shelters had been erected on the upper green of the outer bailey, around the main arena, to accommodate the visiting lords and their kin. In the main arena, one could view Dyfed as they thrashed Dumnonia in the first round of the challenge, which was archery. The King kissed his bride then left her to join Rhys, Angus, Tiernan and Brockwell for the challenge.

'Lady Goddess, come quick.' Bryce came racing up to Tory. 'The men will not let Ione enter.' He took hold of her hand and raced away with her to the lower green, where the initial heats were about to commence.

Tory strode up to address Cedric, who was in charge of the proceedings. 'Sir Cedric, I have been informed that thee forbids Ione to enter my quest. May I ask why?'

'Lady.' He bowed slightly, surprised she even knew the crazy woman. 'To compete one hast to be a knight of Gwynedd, or be nominated by a knight or one of nobility. And with good reason! This prevents those unready to meet the challenge from being able to enter and be unduly harmed.'

'Do I qualify to have an entrant, Cedric?'

'Why, I . . . I guess.'

'Good. Then I shall nominate Ione as my representative.'

'Excellent!' Taliesin slapped a hand on Cedric's shoulder. 'The fee shall be on me, and here be the fee for my own entrant.' The money went into a pot, and 'winner takes all' were the stakes. Taliesin motioned to a short but well-built knight as he dropped the gold pieces into Cedric's hand.

The knight was quite unlike any warrior Cedric had ever seen, and wore no armour. He was dressed totally in black, even his face was covered by a tight black balaclava. Dark glasses covered his eyes, and black gloves concealed his hands. The only trace of him that could be seen at all, was the long brown braid that fell over his broad shoulders to his waist.

Cedric was disgusted by all this; first a woman in the tournament, and now a demon or the like. 'What manner of knight be this, High Merlin?'

'Why, he be the Black Knight, of course. Every tournament hast to have one.'

'His Majesty will have to consent, I do not have the authority —'

'What art the two of thee doing to poor Cedric?' Maelgwn, having caught the last part of the conversation, relieved the knight of his woes. 'Whatever they ask be fine, Cedric. What my lady wants this day, my lady gets.' Tory squealed as the King lifted her high in the air. 'What mode of contest shall proceed this day, as if I did not know?' he asked her as he brought her back to earth.

Tory returned his knowing smile, holding up her fists to confirm. 'But there art rules. Gather the competitors and I shall enlighten everyone.'

Cedric appeared rather bothered by this break in tradition, as he watched the King and Tory make their way to address those concerned.

'By jove, I am having fun! Be this not truly exciting?' Taliesin implored Cedric with a slap on the back.

Cedric managed a meagre sneer as they followed the royals.

Maelgwn called for the attention of everyone and thanked the competitors for their participation. Then Tory came forward to make the announcement they had all been waiting for. 'Warriors of Gwynedd, thee will compete this day with naught but what the Goddess gave thee at birth,' she decreed, before going on to explain the rules.

Anyone who failed to comply with them would immediately forfeit the match to their opponent. Tory had four large circles marked out on the lawn with long pieces of thick rope. Each circle would yield, after a series of knockout rounds, one of the four finalists. If one could force their opponent out of the circle, it was worth a point. If one wrestled their opponent to the ground and held them for a count of five, it was a point. A clean, undefended punch would also fetch a point, but one's opponent must refrain from retaliation until the point was awarded. Any combination of these, for example, forcing one's opponent out of the circle with an undefended punch, was worth two points, and so on. No biting, hitting below the belt, or head butting was allowed, and the first to gain a lead of three points won the match. This form of challenge was fast, effective, and comparatively less harmful than some of the alternatives she could have chosen.

Not only were these rules to Ione's advantage, but they gave Tory a chance to investigate any undiscovered talent that she could train as one of her masters — who would, in turn, become her trainers for the masses.

She already had her female contingent, and had spoken to the King about training Rhys, Tiernan, Calin, Angus, and perhaps Cedric, over the autumn and through the cold seasons. This would mean that the knights and their families would have to stay in the house at Aberffraw throughout the long cold spell (known as sleep or burgeoning) instead of returning to their own estates. Of course, this would be their choice.

In the first clash of the knockout competition, Sir Cedric thought he was being smart when he matched

Ione to fight against Sir Rhys. The poor knight was subsequently humiliated when he lost three points to naught. Sir Cedric, after bearing witness to the unfortunate occurrence, didn't sacrifice any more of his valued knights to her fury so early in the competition. If this woman did manage to make it to the finals, she would be weary and one of his finer champions, Brockwell or Tiernan, would surely finish her.

Ione silently basked in her win. She waited in the circle, arms folded, eager to take on the next challenger. The wind blew the long, brown strands of her hair about the striking features of her face, and she looked rather fine dressed in men's attire. In fact, she quite reminded Tory of one of the proud women of ancient Gaul.

Tory kept the company of Bryce and Taliesin for most of the afternoon. On the lower green they witnessed their representatives go on to win their heats, and make the final four who would compete for the title and the pot of gold.

Taliesin's entrant, whose fighting style was quite like that of the Queen's, had all speculating as to what Otherworld ancestor the Merlin had conjured up to compete on his behalf. Or perhaps he was a warrior from the future or the distant past? But the Merlin was tight lipped and refused to comment.

The Black Knight became the third of the final four, and Ione the last. Calin and Tiernan had won the first two placings, managing also to aid Gwynedd to victory against Gwent Is Coed in the challenge.

Things had looked bad for Gwynedd at first, as the knights from Gwent in the south, who were constantly plagued by seafaring attacks on their harbour ports, had won the archery competition. The warriors from Gwynedd, who were more accustomed to ground assault both on foot and horseback, triumphed in the end, however, winning the greater points in the jousting and swordplay events.

As Dyfed had only just defeated Dumnonia in all three trials, Vortipor had got his wish and would compete against the legend of Gwynedd. It was plain to all that the two young leaders were greatly looking forward to the match, as they raised a goblet of mead to each other's success and wellbeing.

Once again, the boys from the south clenched the greater points for archery, and although Maelgwn shot much better this time round the more experienced bowmen from Dyfed won out in the end.

Tory found the jousting and swordplay hair-raising, yet after Angus, Rhys, and Tiernan had won their heats it was plain to all who the greater horsemen and swordsmen were. Dyfed, having seen little hostile action of late, found their battle skills in this area somewhat lacking.

Brockwell managed to conclude his heat against Vortipor's champion, Sir Queron, in a matter of minutes. Calin was just as amazing to watch in action as Brian had been, Tory thought. So at home on a horse and with his weapons was he, that they seemed a mere extension of himself. He dismounted his opponent on the first pass of their joust. Brockwell then sprang from the charging horse and had his sword poised at the throat of his adversary before Queron realised what had hit him. Sir Queron, twice his opponent's age and far more experienced, could hardly believe it.

'Wast thou born on a horse with a sword in thy hand, boy? I have never seen such skill in one so young. I do humbly yield to thee, Sir Brockwell of Penmon,' Queron said, holding out a hand for Brockwell to help him up.

Under normal circumstances, Brockwell would probably have taken offence to the older knight referring to him as a boy and run him through. Yet, Sir Queron was quite notorious himself, so Brockwell considered this to be a compliment and gladly helped him to his feet.

Maelgwn hoisted himself onto the black stallion, Aristotle, and Tory grew nervous as she watched. She sat forward in her seat, unsure if she felt thus because he appeared so gallant, or if it was a premonition. 'I do not know about this,' she uttered, feeling uneasy.

Brockwell claimed the seat beside her, lifting Bryce to sit on his lap. 'Fear not. Maelgwn be good at the joust.'

'Aye,' Catulus seconded Calin's view. 'The best.'

Cedric sounded the cry and the two began their charge towards each other.

Tory's pulse was racing but she couldn't look. She heard the sound of the lances meet.

'Wooh!' the crowd cried, before breaking into applause.

'What happened?' Tory asked, not opening her eyes.

'Tory!' Brockwell sounded disgusted. 'Thou art supposed to watch. Nothing hast happened.'

Upon daring to open her eyes she found them lining up for another pass. 'Damn.'

She was not to be put out of her misery upon this clash either. Five more passes followed before Maelgwn finally toppled Vortipor from his horse and they drew their swords to do battle.

'Good show, Maelgwn! Finish him off,' Catulus yelled in encouragement, holding up his mead to the young King.

Both men used swords rounded blunt at the point, although one could still inflict a nasty gash if desired, as the blades were left quite sharp.

The two leaders battled and sidestepped each other for a time to the great excitement of the spectators. Finally, Vortipor took advantage of the sun setting behind him, and Maelgwn sustained a gash to the upper left arm.

Tory stood and called out to her husband's assailant. 'Thee will pay for that one, Vortipor.' She gestured to Maelgwn in a sign language only they understood.

He gave her a nod of understanding and returned his attention to the fight, again clashing swords with Vortipor. Maelgwn held his attacker's blade at bay with his own and startled Vortipor with a numbing kick to his jaw. When the Irish warrior hit the ground, Maelgwn stepped hard onto his sword arm, forcing him to lose his weapon. The King rested the blunt end of his blade against Vortipor's jugular. 'The Goddess warned thee friend, dost thou yield?'

'What happened?' Vortipor rested his free hand against his bruised jaw.

'Dost thou yield?' The King looked down at his stunned foe.

'It would seem thou hast left me little choice,' Vortipor granted, and Maelgwn gave him a hand to his feet. 'Congratulations Dragon, thou art a formidable opponent. And ah, sorry about the scratch, got a tad carried away.'

Maelgwn shrugged as if it were nothing. 'Come, let us relax with a drink and watch for a while.'

The King reclined in the marquee while his cut was dressed. Gwynedd had won and there was much cause to celebrate, especially for King Catulus, who'd clenched the wager he'd held with Vortipor and Aurelius Caninus.

'I told thee, he never loses,' King Catulus chuckled, merrily pouring more mead for them all.

Tory's attention drifted to the arena where Sir Tiernan and Ione stood opposite each other, ready to commence the first of the three final fights of the day. The winner of this would meet the Black Knight and the winner of that would fight Brockwell for the title, as he was ranked most highly.

As soon as Cedric gave them leave, Ione charged Tiernan. The shock tactic worked, as she was able to throw him off balance and out of the circle.

Tiernan protested and cursed his ridiculous situation, insisting he could not fight a female.

'Get used to it,' was Tory's response, and Maelgwn merely shrugged; it was Tory's day, her quest, her rules.

Tiernan reluctantly returned to the arena to lose three to one.

None too happy, he entered the marquee to join his fellow knights. 'Do not feel bad, Tiernan, she licked me first round.' Rhys, who had recovered from the embarrassment, held a drink out to his friend.

With his pride and body still freshly bruised, Tiernan was not yet ready to laugh it off. 'It be ludicrous!' he insisted, accepting the goblet of mead.

Tory stood to face him and Maelgwn rose beside her, a mite worried she would cut loose. 'Then thou art not serious about my instruction, Tiernan?'

The knight cooled at the sight of her, nodding his head to confirm both her statement and his mistake. 'I did not think. Apologies lady, if I have offended the Goddess.'

A commotion erupted in the arena and Tory turned to see soldiers dragging Ione away from the Black Knight, kicking and screeching in protest. Cedric approached the royal marquee, appearing rather pleased.

'I be very sorry, lady, but thy entrant hast attacked her opponent before we commenced. That warrants disqualification doth it not?'

Tory appeared disappointed. 'Those art the rules.'

'Match to the Black Knight, he shall meet Brockwell for the Queen's title,' Cedric decreed.

Rhys and Tiernan were overwhelmed with delight, clinking their goblets and taking a swig.

Tory rolled her eyes at this. 'Typical.'

Before the last match of the day began, both contenders were brought before Tory for her blessing. The knights knelt before her, heads bowed low.

'Brave warriors of Gwynedd, who have fought so gallantly this day, I wish thee the best of luck in thy quest for the title and the gold. May the greater warrior win.'

The two knights rose, the Black Knight returning immediately to the arena. Brockwell, however, lingered near Tory to ask her in a whisper, 'Where be Katren, she be missing this?'

'I did speak with her earlier, and I hate to say it but she sounded a mite upset with thee. But I feel sure she will be watching in any case.'

Calin was most perturbed as he returned to the ring for the challenge.

As Tory took her seat next to Maelgwn, appearing rather pleased with herself, he leant over to her. 'What art thou up to? Something be going on, I can feel it.'

'Trust me,' she advised, patting his knee.

Bryce came racing up and sat on Tory's lap. 'Calin be going to win!' The boy was convinced, having witnessed his idol undefeated this day.

'I would not count on it,' Taliesin commented, quietly confident of a win himself.

'Who be this knight, Taliesin?' Maelgwn was finally curious enough to inquire. 'He cannot be a local, I would surely know such a fine warrior.'

'I assure thee, Majesty, my knight lives up to all of thy requirements.'

'In other words, thou hast no intention of telling me.'

'Correct.' Taliesin looked back to the arena where the clash was about to commence. 'The Black Knight's identity shall be revealed to thee upon my victory.'

Cedric sounded the cry and the two warriors began stalking each other in a circle round the edge of the rope. Calin was about to make his move when the Black Knight spun round and planted a heel in his stomach with such force that Brockwell was driven to the ground well outside the circle.

'Two points to the Black Knight.'

Cedric's announcement angered Brockwell; he hadn't lost a point all day. 'Who art thou, sir? I want to know.' He rose, angered.

The Black Knight stood in defence, urging Calin back into the ring.

'Now Sir Brockwell, let's not do anything rash,' Cedric cautioned. He did not want his last hope disqualified for misconduct.

'Nay, let us get on with it,' Brockwell growled, taking his place.

'Match point,' Cedric informed the crowd to Calin's further irritation. 'Begin!'

Again they circled, yet Calin was more cautious this time and stayed further inside the ring. The Black Knight seemed to be taunting him, darting around his attack with apparent ease. In the glossy black shield that covered his opponent's eyes, Brockwell could see his own clumsy attack, and he now wished he'd encouraged Tory to train him sooner. Calin lashed out with a punch, and his arm was unexpectedly trapped mid-flight. The next thing he knew, he was twisted around to land face down in the dirt.

As Cedric started the count, Brockwell struggled in vain to break loose. His arm was pushed hard up across his back, and the Black Knight's knee was firmly embedded in his back.

'Four and a half . . . ?' Cedric tried to stall and was finally forced to concede defeat. 'Five. I hail the Black Knight to be the Queen's Champion and victorious this day.' He didn't sound at all excited about the announcement.

There was a silent pause as Brockwell rose and turned to face the Black Knight. 'Show thyself,' he demanded in anger, planning to kill him, whoever he was.

The Black Knight bowed politely, conforming to his wish. As the knight removed the head cover, all gasped in awe.

'Lady Katren!' Brockwell went weak at the knees, stunned.

'Aye, a woman be capable of so much more than just warming thy bed, Calin. Here endeth the lesson. Now if thou would excuse me, I shall be off to collect my due.' She turned to make her way to the King and Queen, looking back briefly to add with glee, as she removed her gloves, 'Fair fight.'

Calin was totally beguiled as Cedric placed a hand on his shoulder to comfort him. 'It be a shock to me too, Brockwell. I think we had best take up the way of the Goddess before the women take over!'

Ione held her hand up to Katren as she approached the royal tent, and Katren served her a high-five as she passed.

Maelgwn couldn't help but smile at this. 'Katren, thou art all swollen.' He made jest of the padding of her disguise.

'Ate too much at thy wedding, Majesty.' She curtsied to him, very pleased with herself.

Tory, Cara, Alma, Ione, Lady Gladys and Taliesin gathered around Katren. The Merlin placed a goblet in her hand, as the group of women raised their drinks in the air.

'A toast to the Goddess, ladies,' Taliesin said, briefly admiring the lovely women around him. 'The Goddess returns!'

'The Goddess returns!' the women repeated after him, clinking goblets to drink to their first victory.

After claiming her gold, Katren made her way back to her quarters to clean up before the night's celebrations. She was not surprised when Calin followed her.

'Why, Katren? Why hast thou done this to me?' he asked. 'I even saved thy virtue not so long past . . .'

'Only to try to steal it last night!' she snapped back. 'I do not regret my actions, Calin, thou deserved it.'

'Alright, I deserved it,' he agreed, not wanting to fight. 'I apologise for what I said last night, can thou not forgive me?'

'Of course,' Katren said without hesitation. 'Thou art forgiven.' She turned and continued her stride up to the house.

Brockwell was stumped for a moment by the ease of his absolution and ran to catch her up. 'Katren.' He caught her arm. 'I wish to court thee,' Brockwell blurted out, barely believing the words that had left his mouth.

Katren smiled, patting his cheek. 'I do not think so, not yet. Next spring perhaps, if thou art still so inclined.

I have a fair idea thy feelings for me may change in the near future.'

'Why spring? I shall surely die before then.'

'Art thou intending to train under Tory this coming autumn and beyond?' She slipped her arm away and ever so gently pushed him back a little.

'Aye.' His brow became drawn. 'Why?'

She began to move off, her eyes still fixed upon him. 'I do look forward to it then — as I am to be thy sparring partner.' She punched the palm of her hand and laughed.

Brockwell wasn't quite sure how he felt about the news, but recalling the way Maelgwn and Tory were always rolling around on the floor together, he shrugged and grinned. 'How bad could it be?'

13

WINDS OF CHANGE

Tory's first day in court with the knights and advisers of Gwynedd was going to prove every bit as difficult as she'd imagined. The men were riled after their defeat at the hands of the female warriors the day before. Tory deemed that the demonstration had been necessary, however, in light of the proposal she was about to put forth.

On the court's agenda were four main items for discussion — Chiglas' wedding gift being the first. The laws regarding provision and protection of the women and children of Gwynedd would follow, along with the new marriage laws. The meeting would conclude with an outline of the role and standards that would be expected from the elite group of masters that Tory planned to train.

With so much to discuss before the court convened, Tory and Maelgwn retreated to the comfort and privacy of their chamber. There the King read Tory's proposal thoroughly, which they had discussed in part before his inauguration. Lady Gladys had advised Tory well, and Maelgwn agreed that the work displayed much foresight. Although he was quite sure some of his men would not take too kindly to the restraints of the new laws, Maelgwn agreed that the plans would undoubtedly benefit Gwynedd and the Goddess in the long run.

A State-subsidised orphanage would be opened where old Hetty's brothel village now stood, to house and protect the neglected children of Caswallon's rule. It was to be run by Hetty and two of her older girls, thus giving them gainful employment and ridding them of the need to solicit. The bastard children would be given every opportunity to advance socially of their own accord and initiative. A school and playground for the village would also be opened in the spring. From then on, every child between the ages of five and fifteen who could travel to the school in Aberffraw, would be required to attend.

Tory proposed that Selwyn, who was fairly well educated, could train under Taliesin over the cold season and teach at the school when it opened. The King obviously didn't fancy the idea of giving up his page, but Tory pointed out that the aspiring bard could be far better employed as a teacher. Selwyn could instruct the children in basic mathematics, language, history and music while one or two of her ladies instructed them in self-defence, meditation and basic combat skills.

The parents of the children, where applicable, would be required to pay a small fee in addition to their normal taxes for each child. In return, their children would be educated, fed, and upon reaching the age of fifteen, taken off their hands completely. This was already the case with the males of the kingdom, and by the spring a new hall would be erected in the outer-bailey grounds to house the young females. From then on, rather than being sold to the highest bidder, the daughters of Gwynedd would be sold to the State; this was also true of the young unwed girls of old Hetty's keeping. That way, women would serve the royal family for a term, in the same fashion the men did, giving them a few years to discover their calling. Tory hoped this would make it easier for the young men and women of the kingdom to meet, mix, and hopefully match, as it should be.

In future, all marriages would have to be not only recorded, but approved by the State. Both parties would have to freely consent before the court and their immediate family, and if there was no serious cause for objection, the couple would be granted permission to wed. Hence the buying and selling of human beings would become a criminal offence. Dowries were an exception to this rule, as they were considered more of a savings plan to support the daughter in married life. The wife would bestow this wealth on her chosen husband, and should the marriage end in divorce, she could reclaim the same amount to support herself and any kin for whom she may have to provide.

The beating of women and children would become a punishable offence throughout the land, as would rape. Tory knew these cases would be hard to try in court, especially in that period in history, yet until some sort of deterrent was put in place, the culprits would not be dissuaded.

Maelgwn found the outline for the master's training scheme fascinating. First and foremost, these men and women would be required to abide by the new laws as set by the Goddess. Those chosen would guide and set the standard for the many who would follow. If her masters didn't display consideration and understanding for each other, they could not respect the Great Mother and would cease to serve her. The masters would also be asked to take a vow to Gwynedd — that they would never instruct or speak to another outside their ranks about their skills without the Queen's personal consent. To break this vow would be punishable by death.

Tory decided to follow the traditional belt colour-coding system to define the achievement of each individual. The masters would wear white uniforms, like her own, while they were students, and black once they became teachers. The belts would define how masterful one was personally. In Tae-kwon-do there were ten different coloured grades before the black belt, these lower grades were known as Kyu. Kyudan, dedicated to the refinement of the self, consisted of ten different grades of black belt, of which Tory had only reached the second grade.

Maelgwn was inspired by the thought of so much learning. At present, once one became a knight that was as far as it went, except for the odd title challenge. With this proposal his men would have something new to strive for and he, like never before, could compete alongside them.

As the teachers, champions, and representatives of Gwynedd, this elite group of masters would be the first to be awarded special privileges, like a weekend. With intensive training all week, these two days would be set aside to relax, practise, or study.

There were other details to be finalised but on the whole, Maelgwn conceded that Tory could do a fine job of running his kingdom, all on her own. Yet as he embraced her, claiming she was the most miraculous woman he'd ever known, Tory had to wonder if he'd still think so on the morrow, when his men wanted his head for agreeing with her.

In court the next day, Tory wore the gown of black, representing the Crone or wise woman of the Triple Goddess. With the same cut as the other two dresses, this one laced up the front from her hips to a sweetheart neckline, and the collar sat stiff about her shoulders, framing her face. Her hair had been bound up tight in a bun at the top of her head, and her make-up was dark and striking.

Chiglas' messenger had presented his case to the court, yet the King gained no further insight into either Chiglas' or Cadogan's true intent. For Chiglas to offer only Cadogan in exchange for Caradoc's list of offences was laughable; surely Chiglas must realise that Maelgwn could never accept, and this made the new King uneasy.

If Cadogan was lying about his imprisonment, he was very convincing. Still, Tory noticed he didn't appear any worse for it, and she could hardly blame the man because he'd managed to come through his ordeal unscathed. To be sure, she didn't know what to think. Her solemn glare of accusation failed to make him flinch from his story, and pretty soon even she began to question her doubts about him.

In the end, the King decreed that Cadogan was by no means enough ransom to buy Caradoc's freedom or pay for his grievous crimes against the kingdom of Gwynedd. He thanked Chiglas' messenger for Cadogan's safe return and bid him tell Chiglas that if he wished to make a more substantial offer, he would consider it. If not, come spring he would feed Caradoc to the dragon of Keridwen, as promised.

This decision worried Tory greatly; if Cadogan was conspiring with Chiglas, this would be exactly what they wanted Maelgwn to do. Cadogan would be snowed in for the whole of the cold season at Aberffraw, and with Tory's training about to commence, she didn't like the idea one bit. She would wait, however, and discuss it with Maelgwn when they were alone and at liberty to speak their mind.

As Tory refrained from commenting on the matter of Cadogan, Maelgwn wondered if perhaps she'd changed her mind in regard to his knight's loyalties. Yet when she politely refused to begin her address to the court until Cadogan had left the room, the King realised their difference in opinion still remained.

Following a heavy day in court and all the frivolity of the feast that followed, Tory and Maelgwn finally returned to the solace of their chamber for some well-earned time alone. Tory collapsed onto a chair exhausted, unwinding her hair from the tight knot on top of her head.

'Thee spoke like a true Queen in court today. And I must say, the men accepted thy proposals more readily than I expected. Well done.' He took a seat beside her, planting a kiss on her forehead.

'Why thank you, kind sir.' Tory conjured up a smile. 'We shall see if they art still so agreeable when the laws come into force.'

Selwyn knocked on the door before bounding into their room, appearing as if he'd just won a prize. 'Forgive me for disturbing thee, but I have just heard of thy plans for me. Oh lady, could it be true?'

Tory delighted in his excitement, holding out her hands to him as he approached. Selwyn grasped them and fell to his knees before her. 'Aye Selwyn, if thee wishes it.'

'Oh lady, I do, I do. And with all my heart, I thank thee.' He kissed her hands repeatedly.

'Enough.' Maelgwn swiped his page across the back of the head.

Selwyn apologised to his lord and turned back to Tory.

'There be no need to thank me, Selwyn. Thou art the best one for the appointment, and I believe Taliesin will be well impressed with thee.'

'I do hope so, lady. I shall do my very best to make thee proud.'

Again, she was amused. 'Selwyn, I am already proud of thee. Always remember that.'

'Aye lady, I will.'

'Go now.' She smiled down on him, gently stroking aside a long strand of golden hair that fell across his face. 'I believe the High Merlin awaits thee in the library.'

Selwyn jumped to his feet, startled by the news. Then remembering his place, fell on one knee again to kiss her hand, then stood and ran backwards to the door. 'I owe thee everything, lady. I cannot thank thee enough.'

Maelgwn turned to Tory, 'I wonder at times whose squire he be.'

Selwyn knocked and entered again. 'My greatest apologies, Majesty. I do thank thee also and bid thee a very goodnight.' He left again before Maelgwn had a chance to respond.

The King turned to Tory, a mite surprised by just how well she understood his subjects. 'I think he likes the idea.'

'I think thou art right.' Tory was elated to have made the youth so happy.

'Thou dost not think me right about Cadogan though?' Maelgwn asked, though he seemed reluctant to bring up the subject.

'If thee wishes to give thy knight the benefit of the doubt, I will accept thy judgement. I do realise there be no solid evidence against him.'

'But?'

Tory shrugged. She really didn't want to discuss Cadogan now, when they finally had a few hours alone together.

'Tory, I am thy husband, thus I hope thee will feel at ease to speak thy mind.'

The tenderness in his voice both touched and infuriated her. 'Must we pursue this now?' Tory asked meekly, so as not to anger him.

'Tory?' Maelgwn was alarmed by her timid stance and reluctance to speak with him. He took up her hands and held them tightly. 'I will not be angry with thee, I could not! Thou art my wife. I respect thy judgement and need to hear it. Please.'

'Maelgwn, thou art most frustrating at times.' Tory stood. 'Thou art already well aware of how I feel about Cadogan, why push the issue?'

'I had thought perhaps thee might have changed thy mind.'

'I have not, nor will I ever.'

'I see.' He was displeased. 'And what would thee now have me do with him?'

Tory could feel her adrenalin rising and paused briefly to retain her composure. 'I would send him to Degannwy for the cold season and away from thy training ground.'

'But Aberffraw be Cadogan's home, as well as it be my own.'

'Not only that. I would have someone keep a close eye on him while he was there, in case he should seek out Caradoc.'

Maelgwn stood, outraged. 'Tory, thou art being unreasonable. Cadogan hast done naught wrong, and he's been through a great ordeal. Now thee would have me send him from his home, for the whole duration of the autumn and burgeoning? Nay, I will not do as thee suggests.'

'Be that what Caswallon told Sorcha when she warned him about Cadfer?' Her retribution, so swift and to the point, stunned Maelgwn to silence, and he slowly sat down. Tory feared she had hurt him and rushed to kneel at his side, resting her head on his lap. 'Maelgwn, forgive me. I had no right —'

'Nay, thou hast every right. I had near forgotten myself.'

Tory looked up at him to hear his resolve.

'I shall do as the Goddess bids me. But if Cadogan remains at Degannwy without incident till spring, will thee accept this as proof of his loyalty?'

'I would certainly reconsider the matter.'

Maelgwn smiled at her as he stroked her hair. 'Then it will be done.'

The morning came too soon in Tory's opinion. She felt the warmth of Maelgwn's body leaving hers, and dreamt of the weekends that lay ahead when they might spend the whole day snuggled together. This morning, however, she would not be allowed to escape her duty. For today she was to be crowned Queen, and address the great leaders of Britain.

She hadn't the slightest idea of what she was to say to them. Maelgwn had conveyed to her the words of

Keridwen, so Tory could only presume that she had another cosmic episode to look forward to. *So much for being well informed.*

When Sorcha had held control over her, she and the Queen had seemed to Tory as one. She felt what Sorcha did, she knew her mind, and she even recalled some of her memories. When Sorcha had addressed Sir Tiernan at the time of Caswallon's death, Tory saw and felt things between the two that she was quite sure none of the kindred knew about. Tory couldn't imagine how it would feel to have the entity known as the Triple Goddess inside her, so she was as nervous as hell.

All the women of the household were fussing about her, fixing her dress and combing her hair. Tory was pleased that today was the last day of celebrations; the novelty of dressing up had worn thin.

The tunic-style dress of green had a bodice and skirt the like of the others, but it squared at the neck and was sleeveless. A shirt of the palest green silk was worn under it, and the underside of the sleeves fell to the floor. Her hair was left to fall naturally, crowned by a wreath of ivy, pink roses and lily of the valley.

'Tory, thou art as pretty as a nymph,' Lady Gladys concluded. 'Doth thou now feel prepared to face thy subjects?'

Tory rolled her eyes at the question. 'If we wait until I feel ready, Lady Gladys, Gwynedd may well remain without a Queen for Maelgwn's entire reign.'

Lady Gladys chuckled, taking Tory by the arm. 'Thou art the fairest, strongest, and dare I say, wisest Queen this kingdom hast ever known. Thee shall do well.'

In Tory's mind, the processional walk to her crowning was far more gruelling than that of her wedding. Today she was not expected to be a blushing vision of sweetness, but a wise and fearless leader.

Just who am I fooling, I can't do this, she thought. What in hell's name was I thinking when I agreed? I'm not even supposed to be here! Her stately air did not waver as she made her way up the long aisle. All alone, she felt every eye in the hall upon her, and this knowledge made her temperature rise to near boiling point. How could you do this to yourself, the voice in her mind scolded as she approached the stairs at the end of the aisle, where Maelgwn met her. His smile was a revelation. *That's how.* Tory's fear subsided, as she placed her hand on Maelgwn's to accompany him up the stairs to the throne.

Taliesin led Tory through her pledges, both to Gwynedd and the Goddess. Maelgwn then removed the garland of flowers from her head and took great pleasure in bestowing the crown of Gwynedd in its place. The silver counterpart to his own of pure gold had been worn by the queens of his kingdom for generations, and it fitted perfectly.

As all present joined to hail the new Queen by kneeling before her, Tory marked how heavy the crown felt on her head and took hold of Maelgwn's hand to squeeze it tight. Suddenly she had gained a greater understanding of what must have been for Maelgwn a lifelong plight.

Tears rose in Tory's eyes at the overwhelming scene before her, yet she held her head high and smiled for all to see. None, bar Taliesin, knew how deeply dismayed the young Queen really was. The High Merlin wasn't at all worried about this, as Sorcha had been the same. The position would seem a little overwhelming at first, of course, but after witnessing how Tory had handled the men at court the day before, he held no doubt she would cope well enough.

All was going according to plan for the High Merlin. The Prince had fallen in love with Tory and brought the British leaders of the land together for conference; now they entered an unknown future. The three of them, this very day, would change the course of history forever.

King Maelgwn, his new Queen and Taliesin dined in Gwynedd's court with the other noble personages of Britain. The room had been beautifully adorned with fresh flowers to honour the coming of the Goddess, a great feast had been laid out for their guests, and the sound of Selwyn's harp echoed softly in the background.

Over good mead and fine food, old King Caninus, King Catulus and Vortipor each expressed the great pleasure they'd savoured during the past few days. So much so that they were tempted to stay at Aberffraw for the whole of the cold season!

Once the feast had been cleared away, Selwyn was excused, for it was time to get down to the business at hand. Tory sat in a throne at the end of the table. Maelgwn sat at the opposite end, which was too far away for her liking.

'Art thou ready, Majesty?' Taliesin stood up.

'I am.' Tory sounded confident, yet inside the butterflies almost made her sick.

Taliesin laid his hands on Tory's shoulders as he came to stand behind her, proud of how well she concealed her doubt from their guests. The High Merlin calmed her with his healing energies, and Tory's eyes closed with the relief she suddenly felt. Taliesin took this opportunity to formally introduce himself to the representatives of Britain as he opened the proceedings:

> The Books of Bede do not lie,
> the chair of the guardian is here,
> and shall so continue in Europe till the judgement.

The High Merlin's eyes became glazed and his voice monotone. The leaders looked on with great anticipation, hanging on his every word.

> I am Taliesin, son of Keridwen,
> my charge be to protect her true descendancy.
> For all time I shall be here
> as prophet to Gwynedd and her allies.
>
> My knowledge is the wisdom of the Ancients.
> I foresee danger from afar,
> and devise strategies for protection.
> And I serve only the offspring,
> who uphold the way of the Goddess.
>
> Today I come before these men at Mon,
> seeking their esteem and blessing.

An eternity I have endured this
earthly existence,
dwelling in the shadows with the elements.

I alone bespeak the custom of our forefathers,
as they have nominated me as one of the three
great judges.

Taliesin paused to take a deep breath. Tory did likewise. Next thing she knew, the room seemed to be throbbing in time with her heart. Her head felt heavy and, no longer able to support it, she let it drop forward.

Bountiful Mother, fair as the dawn,
wonder to the land of Britain,
cast thy rainbow around this court,
that we may drive back the attack against
our land.

Pray, great lady, show thyself
so that on this day we may all be graced with thy wisdom.

Taliesin gently lowered Tory's semiconscious body so that she was slumped over the table. She groaned, appearing to be in a bit of discomfort.

When the King rose concerned, the High Merlin sternly motioned to him to stay put, and they all waited breathlessly for Tory to rise.

Tory's body slowly sat up in the chair, and the four nobles knelt and humbled themselves as they beheld the fairy features of Keridwen and the angelic green glow of the Divine Mother.

'Mother of God!' King Caninus uttered aghast, as he strained his old bones to kneel for the first time in nearly twenty years. Although he didn't recognise the Goddess by sight, something miraculous had happened to this woman's face; her entire demeanour, bone structure, and eye colour had changed right before his eyes.

'Greetings gentlemen, I thank thee for thy attendance and the new King of Gwynedd for his pains in calling this meeting in my name.' The large, dark eyes of the Crone looked at Maelgwn. 'My son's expectations of thee have not fallen short of his boast. Thou art truly one of the Chosen and do serve thy forefathers proud.' Again her voice resounded with the voices of all three aspects of her nature.

'I live only to serve the Great Houses, my lady,' Maelgwn replied, full of ardour.

'And we art most gratified by thy devotion, Maelgwn. Please be seated, lords, as we have much to discuss. I should not tax this sweet child any longer than necessary.'

The Goddess kept her address short and to the point. She outlined the problems that Chiglas and the raiders posed, and the future of the native Britons if they did not pool their resources to defend their lands. 'These raiders art not as the Romans were. They do not seek to control my people, but to eradicate them completely! By the year two thousand and twenty, no trace will remain of our culture or our people. Our land stolen from beneath us, will wither and die with the exile of the folk. Forever barren, no life shall be able to sustain itself and Mother Earth shall be lost for eons.'

This insight rang true with Maelgwn in particular, as this confirmed many things that Tory had told him of her time.

'In this knowledge shall ye unite under one banner to defend the mother country?' The Goddess cast her eyes over them.

'Dumnonia merely awaits thy instruction lady, thy folk and ways shall be honoured henceforth throughout my kingdom. And I assure thee, King Maelgwn and Gwynedd have held and will continue to hold my allegiance for the duration of my lifetime,' Catulus answered her. He felt a new man for his adventures. He cared not what the priests of Rome would say or those who followed them; anything that made him feel so alive was worthwhile in his mind.

The Goddess nodded to Catulus, thankful for his support. She then shifted her gaze to Vortipor, who sat beside him.

Vortipor slowly shook his head as he smiled. 'I have been witness to many a strange occurrence in my time, but since the fateful day I met the good King of Gwynedd here, I have never known such wonder. I wish nothing more than to link our nations against thy foe, lady.'

As the Goddess looked to Aurelius Caninus for his thoughts, Maelgwn and Vortipor silently prayed that the old King of Gwent Is Coed wouldn't complicate the issue.

The King's eyes, still wide with wonder, suddenly lowered as the Goddess turned her attention to him. He was attempting to hide the tears of shame that welled in them. 'Great lady, I fear I am an old misled fool and a great disappointment to thee. I do solemnly swear that I shall dedicate my every free moment in the short time I have left on this earth, to studying and honouring thy greatness. I beg thee forgive my ignorance, for I have truly known no better. I ask that thee accept my humble offer of service to aid thy cause.'

The Goddess reached out and took up the old King's hands, smiling in delight at her prodigal son. 'My good King Caninus, thou doth cause naught but much rejoicing in my heart, and thy noble ancestors art appeased by thy faith this day. I do wholeheartedly welcome thee home.'

'Oh praise thee, lady.' A couple of tears trickled down his wrinkled face. 'Thou art far too forgiving.'

'Nonsense, that be my way, Aurelius.' She turned to motion Taliesin forth.

The Merlin unrolled a scroll on the table to present his outline of the treaty for all to consider.

The Goddess remained with them only long enough to witness them sign the pact. Once her task had been accomplished, she bid her new representatives farewell. 'Henceforth, thou art all delegates of the Otherworld and the esteemed protectors of Britain. Be as brothers, for thou art one, and let none divide thee. This be the will of the great Houses Don and Llyr.'

Maelgwn placed his hand face down on the treaty. The other three followed suit, placing their right hands on top of his. 'So be it.'

Tory slumped forward onto the table, unconscious.

14

A WINTER SOLACE

Tory woke two days later to find Maelgwn by her side, he'd been keeping a constant vigil since her collapse.

'Praise the Goddess,' he uttered as he wiped her brow gently. 'I feared I had lost thee indefinitely.' Maelgwn poured a drink of water and helped her up so she could take a few sips. 'How art thou feeling?'

Tory leant back, smiling, thankful for his aid; she had barely enough strength to keep her eyes open. 'Out of it,' she mumbled, slowly raising a hand to her head as she became more coherent. 'My face aches. What happened? Did we succeed?'

'We did indeed.' Maelgwn took hold of her wandering hand and kissed it. 'Thou wast simply magnificent, and have made me the envy of every leader in Britain.'

'So they agreed with us?' Tory pressed for confirmation, the matters of State still foremost in her mind.

'Aye. The pact hast been set in place, and the Kings have returned home for the cold seasons with their legions. Taliesin, too, hast taken his leave. He decided to retire to Llyn Cerrig Bach last night and hast invited us to visit him there as soon as thou art able. All were left swooning by thy address, Tory, and did ask that I pass on their humble gratitude and good tidings for the festive seasons ahead, all bar Vortipor.'

'Why not he? Did I do something to offend our guest?'

'Nay, to the contrary, he wishes to remain over the fall and burgeoning.' Maelgwn laughed. 'It would seem that the dear Protector of Dyfed hast got it in his head to persuade thee to train him as one of thy masters. I told him he would have to take it up with thee, once thou hast fully recovered.'

Tory only smiled in response, patting his hand as she closed her eyes to rest.

'What amuses thee? Dost thou like the idea or not?'

'Whose idea was it, exactly?' Tory opened one eye to view him.

Maelgwn reacted with surprise. 'Why dost thou ask?'

'Just answer the question, if thee please,' Tory said, giving him a whack of encouragement.

'I do not understand how, but thou art obviously aware the idea was my own.'

Tory sat down, stunned. 'Maelgwn, I knew that! I swear, I just read thy mind!'

'Could thou have acquired it too?'

'Thou hast this ability, Maelgwn?'

'Aye, that be how I bespeak the dragon and Taliesin, at times. But alas, there be a fine art to it that I have had neither the time nor inclination to refine. The little use I have made of the gift, I have left to pure faith. Sorcha, however, had perfected the art, which be why Cadfer killed her, for fear of her truth saying.'

They were both quiet in thought a moment before realising at the same time, 'It must have been the Goddess.'

'Aye, I think so.' Tory began to remember her experience. 'I recall that when the Goddess came over me, it seemed that I had gained, for that time, total knowledge.

'I know this feeling,' the King said, recalling his inauguration and similar Otherworld rites where this experience had occurred.

'Everything from the beginning that would go on without end, was made known to me,' Tory excitedly explained, as Maelgwn nodded in confirmation. 'Past, present and future existed simultaneously. All the secrets of the ages, the meaning of the universe, the stars, the moon, I understood. Wow, I feel great!' But she spoke too soon, as she immediately became woozy and lay back down.

'So what dost thou say about Vortipor? Doth thou not think it would be a grand gesture, like the sword he gave to me?'

Tory ran her fingers through the long smooth strands of Maelgwn's dark hair. This was the trouble with the Celtic people, Tory thought, they were generous to a fault at times. Such a show of goodwill could easily backfire. Yet, if indeed I can discern whether or not a person is telling the truth, she decided, then I will personally interview every aspirant before I agree to train them. If I believe Vortipor is truly loyal to the treaty, which I must admit I do at present, I see no reason why I shouldn't agree. Thus Vortipor, upon his return to Dyfed, could begin the instruction of others.

'I suppose I could allow Vortipor to stay and play with thee awhile longer. And yes, if I feel him truly in league with Gwynedd, I shall train him as a master.'

'This be grand news.' The King hugged her tightly. 'May I leave thee to rest a moment? I really should let Vortipor know at once.'

Tory nodded with a smile. Yet, as she watched him leave, she had to shake her head. This winter at Aberffraw was shaping up to be like her university days all over again. *Only here, heaven forbid, I'm supposed to be the teacher.*

Most of the senior staff of Caswallon's old court had died during the battle, and those who survived had their hands full maintaining the other estates within the kingdom. Besides Sir Percival, the old accountant who kept pretty much to himself, Sir Cedric, aged roughly in his mid-forties, was the oldest amongst those staying at Aberffraw over the cold seasons.

Lady Gladys had decided to leave all the young people to it and retire to her estate at Penmon. Bryce would be going with her, as Tory could hardly deny the lady time with her grandson. The boy could recommence his tuition in the spring with the other children from the village.

Thus, from autumn, only the masters and the immediate staff would occupy the house. Many of the soldiers returned to their families, homes and farms. Those with no kin stayed in the huge hall in the outer bailey and saw to the chores around the house, as little defence was required during the weather that was to come.

After a few days, Tory's health gradually began to improve. So, at Taliesin's request, she accompanied Maelgwn on Aristotle to Llyn Cerrig Bach.

As they neared their destination the sunlight filtered through the canopy above, and Tory closed her eyes. The huge black stallion lulled her to rest with its gentle steps. She leant back against Maelgwn, her head rested on his shoulder, as they proceeded down the forest track to the temple ruins.

'I have never seen thee so at ease on a horse,' the King commented.

'It be this place . . .' Tory held her arms wide, admiring the wonders of Mother Nature all around her. 'I feel strangely at home here.'

'My mother did love this valley also. She claimed the earth energies were very strong here.'

'Really? Did she mention why?'

'Sorcha thought it because of the fairy folk, as they live here in great numbers. And Taliesin explained that the folk art attracted to such places because it be where the invisible paths of power, that pass over and under the land, cross over.'

'Ley lines,' Tory surmised, thinking she would have to discuss this further with Taliesin.

Before long they reached the overgrown temple ruins. Aristotle was left to roam the wood, and, hand-in-hand, Maelgwn and Tory walked towards the large stone altar inside the temple.

Maelgwn lifted Tory up onto it, and leapt up after her. 'Taliesin!' No sooner had he called the name than the misty haze began to rise; a brilliant white light came bursting forth from the altar and engulfed them.

The High Merlin was overjoyed to see the pair. 'Majesty.' He bowed to Maelgwn and held out his hands to Tory. 'My dear Queen, thou art simply radiant.' Taliesin knelt to kiss her hand, which made Tory uncomfortable.

'Taliesin! I do thank thee, but surely thou art aware of how I detest formality. Thee of all people hast no need to kneel before me, not now or ever!'

The High Merlin smiled as he stood, her hand still in his own. 'Sometimes, dear lady, honour and gratitude art well deserved. For thou hast accomplished more in the last few days than thee could possibly realise. Thus, on behalf of the Goddess and her folk, thy ascendants and descendants, I humbly thank thee.'

'What have we done exactly?'

'Hard to say really, but thou art the ones who shall find out.'

'What? Taliesin, thou art speaking in riddles again.'

'I shall explain over lunch. For I am very pleased to inform thee, that for thy selfless efforts and loyal service to the Goddess, thou hast set thyself apart as one of the Chosen.'

'Which means?'

'Oh, a great many things,' Taliesin said. 'But simply put, thou art spiritually moving up in the world. In a karmic sense, it be *pay back time*. Now if thee will just follow me, all shall be made clear.'

Tory, a little perplexed, looked at Maelgwn.

'Fear not. Thy power to bethink others be part of being Chosen.'

Taliesin swivelled around, 'Tory! Thou hast bethought another?'

'Aye,' Maelgwn informed him, proudly. 'Myself in fact.'

'Wast thou touching Maelgwn at the time?' the Merlin queried.

'Well,' Tory had to think about it. 'Yes.'

The Merlin's smile broadened. 'Still, this be much sooner than even I anticipated. One day thee may learn to bethink others without needing to have physical contact with them.' *Such refinement be truly astonishing in one so inexperienced. Perhaps Sorcha and her teachings are more deeply embedded in her soul mind than I'd first imagined*, Taliesin thought.

Lunch was to be served in the cosy room where Tory and Brockwell had dined during their last visit. Tory was invited by their host to choose whatever she desired to eat, and as Taliesin so enjoyed these little challenges, Tory played along. After careful thought, she requested something that she would not otherwise be able to indulge in. 'Mexican food and perhaps a large strawberry marguerita, or two.'

Maelgwn, always open to a new experience, decided with a shrug to join her. He considered it might be nice to learn a thing or two about Tory's old way of life.

No sooner was her request noted, than Taliesin waved his arm over the table and the lavish feast appeared. Tory gasped in delight at the sight of all the dips, tacos, burritos, enchiladas and the like. These were accompanied by a varied array of seafood, salad, garlic bread, cocktails and desserts.

'A Mexican feast.' Taliesin smiled at Tory, flicking his fingers and igniting every candle on the table.

Tory applauded his display. 'I am most impressed, sir.' She reached out for a large pink drink. 'Cheers.'

Maelgwn followed her example. 'Looks most agreeable, I have to say.'

'Indeed, my young friend, I believe thee will find many aspects of twentieth-century life to thy liking, but then there art many things that art most disagreeable, like the air,' Taliesin informed him, as he peeled a large green prawn.

'Thee speaks as if I were going there.'

'Why thou art. It be thy destiny.'

'But I cannot. I have a kingdom to rule. I have —'

'Maelgwn, Maelgwn, Maelgwn, trust me. There be a way and I, of course, have found it. In theory anyway.' Taliesin's excitement waned momentarily. 'In truth, the exact calculations art going to keep all my computers and my brain very busy throughout the cold season.'

'Calculations for what, Taliesin?' Tory cut straight to the heart of the matter, her smile broadening.

'Well, I believe I can send thee into the future for a year, then bring thee back to find that only an hour hast lapsed here.'

'Wow! Now that's a concept. Thou art truly brilliant.'

'Aye. But there be something I have not told thee,' he said.

Tory placed her glass aside and sat back in her seat. 'I'd say there be many things thou hast not told me, High Merlin. Please be more specific.'

'I have already stated that we have altered the future, just how much I cannot say. One thing be for sure though, thou shalt not be returning to exactly the same reality thee left. I can only send thee to the parallel existence in accordance with the destiny of the world, as it stands next summer solstice.'

'Surely I have not changed history so much in such a short time?'

The Merlin nodded to confirm. 'In the many differing dimensions through time and space, every possibility comes to pass to determine each conceivable outcome. It be impossible to predict what scenario many have eventuated by thy return.'

'Wast thou aware of this when thou brought me here, Taliesin?'

'Aye, I was.'

Tory stood as her anger mounted. 'Well, dost thou not think that just a tad presumptuous?'

'I acted only upon thy instruction, Majesty.'

'Look, just because I had a romantic interest in the Dark Ages did not necessarily mean that I wished to take up permanent residence here.'

The King chose to stay well out of the contention, a little hurt that Tory seemed not entirely happy with sixth-century life.

'I refer not to the past, Tory, but to the future. I assure thee, that upon thy return to the twentieth century, thee will seek me out and tell me of this very conversation and of thy destiny.'

Tory was stunned. 'So again I must blindly trust in thy word, High Merlin.'

'My dear Queen, I would not leave thee without a means of escape. A back door, so to speak.' Taliesin felt Maelgwn's quiet dismay, but Tory had the right to know. 'For thee may choose not to return here, which will break the cycle of thy destiny and undo all that hast taken place here. Thee would return home, all being as thee left it, and lead a totally different life. Maelgwn will find himself married to someone else, and thee will remember naught of each other, or indeed, any of this. Alas, there would be no chance of a reversal then, as none of this will ever have happened.' Taliesin paused. 'The choice of thy destiny be thine own now, Tory, and I shall abide by thy wish whatever it may be.'

Tory sat silently staring into space, remembering those she'd left behind. *As much as they might grieve for a time, I cannot imagine that I have left anyone who needs me as much as these people do.*

Maelgwn placed his hand over hers, and at once she felt his deep fear of loss. Tory thought her heart would break and she turned to him. 'I could never bring myself to leave thee, Maelgwn, *never*.' Tory cast her eyes to the High Merlin, feeling a mite ashamed by her behaviour. 'How can thee be so good to me, Taliesin, when I constantly take thee for granted and misunderstand thee so. I feel totally unworthy of any of this.'

'Enough said,' he insisted. 'Thou art obviously very much in love, and therefore most worthy. The food be getting cold, so please, dwell on it no longer and start to eat. There be something I wish to show thee after lunch.'

Uh-oh, Tory thought. *What next?*

'Fear not. I promise it will be very much to thy liking.'

Taliesin led Tory and Maelgwn through his maze, stopping in front of a door identical to all the others. 'This be a small token of my personal appreciation, lady, and I have waited an eternity to present it to thee.' He smiled, swinging the door wide open.

Tory gasped, holding her hands to her face in amazement. 'Where on earth? I don't believe it!' She wandered slowly around the large room, full of gymnasium equipment. The King, even more surprised, followed her.

'I thought thee might find it useful when training thy masters.'

'Useful. It shall be invaluable!' Tory walked up to one of the punching bags that appeared older and more worn than the others. Her brow became drawn when she noticed her initials on it, those of her brother, and others she'd known. 'Taliesin, I recognise this, it belonged to my old *sensei*, a young master who went by the name of Teo.'

'Really?' he smiled. 'What a coincidence.'

Tory looked at him, hands on hips, feeling not entirely satisfied with his response. 'Do not try to tell me that the all knowing Taliesin did not realise?'

'I must have overlooked it, some of the equipment was secondhand.' He carefully avoided her query. 'In those boxes yonder, thee will find the uniforms thee desired with the various coloured belts.'

Tory and Maelgwn, like a couple of kids at Christmas, quickly investigated.

'Old man, thou art a wonder.' Maelgwn was most pleased, seeing the Dragon motif embroidered on the back of all of them.

'Come on then.' Tory encouraged the King with a slap on the shoulder. 'Allow me to run thee through a proper workout.'

'Splendid idea,' Taliesin announced, pleased that Tory had forgotten the other matter. 'After that, thee may refresh thyselves in the room opposite. Then perhaps a stroll around my garden before dinner?' He gave Maelgwn a wink. 'Thee must both stay the night as my guests. I shall have this equipment transported to Aberffraw on the morrow. Till then, enjoy.'

'What was that all about?' The peculiar intonation in Taliesin's parting words had her curious.

'Pardon?'

Tory winked at him to clarify.

'Oh that!' Maelgwn shrugged. 'I cannot imagine.'

His smile was far too mischievous for Tory to believe him. Still, when even physical torture failed to prompt him into disclosing what he knew, she gave up, figuring she'd find out soon enough.

They spent a few hours running through the use of each piece of equipment. Afterwards, when they retired to their room to bathe and dress for dinner, they each found a change of clothes laid out on the bed.

Tory was not surprised to see that Taliesin had chosen a dress for her to wear and, funnily enough, she liked it very much. Made of a white shimmery fabric, the garment hugged the body in the torso and was cut very low to the cleavage, akin to the more romantic and revealing attire of the seventeenth-century ladies. It was v-waisted, as suited her figure, and fell to the ground in wisps of fabric, which parted when she walked to reveal her bare legs. The shoes, of the same fabric, were like ballet slippers.

'I could never get around wearing this in thy court, Maelgwn.' Although Tory was positive she'd never seen the garment before, she was just as sure she recognised it.

'If Taliesin was not such an old man, thee would not be wearing it here either.' Maelgwn admired her a moment. 'So, art thou ready?'

'Aye . . .' Tory was forced to grin, turning to face him. 'What art thou up to, my lover?'

'Thee shall see.' He took her hands to lead her out the door.

'Nay, we should not. Taliesin warned me about wandering off in this place.'

'Believe me.' His smile did not waver. 'I know where I am taking thee.'

Maelgwn led her out into the hallway, and upon reaching the end they entered a maze of stairs, doorways, archways and open chambers that could have been designed by Escher himself.

She leant over a banister to admire the grand feat of illusion created by the stairwell. It seemed to twist for miles below her and, although it was difficult to tell, Maelgwn seemed to be leading them downwards. The King amused her with stories of his childhood adventures within the labyrinth as he confidently guided her through the maze. Finally, they entered one of the many long hallways that extended off from the central area of the house. When they reached the door at the very end of the corridor, Maelgwn turned to her.

'Close thy eyes.'

Tory did so gladly, eager to learn what was amusing him so. As soon as the door was opened she knew they had stepped outside, as the sounds of little creatures met her ears and the fresh, scented air filled her nostrils.

'Now.' Maelgwn gave her leave to open her eyes.

Tory beheld a woodland garden that was so beautiful it took her breath away. The life force emanating from it was overwhelming — it was purer than anything she had encountered before. She sensed that they were being watched, yet not a single animal could she see. There were, however, an abundance of tiny earth lights that hovered around the trees. Yet as she approached them to investigate, they twirled off, beyond her scrutiny.

'There be something altogether familiar about this place.' She turned to see where they'd entered, to find only a door and frame standing alone in the middle of paradise. A smile swept over her lips as she experienced deja-vu.

'Thee may know it as the Land of Fairy. As thou art one of their Chosen, thou art now permitted to enter their realm.' Maelgwn took up her hand and began to walk with her.

Tory felt as if she would burst with happiness as the tranquillity of the surroundings engulfed her. 'I remember this place now, I dreamt of it several times after we met.'

Maelgwn stopped still and turned to face her. 'As did I. Many times.'

Upon the King and Queen's return to Aberffraw, they were besieged by all at court. From the little they could discern from their subjects' garbled reports, they guessed that Taliesin must have delivered the gymnasium. The royal couple were whisked to the Great Hall to view the mysterious manifestation that had fascinated their subjects.

The magician hadn't just delivered the equipment, he'd installed it as well. The weights, benches and other equipment were well spaced around the walls and the punching bags hung from the high timber beams overhead. The walls of the court were now lined, between the windows, with the same huge mirrors that had been in the gymnasium at Llyn Cerrig Bach. In the centre of the hall was a padded mat to be used for sparring. It had a large black circle marked upon it and a huge motif of the Dragon in the centre.

'How?' Tory shook her head, mystified by the High Merlin's means.

'The folk,' Maelgwn answered simply, then he began to show his men a thing or two of what he'd learnt.

After all had enjoyed a bit of a play, Tory summoned her masters together, asking them to sit on the perimeter of the circle marked on the mat. She had to laugh when she found all the men seated to the left of her and the women to the right, with the gaping space of the circle between them. 'This will never do,' she concluded, clapping her hands to draw their attention. 'Right, it be high time that I enlightened thee all to exactly what thou art letting thyselves in for. I assume that everyone seated around this circle aspires to study under me through the cold seasons. If this should not be the case for any of thee, please leave the room at once.'

Old Percival, the accountant, and the very pregnant Jenovefa, who stood looking on from the outside of the circle, moved to leave at the Queen's request.

'Nay,' Tory called after them, waving them back. 'Percival, I believe one could regard thee as well trusted.'

The old man smiled, delighted that he might still observe, as it was extremely interesting to him.

'And Jenovefa, thee may want to hear what I have to say for future consideration.'

Jenovefa could hardly believe that the Queen would even consider her, and she opened her mouth to answer.

'Nay.' Rhys laughed at the ridiculous notion. 'My wife hast no desire to be a warrior! She shall be a mother before long and will have plenty to occupy her time.'

'With all due respect to thee, Sir Rhys, I do believe I am addressing thy wife.' Tory didn't even look to him. 'I am sorry, Jenovefa, thou wast about to say?'

'I am most honoured by thy suggestion, Majesty, but I feel I must decline.' Though she smiled, her expression was cold as she curtseyed.

'The choice be yours, Jenovefa, but should thee change thy mind . . .' Tory added with regret as she watched her go.

Jenovefa nodded back to her and quietly left the room.

'So, am I now safe in assuming that only the potential initiates remain?'

'Aye,' they all responded in good cheer.

'Then know this,' Tory's voice resounded in the large room and all her pupils hushed in anticipation. 'My role for the duration of thy training be that of thy *Sensei*. Whilst thou art in training under me, ye will all refer to me as such. *Sensei* means head teacher, and my word henceforth be law for all the initiates of the Goddess. Anyone who finds themselves unable to adhere to my conditions, now or at any time, need only leave.' Tory raised her arm and pointed to the door. 'These terms and standards of behaviour will be adhered to without exception or question. I will, of course, be more than happy to explain anything thee may not understand. I suggest thee all consider carefully thy actions before withdrawing, as there will be no second chances for the indecisive.' Tory took a long pause to allow them a moment to absorb her words. 'Upon thy arrival in this room tomorrow at noon, I expect all or nothing, ladies and gentlemen. Have I made myself plain?'

'Aye,' they responded, a few of the men sounding more wary now.

'Alright then, it be time thee all became acquainted with thy sparring partners.'

Brockwell's eyes darted straight across to Katren, who had seemed to be avoiding him since their day of combat. He was pleased to find her eyes rested upon him also, a gentle smile of confirmation gracing her lips.

'These partners art permanent and again, not negotiable.'

She called them forth in their set pairs, directing each to their designated places alongside the other around the circle's circumference. As they numbered twelve, including herself, Tory gave them all a position in the circle, corresponding to a number on the sundial in the courtyard. The head of the Dragon marking twelve was Maelgwn's position, so Tory asked the King to take his place.

'Thou art still my partner, I hope,' Maelgwn said on his way past her.

'Eternally,' she assured him. 'Now remember these places when I call thee to meditation, before and after training each day.'

Tory looked at Calin, who appeared miles away as he gazed at Katren. 'Sir Brockwell.' She gave him a

330

start. 'Thou art number one, next to Maelgwn.' Tory felt the two of them still had a few problems to work out. 'Lady Katren, as two, shall be thy partner. For as we have already witnessed, she be a fine challenge for thy capabilities at present.'

The rest of the men laughed and made jest of the match. Yet Katren and Brockwell happily stepped forward, ignoring them all to take their places alongside each other at one and two o'clock.

'Just wait,' Tory warned the rest of them. 'I have not finished yet. Sir Angus, thou art number three and Alma shall be thy partner as number four.' The reason for this match was obvious, as they struck Tory as having the same problem — they were both very shy when it came to dealing with the opposite sex. Tory hoped that if thrown together, they might stumble upon the understanding they lacked and secretly longed for.

Angus and Alma, who'd barely exchanged more than two words, coyly acknowledged each other and quickly took their places. Poor Angus, a few years older than Brockwell and having only a fraction of his experience with women, found himself between two of them.

'Vortipor.'

'Lady.' He stepped forward, ever so eager to see who the Goddess had chosen for him.

'Five o'clock. Cara . . .'

The girl came bounding forward, just as eager. 'At thy service, Majesty,' she announced, admiring the great leader beside her.

'. . . six.'

Vortipor had already led Cara to their places. This made Tory smile; if their ally was going to take a bride, it may as well be one of her own flock.

'My dear Sir Tiernan,' Tory beckoned him closer, with a sweet smile.

'Aye, lady.' He approached, a mite reserved as only Sir Rhys, Sir Cedric and Ione remained.

'Thou art number seven. Ione, thou art eight.'

'Nay!' Tiernan cried in protest, as he and Ione both stubbornly headed to opposite ends of the room.

This was so predictable it made Tory furious. 'Listen, I have very good reason for this which we will discuss later.' Tory lowered her voice. 'But for now I ask that thee kindly take thy places, or take thy leave.'

With a certain degree of disfavour, Tiernan and Ione took their mark.

Sir Cedric was number nine and was positioned to the other side of Ione. Rhys, the other married man, was number ten and was Cedric's partner. Maelgwn had mentioned that the two had had contentions of late, so this was the perfect opportunity to knock that on the head.

Lastly was herself at eleven, beside the King. The Knights of the Round Mat, Tory thought amused, as she took up her position. *Just doesn't have the same ring to it, really.*

Tory instructed them all to take a few deep breaths and still their minds, before taking hold of the hand of the person on either side of them. After much complaining, they finally followed the simple instruction. 'Culprits pay for time wasted.'

'I can vouch for that,' Maelgwn added to lighten the mood.

Tory flashed him a smile, ever thankful for his constant support. She drew another deep breath, of the mind to unite this mismatched bunch by spring if it killed her. 'Take a look around this circle . . . at each other. Thou art going to be spending much time together, and thus it will be far less painful for us all if everyone makes an effort to get along.' Tory's eyes rested on Ione and Tiernan a moment as she said, 'Remember, thou art all on the same side, a team, one whole. Thou art the future teachers, protectors and representatives of Gwynedd, of the Goddess and her mysteries.'

Tory noted they all sat a little taller, proud to have been chosen to be a part of this elite club. If she could just keep this momentum going, all would be well. 'I want everyone here to consider the people seated around this circle to be as sacred to thyself as thy right arm. Regard them, at all times, with the same respect thee would want for thyself. This be the will and the way of the Goddess.'

'So be it,' came the reply, with good cheer from most.

She went on to inform them of the advantages, like the weekends of leisure time, and of the grading system and how it worked. The King and Tory then presented them with their uniforms of white. For now, only Tory's clothes would be black. Her belt was also black, with two white bars. Those who were beginning were given white belts (tenth Kyu), the lowest grade. She considered Katren, Maelgwn, Cara and Alma to be a grade above (ninth Kyu), knowing more than the others, and thus they had belts of white with a yellow bar. She then explained to them all that these grades were only temporary and that the first real grading would take place two months hence on the feast of Samhain.

This feast marked the beginning of the year for the Britons. The official date was the fifth day of Pethboc (November first), and it was celebrated the night before. Tory had decided upon this date when informed that it was also the traditional feast day of the War Goddess.

Sir Tiernan sought out the Queen that same night, and finding her alone in the library, he beseeched to know why she disfavoured him so.

Tory was surprised by his words. 'On the contrary, Sir Tiernan, thou art very dear to me.'

'Then why hast thou placed me with Ione, when thou art well aware we do not like each other.'

'Really? I have spoken with Ione and she hast no problem with the arrangement. She only reacted as she did because you were so obviously opposed to the idea. What's more, I feel quite sure that it be not Ione that thou art objecting to, but rather an idea of her and "her kind" that thou hast built up in thy head.'

'Perhaps.'

'Tiernan.' Tory's tone softened. 'There be another reason, which I hope thee will be sensitive enough to understand. I ask that it will go no further than thyself, as indeed I have not even told Maelgwn.'

This was the tone Sorcha often used, and he looked up, almost expecting to see her. 'Pray speak, Majesty. Thou hast my strictest confidence.'

Tory invited him to sit down. She took a deep breath before beginning and spoke softly so that none might overhear. 'This much I know of Ione for true. She was raped and relieved of her tongue at the tender age of eight. I have asked her about the incident, but she cannot or will not confide in me. Still, I have a fair idea who was responsible.'

Tiernan felt remorse for his rash judgement, and he hadn't yet heard the half of it.

'This be where, I believe, her intense hatred of men — soldiers and nobles in particular — stems from. This also explains why she pretends to be crazy and why she hast built herself up so, to protect herself and others like her who may fall victim to the same fate. Ione be no whore, Tiernan. She can scarce tolerate a man near her, let alone . . .' Tory waved her hand around a second, trying to find an apt way of putting it.

'I did not realise.'

Tory was warmed by his apparent change of heart and placed both her hands upon his. 'Tiernan, thou art one of the most sensitive men I have ever known. I do not expect thee to court the girl, for heaven's sake, but if she can see that not all men art violent, mindless barbarians, perhaps she might lose some of her hatred and fear. I realise this shall require much patience on thy behalf, but I believe thou art well able to cope with the task. The question be, however, art thou prepared to?'

'Aye, Majesty.' He seemed lost in thought for a moment, before he gave half a laugh. 'It would seem I do not understand women half as well as I would like to believe.'

'I would say that most of the men here art of the same mind at present. I do thank thee for thou consideration and kindness.'

'Thou art the considerate one, Majesty.' Tiernan stood to kiss her hand in leaving. 'May I ask, who dost thou suspect the attacker might have been?' The Queen seemed hesitant to answer, so he added, 'I might be able to assist in some way.'

Tory resolved to confide in him, feeling Sorcha quietly influencing the decision. 'Cadogan, and perhaps Caradoc as well.'

Tiernan didn't seem at all surprised by the suggestion. 'I would say that thy instinct serves thee well. I would certainly not put it past either of them, especially in their younger days together.'

'Dost thou think Cadogan loyal to Gwynedd, Tiernan?'

'My good Queen,' he answered, knowing that this had been a point of contention between herself and the King, 'in truth, I think Cadogan be loyal to Cadogan. I shall keep my eyes and ears open for thee.' He bowed and departed.

As she watched the knight leave, she recalled what she'd learnt of him from Sorcha's memories. Tory feared that he still pined for the Queen he'd loved so dearly and, moreover, blamed himself for not being there to save her from Cadfer. This was the reason Tory had placed the two together, for deep down they had the same problem. Ione and Tiernan were both consumed by past tragedies, making them feel unworthy of love, or oblivious to it. This was a pity, as both were intelligent, handsome and deeply caring souls. How sad that people couldn't see through society's facade to behold the simple truth about each other, she thought.

15

FULL MOON

O n the Saturday that marked the masters' first full moon together, Tory woke earlier than usual. Her sleep had been disturbed by a dream, though she couldn't remember the details. Maelgwn was still blissfully asleep beside her, and as it was not very often that he slept so well, she decided to leave him to dream on in peace.

After she'd slung on her training gear, Tory headed down to the huge kitchens to see what she could find to eat. As she crossed the entrance hall, she was surprised to spy Sir Angus slipping out the main doors that led to the inner bailey. Tory moved quietly to see what he was up to at this early hour.

Angus had taken a seat at his appointed position on the sundial, to watch the sun rise in the dawn sky beyond the bailey wall.

'Am I disturbing thee?' Tory asked softly, as Angus seemed miles away. Her voice startled the knight.

'*Sensei.*' He went to stand.

'Please, stay as thou art, Sir Angus. Sorry I gave thee a fright, it was not my intent.'

Angus just couldn't stay seated while he addressed his Queen and *Sensei*, so he stood in any case. 'I did not expect to see anyone else up before sunrise.'

'Nor did I,' Tory smiled, aware of his discomfort, and took a seat on the ground. 'Why art thou up so early, sir, can thee not sleep?'

As he sat down again, his eyes drifted back to the sunrise. Angus didn't have the good looks shared by most of his comrades, yet he was by no means unattractive. And his angular face seemed very open and honest.

'I come here every morn, in homage to the Goddess who hast chosen me as a master.'

'Thy progress be most pleasing to her, Angus. Thee cannot honour her more than by giving her thy all.' Tory didn't really go for the idea of ritual worship; if one was doing what the 'Divine' intended, what greater form of worship was there?

'But there be no chore in it, *Sensei*. I have never known such joy as thy lessons bring me.'

'My dear Sir Angus, in thy short life, thou hast already endured enough perilous tasks to keep the Otherworld and thy country indebted to thee for six lifetimes! Thou dost well deserve the rewards thou art only now beginning to reap.'

'Still,' Angus appeared fit to burst. 'I want to do more for her.'

Tory was pleased to notice that his eyes had drifted to the number four on the sundial, Alma's place in the circle of twelve.

'She hast been so good to me.'

'Well, a man hast got to do, what a man hast got to do, Angus.' She stood, adding with a smile as she departed, 'Please stay, and by all means continue.'

Later that day, Tory and Maelgwn sent Selwyn on his way to Llyn Cerrig Bach to study under Taliesin till spring. The Queen had never seen the young man so excited, and although she knew he was in for the time of his life, she would miss him and his harp through the cold time.

"I shall think of thee, Majesty, every half noon.'

'Oh Selwyn.' She gave him a huge hug, which he returned in earnest. 'I believe the High Merlin shall put my playing to shame.' They drew back to look at each other. 'And besides, thou shalt be so engrossed in thy studies that flowering shall be here before thee even realises. I feel sure Taliesin shall bring thee to visit us on Samhain. We cannot have thee missing all the fun, who shall play the harp for us?'

'I shall be here if I have to come through a blizzard, Majesty.' Selwyn stepped back and bowed to them both. He then took up the reins of the mule that lugged his few belongings and led the animal towards the portcullis.

That same evening, when Maelgwn and Tory were engrossed in a game of chess by the fire, Brockwell came knocking at their chamber door.

'Forgive the intrusion, Majesty, but I was wondering if I may speak with my sister a moment.'

'Of course thee may, Calin.'

When Maelgwn showed no sign of leaving, Tory said, 'I think Calin meant alone, Maelgwn.'

'Why?'

'Why not? Checkmate.'

Maelgwn stood, a little hurt not to be included. 'Again, after dinner perhaps?'

'My pleasure.'

Calin recognised this kind of abrupt behaviour in his friend and wanted to clear up any misunderstanding he might have. 'I be seeking naught but a female's advice, I assure thee.'

'Take thy time,' Maelgwn replied, as when it came to Tory's free time he had been a bit selfish of late. He left the room, closing the door on his way out.

Tory looked at Calin and had to laugh. Everyone else's uniform was perfectly neat, but the way Calin wore his it looked more like pyjamas. His pants were rolled up at the bottom as they were too long, while his shirt hung open and was all caught up at the belt. Calin looked just like Brian after a workout; he had never been shy when it came to flashing his robust body either.

'What?' Brockwell couldn't understand her amusement.

'Thee could have tidied thyself before coming, Calin. What be Maelgwn to think when thee arrives to speak with me appearing thus?'

'But I did.'

Tory laughed again. 'Why art thou here? No wait, let me guess . . . Katren.'

'What am I to do, she hates me.' Calin collapsed onto the chair in front of her.

'Of course she doesn't.'

'She does! She flatly refuses to so much as see me outside of mastery.'

'Perhaps she's just looking for a more permanent relationship than thou art willing to offer.'

'But I asked her to marry me!' he declared, exasperated with the whole affair.

'I said permanent.'

'Awe, thou art no help.'

He was about to storm out when Tory suggested, 'Why dost thou not write to her, Calin?'

Brockwell turned back to her, struck dumb by the notion.

'Anything, a poem, a letter. Maelgwn wrote to me the day we wed and Katren thought it very romantic.' Tory felt that as he would one day be her brother, she did owe him a little advice.

'I am no good at that sort of thing,' Brockwell groaned. 'Would thou help me?'

Tory laughed, considering it was unfair to assist him when she was also advising his foe. 'I am no poet. Why not ask Maelgwn, he be most accomplished.'

'Nay, he would laugh.'

There came a knock on the door and, as luck would have it, the King entered.

'Sorry, we need the chessboard,' Maelgwn said, to explain his intrusion.

342

Tory looked at Calin who shook his head in response. She frowned, for she was determined to bury the hatchet between these two. 'Maelgwn?'

Calin repeatedly motioned her no, but stopped still as Maelgwn turned around.

'Calin requires thy assistance in a small matter, could thee spare him some time?'

'Sure, I owe thee a favour or two if memory serves. What be thy trouble?'

Tory approached the King, sliding her arms about his neck. 'Remember the note thee sent me on the morn of the day we wed?'

'I do.' He wondered what that could possibly have to do with anything.

'Well, Calin be wanting to write something similar and doth not feel himself very gifted with words.'

Maelgwn turned to Calin, delighted. 'Art thou in love, Calin?'

Calin nodded, unable to say it.

'My darling,' Tory said to the King, 'for a scholar thou art totally unaware at times.'

Maelgwn cocked an eye at her. 'The lady in question would not be Katren, by any chance?' He recalled Tory and her maid plotting Calin's entrapment months ago.

'Aye,' Brockwell grumbled. 'The most stubborn, chaste maiden, one could ever come across.'

Maelgwn turned back to Tory. 'My but thou art a crafty woman.'

'The Goddess works in strange ways,' Tory rolled her eyes off to the side, not prepared to plead guilty.

'As far as I be concerned anyway, damn her,' Brockwell said, becoming all hot and bothered.

'Now, Calin, fear not! If thou wants this maiden, thou shalt have her. I feel sure between the two of us, we can have her won by Samhain.'

'That be less than one month hence, Maelgwn, Katren swore she would not wed till spring, at least!' Brockwell replied.

'Indeed, and the Goddess will not take kindly to those who disclose her secrets,' Tory cautioned the King. If Calin thought that his infatuation had been carefully devised and not of his own invention, he would lose interest at once.

'Trust me.' Maelgwn winked at her as he escorted Brockwell to the door. 'End of the month.'

Tory stared at the full moon from her window. Its intensity was apparently being felt by all, as it was not long before Alma, Cara, and Katren arrived at her door.

Katren was overjoyed to hear of the King's suggested date of Samhain, she was sure that she couldn't deny Calin his will, or indeed her own for much longer. 'Oh Majesty, less than a month,' Katren hugged her. 'Thee said I would know this joy, but I did scarce expect it would be so soon.'

'I wish,' Alma sighed.

'Me too,' Cara added.

'Still, there be much work to be done before then. The fact that Calin wants thee be not enough in his case, I fear. He must want thee beyond all others, so again I caution, do not make it too easy for him.'

'I have no intention of it,' Katren told her. 'I plan to enjoy my independence while it lasts.'

'Good for thee. Now,' Tory turned to Alma and Cara, 'what art the two of thee pining about?'

'I find Vortipor too forward, Majesty,' Cara sulked. 'How doth one control a man?'

'Try not leading him on?' Tory fluttered her eyelids at the girl, mimicking her manner of late. 'Thou art rather forward thyself, Cara. He misconstrues thy affections as an open invitation to thy favours. Thee would do better to treat Vortipor as Katren dost Brockwell if thee wishes to win him for thy husband,' she warned.

'But I want him to pursue me.'

'And he shall, whether or not thee gives him any encouragement.'

Cara pouted, dissatisfied with such a boring instruction.

'Listen to her, Cara,' Katren urged. 'The Goddess knows best, believe me.'

'We need to swap,' Alma softly stated her woes. 'I do not think Sir Angus likes me at all.'

Tory was amused, knowing otherwise.

'Majesty please,' Alma asked, 'I like him very much. What should I do?'

By this time, Tory was beginning to feel like a marriage counsellor. She had decided to match all the single folk in male–female pairs, not in an attempt to play Cupid, but rather to give those not in a steady relationship a greater understanding and balance of Yin and Yang in their lives. 'Thee should arise on the morrow before dawn. Go sit on thy number on the sundial in the courtyard, and as thee bears witness to the dawn of a new day, I grant that the Goddess shall bring thee inspiration, Alma.'

The girl's eyes opened wide with intrigue. 'Dost thou really think so, Majesty?'

'Indeed, but thee must not be too impatient with Angus. He be known as a loner and shy of women, so thou shalt have to take a few pages from Cara's book to lure him out.'

All in the room fell silent with the sound of a knock at the door.

'Enter,' Tory bade.

The door burst open and Brockwell came charging forth. He was holding a sheet of parchment in his hands, paying no mind to who was present. 'I did it!' he announced, appearing rather pleased with himself. But as he looked up to see all the women he was startled back a few paces, and hid the parchment behind his back.

'Did what?' Katren asked as she bounded playfully towards him.

The King had followed Brockwell into the room, and was staring sternly at Tory with his arms folded.

'I have said naught of it,' Tory assured Calin and her husband.

The shock of seeing Katren so playful made Calin easy prey, and she succeeded in procuring his master work. 'What be this, then?'

Calin, embarrassed, would have retrieved the letter, but the King quietly motioned him against it.

346

The smug grin slowly slipped from Katren's face and for a magical second she couldn't hide her true self. 'Thee wrote this for me, Calin?' Katren gasped in shock.

'Aye,' he was almost keen to admit, surprised by the effect it seemed to have had on her.

Calin took a step closer so Katren took a step away, her defences raised again. 'I do not believe thou art capable of such feelings,' she coldly concluded. 'The King hast been putting his sweet words to thy pen.'

'Lady Katren, thou hast my word as a King that I did not string two words on that parchment together. In fact, Calin would not even let me read it.'

This proclamation left poor Katren dumbfounded; her image of Brockwell as an unfeeling womaniser was shattered forever. How could she be expected to defend herself till Samhain? 'Then I do owe thee an apology, sir. Thy words art deeply moving.' A lump rose in her throat as she read his letter.

For the first time, Calin was overjoyed to have a woman so upset in his presence. Quite unable to believe that the truth had actually worked, he moved on to plan B. 'If thou doth believe these words art my own and true, I seek to make a request.'

'And what might that be, sir?' Katren asked.

Calin took another step closer, a little more confident, and this time Katren didn't back away from him. 'The King hast suggested we might like to join him and the Queen for dinner and chess this evening?'

Tory looked at Maelgwn, amazed at his ingenuity. 'Brilliant,' she mouthed in approval, and the King gave her the thumbs-up in return.

'Why, I would love to,' Katren answered, taking Calin by the arm. 'Very much.'

'I shall take thy advice, lady,' Cara resolved, watching the love-struck knight lead Katren from the room.

'Aye.' Alma could barely talk, she was so overcome by the sight.

'And what advice might that be?' Maelgwn thought he'd scare them all out of his room.

'Good day, *Sensei*, Majesty,' they both said as they bowed and quickly took their leave.

'Not Angus and Vortipor too?' the King asked. Secretly he was pleased; everyone deserved to feel such bliss as he and his lady.

'Looks that way.'

The young couple joined the King and Queen for dinner, and the evening was well spent with much good mead, fine food and amicable conversation.

Afterwards, Tory watched the pair laughing and chatting by the fire like the oldest of friends. 'There be a lot to be said for the tradition of chaperoning.'

'Aye,' Maelgwn agreed. 'Still, I hope we shan't have to provide this service for every couple in the kingdom.'

'Here, here. But I think we would both agree we have a vested interest in this case.'

'Indeed.'

Maelgwn remained so absorbed in the book he was reading that Tory, who couldn't follow much of the handwritten script, had to inquire, 'What art thou reading about that keeps thee so fascinated?'

'The female reproductive system,' he told her, with glee almost.

'Did someone call?' Calin, a little tipsy, commented to the amusement of them all. He appeared most impressed with himself, as he made his next move on the chessboard. 'Check.'

Katren quickly made a move and announced, 'Checkmate. I win. Now, let us depart and leave our King and Queen in peace.'

'Dost thou feel like a walk?' Brockwell jumped to his feet to assist her up, inspired by the idea.

'Perhaps.' She took his hand to lead him away. 'Thee understand, Majesties, that the last thing Calin requires be any more information on the female reproductive system.'

'Goodnight.' Calin waved on his way out, glad to follow her anywhere.

'A lovely couple,' Tory commented, admiring their work. 'Now, why on earth art thou reading about reproductive organs? If thou art wondering why Gwynedd doth not yet have an heir, it dost take at least nine months.'

'Tell me something,' Maelgwn inquired politely, ignoring the fact that she was mocking him. 'If a woman hast one turn of the moon cycle and we have been married well over that now, when art thou due?'

Tory's good cheer waned, she had been so busy of late that she hadn't even given the matter a thought. Her hands gripped her face as she admitted with a tortured strain, 'Ages ago!'

'Art thou ever late?'

'No!' she whined, thumping the lounge with both her fists. 'Never.'

'Praise the Goddess!' Maelgwn jumped to his feet, letting loose a laugh. He tossed the book aside and took hold of Tory. 'That be it then, thou art with child already!' The King noticed that his wife didn't appear to be as happy as expected. 'Tory, thou could not make me more proud.'

'I know.' She pulled away from him, unable to look him in the eye. She didn't want to put a dampener on his dream, but he wasn't the one who had to give birth. 'But thy greatest infatuation of late, would seem in truth my worst nightmare.'

'But thus our marriage shall be recognised.'

The tone in Maelgwn's voice said it all to her, *'tis not his want of a child that motivates him*. 'Legal marriage or not, favoured or not, I shall do whatever I must to stay with thee, just as thou hast done for me,' she said, looking at him, her face suddenly pale. 'It be just that, I know how dangerous childbirth really be, Maelgwn, not like these poor woman who enter into it in ignorance.'

Maelgwn had never seen Tory frightened before and as he moved forward in an attempt to comfort her, she kept the distance between them. 'Even in my time, I would have a difficult labour with thy child, but here . . .' She slowly shook her head, petrified by the thought.

'Tory, stop right there, or thee will work thyself into a state,' Maelgwn quietly cautioned her. 'Dost thou think I have not considered this? Thou hast no need to fear birthing here. I know the best midwife thee could wish for, in any age.'

Although Tory was fairly sure Maelgwn still wasn't getting the full picture, she decided to give the King the benefit of the doubt. 'Who then?'

'Why Taliesin, of course.'

With the mere mention of the High Merlin's name, her fear dwindled. *God knows what tricks he might have up his sleeve.* Tory gave a slight smile at the notion. 'Was he midwife to Sorcha?'

'Aye, and she was no better equipped than thee,' the King answered, simply beaming with delight. 'I shall never allow any harm to befall thee.'

'What dost thou mean?' Tory pulled away, making sport of his ardour. 'I do not want to get fat, Maelgwn. I have never been overweight in my whole life.'

'Tory, it will not be fat. It will be flesh and blood. Thine and mine — ours.'

Tory relaxed, so pleased she'd married this extraordinary man. 'What if the baby is a girl?'

'I should love her just as well as her mother, I expect. But he not be a girl.' Maelgwn sounded very sure about it, and with a slap of his hands he returned to the book. 'I can hardly wait to make the announcement, Taliesin will be beside himself.'

'I want thee to know, Maelgwn, thou art the only man in this entire universe I would do this for,' Tory said solemnly.

'And I do love thee for it.'

The King's new wife falling with child so soon would be regarded by all as an Otherworld blessing — a sign of both a fortunate reign for Maelgwn, and of rich harvests ahead for Gwynedd and her allies.

Consulting an old calendar of her own, Tory figured that the baby was due in mid-June (Duir), just before she was to return home.

So much for the hope of giving birth in comfort, she decided. Still, Taliesin was not a bad consolation. *No fear.*

16

SAMHAIN

The festival of Samhain, better known to future generations as Hallowe'en, was only two days away and tension amongst the masters was high as they approached grading.

Sir Brockwell, under Maelgwn's guidance, had been favourably courting Katren. Finally, he plucked up the nerve to pop the question for the second time, asking her to marry him at the forthcoming feast. To Calin's great amazement, Katren accepted and they would be wed the following week.

As fate would have it, however, this arrangement was short-lived. Brockwell's recollection of the tradition of taking one's intended to thy bed the week before the wedding, thwarted him within the hour. He tried as subtly and as sweetly as he knew how to entice Katren's favours from her in advance, but she only took offence to the suggestion. She accused her 'briefly intended' of being fickle, presumptuous, and displaying a total lack of respect for the Goddess. Katren promptly withdrew her acceptance, vowing she would never consider him as a suitor again.

Calin was crushed, and he'd failed to sway her in the two days that had since passed. His written words of explanation, which had proved far more eloquent than anything he could say, had not managed to appease her this time.

Tory tried to allay her fears on Calin's behalf, explaining that even King Maelgwn endeavoured to uphold the old tradition, but Katren was adamant. She explained that if he didn't respect her now, he never would. ''Twas not the act so much, more that he expected it — as if I owed it to him. If becoming his wife means favours on demand for life, I do not want to be wed. It be not that I do not find Calin attractive, as thou art well aware. But right now, my will be my own. Why should I give up my freedom to satisfy what is obviously nothing more than a lustful whim?'

'A lustful whim, Katren? Be that really all thee believes Calin holds for thee?'

'Aye, I do. I think to marry the man I love would be entrapment. In fact, the only way I shall ever really know if Calin loves me for sure, would be to do as he wishes. Then at least when he discovers that *this great love* he boasts for me disappears upon consummation, he will thank me for not trapping him. If he continues to pursue me then perhaps it be love. Now I see why the other women who have lusted after Calin have resolved thus.'

Tory couldn't argue with her reasoning; the decision was Katren's to make. Since the Queen had become the confidant of so many, she tried to listen and advise without interfering with anyone's views.

Despite Tiernan's constant efforts to befriend Ione, no amount of patience and understanding seemed enough; Ione had not warmed to him at all. Tory thought this rather strange as they appeared so in tune when they worked together, especially during kata. Still, the more determined Ione was to ignore Sir Tiernan's goodwill, the more determined he became to win her trust. Tiernan was going to see this woman smile, or even better laugh, if it killed him, and Tory had faith that he would finally succeed.

Vortipor wasn't disillusioned by receiving a cold response from Cara of late. He was charming, good-looking and quite used to getting what he wanted. The young maiden was delighted when he merely doubled his efforts to impress and pursue her. A vague suggestion of marriage was underlying his advances, Cara felt sure of it.

After following her *Sensei*'s instruction, Alma took to meeting Angus at the sundial in the courtyard every morn at sunrise. Much to Tory's satisfaction, the two had actually realised why she had matched them as a team and were using it to their individual advantage. They'd agreed not to become romantically involved just yet, as neither wished to be distracted from their studies. Thus, with the aim of reaching the highest standards, Alma and Angus spent most of their free time together practising, meditating and talking, content to avoid the misadventures of others.

The weather grew ever colder, and a howling wind ripped at the trees outside the long windows of the Great Hall. As grading was nearly upon them and the masters were all so malcontent for one reason or another, Tory decided to try something a little different this morning and prepared herself for a drama. Ione was late to arrive, probably because of the frightful weather. She refused to stay overnight in the castle with the others, due to her aversion to soldiers. Her absence gave Tory time to brief Sir Tiernan on her intended exercise and the special part he may have to play in it.

Rhys and Cedric seemed a mite perturbed when the Queen sent for their wives. Tory didn't attempt to ease their troubled minds, concluding that the pair of chauvinists deserved to sweat a little.

Everyone had gathered when Ione finally joined them, wet and windblown after her trek up from the village. She begged forgiveness by bowing before Tory, holding her cupped hands to her heart.

'My dear Ione. I do wish thee would stay in the house with us. Thou shalt catch thy death making thy way up here every morn, come snowfall.'

Again Ione gestured that she was sorry, but motioned a firm no, before she took up her place between Tiernan and Cedric.

Tory led the masters through a meditation. Today they were exploring the seven chakras located in the subtle body, where the spine is found in the human physical form. 'These seven concentrated centres of energy convert Otherworld, or cosmic, energy into body energy, and vice versa. Thy chakra system transcends the constraints of time and space. It connects thee to the Otherworld, thus uniting all of creation into one force. This be what I mean when I say that we art all one,' Tory explained.

After much deep breathing and chanting, all seemed relaxed and elated. Satisfied that this was as amiable as they were going to get, Tory asked them to stand and face their partners. She requested that Jenovefa take a place in front of Rhys, likewise with Mabel and her husband, Cedric.

'I have noticed that thou art all seeming rather tense,' Tory began to a mixed reaction. 'Thus today we art going to try something a little different. Please allow me to explain.'

Tory walked into the centre of the circle and Maelgwn followed, coming to stand behind her. 'When I give the word, I want all of thee to hug thy partner as thee would a wounded child.'

There were a few disgruntled murmurs until Tory reminded them, 'Anyone who wishes to object be free to leave.' She waited for silence again. 'Now thy aim in exchanging this energy be to comfort the other person to the very best of thy ability. I would like to stress *this be not* for thy sexual stimulation, gentlemen. I expect as adults thee will be well aware of the difference.'

They all laughed as Tory drew the long drapes to dim the light in the room. She had participated in similar exercises in the past, during various self-development courses, and even if there were no truly amazing breakthroughs this day she considered every person in the room could use a good hug.

'Face thy partners.' Silence again fell. Tory nodded to Maelgwn by the CD player, and soft ambient music began to filter through the room, creating a perfect mood.

'My instruction be this . . .' Tory said, her tone as soft and soothing as the music, 'thou art to hold thy partner, eyes closed and in silence, until I ask thee to stop. No matter what may be going on around thee, under no circumstances art thou to open thy eyes or let go of thy partner. Be aware of how this exercise makes thee feel, perhaps it will stir a memory, perhaps an emotion, but only the truth shall serve thee well. For if one cannot face the truth about one's self, one can never expect to understand another. This interaction be part of the quest of the *spiritual* warrior who strives for total self-awareness and understanding. Please begin.'

Katren and Brockwell, who were still not on speaking terms, seemed somewhat reluctant. So in a gentle voice, Tory advised the whole gathering, 'Forget the past, forget the future, there be only here and now. We all have troubles and sorrows in our lives, but just for this moment I want thee to relax and forget them. Forget from whom thou art seeking comfort at this time, they art whoever thee wants them to be.' Tory smiled as Calin and Katren now appeared more absorbed.

Angus and Alma stood perfectly still, smiling blissfully in their embrace. As they appeared to have nothing to resolve, Tory instructed that they could stop.

Neither flinched and with a giggle, remained as they were.

Tory moved on to Vortipor and Cara. 'For holding a child thus, thee could be charged, sir,' she commented quietly in jest, removing Vortipor's hand from Cara's behind.

Vortipor smiled, raising his eyebrows, but didn't stray from Tory's instruction and remained silent with his eyes closed.

Tiernan and Ione, funnily enough, seemed quite content, gently swaying to and fro to the music. When Tory had given them leave to begin Ione had seemed hesitant, yet she was quite relaxed now. How odd, Tory thought. She had felt sure this little exercise would spark some diverse reaction in Ione. Perhaps she was wrong about Ione's motives?

Rhys and Jenovefa had opted to sit on the floor and thankfully appeared to have overcome their differences. It had not been Tory's intention to divide the pair when she'd invited Jenovefa's interest in her craft, she'd only wanted her to feel included. She was about to give them leave when suddenly Katren burst into tears. Tory knew Calin was uncomfortable with such behaviour in women, and held back to see if he could cope with the situation on his own.

Even though Katren pushed away from him, Calin wouldn't let her go. He broke Tory's instruction, determined to console her and asked, 'What upsets thee?'

'Thou dost,' she sobbed, thumping his chest with her fists, too dismayed to put any strength into the struggle. 'Thou art the one . . . doth thou not see?' She broke away from him. 'Forgive me *Sensei*.' She bowed quickly to Tory and ran from the room.

Calin looked to Tory, at a loss for what to do. Tory indicated for him to go after her.

'*Sensei*,' Tiernan drew Tory's attention to Ione, who had suddenly begun to struggle. When she could not break free from his restraint, the woman began to shriek.

I was right after all, Tory thought, as she approached the pair.

Tiernan held Ione firm, as Tory had instructed, and spoke gently to calm her.

'Sshh, thou art fine.' Tiernan persisted warmly, despite Ione's protest to the contrary.

Tory asked her to look her in the eye. With a grunt, Ione ceased her struggle. 'What disturbs thee so?' the Queen said, wiping the hair and perspiration from the woman's forehead.

Ione shook her head repeatedly and began to push away again. Then with one almighty screech, she collapsed into tears.

Sir Tiernan, who was handling the situation very well, was close to tears himself. Tory smiled to him in quiet support as she gently rubbed Ione's back. As Ione began to settle and her breathing grew more regular, Tory was gripped by fear. Her heart began to pound, the room rushed away from her, and she found herself running scared through a forest.

'*Sensei*?' Tiernan called as she began to tremble, and beads of sweat formed on her skin.

'Stay away,' Tory uttered, no longer aware of their presence as she dropped to her knees.

Ione's weeping ceased and her eyes opened wide in recognition. She gripped the Queen's hand in desperation.

'Tory?' Maelgwn approached.

'Nay! Stay away!' She cried out, her eyes open and staring straight ahead.

Kicking and screaming she struggled to break free from her attackers, who were boys of no more than fourteen or fifteen years old.

'Hey, brothel bitch, save your energy,' a very young Caradoc advised her, with a sharp slap to the face. 'We're only just getting started.' He unbelted his trousers, then forced his pelvis between her legs.

'We shouldn't be doing this,' she heard the boy behind her say, as he restrained her arms. 'What if she tells somebody?'

'I always said thou wast a whimp, Cadogan,' Caradoc snarled, looking back to his victim and gripping her about the neck to draw her face closer. 'She won't utter a word.' He opened his mouth wide as it converged on hers.

Tory began to shake her head, letting loose a bloodcurdling scream, before she began to choke.

The King dragged her away from Ione and she broke from her trance. She freed herself from Maelgwn's restraint to run back and embrace her harrowed pupil.

'I saw them, Ione, I saw their faces.' Tory was barely able to breathe from the shock of the horrid scene she'd just witnessed. 'I know them, I know what they have done and they will pay. I swear to thee, Ione, they will pay.'

Ione collapsed into her arms, not knowing whether to laugh or cry from relief. Though tears streamed down her face, Ione's smile had warmth.

Tory looked at Tiernan, who appeared most gratified by what he'd helped to accomplish this morning. He took Ione in his arms, rocking her ever so slightly. Tory left her in Tiernan's embrace, giving the others their leave. 'Those who wish to break may do so.' Nobody moved.

'Ooh!' Jenovefa gasped in pain. 'The babe . . .'

Rhys was besieged by panic and managed to incite the whole room into a state of alarm within seconds.

Brockwell pursued Katren to the women's quarters. Once inside she closed the door behind her. Under normal circumstances, Brockwell would not have entered unannounced. In fact, he hadn't been inside these chambers since he was knighted. However, as he had the leave of the Queen this day, he barged in after her. 'Katren, I give up, thou art driving me insane.'

'Thou art not allowed in here!'

'Katren please, talk to me. I so want to understand. Be my embrace so horrible, did I hurt thee?'

Her stance weakened, the tears silently falling from her eyes. 'Nay,' she confessed, 'Thou art the one I wish would hold me all my life.'

'Then marry me!'

'I cannot do that, Calin.'

He rolled his eyes, 'In the name of the Goddess, Katren, why not?'

In the midst of her hysteria, Katren unexpectedly found some clarity and she replied, 'Because thou art not in love with me.'

'Nay, Kat—'

Katren placed her fingers to his lips to silence him. 'Aye, it be true enough, and I can prove it,' she whispered, before bestowing on him the most luscious of kisses.

This was quite a change for Katren, and Calin was more than happy to go with it. But when she slid her hands inside his jacket, he backed off. 'What art thou doing?'

'I want to Calin, really. It be alright.'

'So thou shalt marry me?'

'Nay.'

Her reply made him frown. 'Art thou saying thee will be my mistress, but not my wife?'

Katren nodded to confirm.

Brockwell paused, appearing rather bemused. He slipped Katren's hands from his chest and stepped away from her. 'Nay, Katren, I shall have thee as my wife or not at all.'

'Calin, see reason! Why should I be different from the others? If thou would just take me thee would find that thou art not really in love with me at all, and thus we will be saved a lifetime of heartache.'

'How can thee say that? I have sworn on my honour that I love thee, why will thee not believe me?' He took hold of her. 'Should I swear by the elements for thee, Katren? Send me on a quest to prove my love, anything, just tell me what I should do.'

She gently held her hand to his face and smiled as she caressed his skin. 'Make love to me.'

The answer brought a tear to his eye. Maelgwn had warned him many times that his past would catch up with him, but only now did Calin truly realise what the Prince had meant. Here he had finally found the one woman to whom he could remain loyal, yet no amount of assurances would convince her of it.

'Katren, come quick,' Alma called, racing into the room, too preoccupied with her news to notice she'd interrupted anything. 'It's Jenovefa, her water hast broken.'

Katren looked at Brockwell. She was reluctant to leave him when he appeared so forlorn.

'I am not going anywhere.' He gave her leave to tend to the emergency. 'Thee should go.'

For nine hours the Queen remained at Jenovefa's side. Ione had fetched Old Hetty from the village to attend the birth. The old woman had delivered more children than everyone else in the area put together, and Tory felt Jenovefa was in the best of care.

This shall be me before too long, Tory gulped, as she watched Jenovefa, sweating and screaming through her agony. *I must be insane*, Tory concluded as she left the room.

'How doth she fare, Majesty?' Rhys was upon her as soon as she emerged.

Tory smiled. 'As well as one could expect, sir, but she be only halfway there at best. So thee may as well get some rest.'

'Who could sleep? I want to see her.'

'I would strongly advise against that. At this stage, Rhys, I think she would probably kill thee. Tiernan, would thee take Rhys and fill him with food and mead until he passes out.'

'With pleasure.' Tiernan took hold of him.

'Nay, I do not want —' Rhys protested, but Tiernan was by far the stronger of the two.

'That be an order, sir, not advice,' Tory raised her voice, too tired to argue with him.

'How art thou faring?' Maelgwn approached to ask.

The look she gave him implied that it was a stupid question. 'That shall be me in seven months.'

'Aye.' He smiled.

'Thee need not appear so happy about it. Thee shall owe me big for the favour, believe me.'

'Indeed, I shall,' he agreed, in good spirits. 'But right now thou art tired, and well in need of food and rest thyself. Come.' The King could see a protest surfacing. 'That be an order,' he cautioned, leading Tory off down the hall.

Maelgwn let Tory sleep till after dawn the next day. When he entered their chambers to wake her, he found the Queen tossing about and saturated in sweat. 'Tory, Tory wake up, thou art dreaming again.'

Her eyes opened wide and she sat up. 'Jenovefa's babe?' she asked in a panic.

'Jenovefa be fine and very close now,' he assured her, surprised to see her scrambling out of bed. 'What be the matter?'

'I have had another prophecy,' she explained, pulling on her clothes.

'What hast thou seen?'

'Blood.' She tied her belt and made for the door. 'Lots of it.'

Tory arrived at Jenovefa's side, finding all as it should be.

'Majesty.' Jenovefa reached her arm out anxiously for Tory.

'I am so sorry, Jenny. Maelgwn did not wake me.' Tory clenched her hand tight.

'The King only be watching out for his own heir,' Jenovefa uttered. She gasped for breath, too fatigued to scream anymore.

It seemed that she had something to say, if only she could find a moment's peace.

'I have changed my mind, Majesty. I wish to study under thee, with my husband's permission or no. I will not spend the next twenty years thus,' she panted heavily, a groan escaping her lips.

Mabel, one of the other noble women of the court, gently wiped her brow with a cool cloth. 'Shh Jen. She be delirious,' she informed Tory.

'I do not think so somehow,' Tory replied.

'Nay, I am not!' She pushed Mabel away. 'Majesty please. Better I die now than my life amount to naught but that of a glorified mare.'

'Jenovefa! What art thou saying?' Mabel, the mother of four, was horrified.

'Thee understands, Majesty.' Jenovefa ignored Mabel's protest, awaiting the Queen's word.

'Aye.' Tory politely asked Mabel to fetch some more water. Once she'd closed the door behind her, Tory consoled Jenovefa. 'I be not sure how we shall get around thy husband, but we shall work something out.'

Although the agony of the moment seized her, Jenovefa managed to smile.

'Push child . . . I see the head,' Hetty instructed.

With that, Jenovefa screamed with all her might.

'What be going on in there?' Rhys demanded to know, heading for the door.

Maelgwn and Tiernan advanced to stop him. 'Tory shall let thee know as soon as there be any development,' Maelgwn instructed, leading him back to his seat.

'But listen to her!'

'That be nothing.'

They turned to find Taliesin and Selwyn striding down the hall.

'Thee ought to have heard Sorcha giving birth to this one,' the High Merlin chuckled, making light of a serious situation.

'High Merlin, praise the Goddess thou art here. I think she be dying!' Rhys raced to meet him.

'Nay.' Taliesin rested a hand on his shoulder, sending surges of calming energy through the expectant father. 'She be in agony, I'll grant, but fear not, she shall survive.' The High Merlin looked at the King, his old face filled with pride. 'And there be more congratulations in order, I believe.' He embraced Maelgwn as he had not done since the Prince was a small boy, overwhelmed with delight.

'I suspected the news might please thee.'

'Pleased! I couldn't be more so. I am to be his tutor, of course?'

'Who else?' Maelgwn answered with a smile.

'Please, High Merlin, can this not wait?' The screams from his chambers caused Rhys to fret more.

Suddenly all was was quiet. The men held their breath, looking to the closed door, until the sound of a babe crying caused them to break into rejoicing. Rhys rushed through the well-wishers as the door opened.

Tory came forth, quietly closing the door behind her. 'It be a boy.' She burst into tears, as did Rhys as he embraced her, elated and relieved.

'A son! May I see them?'

'Jenovefa asked that thee give her a moment, but I assure thee, both mother and child art in fine health.'

'So, by what name shall thy son be known, Rhys?' Maelgwn handed the proud father a goblet of mead to toast the new babe's health.

'We have agreed on Gawain.' The name meant hawk of battle.

'Splendid choice.'

Everyone raised their goblets as Taliesin made a toast. 'To the young Lord Gawain of Din Lligwy. May he find beauty, wisdom and joy in life. And may the Goddess bless him with the health and strength to do his father and his forefathers proud.'

'So be it!' One and all resounded as their goblets met.

The herds and flocks of Aberffraw had been gathered together over the weeks prior to Samhain. The choice animals were spared for breeding purposes, but the majority had been killed the night before the feast for the winter stores. The King and Taliesin had both seen this as the possible inspiration for Tory's dream. As Taliesin had experienced no such premonition, he felt that in this case Tory was perhaps confusing prophesy with a nightmare. But the Merlin did not say so in front of her. He explained that he felt the Queen so in tune with the Goddess and the land that she must have sensed the panic of the beasts led to the slaughter.

Tory had seen naught but blood, gushing down walls, stairs, floors and eventually all over the earth, staining everything in its path a coat of red, so dark it appeared almost black. As life in the castle was calm now and Jenovefa and her child were well, Tory accepted this conclusion.

By evening every fire in the kingdom would be extinguished, only to be rekindled from a ceremonial fire lit by a druid. From this fire, others would be lit in the outer bailey where the folk from the surrounding common could offer sacrifices to the Goddess in the hope of gaining good fortune for the coming year.

Samhain was a very magical and spiritual time for the people of Britain, for it was thought to be the day when the Otherworld became visible to all humanity. Under the veil of night, the ghosts of the dead set out to wreak vengeance on the living, and evil marched unbridled across the land. Hence everyone was very aware of their behaviour at this time; if one angered the spirits, one would surely bring misfortune upon themself and their kin.

This last day of the year had a sacred name of its own in the darker mystic circles. So dreaded by the ancients was it, that its true name was never uttered aloud and its rituals were never committed to parchment. The Nameless day, when an old King was dead and a bright new King not yet born, was especially sacred to the dark Queen in her destructive aspect. The shadow of the triple Goddess, and patron of all that is unwholesome in nature was a deity that thrived on humanity's most selfish desires. Like her day, she too was nameless to the pure of heart. For once invoked she was a negative force to be reckoned with, as Sir Cadogan was about to discover.

Cadogan had been drinking with his old comrades, Sir Vaugnan and Sir Jeven, who were also stationed at Degannwy for the cold seasons. Later that evening, Cadogan, who was good looking in a snakish kind of way, had managed to win the favour of a young maiden staying at the citadel, and had whisked her back to his chambers for a night of mischief. Samhain, like Beltaine, was renowned for it.

The girl collapsed onto his bed as intoxicated as the knight, her arms outstretched high above her head. 'Do what thou will, sir,' she invited, as he crawled on top of her, eager to oblige.

Cadogan fumbled with her clothes, his fingers lacking any coordination due to all the mead he'd consumed. The girl giggled as she returned his affection, yet as his lips caressed her neck she began to quiver and shake. Cadogan, assuming this was due to his personal magnetism, thought nothing of it until she suddenly thrust him from her.

'Get off me!' Vanora's harsh voice thundered, as she raised herself and stood beside the bed.

'Art thou playing me for sport, child?' Cadogan was rather annoyed.

'Imbecile, it be me, Princess Vanora. Remember? Daughter of the great Chiglas? So much for thy proclaimed love for me and desire to assume the role of my father's heir.' Vanora was most displeased, as she observed the body of the maid she had seized.

It was Vanora's voice alright and her manner, yet it was the same maiden he'd been entertaining all night who stared him back. 'Princess Vanora! How can this be?'

'Never mind how I did it,' Vanora commanded. 'What of thy vow?'

Cadogan finally got a grip on the situation and fell to his knees before the maiden. 'But thee called my love a farce, claiming thy heart was already lost to Prince Caradoc.'

'Well, I have changed my mind. My father hast decided Caradoc to be a mindless cretin, and thus unfit to succeed him. Hence he be most certainly unfit to claim my hand.'

'Oh Majesty.' He took her hand to kiss it, but she withdrew it immediately.

'Not so fast,' she walked away from him, observing his quarters with apparent distaste. 'I have consulted with the dark forces and my father on the subject of thy origins, Cadogan. It would seem that thou also hast the right to claim the title and power of a prince, as thy father was the once King of Dyfed. Apparently he was unjustly done out of his title and kingdom by the Desi Clan, with the help of the damn Romans.'

'Vortipor,' Cadogan uttered the name with a vengeance. 'Art thou sure of this?'

'Of course I am!' Vanora snapped. 'Dost thou think for a moment that we could even consider thee if it were not the case?' Her tone and manner became more ardent. 'So, if thou dost still desire to lay claim to my hand, Sir Cadogan, to rule Powys one day in my father's stead and claim back thy rightful seat in Dyfed, then,' she moved closer, in encouragement, 'my father, as with Caradoc, hast set thee a task to prove thy worthiness. If thou art successful, then my hand and title shall be thine.'

Cadogan grinned broadly. In his drunken stupor her proposal sounded even more enticing than the maid's. 'Whatever service thy mighty father requires of me, consider it done. Just name the quest.'

Vanora smiled broadly, pointing to his bedside table where a tiny black bottle slowly materialised. 'It hast been made known to us that the new Queen of the Dragon, the War Goddess, already carries his heir. King Chiglas wants the Otherworld warrior from the future for himself. It be his wish that, come the first snowfall, thee take this bottle and make with it to Aberffraw. Then, without alerting any to the fact, give the contents to the Queen.'

'What will it do to her?' Cadogan didn't seem as keen now.

'It will sedate her for the journey to Powys and help rid us of Maelgwn's troublesome seed.'

'I do not know about this, the risk involved in just getting her out of Aberffraw unnoticed be very high indeed.' He seemed to have sobered somewhat, giving the matter closer consideration. 'Let alone the trip back to Powys! The mountains will be perilous come snowfall, I cannot guarantee she will survive.'

'My love.' Vanora crouched beside him, aroused that Cadogan, unlike Caradoc, actually seemed to be mildly intelligent. 'My father shall send a boat that will await thee at the end of the Menai. This can bring thee all the way back to Powys — no mountains, just a short ride inland to our capital, Arwystli. What could be easier?'

'It shan't be easy, I assure thee.' Cadogan, knowing Tory better than Vanora or her father did, thought it would be near impossible. Yet, he had so much to gain.

'But thou art so smart, Cadogan. Thou hast not been caught out yet for the treacherous leech thou art.'

'True.' He took hold of her around the waist as the Princess seemed rather amiable at present.

'So thee shall do it?'

He nodded.

'Excellent. Oh, there be one more thing, if I may?' she flirted, aware this was the only way to persuade him.

'Ask and it shall be done.'

'We also want her maid, Katren, as we might need her for persuasive purposes.'

'Wise move.' Cadogan considered he could use her to the same end.

'Stay in thy room this night and take advantage of this silly child, as she shall prove thy perfect alibi.'

'But we have planned nothing for this night, why should I need an alibi?' Cadogan was afraid he might have missed something.

Vanora smiled, dropping her voice to a whisper. 'So that when Caradoc escapes, thou shalt not be suspected. King Chiglas wishes to punish him for his bungling. Caradoc, of course, will believe his love coming to his rescue. But after he hast made it all the way back to my father at Arwystli, he shall find a very different reception awaits him.' The pair grinned mischievously.

As Cadogan broke from a kiss with her, he was startled to find the young maid had regained her own drunken sensibilities.

'How did we end up on the floor?' The girl burst into laughter.

The knight didn't bother with an explanation.

Come grading day, the masters had burnt off much of their nervous energy at the Samhain celebrations. As they'd also had a day to rest and recuperate, they were all in a much improved frame of mind.

Tory began with a simple meditation to relax them. 'The perfect balance of mind, body and nature be what I expect to see this day. We have come a long way in just two months, so remember what I have taught thee. Remain calm, balanced and focused. I wish thee well.'

Percival was seated at a small desk with pen and parchment, keeping score and jotting down the Queen's notes as she discreetly conveyed them to him.

Tory ran each master through what they'd learnt: kata, Tae-kwon-do exercises, kicks, and strikes on the bag. As this grading was a test of the self, competition through sparring wasn't a factor. But when the masters had completed the program, they were given the option of taking a breaking test.

Tory had been training Maelgwn in this technique, known as Shiwari, since their first lesson. The King had spent many hours hitting the straw pad, which hardened the hands, fists, and outer edge of the foot. Most of the masters had taken up the practice, yet none bar the King and Queen had ever tried it out on a wooden board.

Some of the masters declined the test when informed that if they did not succeed, it would be deducted from their grade. This stipulation differentiated between those who truly believed it within their capabilities and those who did not; this belief was essential if one was to succeed.

Most of the men opted to test their new skills, except for Rhys and Angus. Only Ione stepped forward to represent the women. Tory knew Katren was procrastinating, but her fear of loss prevented her from stepping forward. Tory thought this a shame, as Katren was quite capable and the planks were not very thick.

First up was Brockwell, as he was so sure of himself.

'Calm and focus thyself, Calin,' Tory instructed gently. 'Thought and action must be one, no hesitation.' At the point where Brockwell unleashed his power, Tory realised that she was witnessing the warrior she'd known in Brian. A tear escaped her eye as she watched his unmistakeable technique, the wood splintering apart under the force of his blow.

Vortipor, who hadn't been concentrating from the start, was next. The trouble with Vortipor was that everything was a game to him, thus he accomplished naught but a bruise for attempting the feat.

Cedric also failed. Tory knew that he'd only attempted the blow because he felt he had something to prove to everyone, which subsequently he did not.

Ione had no problem with the test. Tory's heart warmed when Ione then encouraged Tiernan with a light thump on the shoulder and a smile, as it came his turn. The knight, in the quiet realisation that his own personal mission had been accomplished, stepped forward confidently to face the breaking test. When Tiernan accomplished the deed, he and Ione actually hugged each other voluntarily. He then took the liberty of declaring them the supreme team, as they were the only pair to successfully perform the task.

The last to step forward was the King, who did so with a huge smile on his face. 'Two,' he motioned, holding up two fingers.

'Two!' Tory just adored his spunk, challenging him in fun only as she felt confident he could do it.

'Aye.'

Tory gave him the go ahead. He has worked so hard on this skill, she quietly prayed, Goddess grant him victory.

His subjects watched breathlessly as the King brought his closed fist down to shatter the two pieces of timber, and a round of applause was raised to commend the achievement. With this the examination was over.

After tallying the points scored throughout the day, Tory gathered her students in the circle to award them their new colours. She first addressed those who'd made the least rate of progress.

Cara had jumped a half grade from white belt-yellow tip (ninth Kyu), to yellow (eighth Kyu). Her progress and fighting style were good, but her concentration was not. Rhys, Cedric, Vortipor, and Angus had jumped a grade from white (tenth Kyu) to a yellow belt.

Katren and Alma achieved a whole grade, from ninth Kyu to a yellow belt-green tip (seventh Kyu). Calin, Tiernan and Ione, who'd proven themselves outstanding, progressed from their white belt (tenth Kyu) up one and a half grades to the yellow belt-green tip (seventh Kyu).

The star of the day was, of course, the Dragon himself, who proudly stepped up to receive his green belt. Maelgwn had jumped one and a half grades to sixth Kyu. He tied on the new belt that represented all those months of hard work, and wore it with great pride.

17

THE FÍVE
DARK DAYS

Over a month had passed since the news of
Caradoc's escape reached Aberffraw, and still
the soldiers at Degannwy had failed to find any
trace of the treasonous prince, nor had they determined
how he'd escaped.

'Cadogan had a solid alibi,' Sir Vaugnan, who had
been keeping an eye on the knight's movements for the
King, told the court. The guard who held the prison
keys had been in attendance all night, and vowed he'd
not lapsed into sleep at any time. Still, come the
morning after Samhain, Caradoc was not to be found in
the supposedly impermeable oubliette.

The report had set Maelgwn on edge for a week or
so. But when Caradoc didn't rear his ugly head to
avenge him, the King felt he could safely assume that

his half-brother had run back to Powys where he would hide out until the snow had passed. The next day, the nineteenth of December by a modern calendar, marked the first of the five 'Dark Days'. The Britons called this five-day period of sorrowing, when time stood still, the dead of the year. Soon the land would be covered in snow for the sleep time, better known as burgeoning.

Maelgwn was rather pleased at the prospect that he could beat Caradoc senseless all over again come spring. For his brother would most certainly return then, to atone for his past failures and imprisonment.

Come dawn of the first of the five days of sorrowing, Tory awoke from a frenzied dream.

'Tory, what ails thee?' Maelgwn hugged her close, trying to calm her.

'Blood, so much blood . . .' She could not convey how nauseous the vision made her feel. But this time there had been something else — Tory recalled a face. 'I saw a man! At least I think it was a man. He looked more like a slug.' She shuddered. 'And he was reaching for me.'

Maelgwn's embrace tightened, and he went very quiet.

Tory could sense that fear of loss in him again, and pulled back a little. 'Who be it that I see, Maelgwn? Be it Chiglas?'

'Aye.' He hesitated then agreed, 'There be no mistake by thy description of him. Caradoc may have told him something of thee.'

'But he knows little. None of Chiglas' kindred saw me fight. The only way Chiglas could know anything of my skills or origins would be if *Cadogan* had said something to him.'

'Thou art right. Still, a dream cannot be deemed as proof of his treason, Tory, and Taliesin warned thy dreams could be misleading whilst thou art with child.'

'Oh please, Maelgwn, don't patronise me. I do not wish to start arguing about Cadogan again, I am just telling thee what I saw.' She climbed out of bed, annoyed with him.

Taliesin had also warned that Tory would be much moodier while she was pregnant, so the King was patient and held a good mood. 'Of course. I shall be alert, I promise.'

'I am sorry. I did not mean to snap. Oh look!' Her whole manner softened as she looked outside.

'Aye, an early snow.' Maelgwn watched with a smile as Tory approached the huge long windows; now their winter seclusion had truly begun. *Peace at last.*

That evening, the King met with a rude shock when he was informed that Cadogan was on the doorstep bearing a grave message from Degannwy.

'Thee must forgive my setting foot on Mon before spring, Majesty, but I am the only courier of merit who be fit to ride in such weather. There hast been a murder at the citadel.' He pulled a scroll from inside his clothes and handed it to Maelgwn.

'And there seemed no cause for the attack whatsoever, sir?' the King asked after reading.

'Nay, Majesty. Some have speculated that perhaps Prince Caradoc never left Degannwy after escaping the oubliette. It could be possible, I suppose . . .'

'Aye, Sir Vaugnan stated thus in his note.' Maelgwn was thoughtful a moment. 'I shall have Sir Rhys and Sir Brockwell accompany thee to Degannwy at once. I feel sure they can resolve this in my stead.' He felt nervous about having Cadogan so close at hand after Tory's warning this morning.

'Majesty, please.' Cadogan's voice was meek, as he dared to make a request. 'The weather outside be truly fierce. Could I not rest the night and set out in the morning?'

The King was disinclined to agree, but he could hardly expect the man to turn around in near darkness and head back through the snowfall. 'Of course. I shall send Sir Rhys and Sir Brockwell on ahead of thee to investigate, just in case the situation at Degannwy worsens overnight.'

'Very good, Highness. I do appreciate it, I assure thee.' He bowed.

'Send Tiernan, Brockwell, and Rhys to me,' the King commanded.

After the King briefed Rhys and Brockwell on their errand, they left at once. They were eager to return to Aberffraw and their training before the weather became too bad to permit safe passage home. The King instructed Tiernan to ensure that at no time while Cadogan was in the house was the Queen to be left alone.

Heeding the implication of mistrust in the King's voice and having just cause to be suspicious of Cadogan himself, Tiernan swore this would be done.

As the five days of sorrowing were observed as a holiday, the courtiers were at leisure to do as they pleased. Katren was taking an early morning stroll along the east hall when she spied Sir Cadogan, sneaking around. *What be he doing here?* She was quick to conceal herself in a doorway to observe his movements. The knight glanced back in her direction, and Katren flattened herself hard against the door. When she ventured another glance down the hall, Cadogan had vanished. *Did he see me?* She proceeded cautiously along the corridor, keeping her back to the wall. The large stone buttresses, which jutted out between the doorways, provided many a place to hide.

'Lady Katren.'

The maiden was startled as she felt the cold steel of a knife against her throat.

'Just the maid I am looking for,' he hissed, dragging her into the room from which he'd emerged. Cadogan closed the heavy door behind them, keeping the knife hard pressed against his captive's jugular. 'Where be the Queen?'

The tears welled in her eyes. She so wanted to test her skills, but could she move fast enough to escape his blade? 'I am no longer the Queen's maid, sir,' she said. 'I do not follow her schedule as closely as I once did.'

'Do not test me girl!' Cadogan turned her around, and thrust her hard against the wall.

This was the break Katren had been waiting for. She drove her knee deep into his stomach and, clenching her hands together, took a swing at his face. Half keeled over, Cadogan stumbled backwards. Unable to believe her own strength, Katren raced for the door.

'Damn it!' Cadogan lunged forward to grab her, but fell short.

As Katren fumbled with the door handle, she lashed out with a kick to her attacker's jaw to buy her some time. The door swung wide and she escaped into the corridor, only to be tackled to the hard stone floor and dragged back inside the room.

'Blasted bitch!' Cadogan rolled her over and belted her across the face repeatedly, until she was too delirious to resist him. 'Now.' He raised the maiden up and shook her, to make her conscious. 'Thee will tell me where Maelgwn's whore be, or I shall gut thee before thy own eyes.' He made the knife at her belly felt.

'The north tower,' Katren mumbled, ashamed.

'Much better.' He roughly locked arms with her again.

Tory was taking a bath in the north tower this morning, as the bath in the royal chamber was being cleaned and refilled. Sir Tiernan had instructed Ione to keep an eye on her until she joined the King for supper, as Maelgwn was attending to some matters of State. Tory laughed when there came a knock at the door, sure that it was Maelgwn neglecting his duty yet again for a little play. 'Enter.'

'It be Katren, Majesty,' the maid announced through the door without entering.

'Well, thee may enter, my sweet.'

'Could thee get the door?'

Tory nodded to Ione, who moved to oblige. As the door was unbolted, it burst open on her and the heavy oak wood knocked Ione unconscious. Katren came hurtling into the room, followed by Cadogan who strode in, closing and bolting the door behind him.

He stepped over Ione's body and drew his sword, thrusting it towards Katren. 'Get out of there,' he instructed Tory, a lustful glint in his eye as he watched her huddled in the bath.

'I am so sorry, Majesty,' Katren cried.

'Thou art a spineless snake, Cadogan.'

'Thou art so right,' he was pleased to agree. 'Do it!'

Tory stood up, as Cadogan's sword was getting awfully close to her friend. As his eyes ravished her naked form, Tory recalled her wedding gift from the King. She quickly let down her long hair, which fell about her like a cloak, and she wondered if she'd acted fast enough to prevent him noticing the waistlet. She climbed out of the bath and retrieved her jeans and jumper from the back of the chair, pulling them on. 'My, but thou art a sucker for punishment,' Tory decided to try to provoke him in the hope of drawing him closer to herself and away from Katren. 'Doth thou want to tell me of thy game before I beat thee senseless?'

Cadogan pulled the black bottle from his bag, placing the potion on the ground before stepping away again. 'Come here.' He took hold of Katren by the hair, jerking her head back and placing his blade across her stretched neck.

'Drink the contents,' he instructed Tory.

'One of Vanora's concoctions, I presume. Poison?' She slowly knelt down to retrieve the bottle. It made her hand ache just to touch it; this brew had dark origins indeed.

'Nay, it be not designed to harm. It would seem the great Chiglas hast taken an interest in thee and requires thee still functional.' Cadogan didn't disclose that he knew of her pregnancy. 'It be naught but a sleeping potion, so drink it.'

As she appeared to have little choice in the matter, Tory did as she was instructed. She raised the bottle to her lips, spying Ione coming round out of the corner of her eye. The taste of the evil brew made her gag as it trickled down her throat. Tory stood, casting the empty bottle to the floor. It smashed into pieces on the stone flagging confirming that the contents had been consumed. 'Now release her.'

Cadogan scoffed at her command. 'I am the one giving the orders now, Highness.'

Tiernan made his way through the house, inquiring as to the whereabouts of the Queen. He was not alarmed by her apparent absence, safe in the knowledge that Cadogan had left Aberffraw early this morning.

'Lady Cara.' He spied someone who was sure to know.

'Sir Tiernan,' she bowed to him.

'Where be the Queen hiding herself?'

'Why I do not know, sir. I have not seen the Queen or Lady Katren all day. Perhaps they took a walk together?'

Tiernan became concerned. 'What about Ione, hast thou seen her?'

'Nay. Be something amiss?'

'Fetch the King from the library, I shall be in the north tower.' Tiernan urged her to hurry. He should have thought of the tower earlier, as Ione and the Queen had been headed there when last they spoke.

Tiernan entered the tower and froze as he beheld a pool of blood, intermingled with water and glass on the stone floor. 'Please not the Queen,' he prayed. He couldn't bear to be responsible for failing her twice in his lifetime.

He followed the trail of blood that led around the large stone tub, and spied a body which had been dumped there. Tiernan, realising it was Ione, rushed to her aid. 'Unmerciful Goddess. Hast this one not been through enough!' He crouched to hold her in his arms, washing the blood from her face with cool water in the hope of reviving her. 'Ione. What happened . . . who did this?'

As he cleaned the gash on her head, Tiernan realised that it didn't seem so bad as to warrant so much blood. He desperately sought another source, finding a bump on the back of her head and a gash on her upper arm also. 'Please Ione, open thy eyes.' He took the belt quickly from his waist and bound her arm tight near her shoulder to stop the loss of blood.

Ione's eyes parted and she silently watched Tiernan, who tended her unaware that she had regained consciousness.

'Thou art too a fine a woman. Damn it, wake up,' he pleaded as their eyes met. An awkward feeling beset the knight's stomach as he caught the look of perfect wonder that graced Ione's face, as if she were witnessing a miracle. She reached out slowly and wiped a tear from his cheek, then she watched it trickle down her finger as if it were an incomprehensible phenomenon.

The door burst open and the King paused a moment upon sighting the blood. 'Tiernan!'

'Here, Majesty.'

With the spell suddenly broken, Ione gripped Tiernan's shirt and pulled herself up as she recalled what had befallen the Queen. Ione had regained consciousness before Cadogan made his getaway. In her bleary state she'd endeavoured to overpower him, resulting in the further injuries she'd sustained.

'Ione, what hast befallen you? Dost thou know who attacked thee?' The King was getting more used to communicating with her now; simple yes or no questions saved a lot of guesswork.

Ione nodded to confirm and pointed to the stub which was all that remained of her tongue, the expression on her face appearing hopeless. If she'd never been able to convey the identity of her attackers before, how was she going to do it now. The Queen was the only one who knew her secret.

Maelgwn frowned, frustrated, he didn't understand. 'What doth that mean?'

'The same man who attacked thee?' Tiernan asked.

Ione nodded, rather surprised that he'd guessed. The Queen must have told him how she'd lost her speech.

'Caradoc?' Tiernan presumed, as the bastard prince was still on the loose and hot for revenge.

She shook her head with a frown and encouraged him to guess again, wondering how long he'd known about her ordeal.

'It was surely Cadogan then,' Tiernan informed Maelgwn, and Ione nodded.

'He hast taken Tory?' Maelgwn was seeing red.

Ione nodded again, holding the tips of her fingers together before drawing them apart. She repeated this action a few times.

'What doth that mean?' The King was stumped again and rose frustrated. If Cadogan had Tory out in this cold too long, she could lose their child; perhaps that was the whole plan. 'Damn! This be impossible! Why did Taliesin not foresee this?'

'It means ... longer?' Tiernan ignored the King's panic, remaining focused on Ione, determined to solve the mystery.

She motioned *no* and repeated the movement.

'She means more,' Cara uttered as she walked in and saw the blood covering the ground.

With this established, Tiernan surmised. 'Cadogan hast taken more than the Queen?'

Ione slapped her hands together with a nod.

'He hast taken someone else? Who?'

Cara crouched down beside Ione to look over her injuries. As she'd seen everyone else this day, she concluded, 'Katren?'

Ione again slapped her hands together to confirm.

The King was saddened to learn this, as Cadogan would never cart an extra body without good reason. No doubt he intended to use Katren to threaten Tory into submission. *I had best get word to Brockwell at Degannwy immediately.*

'I do not understand.' Tiernan stood to address the King. 'Majesty, how could Cadogan have taken both of them out of the house without detection? 'Tis impossible.'

'The same way we entered the house when Cadfer seized power,' Maelgwn surmised.

Tiernan looked to the King: 'The west tower.'

'Cadogan knew about the passage, we used to play in it all the time when we were boys,' the King explained as he scaled the northern caphouse steps, with Tiernan in hot pursuit.

They followed tracks left in the snow on the open wall-walk, between the north and west towers. When they descended the stairs from the west caphouse, the King's fears were confirmed. The furniture and rug that usually concealed the passage had been pushed aside. Beneath the trapdoor lay a secret path that led one way to the prison level, and the other way to an underground passage that brought one out at a cave in the cliff face some distance down the beach. This exit could only be used at low tide, which it had been earlier this morning.

'The Queen warned me, over and over. Why did I not listen?'

'He cannot have gotten far in this weather, Majesty.' Tiernan attempted to keep him rational.

'If Cadogan be taking her to Chiglas, as the Queen foretold, I suspect he will have sent one of his larger boats to speed their journey to Powys.'

'Goddess forbid, Majesty, Chiglas! What dost thou propose to do?' Now Tiernan was panicking.

The King's eyes narrowed, his remorse and anger consumed him. 'End this damn blood feud.'

'An attack on Powys in spring would be difficult enough. We would lose hundreds more men in this weather,' Tiernan reasoned.

'No forces this time, Tiernan, just thee, Angus and myself. We leave for Llyn Cerrig Bach within the hour.'

It had been some time since the Dragon had overshadowed Maelgwn's demeanour, thus Tiernan didn't question his instruction. 'As thee wishes, Majesty. We shall make ready.'

When the party met in the stables, the King was surprised to find Vortipor in attendance. 'This be not thy fight, friend. I advise thee stay well out of it, to avoid any repercussions on Dyfed.'

'Sorry friend,' Vortipor corrected him politely. 'The Goddess hast clearly stated to the contrary. Be as brothers for thou art one, and let none divide thee. Thy woes art my own. Besides, if thee believes for a moment that thou art taking off on an adventure without me, thou art much mistaken.'

Maelgwn shook his hand, more than thankful for the support. 'So be it then,' he resolved, slapping Vortipor on the shoulder. It would seem the Protector of Dyfed did take some things seriously after all.

As they mounted their horses, Ione rode into the stables, of a mind to go with them.

'What art thou doing here, thou art ill,' Tiernan declared, knowing she was going to dispute the issue.

Ione flipped the fur cloak from her shoulders and flexed her muscles assuredly to imply that she felt fine and was raring to go.

'I do not care, Ione, thou art staying here,' Tiernan instructed.

Ione, who answered only to the Queen, held up her middle finger in protest; Tory had been teaching her a few silent expressions of her own. She motioned to her mouth, adamant about her right to go.

'I know thee owes him —' Tiernan began.

'She will be useful, Tiernan. She may come,' the King intervened, then he dug his heels into Aristotle and rode out the stable doors.

Ione gave Tiernan a smug grin as she took off with the others to pursue the King.

The party sped across the white countryside. The snowfall had eased for a time and they made Llyn Cerrig Bach just after nightfall.

Tiernan and Angus knew that the derelict site housed more than met the eye. Yet Vortipor and Ione were left to wonder why the King would ride for hours in the opposite direction of his foe to visit such a desolate place.

'Maelgwn, old boy.' Vortipor was quite sure the King had taken leave of his senses. 'I hate to point out the obvious, but if thou art seeking assistance here, thou art about five hundred years too late. There be naught left but a pile of old ruins.'

'Let this be a lesson to thee, Vortipor,' the King answered, then turned and headed for the temple remains. Angus and Tiernan smiled broadly as they fell in behind the King and followed him towards the entrance. Neither had ever been granted entrance to what lay beneath the altar, but they had heard Brockwell and the King speak of the High Merlin's abode.

Taliesin hadn't been informed of their arrival, yet the torches within the temple were lit and the top of the altar was free of snow. 'It would appear we art expected,' Maelgwn observed, taking a stand on top of the large stone tablet and helping the others up after him.

No summons was required this time as Vortipor, who was the last up, barely had the chance to get on the large stone before the illuminated mist began to billow forth from the cross.

Ione appeared ill at ease, so Tiernan thought he'd do the right thing and put his arm around her for comfort. This only served to score him an elbow in the side for his trouble. She looked at him sternly, standing firm, with her arms folded. If he wasn't afraid, she wasn't either.

Vortipor, beholding the mystic event, began to laugh. The bright light bursting forth from beneath him felt like pure life force, it cleansed and empowered him as it penetrated every fibre of his being. 'Dragon, thee never disappoints!'

As the mist gave way to the great entrance room of Taliesin's abode, the new arrivals were awestruck.

The King didn't share their elation. He thundered forward to address Taliesin, who awaited him with Selwyn. 'Why hast thou not told me of this, old man?

How could thee allow Tory to fall into the hands of Chiglas?'

'Calm thyself, Dragon,' the Merlin cautioned, appearing rather angered himself. 'Do not blame me for thy shortcomings. The Queen warned thee only yesterday, which be far more warning than I had.'

The truth hurt and only served to fuel Maelgwn's fury. 'Thee cannot tell me that the eminent, infallible, Taliesin Pen Beirdd did not know of this. What kind of a fool dost thou take me for!' The King's harsh words resounded around the room as he glared at his mentor.

Taliesin slowly walked forward to address Maelgwn, and he appeared to be calling on such restraint to remain civil that it caused his whole body to tremble. 'I cared for her long before thee ever knew she existed! Doth thou think for a moment that I would have gone to such pains with her, so that I could lose her to Chiglas?' Taliesin calmed himself once more. 'Understand that we art history in the making, my friend. From the time thee wed Tory and signed the pact with the neighbouring tribes of Britain, we entered an unknown future. How can I be expected to recall this incident in time, when it hast never taken place before?'

Maelgwn realised that he had no one to blame but himself. 'It would seem I am the fool, High Merlin.'

'Nay, thou art human, Majesty.' Taliesin placed a hand on his shoulder. 'And if thou art through with feeling sorry for thyself, we can see to the rescue of thy Queen.'

Before news of the abduction reached Brockwell at Degannwy, he and Rhys were approached by the young maid whom Sir Cadogan had vanquished on the night of Samhain. She appeared very ashamed of herself, not looking up from the floor as she quietly announced, 'Call off the murder investigation, I know who committed the grievous crime.'

Cadogan hadn't pursued her since the festival and, sure that he had another lover, she'd been secretly observing the knight's movements. 'Please understand that to witness such an act 'twas a terrible shock.' She began to sob. 'That be why I have not come forth before now.'

Brockwell, considering what Tory would do in his place, approached the girl and placed a hand on her shoulder. 'We understand, please take thy time.'

Rhys sighed at Brockwell's patience. 'However, we would like to catch the offender before he strikes again,' he added, hoping to move things along.

'He will not,' she sniffled.

Brockwell went down on one knee before her. 'How art thou so sure?'

'He be no longer here, sir. He was sent on an errand to Aberffraw yesterday.'

'Cadogan.' Both men resolved at once.

Rhys rushed forward to question the subject more closely. 'What just cause did Cadogan have to murder the soldier?'

'I do not know, sir.' She was flustered by his forceful manner and began to weep again.

'Thee must suspect at least?' Rhys pressured her harder.

'Rhys,' Brockwell stood and gently urged him to back up a little. 'Please, permit me.'

Rhys agreed to Brockwell's request, moving to answer a knock at the door. He was handed an urgent communication from the King at Aberffraw.

'Calin.' Rhys appeared rather ill as he read. 'Forget her, I know his motive.'

'What hast happened?'

Sir Rhys stepped forward and handed Brockwell the note.

Calin read, then crushed the parchment in his hand. His eyes moistened with the thought of the horrors that may lie in store for the women he loved. He inhaled deeply to control the anger brewing within him. 'Let us be gone, sir.'

As usual, Taliesin insisted that everyone eat before he explained what he knew. Maelgwn protested, anxious about his wife and unborn child.

'Thee may leave tonight, unprepared, or leave on the morrow with some hope of saving her.'

'Explain.' Maelgwn hated the fact that Taliesin always got his way, and the Merlin raised his brow, aware of this.

'I shall, after supper.'

Once the party had dined on the beef of two white bulls that had been slaughtered and cooked according to an old druidic tradition, the Merlin began to explain the reasons for their delay. 'I can safely say that thou art one of the most fortunate men I have ever known, Majesty.'

The look the King gave him implied that the remark didn't even warrant a response.

'Tomorrow happens to be the sixth day of the moon, when the influence of the orb be at its height. At this particular time of year, after a traditional sacrifice and an elaborate feast . . .' he waved his hand across the food on the table before them, 'one can cut mistletoe from the sacred oak to make an antidote for all poisons.'

'Be Vanora intending to poison my wife?'

'Nay, not the Queen, but thy heir.' The King rose immediately, but Taliesin gripped his arm. 'Thou art already too late, Maelgwn. Cadogan forced Tory to take the brew before she'd even left Aberffraw, under the premise it was just a sleeping potion. But fear not! Thy enchanted wedding gift still protects the child. But without the potion, that I can only make on the morrow, thy heir shall surely perish.'

The King's eyes closed and he resigned himself to be patient and trust in the Goddess, as she'd never steered him wrong before.

'There be one other very good reason for delay,' the Merlin informed them, his spirits lifting. 'If thee would all care to follow me.'

Taliesin guided them to the room housing his hexagons. The party was astonished to behold within the largest of these a holographic image of Chiglas' capital, Arwystli, and the surrounding terrain.

'Sacred Mother!' Angus mouthed the words as his voice escaped him.

'Great wonders of Britain, High Merlin!' Vortipor cried in amazement. 'I am mighty glad I am on thy side.'

'Arwystli?' Maelgwn sought to confirm, leaning against the glass to try to find whatever was amusing Taliesin so.

'Aye,' Taliesin smiled, waiting for the King to spot their saving grace.

Maelgwn had no fear of the technology, as they'd used this equipment to crush Cadfer fifteen years ago. 'What be all that commotion in the mountains yonder?' The King assumed the control position behind the panel and proceeded to zoom over the countryside, to take up a vantage point closer to the mountains.

'They look like Saxons, Majesty,' Tiernan said as he ventured closer.

'Undoubtedly,' Taliesin said. 'It would seem Chiglas did not see fit to pay them for their unsuccessful attempt to seize Gwynedd. And with no spoils to cover the plundering scavengers through winter, they intend to take their due by force. And they will, on the morrow.'

'Saved by the Saxons, well I never!' Maelgwn almost had to laugh.

'Indeed, the perfect diversion. Wait for them to break through the outer defences, sneak in while all art engaged in battle, and make for thy Queen. Unfortunately, I shan't be able to tell thee her situation within the city until morn, when she hast reached Arwystli.'

'Excellent!' Maelgwn greatly approved.

'I thought so.' Taliesin was gracious.

'Excuse me,' Vortipor interrupted politely. 'I know this may seem a stupid question, but if we do not leave now, how shall we make Powys in time?'

'Rufus, I hope,' the King answered, but he could never tell just how much persuading it would take to draw the dragon out into the Middle Kingdoms.

Sir Brockwell and Sir Rhys reached Aberffraw in the early hours of morning. Brockwell charged into the house, yelling at the top of his lungs to draw the attention of anyone who could tell him what was going on.

Cara, Cedric and Alma came racing to him.

'Where be the King?' Calin panicked.

'He makes chase,' Cedric assured him, taking hold of the young knight's arm to prevent him from dashing off in pursuit. 'He said thou art to remain here, for the way the King hast taken the others, thee cannot follow, Calin.'

'What art thou saying, Cedric? Chiglas holds my lady captive!'

'The King hast got Vortipor, Tiernan and Angus with him, they shall see to Katren's rescue. We need thee here, in case this be another damn trick.'

'Cedric, my love, my sister and my King art out there!' He pointed to the darkness beyond the frosted windows. 'Without them, there be nothing left here for me to protect. I am the King's Champion, I should be with him now. Please, tell me which way they went?'

Cedric let Brockwell's arm go. 'Llyn Cerrig Bach. The King sought the High Merlin there.'

'Bless thee, Cedric.' Brockwell backed up in haste. 'I shall make thee glad thee told me, I swear.'

'I am coming with thee,' Rhys resolved.

'Nay Rhys, stay with Cedric, thy wife and thy child. No offence, but I will get there faster on my own.'

'May the Goddess speed thee,' said Rhys in parting.

'How could she not,' Brockwell reasoned, as he made for the door.

Taliesin performed the ritual at the first rays of dawn, and, with the aid of a golden sickle, he cut the plant known as mistletoe from the oak tree. The Merlin was mindful not to cut the oakwood, as this would be considered unfortunate and thus condemn their mission.

On the pure white blanket that covered the fairy wood, the small group of warriors observed the rites taking place. They made the most of the opportunity to focus and centre themselves, for it had been decided that they would go into Arwystli without their cumbersome armour to gain the vantage of speed and agility.

Whilst the potion brewed, the party returned to the Merlin's control room to view the current situation at Arwystli. Taliesin's tiny satellite camera was homing in on a microscopic device that lay inside the charm Tory wore around her waist. As it shot past on the screen before them, the masters noted the course they would take. After passage through the outer and inner baileys on the screen, they entered the huge dark fortress that housed Chiglas and his forces. There they found the Queen and Katren in the throne room, standing before King Chiglas and the Princess Vanora.

Tory had been unconscious for most of the icy crossing from Mon to Powys. The potion had drained every ounce of strength from her body, and the cramps in her stomach were becoming harder to ignore. Katren grasped her tightly around the waist to help support her in a standing position. Tory had never felt this vulnerable, ever. She recognised the man seated on the throne from her nightmares. This disgusting individual was obese to the extreme, with sores covering his face, hands and feet which indicated that he was riddled with disease. The advisers standing around his throne appeared to be suffering from the same ailment. Chiglas was bald except for a few strands, and his beady little eyes appeared ridiculously small in comparison to his huge crooked nose and large lips, which were almost purple in colour.

Vanora watched her father intently as he grunted and snarled, his tongue quickly lapping over his lips on occasion to keep them moist. She nodded ever so slightly in acknowledgment, then stepped forward to speak on his behalf. The evil King and his daughter were using telepathy to communicate, which made Tory wonder how they had the power to bethink each other. Surely they had not been set apart as Chosen.

'Sir Cadogan, we art greatly pleased that thou hast delivered the War Goddess as promised. We find thee worthy to bear the title of Prince of Powys, heir to our kingdom.' Vanora paused, her cold black eyes looking to Tory. 'Did thee give her my potion as instructed?'

'Of course, Highness.' Cadogan placed his right hand on his heart.

'Then where be the blood of the Dragon's heir?'

What! Tory turned to Cadogan who was standing next to her. She summoned what strength she had left and served him a punch to his temple. Such a strike was known to cause loss of vision, balance, consciousness, even death through a brain lesion.

Cadogan dropped like a ten tonne weight to the floor, bleary eyed and shaken.

'Thou art a lying maggot, Cadogan. If my child dies I shall crush every bone in thy body, one by one.'

Cadogan's eyes rolled back in his head as he passed out.

Tory received a backhanded blow to the face from the guard closest to her, but she only smiled in satisfaction. 'Weak as piss,' she claimed, as the guard raked her arms behind her back to restrain her.

Princess Vanora didn't seem at all bothered by her future husband's affliction; the Queen of Gwynedd was more her concern. 'So then, thee must have on thy person some fairy enchantment that protects thy child. What might that be?'

Think of something else, Tory told herself in desperation, knowing that Vanora would only see whatever came into her mind. The Queen conjured the image of an alien creature from a horror movie she'd seen. She recalled the close-up of the beast's head as it slowly parted several sets of extendible jaws, dripping with saliva and slime.

Vanora screeched as the horrific vision entered her mind, and backed away quickly to escape it.

'I will find it!' she thundered. 'Remove thy clothes.'

Chiglas appeared inspired by the prospect, licking his lips as his arms reached out towards the Queen; this was truly Tory's worst nightmare.

'Eat shit!' She made her resolve plain.

Fortunately for Tory, just then a guard rushed in to inform Chiglas that the Saxons were storming the walls.

'What?' Vanora moved to the window to determine the size of the threat. 'Lock up the Warrior Queen and her servant,' she ordered. 'I will contend with them presently.'

After bearing witness to the scene in Chiglas' courtroom, Maelgwn would not delay his departure any longer. While Taliesin bottled the antidote, the King made haste through the labyrinth to seek the dragon's lair.

Maelgwn walked along the stony track that led up to the cave which Rufus frequented. As the King reached the entrance, he was startled to encounter not one dragon but two. The second dragon would have taken his head off, had he not been fast enough to duck into a crevice in the rock and escape injury.

Albina!

Maelgwn heard the sound of Rufus' familiar voice resounding through his brain, even though nothing but a low growl reached his ears.

That be one's penance to Keridwen, that thou art about to swallow.

Rufus, the larger of the two, came to stand beside the unknown dragon, bringing chunks of rock and dirt crumbling down inside the cave with the vibration of his every step. *Please accept one's apologies. Albina, my mate, be brooding at present.* The dragon motioned with his claw to an egg that was larger than the King. *Not unlike thy Queen.*

'I understand completely. I am sorry if I startled thee, Albina.' The King bowed politely to her. The beast seemed unimpressed, and with a snort returned to her position curled around her spawn. 'I would have sent word of my visit, but I am pressed for time and greatly in need of thy assistance.'

One knows why thou art here. And one could be in favour of helping thee, provided . . .

'Provided what, Rufus?'

In return for a fast flight to Powys, one wants all the dead of all thy foe, including thy brother and the corpulent Chiglas. However, these latter two, one wants alive! Thus the beast claimed their souls and would wipe them from existence forever.

'I shall do my very best to meet thy request, Rufus, but I cannot promise them alive without question.' Maelgwn hoped the beast would see reason.

Done. One shall meet thee and thy masters at the temple, presently.

Brockwell spurred his horse on through the snow, heading down the valley trail to the ruins. He arrived at the site to witness the dragon departing overhead. 'Maelgwn!' he cried in vain, watching the huge beast soar to such a height that he could no longer see it through the cloud. Brockwell slouched in his saddle, disheartened.

'Calin, why so glum?'

Brockwell spun round to find Taliesin on the stairs of the temple. 'I have failed the Lady Katren.'

The High Merlin laughed wholeheartedly as he approached the young knight. Calin, feeling that Taliesin mocked his pain, folded his arms indignantly.

'Thou art discouraged too easily, my young friend. Have I not told thee, where there be a will, there be a way.'

'So thee will help me?' Calin sprang off his horse to meet him.

'Aye, but I do not know if thee will like the form of assistance I have to offer,' Taliesin cautioned.

'I will do anything.' Calin fell on one knee before the High Merlin. 'Just name it.'

18

ANGER TO AVENGE

The tortured screams of anguished souls echoing up from the dungeon rooms mixed with the unearthly groans of the sick and dying. In light of the Queen's performance in the throne room, Katren and Tory were escorted to their cell by several very large armed guards. Tory buried her fear under an indifferent facade, but in truth, she could never have imagined a more horrid place. The stench on its own was near fatal, and she thought it little wonder that half of the populace at Arwystli were diseased.

Katren trembled so much she could barely walk. Yet she managed to hold her head high and not shed a single tear, even as the men they passed in the cells leered and grabbed for them. *I must not fear, Calin will come for me.* Katren only hoped there would be something left of her to save.

The women were cast inside a dark tower, and the door was bolted shut behind them. They needed a moment for their eyes to adjust to the dim lighting. A foul odour hung heavy in the still air, vexing their nostrils as the source was not far away.

As Katren picked herself up from the floor, she heard the scratching sound of rats. 'I think we should go upstairs, Majesty.' She got to her feet, quickly helping Tory up.

'I tend to agree,' Tory said and looked up the stairs toward the caphouse, where glimmers of daylight could be seen.

'Sorcha?' said a voice.

Tory and Katren both froze in horror.

'Caradoc?' Tory edged Katren to a safe position behind her.

'Aye, sorceress, come to finish me?' He inquired in a way that implied he couldn't care less.

Katren noticed something move in the shadows, back against the stone wall. Tory inched closer to investigate, despite Katren's whispered protests. 'Art thou hurt, sir?'

'I feel nothing.' Caradoc's response was spiritless.

Tory considered that it could be a trick. But when she saw him, she realised Prince Caradoc was no longer any threat. Katren shrieked when she saw the pile of skin and bone, covered in gashes and sores. Gangrene and maggots had besieged his body long ago, fuelled by the pool of filth from his own secretions, in which he lay. The rats had also enjoyed a feed. Katren, in spite of her loathing for the man, kicked the scavengers away.

How on earth is this man still breathing? Tory asked herself. Surely not even the lowest of creatures deserves to die like this.

'Well, come on. Do it! Be this not what thou hast always wanted, Mother dear, to rid thyself of thy greatest mistake?' he yelled, overwhelmed by his contempt for her.

Katren urged Tory back but the Queen only patted her hand, crouching down to look Caradoc in the eye. The man was obviously delirious and beyond pain. 'Nay Caradoc, 'tis not true.'

'Liar! Thou hast always favoured Maelgwn over me. Was it my fault I was conceived as I was? Nay! Yet thee drove me away.'

Tory felt Sorcha's presence upon her and motioned Katren away. 'Upstairs.'

'Nay, Majesty, I will not leave —'

'Do as I say child!' Tory roared in Sorcha's voice and her own, startling Katren into complying at once. When she turned back to Caradoc, his mood had calmed somewhat and he stared wide-eyed at her angelic presence. 'Dost thou not recall our time together when thou wast still a young boy? Before Cadfer got hold of thee, before the blood feud and the uprising, my sons were fast friends then.'

'Aye, I do,' Caradoc acknowledged, as if he could see his past before his eyes while they spoke. 'I remember thee would read to us in the shade of the trees in the courtyard. Games, good food, friends ... 'twas the best time of my life,' he resolved with a distant smile.

'The Goddess understands thy plight, Caradoc, and shall be lenient.' At the mercy of Sorcha's will, Tory administered a fatal blow.

In the blink of an eye Sorcha was gone and Caradoc was dead on the ground at Tory's feet; his nose had been broken at the bridge and smashed back into his brain. She stepped away from him, totally appalled by the deed. 'Damn thee, Sorcha, I am sick of doing thy dirty work.' As the rats took to the corpse, Tory's nausea set in. 'Get me out of this place.' She burst into tears. The cramps in her stomach intensified until she was reduced to a huddle on the floor.

'Majesty.' Katren rushed down the stairs to her side, but the Queen's eyelids were already closing. 'Please, Majesty, don't leave me on my own in this place.' The maiden patted her cheeks, losing the battle to keep her conscious. 'We must get thee upstairs.' She hoisted the Queen upright and, struggling with the dead weight, dragged her towards the caphouse.

Brockwell awaited the High Merlin in the hall outside one of the thousands of identical doors within his maze. Taliesin was having words with Brockwell's transport, which was another winged beast — a griffin.

It was said that the creatures were so fierce in appearance that one couldn't help but be afraid of them, and if a griffin sensed fear it would devour thee at once. Thus Brockwell wasn't really looking forward to the test, and he thought of Katren to save losing face. As luck would have it the griffin owed Taliesin a favour or two, so if Calin was dauntless when he met the beast he'd have his ride to Powys.

Calin grew tried of pacing up and down the hall as it only served to make the delay all the more frustrating, so he took a seat on the floor and assumed a meditative position. He drew three long, deep breaths to seek the guidance and blessing of his forefathers. 'Please protect my love until I can make it to her.'

'Calin.' The Merlin finally emerged.

'What did it say?' Brockwell jumped up to confront the news.

'Thou art not going to like it, I fear.'

'High Merlin please,' Brockwell was eager to leave as the distance between himself and his King grew wider with every passing second.

'The situation be this, thee must walk into the centre of the lair. If thee shows the slightest fear, the griffin will turn thee to stone for wasting its time, and thy spirit will remain entrapped thus for all eternity.'

Brockwell looked to the ground to think a second. 'I should rather be turned to stone trying, than risk a lifetime without her.'

Taliesin smiled. 'Bear that in mind and thou shalt do just fine.'

Calin nodded in gratitude and cautiously approached the door.

'A word of advice . . .'

Brockwell looked back, thankful for any assistance the Merlin had to give.

'Do not draw thy weapon, and think only the purest of thoughts. These beasts, although ferocious on the outside, art fools for sentiment deep down.'

Brockwell nodded once again, turning the handle of the door that concealed his fate.

The room was huge — a deep, dim expanse of stone and rock. So high was the roof, Calin could not view it and the wall around the door faded into nothingness on both sides. Torch-lit stairs led downward through the rocky terrain. No wonder the old man took so long, Brockwell concluded, as he began his descent into the beast's dominion.

Brockwell finally reached a large plateau of rock, and from its edge was a sheer drop to infinity down a rocky cliff face. The knight peered into the darkened shadows beyond the torch light. 'Hello.'

The sound of wings came from above like that of an eagle swooping down on its prey, only this was far louder. Calin looked up to behold the huge creature. Its head, chest and wings were feathered and it displayed the forelegs and talons of an eagle. This one, however, was about ten times larger than the average eagle, and was plummeting head first with its claws outstretched towards him.

Brockwell's first reaction was to draw his sword, but he refrained as advised. He waited until the beast was near upon him before ducking away from its sweeping grasp. Brockwell quickly turned to face the beast, so it would not think him trying to flee.

It was only as the creature landed before him that Calin could observe the rest of its form. From its shoulders a metamorphosis took place; the griffin had the hindquarters of a lion, and tawny coloured fur covered the rest of its body. Although legend has it that these creatures have the tail of a serpent, Calin observed nothing more than the normal tufted tail of a lion. The only other unusual feature he could note was that on its eagle head it had the ears of a lion.

The griffin had begun to circle him on all fours. It opened its huge beak and let loose a deep, loud roar, the force of which near blew him off the plateau. Brockwell roared right back at the beast grossly larger than himself, and continued to yell even after the beast's roaring had ceased.

Why art thou not afraid, when one plans to eat thee?

Calin hushed as he heard the words and looked about him. 'Did thou say something?'

Nay. One be waiting around for the good of one's health.

The creature's mouth made no movement, and Brockwell realised that he was not hearing with his ears, but with his mind. 'Thou art bethinking me?' Brockwell said with excitement, simply delighted with himself. 'Excellent!'

The griffin didn't seem to share his rosy view, for a long, slow growl escaped its beak as it continued to circle. *Answer one's question . . . How be it that thou art not afraid?*

Calin shrugged. 'Because thee will only eat me if I show fear.'

Hah! Never listen to human beings. One said one would turn thee to stone if thee showed fear. One did not mention

411

what one would do in other circumstances. The beast's sinister laughter echoed through Brockwell's brain, and the griffin chopped its beak a few times to emphasise the point.

The Knight wasn't alarmed, as he figured the creature was still testing him. 'Thou art not going to eat me.'

Why not? The creature snapped.

'Because I am a warrior of the Triple Goddess. My quest be to the save the life of her greatest representative, thine sister the good Queen of Gwynedd, and my love, the Lady Katren, for they art being held captive by the savage Chiglas. Surely as a creature of the Goddess thee would rather make a meal of her foe, than her humble servant.'

There art precious few of thy kind who art humble, the creature scoffed. *One cares not about the affairs and occupants of the Middle Kingdoms, thou art all just as bad as one another.*

'Nay, thou art wrong.' Brockwell was adamant as he strode forward to address the animal. 'The two women whose lives I seek to save art the purest of souls. If thee could only know what I know of them.' Calin's eyes began to flood with tears as he recalled the fine times they'd seen since they'd been brought together, some six months ago. 'I love them, understand! And I shall not allow thee to let them perish. They need us and thou art going to take me to them.'

Calin noticed the tears that had filled the eyes of the huge animal. It plonked itself back onto its hind quarters and proceeded to cry like a baby.

'I am sorry,' Brockwell said, and he felt as awkward with the sobbing beast as he did with a weeping woman. ''Twas not my intent to upset thee.'

Please stop, one cannot take it.

'Stop what?'

Thinking of her! So beautiful, so strong. The beast's voice wavered with emotion. *One hast decided to help thee, but thee must make me a promise in return.* The creature's sobbing subsided.

'What kind of promise?'

Wed the girl of thy heart and remain beholden to her alone for as long as ye both shall live.

'But I want nothing more.' Brockwell felt the request too easy.

Should thee ever break this vow, thou shalt bequeath thy bountiful mate and all thy offspring to me, never again to lay eyes on them. Dost thou consent?

In light of his promiscuous past, Brockwell took a moment to consider the proposal. Did he possess the willpower to meet the lifelong challenge? 'I do.'

Tory had regained consciousness, but she was still weaker than ever she'd felt before. From the barred windows of the prison tower, she and Katren observed the situation unfolding in the city below.

Arwystli was similar in layout to Degannwy in that it housed a whole city inside its outer bailey walls, rather than just a castle. But as it did not have the same topographical protection Degannwy did, the city's walls were higher than most other British strongholds. Many of Chiglas' soldiers scurried to reinforce the outer and inner-bailey wall-walks, as Saxon troops came down from the outlying mountains and gathered outside the city.

'I thought the Saxons were allied to Chiglas?' Katren tried to assess what was happening.

'It would seem they have had a falling out,' Tory commented, as she heard the tower door downstairs open. She stood to address the impending confrontation, urging Katren behind her.

'Nay *Sensei*, I am ready to fight,' Katren insisted, fed up with being afraid.

'Savour the element of surprise, Katren. They will not hesitate to kill thee. So, if I squeeze thy hand, I want thee to get down and stay down.' Tory again pushed her into the background.

Four large guards emerged, two bowmen and two swordsmen. They were accompanied by Vanora and the revived Sir Cadogan, who came over to stand opposite Tory.

'Thee shall find the charm about her waist,' Cadogan informed Vanora with malice.

'Thou art a son-of-a-bitch, Cadogan! I do solemnly swear that thee shall not live to see this night fall.' Tory seethed as the swordsmen stepped forward to take hold of her, the bowmen covering them from a safe distance.

There be no pain, there be no fear. Tory squeezed Katren's hand and lashed out at the first swordsman with a kick, knocking him back into his bowman and sending them both tumbling down the stairs.

'Get the maid,' Vanora instructed, frustrated by their incompetence.

But Tory had already spun around to take out the other swordsman with a high kick to the side of his head, sending him on a collision course with the hard stone wall where he fell unconscious. There was a momentary pause, then the other bowman tried to get a clear shot at Katren, but Tory was too quick to resume her cover.

Cadogan drew his sword and wielded it back and forth in warning.

Vanora, as usual, sounded completely unaffected by it all. 'The child in thy womb be dead anyway, thee may as well let it out.'

'Like I would take thy word for it,' Tory replied. He wasn't dead, she could feel him fighting it, but god knows what damage the poison had already done to the tiny foetus. 'What hast she promised thee, Cadogan? The same deal as Caradoc? For his loyalty he became a diseased banquet for the rats down below.'

'Caradoc was a fool,' Cadogan snarled; she'd hit a nerve.

'Thou art the fool, Cadogan, for believing this juvenile capable of keeping her word.'

That was it. Regardless of orders to the contrary, Cadogan swung his sword at her, mid-height, and there was no escaping the blow. Tory turned and ducked to avoid the blade making contact with her body, thus taking its full force in her upper left arm. The pain was real. She fell to her knees, gripping her arm as the blood gushed through her fingers.

'Hold her,' Cadogan ordered the guard as he hauled Katren aside by the hair and cast her across the room to the bowman.

'Nay, Sir Cadogan please,' Katren begged him. 'Gwynedd took thee in when thee had no other. How can thee betray her like this?'

Vanora, annoyed by Katren's whimpering, slapped her hard across the face. 'Save thy breath.'

Katren spat at the Princess and for a moment they glared at each other, neither wavering.

'Kill her,' Vanora resolved, as she turned to see how Cadogan was doing.

'Wait! We may still need her.'

'Now what?' Vanora was losing her cool.

Cadogan, with a knife hard to Tory's throat, dug through her layers of clothes to take hold of the charm. But it would not be pulled off. 'It will not break, not even my steel can budge it.'

'Curses!' Vanora thumped her foot like the spoilt child she was. 'Take it off!' she demanded.

'I cannot,' Tory said, remaining very calm. 'Only the Dragon himself can remove it, as he was the one who placed it there.'

Vanora's black eyes were filled with spite as they glared at her. 'We shall see about that.'

The sight of the Saxons raising the portcullis of the outer bailey at Arwystli was satisfying for the young King of Gwynedd, as he watched from the cover of a ridge.

'Won't be long now,' Tiernan affirmed, speaking the King's mind for all to hear.

'Why do we not get the dragon to storm the castle before us,' Angus wondered aloud. Since they had such a show of power, why weren't they using it?

'This dragon and myself art synonymous these days I'm afraid, and I want none to know of our presence,' Maelgwn explained.

The huge beast was rolling around in the snow like a dog with an itchy back. Ione applauded the antics of the creature, simply delighted by its play. She didn't seem to fear it at all as she approached the dragon with a large forked stick to help relieve its frustration. The group of men nearly dropped dead when she served its thick scaled hide with a good scratch, right in the place it sought to reach. This was much to Rufus' satisfaction, as his eyes rolled about in his head uncontrollably, his tongue hung out the side of his mouth, and his tail lashed about, kicking up more snow.

'Ione, it be time,' the King called her back to the others, who pulled black masks over their faces.

Maelgwn drew his new steel sword and held it out before him, then the others brought theirs to rest across it.

'Go forth in the name of the Goddess this day, recalling all she hast taught thee. May the might of Gwynedd prevail and may the Great Houses guide and protect us all.'

'So be it!'

The battle raged on in the city below. From what Katren could surmise from the prison tower, the Saxons appeared to be the stronger force. She turned back to view the Queen, whose hands and feet were now shackled together. The guards hadn't bound Katren, as they obviously didn't consider her to be a threat. She'd wrapped Tory's wounded arm with a strip of material torn from her skirt. Katren had never before seen Tory so despondent. *She certainly be worried about her babe*, she reasoned, for Tory had said naught since the guards departed.

Tory gazed quietly at the shadows on the floor. She was thinking of Caradoc's death, or rather just after it, when she had cried, 'Get me out of this place.' She was considering in retrospect that she'd been referring to her whole situation, not just Arwystli. This truly was the age of darkness and Tory knew her current plight was only a taste of what her future, as Queen of Gwynedd, held in store. Every day here was a fight for survival. What if her unborn child did live? What kind of a future would he have? There would always be someone waiting in the shadows to do Gwynedd out of an heir. Her thoughts turned to home, her parents, her house, and her studies; the tranquillity and anonymity were just a cherished memory. If she returned to the twentieth century next summer solstice, as Taliesin suggested, would she even know her parents, or worse, would they know her? If, of course, they even existed within the new reality she would encounter upon arriving home.

There are three candles that illuminate every darkness, child. Tory recalled her father's voice so clearly that it brought tears to her eyes. *Truth, nature, and wisdom. View life's dilemmas with their combined enlightenment, and you will always find the right solution.*

As Tory considered this a feeling of intimacy swept through her body, filling her soul with the sweet recollection of the beautiful man she'd managed to secure for herself, and herein she found her truth. For she was bound to Maelgwn, not by patronage or law, but by the very knowledge of his existence. Even if she could escape this nightmare of an age, life without him would be far more torturous than any horror Chiglas or the Saxons could dream up for her.

Once again she heard the door downstairs open.

Come on, Tory, it's your very nature to fight. And if the universe in its wisdom has seen fit to throw this test your way, you must meet the challenge head on and to the best of your ability.

'What should I do, Majesty?' Katren asked, fearful of the outcome.

'Only what thee must to save thyself. If thou finds an opportunity to flee, take it,' she stressed as they looked to the stairs.

They were both very surprised to see only Princess Vanora and a small hooded figure.

Katren remained frozen, her back against the wall, as the hunched little figure hobbled slowly towards the Queen.

'We meet again, Sorcha,' the old creature croaked, removing her hood to view her prey more closely.

The hag appeared older than time itself, and Tory could easily sense the evil emanating from her. Warts covered her face and hands. Her straggly silver hair hung dead around her diseased features, and her fingernails were as long and sharp as knives. Albino in colouring, the witch's pupils were red within an iris of white.

'Nay Mahaud, her name be Tory Alexander, Maelgwn's Queen, brought from the future by the Old Ones.'

Mahaud burst into laughter. 'It be Sorcha, make no mistake. Taliesin hast learnt some new tricks. But, of course,' the old crone looked at Katren and with a wave of her hand the maiden fell unconscious, 'it shan't do him any good.'

That's what you think. Tory attempted to strike at Mahaud but the shackles hindered her attempt.

'And, as usual, I am right.' The witch extended her arm in Tory's direction, the tips of the hag's fingers glowing red as hot coals.

Every muscle in Tory's body suddenly froze, and her shackles fell away to the floor. She then rose to a stable, horizontal position about a metre above the floor. *So, you are the source from which Vanora is learning her craft?*

'Aye,' the witch confirmed. 'Did thee not get my message? I sent it twice, so thee cannot say I did not give thee fair warning.'

The dreams, all the blood, Tory realised, her panic rising.

'It be the future thou hast seen,' the witch taunted, 'thy future! For as thou art about to discover, my sweet, there be a fourth side to the Goddess.'

The King and his small band entered the outer bailey, cutting their way through the commotion. Neither the Saxons nor Chiglas' men could figure whose side the masked warriors were on, and most avoided the party to concentrate instead on the known enemy.

The fighting became more intense as they neared the inner-bailey portcullis. The Saxons could not raise the gate, though many of the barbarian raiders had scaled the fortress walls.

Ione, who was having a field day wielding fatal blows to every man who got between her and the inner bailey, drew the King's attention to the sky.

Maelgwn looked up as the huge shadow of a griffin fell over the fortress. The fighting waned as all gasped in horror at the beast, and many soldiers ran in fear of their lives.

'Now we have a problem.' Vortipor observed the mighty creature circling overhead.

'Perhaps not.' Maelgwn was quietly confident that this beast was the same one allied to Taliesin.

Those Saxon fighters who had been scaling the wall, took their leave and ran away. But one huge warrior decided to stand his ground, cursing those who scampered in fear. The King recognised him as he had confronted this scoundrel in battle before. He was Ossa, the Warlord of the Saxon invaders. Ossa was the son of Octa, who had plagued Ambrosius, High King of Briton, and Caswallon, in his early days as King of Gwynedd. The King and his knights didn't understand much of the Saxon language, but through the Saxons' alliance with Chiglas many of their foe had learnt the native tongue. Thus it was understood by Maelgwn and his band that Ossa accused the deserters of being no better than a bunch of women.

Ione caught the comment, and as she was to the Saxon leader's blind side, she gave him a kick up the butt for the insult. Ione ripped the mask from her head to make her gender plain and held her sword poised to challenge him.

Ossa let loose a riotous round of laughter upon seeing her. 'Well my lovely, want a taste of my sword, hey?'

Tiernan, who was also well aware of the Warlord's status, ran to Ione's aid. But when he saw she was holding her own, he slid to a stop on the wet snow to admire her prowess.

The big, brawny warrior was growing increasingly frustrated with her audacious moves. She was making a mockery of him in front of his men and his foe, and all seemed to be getting a good laugh out of it.

'Great Goddess,' Tiernan uttered. 'She be magnificent.'

As Ossa's anger mounted, his concentration and skills waned. Ione's moves became twice as daring, her strikes harder and more precise. Soon Ossa's sword was sent flying into the distance, and the point of Ione's sat poised at his throat.

'I am sorry if I offended thee,' he grumbled.

Ione motioned him to his knees, indicating that she wanted him to beg. When he refused, she applied enough pressure to persuade him to comply.

'Who art thou?' the warrior asked, more interested than angry.

Ione's beautiful dark eyes gazed down upon him a second, the perfect features of her face devoid of any expression.

As she raised her sword into the air, Tiernan fended off the Saxon soldiers who rushed towards her. With no time to procrastinate, Ione clobbered the Warlord in the head with the iron hilt of her sword, and he passed out in the snow. She turned to assist her partner with the masses but many of them backed away, fearing that perhaps she was the fabled War Goddess who had thwarted their attempt to take Gwynedd.

The griffin came to land on the wall that harboured the inner bailey portcullis. Warriors from both sides fled its path, and the ones who didn't became a fast snack for the beast.

Brockwell, having assessed the situation from the air, jumped from between the wings of the animal and took a stand on the wall to call to those down below. 'Would thee like me to get the gate?' He appeared rather impressed with himself, for his question met with an overwhelming response from all below.

'A champion indeed,' Maelgwn said, and was forced to smile as the portcullis went up and the barbarian warriors rushed into the fortress.

I thank thee, my friend. Brockwell bowed to the Griffin, who'd lived up to its end of the bargain. *Thou art free to go.*

Remember thy vow, warrior, the beast cautioned, as it took flight from the battle scene. *For I will.*

'Speaking of which . . .' Calin made haste inside the castle.

As Katren came round she heard the muttering of an alien tongue being uttered in a deep, malign tone. It sounded suspiciously like an incantation, and without moving she slowly opened her eyes to view the situation.

Tory was suspended in the air. The old crone was standing over her, and appeared totally focused on her task. Vanora, too, had her back to Katren as she stood close by Mahaud to witness the deed.

By the time Vanora sensed the movement behind her, it was too late. Katren served her a punch right in the vital point at the root of the nose, and the Princess dropped like a rock. She then turned her sights to the old woman, who seemed oblivious to the fact that anything had happened. Katren scraped together every ounce of bravery she had and moved to attack.

Without even turning from her hex, Mahaud waved a finger in Katren's direction and the young maid suddenly found herself airborne. She literally flew down the long spiral staircase without so much as touching one stair. The door to the tower downstairs opened to allow her passage and she was cast against the stone wall in the corridor outside, the door slamming shut behind her.

Katren jumped up at once to see if she could regain entry. When she could not, she began pounding furiously on the door. 'Let her alone, witch. The Goddess will damn thee both to the Underworld for this.' She slid down against the heavy wooden door to the ground where she sat, helpless in the face of the tragedy.

'Just the maid I am looking for.'

Upon hearing the sound of Cadogan's sleazy voice, Katren realised she had problems of her own.

'Allow me to show thee my new quarters here at Arwystli.'

'I would rather die,' she stated, defiantly, as she moved to raise herself.

'Ah!' Cadogan drew his sword to discourage her. He brushed the long brown hair off her shoulders with its point then slid the blade under her chin, lifting her face up to view him. 'What a waste.'

As Cadogan raised his sword, Katren closed her eyes and shed a tear. Her only regret in passing was that she would never wed her love.

'Cadogan!' Brockwell charged down the corridor at such speed that Cadogan was forced to defend himself. 'Thou art a dead man,' Brockwell pledged as he engaged his former ally in combat, drawing him away from his lady.

The King's party arrived on the scene in time to see Brockwell disarm Cadogan. Ione cried out in protest as Cadogan was driven to his knees by Brockwell's sword.

'Calin. Leave him,' Tiernan voiced Ione's mind.

Ione walked steadily towards them, casting her sword aside with an ardent look in her eye. She'd been waiting over ten years for this, and no one was going to do her out of the pleasure. She swung open the door to an empty cell, and tossed the key to Tiernan.

Cadogan, foreseeing his fate, became distraught. 'Nay please, Calin, kill me. I beg thee, do not leave me to her.'

'In a couple of hours, perhaps.' Calin laughed as he backed off.

Ione clutched the front of Cadogan's shirt, dragging the spineless weasel to his feet.

'Where be the key to the tower?' Maelgwn demanded.

Cadogan produced the key from his pocket, his eyes flooding with tears of remorse. 'Majesty, have mercy,' Cadogan cried, kneeling at the King's feet.

Maelgwn could not speak to him; the repulsion he felt was so great that he addressed Ione instead. 'Leave him alive, the dragon wants him.' Maelgwn left to unlock the tower door.

Ione dragged Cadogan, still kicking and screaming, into the cell. She cast him in, slamming the door locked behind them.

'I knew thee would come.' Katren flung her arms around her rescuer's neck.

It seemed to Calin as if an enormous weight had been lifted from his shoulders when he cradled her in his arms. 'Marry me?' he whispered softly.

'All the warriors in Britain could not stop me,' she confirmed with a kiss.

The King flung open the heavy tower door and ran up the stairs as fast as his body was able, Mahaud's fervoured words spurring him to move faster.

'Heed me demons at this our desperate hour, abate this charm of fairy power.'

Maelgwn reached the caphouse just in time to witness the chain snap off in the witch's hand, and her wicked laughter filled the room. At this moment Tory's body dropped to the hard stone floor in a pool of blood.

'Die witch!' Maelgwn ran at her with his blade, but he wasn't fast enough to kill the sorceress.

In a blink of an eye the hag changed form into a bat, the waistlet fell to the floor, and she made her escape through the bars in the window.

With the witch's hold over her broken, Tory had drawn herself up into the foetal position. Tiernan dropped to his knees at her side and called out, 'Maelgwn, the potion.'

The King held the tiny bottle in his hand. ''Tis an antidote for poison . . . but this?' Maelgwn slowly shook his head as he bent down beside her, overwhelmed by the excessive amount of blood she'd lost already. It was worse than any wound he'd ever seen; she would surely die within the hour.

As the pain from the explosions taking place inside her body became too much to bear, Tory screamed in agony, 'Forget me.'

'Nay, Tory.'

Maelgwn drew her up in his arms but Tory gripped hold of his shirt, determined to make herself clear. 'I am dead anyway, but Chiglas . . .' she gritted her teeth a moment to endure the pain, '. . . must pay for this.' She cried out, hunching her knees to her chest even tighter.

'Tory, I cannot leave thee, 'tis all my fault, I should have listened to thee.'

'Shh.' She brushed the tears from his eyes, as she felt herself become separated from the pain in her body. 'Maelgwn, my love, do this for me.'

He nodded reluctantly. 'Hold on,' he whispered, softly. 'I will think of something, I swear it.'

The King passed Tiernan the bottle and stood to leave. 'Stay with her, I shall return as fast as I can.' He pointed to Vanora's comatosed body on the ground. 'Bring her,' he instructed Angus.

The King and all the masters, bar Tiernan, made their way to the throne room to confront Chiglas. Even Ione joined them, as Cadogan had lost consciousness for the moment and she'd found there wasn't the same satisfaction to be had in beating his senseless body senseless.

Chiglas was seated on his throne appearing quite unconcerned that he and his advisers were surrounded by the enemy that had every imaginable form of weaponry pointed at them. Ossa, who'd managed to seize control of the fortress, was in the process of announcing that he was going to have the lying mongrel of a king ripped limb from limb.

'He be mine, Ossa,' Maelgwn announced rather bravely, as his warriors entered the room filled with Saxon soldiers.

'Well now, who should appear but Maelgwn of Gwynedd,' the Warlord said, noticing Ione was with him. 'What right hast thou to lay claim to my spoils, Dragon?'

'Chiglas hast slain my father, my unborn heir, and near killed my Queen. I have no argument with thee this day, Ossa, take thy due, but leave Chiglas to me. This be a kindred affair and none of thy concern.'

'Then we do have an argument,' Ossa concluded, not liking being told what to do. 'I took this fort, therefore Chiglas be my prisoner.'

'Thee could not take a horse! I had to open the gate for thee,' Brockwell heckled, and his fellow masters collapsed into laughter.

'Do not play me for the fool, boy, we raised the gate!' Ossa insisted.

Maelgwn, not so amused, replied, 'How would thee know, when thou wast unconscious at the time?'

Ione stepped forward to jerk Ossa's memory, appearing more than willing to knock him out again.

'But for my knight's mercy, thee would be a dead man. And believe me, she will not be so gracious next time,' Maelgwn cautioned.

Ossa observed Ione closely. 'A deal, then, Dragon. Give me this knight and I shall leave thee Chiglas.'

Ossa was not a young man, and his ungainly body was tall and top heavy. Most of the warrior's face was covered by a long, fair moustache and beard, which parted into two long braids. His long, thick hair was as fair as his beard and was beginning to grey with old age. The rest of his face, bar his small eyes of deep blue, was shielded by a heavy iron helmet that bore the face of a wildcat. He was clad in furs and armour, and on the whole was rather fierce in appearance.

Ione looked to Maelgwn for fear he might agree; most of the men she'd known would have.

'The exchange of women for profit be outlawed in Gwynedd, Ossa. But quite apart from that, Ione be one of my finest knights. I could ask her if she wishes to go with thee, but I have a feeling she would much prefer to take off thy head.' The King smiled as Ione drew her sword to confirm.

The Saxon Warlord was outraged at the insult. 'Enough! If thee will not make a deal, then die!' he decreed. 'Take them, but I want the girl alive.'

The room was thrown into chaos at his word. The Saxon cutthroats began to charge Maelgwn and his handful of knights, when the floor beneath their feet began to tremble.

In a flash of lightning, Mahaud appeared alongside Chiglas' throne. 'Fools!' the wretched hag shrieked, mocking the invaders with her laughter. 'Thou art all going to die.'

She raised her glowing fingertips to the closest Saxon soldier, and every man in the room took a step backwards as her victim yelled and burst into flames. Vortipor turned to the King of Gwynedd, and whispered, 'I am beginning to wish I had let thee talk me into staying at home. How dost one compete with this?'

Maelgwn looked at the flaming carcass, twitching furiously on the floor. 'I wish I knew.'

Chiglas' laughter was resonant over the din. He applauded Mahaud's display and continued to delight in it as she randomly picked off his foes. His enjoyment was thwarted, however, as once again the room began to shake, even more violently than before. Upon the first sign of danger, Mahaud suddenly vanished into thin air.

Each of the long windows around the room shattered, one by one, and the large doors burst open sending a wild wind ripping through the chamber. When all had calmed and those present dared to raise their heads, they saw Tory's bloodstained form in the doorway. She floated just above the ground, radiating a green glow so bright that the onlookers had to shield their eyes, and it was obvious to all that a divine force was upon her.

Maelgwn fell on one knee, so thankful he was to see the Goddess; now Tory would surely live. The King was not at all surprised when Taliesin followed Tory into the room with Sir Tiernan at his side. As they advanced, all present fell to their knees to pay homage to the miracle. Except, of course, Chiglas, who was now reduced to a blubbering mass of nerves. He sat on his throne, way too overweight to move of his own accord.

The Goddess first approached Maelgwn, touching his bowed head lightly with her fingertips. 'Fear not my young King, all shall be well with thy Queen. Thy forefathers will watch over thy heir, and I vow he shall return to thee.'

Maelgwn was so overcome, he could barely thank her. 'I am deeply indebted to thee, lady.'

Her huge, green–grey eyes turned to the Saxon Warlord, her expression more sombre. 'Ossa, son of Octa, thy breed have been a thorn in my side, ravaging my people and my lands.'

Ossa raised his eyes to look at the Goddess and was momentarily overcome by the great energy force that confronted him. Amazed, the Warlord experienced the wondrous peace and love that emanated from her, and begged, 'Be merciful on us, lady. We did not know.'

'How soon thy race forgets, Ossa. What of the repeated warnings Ambrosius gave thy father? Take thy due, no more or less, then return to the far east of the land with thy clan. And remember this, the moment any Saxon, Angle or Jute makes war on my native people, thou shalt all be driven from this land completely. If thee cannot live here in peace with us, thee shall not live here at all.'

Ossa nodded to confirm his understanding. 'Thou art too gracious. I shall do as thee bids at once.' He raised himself, rather eager to be gone. At his word, his men rose in an orderly fashion and quietly left the room.

The Goddess then turned to deal with Chiglas, who quivered like a great pile of jelly. 'I have nothing to say to thee Chiglas, although I do know someone who wishes an audience.'

Rufus' huge head appeared outside the broken windows, eyeing the wretched King with relish.

All of a sudden, Chiglas, throne and all, rose from the floor and was drawn closer towards the mouth of the huge beast, squirming and squealing in horror. His advisers, still cowering on the ground, prayed they were not next on the menu as the dragon opened its mighty jaws to swallow their King. The fire of its breath reduced the obese leader to dripping lard, and its mouth snapped shut, doing away with Chiglas' evil soul forever.

A round of applause sounded out, even from those who'd served him.

The Goddess faced Sir Brockwell and Lady Katren. 'As the next of the true lineage of Cunedda, after

Maelgwn, I acknowledge thy right to claim the title of a King, Calin Brockwell, through thy grandfather King Einion Yrth of Gwynedd. Thou hast always done the Great Houses and thy forefathers proud, and hence I offer to thee the throne of Powys. Dost thou accept this as thy destiny?'

Brockwell couldn't believe his ears. Nor could Katren, realising she was to be a Queen.

'I am thy humble servant, lady, and I thank thee for the honour.'

'You must join with Gwynedd, Dyfed, Dumnonia and Gwent Is Coed in the pact against the foreign raiders. For although Ossa hast promised to keep his distance, his race art of feeble character. We must prepare to confront them and others like them when they return.'

'Aye lady, I understand.' Brockwell held his hand to his heart to pledge this.

'Taliesin, I shall leave the Princess Vanora for thee to contend with as thou sees fit.'

The High Merlin bowed graciously.

The Goddess turned to Ione, who'd been watching quietly from a distance. 'Come forth child, I will not harm thee.'

Ione, sword in hand, came and knelt before the Goddess, her head bowed low as her eyes filled with tears of adoration.

'Thou art most pleasing to us, child. So much hardship thou hast known in thy short life, and still thou hast the faith to defend my cause. I could not leave such loyalty unrewarded, and thus my dear Ione, be silent no more.' The glowing figure reached down to hold Ione's face between her hands. The brilliant emanation enfolded her, before it dispersed completely. Thereupon, Tory collapsed and Ione caught her up before she hit the ground.

19

BURGEONING

The whole of Prydyn was thus united with Dumnonia against the invaders of Britain. Brockwell, Sir Tiernan and Vortipor remained at Arwystli to help set the kingdom's affairs in order. Reinforcements in the form of soldiers, accountants and advisers were assigned to the city from Gwynedd, Dyfed and Gwent Is Coed. It had been decided that Awrystli, in Powys, being the point most central to all, would become the official meeting place of the allies.

Sir Cadogan met his end in the belly of the dragon, as Maelgwn wasn't prepared to take any more chances with him. Lady Katren conveyed to the King the story of Caradoc's end and of his mother's last words with him. Hence Maelgwn resolved to have Caradoc's body taken back to Gwynedd, where he would have him cremated and his spirit put to rest in the mountains that he'd loved.

Rufus transported King Maelgwn, his unconscious Queen, Sir Angus, Lady Katren and Ione back to Gwynedd.

Tory remained in a deep sleep for days. Before the Goddess had left her body, Tory's bleeding had stopped and even the gash on her arm had vanished. Maelgwn had the word of the Goddess that his Queen would be alright, so he didn't fret for her physical welfare; it was more her mental and emotional state that worried him. Although Tory hadn't welcomed her pregnancy at first, prior to her abduction she had begun to warm to the commitment. Consequently, Maelgwn felt her ordeal all the more tragic.

On the eve following their return to Aberffraw, Maelgwn entered his chamber and was alarmed to find the bed empty. 'Tory?'

'Aye.'

He turned to see her huddled in the bath, gazing at the candlelight reflected in the water. 'How art thou feeling?' He heeded the sorrowful air about her.

'Empty,' she answered, but did not break from her trance.

Maelgwn's heart sank in his chest. 'I will not blame thee if thou doth despise me for life, I should have listened —'

'Nay!' Tory was jolted from her sad reflection. ''Twas not thy fault, Maelgwn, and I do not blame thee.' Her tone was firm, yet she did not look at him. 'I blame myself.'

'That be ludicrous! How in the name of the Goddess could thee have —'

'I did not want this child!' She interjected, angry at herself. 'I am responsible for everything that happens to me in this life! I create my own reality. My mentors have warned me repeatedly to be careful of what I wish for.'

'But thou wast of a totally different mind before thy betrayal.'

'But by then it was already too late. Dost thou not see?' Her sorrow came to the fore and tears began to roll down her cheeks. 'I had already sealed its fate.'

Maelgwn couldn't just stand by and watch her fall to pieces. 'Come on.' He took up her big wrap to encourage her out of the bath.

Tory was slow to comply. But when she did finally emerge from the water, Maelgwn placed the garment around her and carried her to the bed. It was comforting to feel him close, and Tory hated to feel that she'd let him down. 'I made the wrong decisions and sacrificed thy heir. I am so sorry, Maelgwn. I know how much it meant to thee.'

'Tory!' He placed her on the bed, and took a seat beside her. 'Only so our marriage could be recognised and no other reason. I would not care if we never have a child, so long as I have thee. This law in regard to an heir be totally absurd. And I, as the King, intend to do away with it. If we do not have a boy child, Brockwell and his sons shall inherit the throne of Gwynedd.'

Tory threw her arms over his shoulders to embrace him. 'Doth thou really mean it?'

'Aye, I do. Thou art the only thing on this earth that I care about, Tory. Nothing should overshadow our life together.'

Tory drew away from him as another matter came to mind that was just as disturbing. 'How can I still be living and breathing, Maelgwn? Was I not dying when thee left me in the prison tower?'

'Dost thou not remember?' The King had quizzed Taliesin about this, yet the Merlin refused to discuss it until he had spoken with Tory first.

'Nay, last I recall was when I saw thee leave. Beyond that? Just all the blood, Sir Tiernan's face, and then nothing.' Tory become more anxious as her senses returned to her and she considered all she'd missed. 'Tell me everything Maelgwn, what hast happened? Be everyone alright? What of Katren?'

'Slow down. Everyone and everything be fine, I assure thee. Taliesin said he would visit soon to clarify all that I cannot. However, I can endeavour to tell thee what I understand befell at Arwystli.'

'Please do.'

The King began his tale at the discovery of her abduction, omitting nothing as he described the events that led to her collapse in Chiglas' throne room, where the Goddess left her body cured of all its ailments.

Tory had to admit she was a mite disappointed about the wound on her shoulder. After all that pain, she didn't even have a battle scar to show for it. In fact, as Maelgwn pointed out, even the scar on her neck that Brockwell had given her the day they'd met had vanished.

She was delighted to learn of Brockwell's firm engagement to Lady Katren, and of their plan to wed on Beltaine, just as Katren had originally requested.

Brockwell had also decided to recognise Bryce as his son. He knew how much his intended bride cared for the boy, and he had grown rather fond of Bryce himself. The spirited child, who was already the recognised heir to his estate and title at Penmon, would now be recognised as heir to his throne in Powys, should Calin and Katren not have a male child of their own.

Only one thing remained to taunt Tory in the wake of the ordeal; the crone had escaped.

'Who was Mahaud?' she asked the King.

'I know little, bar that she lives in the land of shadows consorting with the powers of darkness, the lowest forms of Otherworld entities that dwell in the deepest depths of consciousness. To support her earthly existence, she must feed upon the energy generated by the negative thoughts and the low acts of human beings. Hence, she attaches herself to any ruler with evil intent. This be why the dark sorceress cannot exist here in Gwynedd, as there be insuffient evil to sustain her. Cadfer sought her aid to overthrow my father but, as with Chiglas, she fled. Mahaud must have been quietly spinning her evil web in Powys ever since. Taliesin be the one to ask about her, not me. For it be the Merlin whom Mahaud fears and ultimately wishes to thwart.'

'But why, what did Taliesin do to her?'

Maelgwn shrugged, apologetically. 'Taliesin did explain it all to me once, but I am afraid I was too young to truly grasp it. I think he said it had something to do with polarity.'

'What? Like the law of opposites, positive and negative, that sort of thing?'

'Aye, I believe so,' Maelgwn confirmed, wanting to put her mind at rest. 'Please, Tory, forget Mahaud, she cannot seek thee here.'

But the Queen could not forget the old witch, or what she had done to their child. There were still so many questions in her mind, and Tory was sure Maelgwn was hiding something. 'So if Mahaud was aiding Cadfer, she was the reason Sorcha took to studying under Taliesin.'

'Perhaps thou art right, Tory, I really would not know. I was only two years of age at the time.' Maelgwn raised himself from the bed.

'Have I said something to annoy thee?'

'All I know,' Maelgwn replied, 'be that after she took to studying under the High Merlin, her relationship with my father was never the same.'

'Thy father did not approve?'

Maelgwn was silent a moment. 'He did not understand.'

Tory knew she would only aggravate him further if she pursued the issue, so she would just have to wait till Taliesin arrived to get some answers.

The High Merlin made his appearance at Aberffraw late the next morning. He explained over lunch, with those masters left at the house, that he'd been detained at Arwystli, weaning out Chiglas' die-hard supporters. To set Lady Katren's mind at ease, Taliesin remarked that most of the landowners in Powys were gratified to be rid of the tyrannous king and were eager to embrace the ways of the Goddess once more. It was common knowledge that Gwynedd had been well favoured by the Goddess, and as a result had become the most prosperous kingdom in Prydyn and most likely in the whole of Britain. Thus the lords of Powys hoped that now their kingdom would again see peace and prosper as did its neighbours within their allegiance. Taliesin explained that Brockwell, Sir Tiernan and Vortipor would return within the month to see out the rest of the cold season at Aberffraw.

Those present at the castle had continued to train in the absence of the others, but it wasn't the same without the complete circle of twelve. Calin's one regret about his new appointment was that his tuition might have to come to an end. With this in mind, Taliesin suggested that the masters should continue their training during the cold seasons. Though many had kingdoms and estates of their own to run, in the heart of winter there was little required of a custodian to maintain his lands. The individual heads of State could then train their own troops in the warmer months.

All at lunch agreed wholeheartedly to the suggestion and drank a toast to the High Merlin, the Goddess and the Masters of the Dragon.

After they had dined, the King and Percival excused themselves as they had much work to do. Taliesin considered this rather fortunate, as he could now speak to the Queen in private. He led her to the north tower, where they would not be disturbed.

'What is the great mystery, Taliesin? Why are you acting so strangely?' Tory waited patiently while he fumbled with the key in the door. He then gestured politely for her to enter, his eyes of soft mauve meeting hers as she passed him.

Tory climbed the stairs to the caphouse. 'I shall send for some firewood,' she said, as the temperature here was well below freezing.

'No need,' Taliesin replied. He flicked his fingers over the fireplace, igniting the pile of damp and rotting timber as though it were dry twigs.

'I keep forgetting.' Tory smiled, moving to warm herself by the raging fire. 'Do you feel the cold?'

'No.' The Merlin took a seat on the bed. 'Temperature is just the elementals playing tricks on your mind, you know that.'

'Do you feel anything at all?'

'No, I do not feel . . . I experience. So while I do not feel the cold, I may experience it, if I so choose.'

'Does the same rule apply for emotions?'

'The emotions one experiences are always of one's own choosing, Tory. Though I endeavour to surround myself with positive ones.'

'But what of love, Taliesin? Have you never been in love?'

A smile crossed his lovely face, and for a moment Tory could have sworn that he was blushing. 'Why of course I have. I have not always been as I am now.' Taliesin cunningly led the conversation toward another more relevant issue, and Tory took the bait.

'So what are you now?'

'Where, is a more apt question. Have you ever heard of the Spirits of the Seven Rays, or in angelology, the Seven Spirits of God?'

'The *what?* It sounds like something religious, and therefore I would know nothing about it.'

'No it isn't really, though every religion and culture has its own explanation of it. I just have to figure by what term you would know it. Let me see now ...' Taliesin paused to consider. He knew Tory understood this, as in pastlife incarnation, it had been he who had taught it to her. 'Do you know anything of theosophy, or more specifically, the Seven Planetary Chain Logoi, perhaps?'

'Is that something to do with the Greeks?' Tory had a vague recollection of it in one of her courses.

'I've got it!' He held up a finger, bursting into a smile of revelation. 'The seven planes of existence, the seven bodies or principles of man.'

'Now you're talking.' Tory slapped her hands together. 'Yes I do, this physical or earth plane being the first of the seven and that of nature. There are planes to be found lower in density, or hell, as some might choose to call it.'

The Merlin encouraged her to continue, leaning back on the bed to get more comfortable. *Let's see how much she remembers.*

'Alright,' Tory began, a mite bothered that he saw fit to test her. 'The astral plane is the second body or plane, which is comprised of emotion. As Earth's etheric double, it penetrates the physical. On the third plane, the forces of will find expression, as it is the plane of thought. Again penetrating the first two planes, it is of a faster vibrational frequency. Therefore, like the astral plane and the planes that exceed it, it cannot be viewed by the human eye, but may be perceived through the third or mind's eye.'

The Merlin bowed his head as if to compliment her understanding, and awaited the rest of the address.

'The fourth is the plane of wisdom, from whence all imagination and inspiration comes. The fifth plane is spiritual or the plane of the self, from which stems desire, but only the desire for the highest good of the overall plan of creation. Must I go on?'

'Please.'

'The sixth plane is . . . let me think? Oh yes! The sixth is that of involution, the last progression of the soulmind before it again becomes one with the perfection of totality, which is, of course, to be found on the seventh plane. Hence where comes the term "seventh heaven". Good enough?' Tory concluded, rather pleased with herself.

'That's what you meant, isn't it?' she realised. 'When you said you had been forward and backward in time. *Time* meaning the moment when you parted from totality, to the moment you shall become one with it again. Rather than human *time*, as it is known and counted in years or minutes.'

Taliesin smiled, pleased with her conclusion. 'You have learnt your lessons well, Tory Alexander.'

He paused to observe her for a moment, making Tory feel altogether ill at ease. It was as if he was adoring her and she experienced an eerie sense of deja-vu.

'So in answer to your question, "where am I now?"' he sat upright, 'in angelology terms I would be known as a master, as say the Master Buddha before he moved on in his journey toward awareness. This be the last level of consciousness where I may still function in a physical body. Beyond the understanding I have, there are only two higher realms of awareness that exist in the etheric world — Lordship and Godhood.'

'The sixth and seventh planes . . .' Tory uttered, as she attempted to digest his story. 'So what you're telling me is that you are a real, honest to god angel!'

'Angel, deva, etheric world intelligence, whatever you want to call it; as is everyone and everything that has a soul, to differing degrees and polarities.'

Tory was fit to faint. 'But how? Taliesin, you must have been human once, how did you become so aware?'

'Well, to tell you the truth, it was a bit of an accident really, and a very long story . . .'

'Please, Taliesin, I would love to know, if you are in any way disposed towards enlightening me,' Tory pleaded, using her big green eyes to her best advantage as she knelt down beside the fire.

'Well, if you really want to hear it.' He reclined on the bed to tell his tale. 'I've lived many different lives, just as you have, not consciously recalling one from another, until I was born in Britain, the son of Gwreang of Llanfair who named me Gwion Bach. This was about the same time the great Pyramid wars were taking place in Egypt, and here in Britain, it was a time of great sorcery, to be sure!'

'But that was four thousand years ago! I didn't realise Britain was even populated then, by civilised folk anyway.'

'Oh yes,' Taliesin assured her. 'What of Stonehenge and the Glastonbury Zodic? Under the roads built by the Romans during their invasion, there are tracks dating back thousands and thousands of years. The Middle East was not the only area to which the Atlanteans fled,' he explained before returning to his story. 'It was here in Gwynedd that I met a High Merlin, through whom I was eventually introduced to the great Goddess, Keridwen.'

'Your mother?' Tory was confused already.

'My spiritual mother. She transformed my consciousness and thus I was reborn and proclaimed my true name, Taliesin. Keridwen was once a guardian of Britain, as I am. I inherited the position, so to speak. And although she now resides in the Otherworld, she still sees and speaks through the more enlightened souls who remain here in the Middle Kingdoms.'

'I don't understand. What do you mean when you say Keridwen transformed your consciousness?'

'Ahh well, that's where the mistake comes in. You see, I was assisting in an experiment, the creation of a brew of knowledge that was intended for her son. Keridwen had many children, two of which were twins, a boy and a girl as it happens. Her daughter, Creirwy, was a raving beauty, intelligent and perfect in every way.'

'But he was just the opposite, right?'

'Right. Monfan, which meant great cow, was nicknamed Afagddu, meaning utter darkness.'

Tory burst into laughter, but her expression reflected disgust. 'Didn't have much of a chance either way, did he?'

'Not really, no. He was so ugly that no man would fight him at the battle of Camlann, mistakenly thinking he was the devil. Hence with her brew, Keridwen sought to make Monfan wise, to overcome his other more obvious disadvantages.'

'You didn't drink it, Taliesin?'

'No, but just as the cauldron had almost burnt dry, after a year and a day of careful tending and stirring, one drop of the three that remained accidentally splashed on my hand, and I was rushed by waves of knowledge for which I was totally unprepared. Needless to say, Keridwen's potion was ruined.'

'She must have been furious,' Tory said, fascinated. 'What did you do?'

'What did I do? I changed into a hare and fled as fast as I could.'

'Can you really change form?'

'Even Maelgwn could change form when he was a child, and was well practised at it. I learnt the craft from a High Merlin way back in the early days of my youth as Gwion Bach. In any case, I needn't have bothered. Keridwen caught up with me in no time.' Taliesin came to sit by the fire with Tory. 'The Goddess knew it hadn't really been my fault, yet I did pose a problem. A soul mind as naive as mine was then wasn't ready for the wealth of knowledge that had been bestowed on it. I became, as most who delve into mysteries and powers beyond their understanding, prone to be led astray by negative or dark forces, like Mahaud, for example.'

'Mahaud!'

'Yes, but I shall speak of her another day,' Taliesin said quickly, as they had already moved too far from what he'd really come to say.

'So how did Keridwen expect her son could cope with all this knowledge?'

'She intended to mould him over the years, and was not so inclined towards awarding me such time and attention. Yet, she did not want to waste the knowledge I had gained. What happened next is hard to explain. She swallowed my soul, and it was how it might feel to you when she takes over your body: purifying, exhilarating, enlightening! She stayed at one with me for nine months.'

'You must have been completely wiped out.'

'Well I was! When I emerged from the daze I was unrecognisable and remembered little. I was sent as a bard to the court and service of Elffin, a distant ascendant of Maelgwn's great grandfather. The rest is history really. In time, I discovered that I had transcended death. I was free to explore all the realms of time and space, those to which one can transport a physical form, that is. I'll grant that the thought of being immortal, free from disease and death for all time, was rather daunting at first. Until I discovered that it was just one simple step in many during my soul mind's evolution.'

Tory leant back against a chair, her brain on overload. 'Is there a reason why you're telling me all this now?'

'Yes there is,' he confessed, not feeling as eager to be out with it now.

Tory closed her eyes, already knowing what Taliesin was about to say. 'I knew it, I should have died at Arwystli.'

'Indeed.'

'So I'm immortal, am I!' She scoffed at the notion.

'Haven't you noticed that your body is no longer scarred or blemished, and all those aches and pains you used to have are gone?'

Tory couldn't dispute this. She wasn't sure that she wanted to know anymore, but she had to ask, 'How, Taliesin?'

'An immortality potion of the ancients. I have been saving it for eons.'

Now Tory really was confused. 'Well why didn't you just give the potion to Sorcha when she was dying? It would have saved you all this trouble?'

Taliesin was somewhat disconcerted by the question. Tory sensed this and what's more, he detected her doing so. 'It wasn't meant for Sorcha, the ancients intended it for you.'

'But why me? Are the Gods following the development of everyone on this planet as closely as they have apparently been following mine?'

'Yes they are, as a matter of fact.' He bowed his head to confess what he must. 'I have been deceiving you, Tory Alexander.'

Tory was taken aback, as a white light began to exude from his body and a transformation began. She stopped breathing as the Merlin's hair, skin colour and very form changed before her eyes. Staring back at her was a totally different man.

'Teo.' Tory beheld her *sensei* of many years. He was, besides Maelgwn, the only man she'd ever slept with. 'God, no.' She rose to her feet, scared of the feelings the sight of him aroused in her. 'It isn't true.'

'Tory, be calm.'

But she turned away, not wanting to look into those dark eyes so full of reason. Unfortunately, Teo had a body and face that would shame Adonis. His long dark hair fell in a braid to his waist and his smooth olive skin had never known a blemish.

'I knew he was too perfect to be real,' she exclaimed.

'This is how I appeared when I was Gwion Bach. Teo was one of my earthly incarnations, long before I ever met with Keridwen. What I felt and did when I was Teo was very real, to me anyway.'

She raised her hands to block her ears, for it was Teo's voice also. 'So why the disguise? Why did you allow me to fall in love with Maelgwn, if you only intended to haunt me thus? Or is this your revenge for my decision, when it was you who served me the ultimatum?' Tory burst into tears.

Taliesin took hold of her arms, his energy calming her at once. 'Listen to me, I did not assume this form to deceive you. With all my travels through time I found a disguise necessary. I have bumped into many of my past-life incarnations in different periods of history, and it saved me from being confused with them, or giving them heart failure upon meeting themselves. Maelgwn is your destiny, I know that now. Please believe I am beyond the concept of earthly love, as you and

Maelgwn know it. I flourish, as do we all, on the pure energy your devotion for each other creates. The last thing in the world I wish to do is to divide you.'

'I did love you, Teo. I remember everything you taught me.' She drew enough courage to reach out and hold his face. 'I always thought you had the makings of an angel, and now you are.'

'See, you made the right decision after all. If you'd stayed with Teo, you wouldn't have ended up here.' He let her go and took a few steps back, resuming his normal form. 'I can be of much greater assistance to you now than I could ever have been then.'

'You are. I want you to know that, no matter how I do challenge you at times.'

'I know.' He put his arm around her and gave her a squeeze of assurance as he led her back to the fire.

'You still haven't explained why the Gods chose me.'

'Why do they choose anyone?' he answered. 'All shall be made clear to you in time. As I have had to seek my own truths, so must you seek yours.'

Tory resumed her seat on the large floor cushions, with Taliesin beside her, finding his reason of no comfort. 'Well how are we going to break this to Maelgwn?'

'A good question, but you must decide the answer on your own, I'm afraid. Although, I will say this, if you wish it, Maelgwn and indeed all around you may witness you age gradually. You can appear to be whatever image you choose to project, as I do. You shall simply outlive everyone and move onto new realms and adventures. But you won't have to die in between, and you won't lose track of your accumulated knowledge.'

'I will see everybody die.' Tory was saddened by the thought.

'And reborn again.'

She tried to comprehend his words, but the concept was too overwhelming to cope with in a second. 'You will always be here?' she asked, seeking some sort of stronghold in the universe she now seemed lost in.

'For some time yet.'

Tory exhaled deeply and her thoughts turned back to the King; this was a tough one. 'I have always been honest with Maelgwn. But I dare say, if he finds out you were an old flame, past incarnation or no, we'd have Buckley's chance of you ever being allowed to teach me anything.'

'Now did I say anything about instructing you?'

'Come on, Taliesin. I may be naive but I'm not stupid. Isn't that what this is all about? You'll want to move on eventually, as Keridwen did, and seek another to take your place.'

Taliesin didn't have to confirm her query, as his grin gave him away. 'Perhaps that is the way of it, but only time will tell.'

Tory and Taliesin talked well into the evening before he bid her farewell. The High Merlin still had much work to do before summer solstice, when he would attempt to send Tory home. Taliesin swore he would return with Selwyn before Beltaine, May first, to celebrate the feast of the Goddess, and indeed his own birthday, with all at Aberffraw.

As predicted, Brockwell, Tiernan and Vortipor returned to Aberffraw within the month, eager to resume their training and the company of their close circle of friends.

The winter cold was well upon the isle, isolating it from the treachery and strife of the outside world. Those staying at the castle were more than thankful for the time to recuperate; their peaceful interlude would span near one third of a year.

20

BELTAINE

By spring the snow had passed and torrential rain had transformed the pure white fields into dirty brown puddles of sludge. It wasn't until late April that the sun really burst through the clouds, awakening the land from its sleep. With the days growing longer, farmers began ploughing their fields, and the animals were freed from their winter confinement. Trees and flowers were budding, and it seemed the whole land was crying out for joy in the warmth of the sun's rays.

The soldiers who'd left Aberffraw for the cold spell, now returned to their posts. Lady Gladys and the young Earl of Penmon arrived back earlier than expected. The suspense of waiting to hear what had happened at the castle over the cold seasons had become too much to bear. Bryce was particularly eager to get back to all the action, and had been so for months. Lady Gladys was overjoyed to learn of Calin's intent to wed Lady Katren, and the old schemer acted completely surprised when he told her. But when Calin sprang on her the news of his Princedom, the old lady became so excited, she fainted. When she was revived the courtiers all teased her by threatening not to tell her the rest of their news as they feared it might be fatal.

Bryce could hardly contain himself when he learnt he was to be a prince, and was addressing Calin as father by the end of lunch. Likewise, the child was thrilled to know that Lady Katren would soon be his mother. He had wished for nothing more since the day they'd first met, and quite openly stated as much. The young Earl of Penmon, unlike his father, had no problem expressing his emotions.

Jenovefa and Rhys introduced Lady Gladys to their new son, Gawain, and she eagerly embraced him.

Amidst all the stories of creatures, sorcery, villains and battles that were being sprung on the wide-eyed boy and his grandmother, Cara and Vortipor brought the whole room to silence with the announcement of their engagement.

Vortipor apologised for having to steal such a lovely lady from the household at Aberffraw, but he could not bring himself to leave without her. The couple planned to leave for Dyfed before Beltaine, also wanting to wed on the feast of the Mother Goddess, but in accordance with the traditions of the Desi Clan. King Maelgwn congratulated his friend, expressing his heartfelt disappointment they would not be able to attend, with Calin and Katren's wedding the same day in Gwynedd. Vortipor understood and promised he would stay with them until after Calin's inauguration, two weeks hence.

In the short time that was left of their winter training, the masters began to practise in the wide open spaces. Tory held kata on the beach, which was quite a spectacle for the locals. Stories of the masters' escapades had spread throughout the land over the long cold months. Common folk and soldiers alike had begun to gather at dawn to observe the band as they practised the art of the Goddess. Within a few days, Tory noticed that some of the onlookers were trying to grasp the movements, especially the children.

This pleased her very much, as the work on their school was nearly complete, and it was obvious that the youngsters would take to the training as ardently as had Bryce. Alma was appointed to instruct the local children in self-defence and meditation over the warm seasons. Angus was training the men at Aberffraw, so the pair could still work together.

The female hall was only weeks away from opening — Old Hetty's girls and the young maidens throughout the kingdom would be able to take up residence after Beltaine. Ione would be their instructor. She was to sort out the warriors from those who were more domestically inclined, and thus develop the girls' individual interests and talents. The maidens who opted for domestic training would be assigned to Lady Gladys and the head maid, Drusilla, for some of their instruction, but all would be taught basic self-defence.

Ione was now enjoying a vastly different lifestyle and outlook. She strutted around dressed like a man, as did the Queen more often than not, her sword at her hip and her head held high. Men who had once abused and looked down on her, now praised and adored her, for she was the woman who had defeated Ossa, Warlord of the Saxons, in armed combat. This was a formidable triumph for any warrior. So Ione, who claimed to be totally disinterested in men, had more suitors than she knew what to do with, though Tiernan wasn't one of them. The gift of speech didn't seem to make it any easier to express her true feelings; after eleven years without words, they did not come easy.

The other masters were basking in the notoriety, as everywhere they went people stood in awe of the uniform bearing the Dragon. No one could understand how such a small group of knights, half of which were women, could seize a whole kingdom. It was said the divine was upon the order and thus everyone wanted to be part of it.

Grading was held two days before Calin's inauguration, and all the students managed to achieve a whole grade this time. The masters could now wear their uniforms of black, for they departed the room as teachers, until next autumn when they would again return to Aberffraw to resume their training.

The males of the household at Aberffraw were joined by the knights and landowners of Gwynedd, as well as the heads of State and noblemen of Powys, to bear witness to Prince Brockwell's inauguration. King Catulus of Dumnonia had made the trip especially and brought with him old King Caninus of Gwent Is Coed, who hoped to gain a further insight into the ways of his ancestors.

Tory waited patiently for Katren to wish Calin farewell. By the time she did finally part with him, some of the men had already begun to leave. As Calin ran to his mount, Tory called after him, 'Calin wait.'

He paused, one foot already in the stirrup. 'Majesty please, I shall never get out of here.'

Tory ran to catch him up, pulling out from behind her back Brian's leather jacket. 'I just wanted to give thee this, for good luck.'

Calin was truly touched and took hold of the jacket as if it were a great treasure. 'But this was thy brother's, all thou hast to remember him by.'

'I have thee,' she proffered assuredly. 'Besides, it was Brian's lucky jacket. Saved his butt so many times thee would not believe! Take it, it belongs to thee.'

Calin removed his woollen cape and pulled on the jacket, which fitted him perfectly. 'This be truly remarkable,' he exclaimed, as he admired the workmanship.

'It will help to keep the rain out, too,' Tory informed him with a pat on the back. 'Good luck on thy quest bro, though I know thee will not need it.'

'Many thanks.' Calin unexpectedly hugged her tight. 'I do love thee, Tory,' he whispered.

She pulled away from him, rolling her eyes that were now moist with tears. 'Men!'

They both laughed and with another embrace, Calin finally mounted his horse.

'I shall see thee soon.' Tory held out her hand for a high-five in parting.

Calin slapped it. 'Count on it.' He dug in his heels and was away after the others.

No sooner had the last man departed, than Tory found Jenovefa at her side. 'Majesty, I have had the most wonderful idea.'

'And what might that be?' inquired Tory, as if she couldn't guess.

'Well, as the men will be gone for the next few days, and I am much recovered from Gawain's birth, I thought that perhaps I could train with thee and the other girls, just to see how I fare.' Her large eyes that looked up at Tory were so filled with ardour that the Queen could hardly say no.

'Thou hast discussed this with Rhys?'

'Nay,' Jenovefa replied, disappointed. 'Not since before the birth, and then he refused to so much as consider it. But, Majesty, thee said . . .'

'I know what I said. It be your choice, Jenovefa, and I will train thee. But thou must take responsibility for thy own decisions, speak up for thyself. And if thy husband does not like it . . . then . . . then, I shall talk to him,' Tory resolved, knowing she was destined to get the blame anyway.

Jenovefa was so ecstatic that she hugged the Queen. 'Oh how can I thank thee, Majesty?'

'Talk to thy husband.'

'I will Majesty, I promise. As soon as he returns.' Her excitement waned a little. 'Still I fear his response will be the same.'

'We will see.' Tory seemed so confident that Jenovefa's spirits lifted, and she escorted the Queen to the gym.

To prove his worth, Calin was sent on an errand to Dalriada, lower Scotland, to see a man by the name of Fergus MacErc who had arrived in Dalriada from Scotta (Ireland), only a decade before. He had established his dynasty at Dunadd with the aid of a mere one hundred and fifty men and his two brothers, Loarn and Aengus. Although the MacErc clan had yet to come to power, it was known to the Goddess that every great Scottish king would be derived from their seed.

The task assigned to Brockwell by the Goddess proved not so daunting as first expected. The leader turned out to be an old ally of Vortipor's kindred, and thus the protector of Dyfed had written a letter of favour sealed with the mark of the Desi. With this letter and a copy of the pact, which now also encompassed Powys, Brockwell climbed upon the griffin and flew off into the sunrise. He was to deliver a message from the Goddess to the Clan MacErc. The message was a warning and pertained to the fate of their descendants and of Dalriada, if they did not heed her call. For as history stood, the Scots, as they were to be known, would spend the next five hundred years trying to establish their kingdom while fending off Viking, Anglo-Saxon and Norman raiders, to whom they would eventually lose not only Dalriada, but their homeland of Scotia as well. Brockwell was to inform the MacErc of the victories the pact had already won and invite the leaders of the clan to the next meeting of the alliance, to be held in the middle of the month-long festival of Lughnasa, at Arwystli in Powys.

The inauguration party arrived back from Llyn Cerrig Bach two days later to feast and await Brockwell's return.

Selwyn accompanied the men back from the temple ruins, where he'd assisted Taliesin in performing the initiation rites. The young musician was truly beginning to look like a bard after spending the winter with the High Merlin. He had a kind of windswept and mysterious look about him, and he appeared not at all like the boy who'd left Aberffraw less than six months before. Selwyn rode back into town on a handsome white horse, his mule lugging his harp and other possessions behind him.

Not in the mood for feasting with a bunch of guys still tripping out on one of Taliesin's concoctions, Tory suggested to Selwyn that they sneak away to her chambers where it was quieter and they could talk in peace. Maelgwn joined them by the fire for a time, and Tory was gratified to see that the King no longer addressed Selwyn in the manner he had when the boy was his page.

Selwyn marked the change also as he excitedly conveyed to Maelgwn the tales of his adventures inside the Merlin's labyrinth. For the first time, His Royal Highness was listening with interest to the boy's words, laughing in delight and recognition at his stories.

Maelgwn had never known anyone, apart from himself and his mother, whom the Merlin had taken under his wing, and he understood all too well the standards that Taliesin expected. If the High Merlin was tutoring Selwyn in the mysteries, the boy must be a fine scholar indeed and no doubt had an important role in Taliesin's scheme.

Maelgwn had acquired another young page to order about in Selwyn's stead. He went by the name of Tadgh, and had served Sir Gilmore before his untimely death. Tadgh seemed too light-hearted to succeed as either a scholar or a soldier, as he was more like a court jester. He was frightfully amusing at times, very polite and entirely trustworthy. Still, the King was disappointed that his new page was not musically inclined like Selwyn. He'd been trying to ignore the humour of his new aspirant, but Tadgh was proving far too likeable. He was determined to win the King's favour and no matter how short Maelgwn's tether, Tadgh kept his good spirits and employed a quick wit. A little smaller than Selwyn and of slight build, Tadgh was aged four and ten. He had waves of thick dark brown hair that fell to his shoulders, green eyes, rosy red cheeks, and was of a fair complexion.

The page was pouring mead while Tory and Maelgwn listened intently to Selwyn tell the tale of how he'd come by his horse. But the enchanting anecdote was cut short by an impatient pounding on the door.

'Please, make haste if thy matter be so pressing,' Maelgwn instructed, not really wishing to be disturbed.

Sir Rhys entered holding a hand over one eye, and he appeared extremely angry as he stormed towards them. 'I am sorry to disturb thee, Majesty.' The knight was so enraged that he had to grit his teeth to articulate his words. 'But I demand to know what thy Queen hast done to my wife?'

The King remained seated as he addressed his knight, sounding not in the least bit bothered by Rhys' foul mood. 'Something vexes thee?'

Rhys' hand half covered his face, as he turned to the Queen. 'Why be my wife practising mastery techniques in our chamber? She near took my eye out when I entered.' Rhys divulged his afflicted eye, which was inflamed and beginning to darken to a bruise.

The King couldn't refrain from laughter, and Tory, Selwyn, and even Tadgh collapsed into hysterics.

'This be no laughing matter,' Rhys beseeched them, indignant. 'Jenovefa was perfectly content to be my wife before she met thee, Your Majesty. To love and obey, that be what our vows stated. Thus, I *forbid* her to train under thee.'

Maelgwn felt Tory's patience snap and he rose to intervene if necessary.

'Then I shall divorce thee.'

They all turned to find Jenovefa standing in the doorway.

'Better a life without love, than a life without freedom,' she resolved, solemnly.

'I thought I told thee to wait in our room.' Rhys moved to physically remove her.

'Art thou not listening! I shall leave thee, Rhys, and then thee will have no say in what I do.' She avoided him and made haste to the side of the Queen.

'She can legally do that,' Maelgwn cautioned Rhys, who was becoming increasingly agitated by the second.

'I blame thee for this, Maelgwn. This whole situation be well out of control and 'twas of thy making.'

'Now wait a minute.' The Queen approached the knight. 'I believe there be one small point thou art overlooking. What would happen if thou wast away fighting a campaign somewhere . . .' Tory circled Rhys as she spun her scenario. 'And thy estate at Din Lligwy was raided? Now most of the women in Gwynedd will have been trained in self-defence, but not Jenovefa. So what becomes of thy wife then? Need I tell thee, she would be dead!' Tory thundered, annoyed by his selfishness. 'How dare thee blame thy King for thy shortcomings. Thine own fear and arrogance hast brought about the ill will between thee and thy wife. Face it Rhys, though thee may have the mind of a great scholar, thee can still not grasp the simple concept that we art all created equal. Every human being hast the right to their freedom, to be heard, to make their own decisions, to live and love as they see fit. Love and respect, sir, art not a condition of marriage, they must be earned!' Tory paused, having exhausted her frustration. 'Am I getting through at all?'

Rhys, whose eyes were downcast, nodded and replied, 'I understand well enough.' The law was on the Queen's side. If he didn't agree with her he would lose his wife and be forced to forfeit his place in the circle of twelve, neither of which he was prepared to relinquish. 'I apologise, Majesty.' Rhys swallowed his pride. 'I did not think.'

Satisfied that her husband had realised his mistake, Jenovefa said she was sorry she'd punched him in the eye and swore that from now on she would confine her practice to within the walls of the gymnasium.

Three days later, Brockwell arrived home from his quest triumphant. He rode into Aberffraw in the company of the High Merlin. Katren made sure the whole household was aware of his return, and everyone rushed to the courtyard to meet them.

Calin jumped from his saddle, appearing most impressed with himself. He took hold of Katren to bequeath a kiss, pleased to confess, "Tis all I have thought about for days.'

As Calin couldn't drag himself away from his beloved, Taliesin took the liberty of informing the gathering of the outcome of the quest. He announced that the pending King of Powys had not only persuaded the MacErc clan to come to the allies' gathering, but had also convinced the leaders to sign the pact. The Anglo-Saxons had already begun to raid their lands in Cumbria, and the Picts, in the upper highlands of Alban, were proving just as troublesome. The men who had witnessed Calin's initiation rites were most impressed, for no one had ventured into the mysterious and savage land of Dalriada and lived to tell of it.

The Merlin dismounted and Maelgwn greeted him warmly. 'Good morning, High Merlin, how is everything with you this fine day?'

'Very well indeed, Majesty.' He thought nothing of the King's words for a moment and then he realised.

'Splendid! Tory hast been teaching thee English.' Taliesin was in the best of moods as he placed his arm around his pupil and accompanied him inside. 'It would seem there be much to celebrate at Aberffraw this night.'

On the eve of the wedding and the feast of Beltaine, the guests residing at the castle at Aberffraw were treated to the story of the first of May which they were to celebrate. The High Merlin took his place by the fire, his goblet filled with mead. Selwyn sat alongside him with his harp to enhance the tale with the heavenly strains of his strings. Taliesin waited for his audience to settle before he began the tale. As a hush came over the room, he asked, 'The word "Beltaine" means?'

'Fires of Beli.' All bar Tory replied in unison; they had obviously heard this story before.

'And Beli was?'

'The God of life and death. The father of gods and men.' The room resounded with amusement.

'Who be telling this story?' Calin added in jest, not moving from his place alongside Katren at the Merlin's feet.

Taliesin gave Calin a look of caution as he resumed. 'Beli's story dates back to a time when the Otherworld and the Middle Kingdom co-existed on the same plane. Beli came to our land from the Honey Isle, which your Majesty,' Taliesin pointed out for Tory's information, 'might know better as Atlantis.'

The Merlin had spoken to Tory about Atlantis when they'd last met, nearly five months ago. The subject had arisen when Tory had asked how Taliesin had obtained his knowledge of the mystic forces that surrounded the planet; how he had learnt the secrets of time travel, the megaliths and the higher realms of consciousness. Taliesin explained that he'd lived year to year through history, growing increasingly frustrated with humanity's decline, and his inability to do anything about it. At his wit's end, Taliesin finally besought Keridwen to help him amend the state of Britain. The Goddess had previously said that Taliesin must acquire these skills on his own to amend his error in ruining her potion. But in her mercy and wisdom, she sent the High Merlin back to Atlantis to learn from the Ancients.

'I follow thee, Taliesin,' Tory told him. 'I recall thee mentioning Beli in one of thy poems, where thee described the land surrounded by deep moats from which he came. I understand that thee referred to Atlantis as the Honey Isle in the poem, because of the sweetness of the forgotten knowledge to be found there. As thee depicted Beli as the Dragon, who became the guardian spirit of Britain, I assume he was a great ancestor of Maelgwn.' Tory had been taking a closer look at the Merlin's writings over the cold season and his riddles were beginning to make more sense to her.

Taliesin confirmed her conclusions with a wink. He then went on to tell of how Beli, the husband of the great Don, gained victory over the powers of darkness in their land. He brought the people of Britain the secrets of the harvest and knowledge of the seasons of the year.

Beltaine marked the birth of the harvest year, and the fires did honour to him.

As the Merlin recounted the tale, Tory thought it strikingly familiar to the story of the great deluge as written in Genesis. It was even closer to the ancient Sumerian account of the tale. In this version it was Beli (under the name of Enki) who advised Noah (who was also known by a different name). When the select few who had been spared from the disaster again found dry land, they built an altar to the god and burnt offerings in his honour, giving thanks and praise.

This led Tory to wonder if the Celts had borrowed the tale from the Jews and Christians? Yet it seemed more likely that the Judeo-Christian saga had been derived from the earlier Sumerian version.

As with Samhain, all the fires in the land would be extinguished to be rekindled from the sacred fire. The fire would be lit by the druids on the morrow at eve, and left to burn all night. Prime cattle would be driven between the fires for purification and fertility. Men and women would take to the fields and make love to enhance the fertility of the earth and ensure a good crop. Come dawn, the people of the land would take the new flame home and light their own fires again. This symbolised a fresh start and gave all the hope of a good yield.

Tory rose early the next day to help Katren prepare for her wedding. As the Goddess' representative at the house at Aberffraw, Tory was required to attend Calin's crowning this morning and so she wore the green dress of the triple Goddess. Tory was the only woman permitted to attend, just as Lady Gladys had been at Maelgwn's crowning.

The bride awoke in a bed covered in fresh spring flowers. Tory and Ione were there to greet her with bread, fruit and a jug of mead to calm her nerves.

Katren had asked Ione to be her bridesmaid, for Ione had helped her to win the title of Queen's Champion and, indirectly, Calin's heart. Ione was thrilled by the honour and had graciously accepted, even though it meant appearing feminine for a day.

Calin wrote a love letter in the early hours of the morning after he'd picked the flowers that now covered Katren's bed. His note explained that this inability to rest stemmed not from nerves but from his anticipation and elation of their imminent union and life together.

Katren, who had been reading the note aloud, went quiet and read the rest of his letter to herself. With a devious chuckle, Katren's cheeks flushed red. She folded the letter and held it to her breast. It was hard to believe the turn her life had taken, considering the way it could have been had Tory never come bounding into it.

'And?' Ione prompted, as it was just getting interesting.

'And then he just reverts into obscene degeneracies pertaining to his lustful intent, but I will not bore thee with my love's unscrupulous appetite.'

'Why not?' Ione protested.

'Ione!' Tory was surprised. 'I thought thou wast not interested in men?'

'True. But there be no harm in learning how they think,' she smiled. 'Know thy enemy. Thee said that, *Sensei*.'

Ione was wrong in thinking that all men were her enemy and Tory had corrected this misconception so many times that she decided a different approach was required. 'It be the key to defeating thy foe, to be sure, dost thou have a particular conquest in mind?'

'Nay, I do not!'

Ione was so disgruntled that Tory and Katren had to delight in her obvious lie.

'Well, whoever he be, I assure thee, he shall lose his heart this day,' Tory said, feigning ignorance.

'Majesty, I beseech thee, there be no one,' Ione stated in a huff. 'Thou art my only concern.' Ione was to assume the role of Queen's Champion in Katren's stead, as she was the highest ranking female warrior among the masters.

Katren decided to put her at ease. 'In that case, thou shalt be breaking hearts all day.'

'Now that be much more to my liking,' Ione informed them.

Tory made Katren a wedding gift of her make-up, and with it they set about preparing Ione for the event. As they did, Tory considered that even the most beautiful models of her time would pale in comparison; this woman had features and a body that superstars would pay millions for. Heaven help poor Tiernan when he set eyes upon the true beauty of his partner. The only trouble was that the knight still pined for Sorcha and might fail to notice even Ione. This certainly seemed to have been the case so far. Nevertheless, over a decade had passed since Sorcha had stolen his heart. It was time Sir Tiernan got over the loss of his first love, who had never really been his anyway, and got on with the rest of his life.

The Queen left Katren and Ione to dress as she was running late to escort Brockwell to his crowning. She knocked before she entered Calin's chamber. 'Calin, it be Tory. Art thou decent?'

'Not since the day I was born,' he replied, motioning to Sir Tiernan to open the door for her.

Tory rolled her eyes at Calin's jest and burst into the room, only to have the heavy oak door near close on her again when it accidentally met with Sir Tiernan's head.

'Tiernan! . . . Art thou alright?' Tory crouched beside him.

'Nice going!' Calin threw his arms in the air. 'As a lady, thou art supposed to wait until the door be opened for thee.'

'I am sorry,' Tory said. 'But I wast running late.'

'Well thee could have picked someone other than my best man.' Tiernan's eyes were rolling around in his head but he was still conscious. 'This doth not look promising.'

'He will be fine, there be no need to panic. Tiernan, look at me. Focus.' Tory endeavoured to keep him with them. 'Can thou hear me?'

Maelgwn came over to give her a hand to get him on his feet.

'Aye, my love, I can,' Tiernan mumbled, smiling deliriously, his eyes lulled closed.

Uh-oh! Tory cringed, as Maelgwn knew nothing of the knight's feelings for his mother.

'What?' The King dropped him back on the floor with a thud.

'Nay, please Goddess, do not let this happen today!' Brockwell pleaded, his eyes raised to the ceiling.

'What doth he mean?' Maelgwn's tone stopped just short of an accusation.

This surprised and angered Tory. Yet, as it was Calin's wedding day, she kept a civil mood.

'Sorcha,' Tiernan held a hand out to touch her cheek in wonder. 'How I have longed for thee.'

'Shh,' Tory consoled him, not knowing what else to do; Tiernan would kill himself if he realised what he was disclosing.

'Sorcha?' Maelgwn was shocked and backed away, trying to comprehend the full implications of the news. 'Tiernan was my mother's lover?' Maelgwn was mortified. 'Mercy sakes, how many did she have?'

'Please, Goddess!' Calin repeated his plea, more desperate this time.

Lady Gladys entered in the midst of the confrontation, wondering what was holding everyone up.

'Stop right there,' Tory cautioned, feeling Sorcha's presence was very close. 'It be true to say that Tiernan was in love with thy mother, it would seem just about everybody was. But he never laid a hand on her, I swear to thee. He was loyal to Caswallon to the end.' Tory gently placed the knight's head on a pillow.

'So, thou art Tiernan's confessor now, I did not realise the two of thee were so close,' Maelgwn said.

Tory stood, trying desperately to contain her rage. *He's just upset, don't take it personally.* 'I know purely by accident, for when thy mother's spirit comes over me, I experience many of her memories and feelings. So please, allow me to tell thee the full story, before thee condemns anyone. When Cadfer raped her, Sorcha decided not to tell Caswallon, fearing a civil war in Gwynedd. But when she fell pregnant with Caradoc, the guilt drove her away from thy father. Not Taliesin and her study of sorcery, not Tiernan's attentions, but Cadfer's spiteful act.'

'She speaks the truth, Maelgwn,' Lady Gladys assured him.

'Thy father, feeling Sorcha no longer desired him, stopped taking her to his bed and took others in her place. With two young sons and thy uncle and his witch ever menacing her, it was only the young Sir Tiernan's adoration and confidence that kept her going. It be true they aspired to be lovers, but their devotion to thy father surpassed their love for each other — this kept them apart and loyal to the crown of Gwynedd,' Tory explained.

Maelgwn collapsed into a chair, overwhelmed by this revelation. 'Why did thee not tell me all this before?'

Tory crouched before him, taking hold of his hands. 'Because if Sir Tiernan chose not to tell thee in all these years, he obviously did not want thee to know. Maybe he thought thee might look back on thy mother in a bad light, or perhaps he feared thee wouldn't understand. I hate to say it, Maelgwn, but he would have presumed right.'

Maelgwn squeezed Tory's hands. 'I am ashamed of my behaviour.'

'No need. It be a rude shock, I know,' she replied. 'I think it might be best if this dost not leave this room. It hast been Sir Tiernan's secret this long, let us keep it that way.'

'Indeed,' Maelgwn agreed. 'That explains why Tiernan never married. How sad.'

'Well, I will never marry at this rate,' Calin exclaimed. 'What am I supposed to do with this?' He motioned to his best man, passed out at his feet.

'Calm down,' Tory took up her brother's arm. 'So he shall miss thy crowning. He'll sleep it off and will be fighting fit by the wedding.'

'I shall see to Sir Tiernan,' Lady Gladys assured her son, before embracing him. 'Thy father would have been very proud this day.'

'I shall do my very best to do honour to his memory.' Brockwell hugged his mother tight.

This took Lady Gladys by surprise as it was very rare that Calin was so affectionate with her, especially when there was company about.

Bryce came running into the room, all hot and bothered. Dressed in his best clothes, he dragged at them in an attempt to improve his comfort. 'Father, thy guests art getting restless.'

'Indeed. Let us be gone.' Maelgwn shuffled them all out the door, picking up the excited boy on his way through. 'Best not keep thy people and thy bride waiting.'

The ceremonies were performed in the sunshine of the inner-bailey courtyard. Taliesin led Brockwell through his vows, and Tory had the honour of crowning him. That afternoon, when they had been wed, Brockwell crowned Katren as his Queen and Bryce as Prince of Powys, whereupon the real festivities and magic of Beltaine took over.

Tiernan regained consciousness in time for the wedding ceremony, although he seemed to be having trouble concentrating on it.

Katren, so tiny and petite, appeared the very picture of a fairy princess in her wedding gown, but it was Ione who stole the show. Her flowing gown of olive green complemented her colouring and muscular curves, and her brown hair had been wound up into a bun and interlaced with tiny white flowers. Whispy curls accentuated her long neck and fell softly about her. As Ione took pleasure in smelling the magnificent bouquet of white flowers in her hand, she truly did appear the very image of a Goddess.

Tiernan was seated next to Ione at the wedding banquet, and was thus forced to witness the endless stream of admirers who approached to address her and dote upon her beauty. The knight's sanity received its final blow when Ione, quite by accident, turned from a conversation with one of her devotees to catch Katren's wedding bouquet. Ione's young suitor insisted this meant their union was fated, and it was at this time that

Sir Tiernan took his leave. With a goblet and jug of mead in hand, he headed toward the bonfires that were now blazing in the outer bailey.

Tory watched him depart, and suspecting it was jealousy that drove him away, she followed him to find out.

The drunken festivities were in full swing on the common ground, and Tiernan found a quiet place under a tree, where he sat down and proceeded to get sloshed.

'It will not help.' Tory looked down at him as he refilled his goblet.

'It cannot hurt,' he replied. 'Please sit, Majesty, I be glad thou art here. I have something I wish to discuss.'

'About this morning?'

'Aye. I am sorry to say, I have since recalled the whole of it. I apologise for landing thee in trouble with thy King, but I also thank thee, thy words to him were most eloquent.'

'I am the one who should apologise, Tiernan. I hit thee in the head with the damn door.' This made him laugh and she was glad. 'I be sorry Maelgwn found out after all these years.'

'Ahh,' he waved it off. 'So it means I must confront the conversation I should have had with him years ago. I have been forced to face up to many things this day.' He watched a group of people, Ione amongst them, as they approached one of the bonfires. 'The most obvious of which was a ten-ton door.' He spurred Tory to laughter and lightened the mood. 'Only joking. In fact I am glad, it seems to have knocked some sense into me.'

'Pleased to be of service.' Tory raised her goblet to him. 'Cheers.'

Tiernan returned the gesture. 'How long hast thou known about the Queen and myself?'

'Since the day I met thee at Caswallon's bedside.'

'Thee told the King that thee felt Sorcha's feelings. What did thou mean by that, exactly?'

He edged around the question he truly wanted to ask, but Tory guessed his mind. 'She did love thee. I know Sorcha never said it outright, as it lingers in her memory as one of her greatest regrets.'

Tiernan let loose a cry of relief. 'I knew it.'

'Sorcha in no way held thee responsible for her death. She was far happier knowing that her champion was protecting her son.'

'She loved me.' Tiernan leant back against the tree, lost in this discovery.

Tory, judging from the smile on his face, considered that this knowledge was perhaps not so good for him at this time. 'More than thee will ever realise, Tiernan. But thy love that once gave her reason to live, now grieves her terribly. She will not be able to rest in peace while thou art still clinging so tightly to her memory. It hast been three and ten years since she died, be it not time thee let her go?'

'Tory.' Maelgwn caught sight of her and made haste to join them.

'Oh no.' Tiernan held his head, not ready to face Maelgwn yet.

Tory sprang to her feet to distract her husband. 'Aye, my love.'

Maelgwn didn't pause to make conversation, he just whisked Tory up over one shoulder and began to make off with her.

'Maelgwn! Where art thou taking me?' She was amused by his playful manner.

'Sorry Tiernan, got to do our bit for this year's harvest. I do love Beltaine!' Maelgwn cried with glee.

'Good form.' Tiernan held up his glass to toast the King. 'Plant a few seeds for me,' he chuckled, watching the young lovers depart.

Tory waved to him, too drunk to be bothered retaliating against her degrading predicament. 'Plant a few seeds for thyself,' she squealed as Maelgwn picked up speed, heading for the outer-bailey portcullis and the fields beyond.

In the midst of the formalities, Katren managed to steal her husband away from their guests. She led him out of the inner bailey, and down the pathway towards the beach.

'Where art we going?' Brockwell merrily inquired.

Katren giggled as she pulled him aside into the trees. 'Here will do.' She obliged him with a fervoured kiss of encouragement.

'What? Now?' The notion made him smile.

'Why not?' She wrapped her arms around his neck and drew herself in close to him. After all, everybody else was doing it and she'd never had the opportunity to participate in the Beltaine festivities before.

Caught up in his rush of passion, Katren could hardly breathe for her excitement. Calin's lips caressed her neck and shoulders, as his hand slid underneath her long skirt and over her bare thigh.

'Oh, aye,' she whispered to spur him on. Yet the next thing she knew, Calin had backed off completely.

'Damn it!' He wanted to hit something. 'I cannot. It dost not seem right.'

'But Calin, we art married now!' she implored him.

'That be exactly my point. Every woman I have ever had, I have taken thus. But thou art my wife, Katren, whom I have vowed to love and respect for the rest of my life.' He took hold of her hands. 'We shall look back on this moment in years to come, and I want thee to remember how special it was, not how quickly it was over. So please, allow me to try to make it so.'

'Of course.' She smiled, her heart near bursting from the sweet sentiment of his resolve.

'Now stop that.' He wiped her tears away. 'Thou art supposed to be having a good time.'

'Then how come everyone else gets to have all the fun, and we have to wait?'

'Why indeed.' He gripped her hand tightly, leading her off towards the inner bailey.

'Where art thou taking me?'

'To bed,' he stated, determined.

'But it be too early to totally abandon our guests.'

'We can sneak into the house via the servants' entrance, no one shall even miss us.'

Ione had been watching Tiernan very closely, and spying him on his own, she excused herself from her present company to join him.

479

'Thou art a worry, friend.' She stood before him. 'On a night such as this, with thy reputation, why art thou all alone, Tiernan?'

He smiled, beckoning her to sit and offering her some mead. 'It is because I have been in love with a memory for the past three and ten years. Why art thou alone?'

Ione accepted his invitation, taking a seat and his mead. 'Because I have hated men for the last ten years.'

'But what of all thy suitors, Ione? Surely one of them must be mildly attractive to thee.'

She forced a laugh. 'Most of them have taken off to the fields with far easier game than I.' She had a long drink to build up her courage. 'The only man that I do find mildly charming at times ignored me all day.'

'Bastard,' Tiernan said in his drunken stupor.

'He seemed to prefer to get drunk under a tree, all by himself.'

Tiernan froze, caught quite off guard.

'Thee did not even mention whether thee thought I looked nice,' she added softly, her eyes to the ground; she was so afraid of leaving herself vulnerable to him.

'Dear Ione, thou art a paragon of beauty to be sure, but . . .' Tiernan was bewildered, how could he put this without hurting her.

'But what?'

'I am too old for thee. Thou already hast thy pick of every eligible young knight in the kingdom. Thee should consider one of them.'

'Thou art only of eight and thirty, Tiernan. 'Tis not like thou art at death's door.'

Tiernan was not amused. 'And thou art not much more than a girl at one and twenty. Thou dost not need an old man.'

'Aye, I do.' She gently grasped the back of his neck and drew him in till his lips met hers.

Tiernan parted from the kiss, rather dazed. 'Now Ione, listen to me —'

Again she kissed away his protest and whispered, 'Only thee can prove me wrong about men, Tiernan.'

This was the moment of truth for the knight. He had been faithful to none but Sorcha — in a rampage of regret, since her death he had broken a hundred hearts. 'I am a fickle lover, Ione. I fear I cannot help thee, as I cannot even help myself.'

Ione smiled. 'Then perhaps we can help each other.' She stood and held out her hands to him. 'Come plant a few seeds with me.'

He took her outstretched hands and raised himself to his feet, finding he was a little more intoxicated than he thought. 'Be gentle with me,' he mumbled in jest, placing his arm over her shoulder to steady himself.

'Do not fear old man, I shall leave thee alive.'

'We made it!' Katren gave a cheer as Brockwell carried her into his room, kicking the door closed behind them. 'Oh, it be lovely,' she gazed round at the flowers adorning the chamber that her bridesmaids had prepared for them.

'Aye.' Calin's eyes did not shift from his new wife. 'My room hast never looked so good.' He kissed her and set her down on his bed.

'What be wrong?' she inquired, as he was staring blankly at her.

'I am just waiting for a protest,' he joked.

This made her smile. 'There shall be none this time.'

'So.' He looked to the laces down the front of her gown and lightly tugged at the bow so it fell undone. 'Thee can see no reason why we cannot be joined in the union of wedlock?'

'None whatsoever,' she confirmed with adoration.

He guided the gown over her shoulders and down her arms. 'Then, so be it.'

His lips pressed into her cleavage and a fever beset Katren's body, her nipples hardening in the warmth of his hands.

Calin looked up, filling his eyes with the sight of her. The sentiment he felt reminded him of a fable he'd once heard. 'And her beauty was so overwhelming that he could no longer deny his love for her, and thus he confessed with all his heart that he did so.'

Katren's eyes filled with tears at his lovely proclamation. She gently held his face between her hands to vow, 'And with his realisation he made her very joyful.' Brockwell's lips then enfolded her own to convey his feelings more eloquently than any spoken word.

The first rays of dawn found Tory and Maelgwn by the embers of a fire in the outer bailey. Most of the villagers had left, and the world was peaceful and still in the wake of the night-long celebration.

'Good morning!' Calin announced very loudly and with much cheer, giving the pair quite a start.

'Well it was,' Tory said sarcastically as Calin took a seat beside them. 'Where be thy better half?'

'Asleep.' He grinned broadly. 'I thought it best to let her rest before the trip back to Powys.'

'We shall miss thee both, Calin, very much.' Tory reached out to grip his hand.

'Aye, we will.' Maelgwn patted his old friend on the back.

'Excited as I am to be a king, I must confess, I do not want to leave. I imagined I would live out my life in thy service, Maelgwn. I have rarely been parted from thee for more than a day since thee returned from the monastery.'

'Life be like that sometimes. But if we always knew what to expect in advance, then what would be the point of living at all.'

'Quite right,' Tory confirmed. 'Less than a year ago, I certainly did not suspect where my life was taking me, but I am mighty glad it led me where it did.' Tory smiled up at her husband who was being particularly attentive this morning.

'And we will be back here come Samhain, I suppose.'

'Aye, and we shall see thee before then at the meeting of the alliance on Lughnasa. What be wrong?' Tory asked when she saw that Brockwell still looked concerned.

'Art thou still planning to return home come summer solstice?'

'Aye, I must. But while our visit to the future shall span a whole year, we shall only be gone from thy reality for an hour. Thee will not even miss us.'

'I wish thee would take me with thee.'

'Nay, Calin. I realise thy woes, but I do not know how my parents would cope with their dead son appearing together with their missing daughter and her new husband, who just happens to be a sixth-century king. I think it all might be a bit much. I can take care of myself, believe me. Nothing will go wrong.'

'Well then, the stones art not far from Powys, so I shall go to them in any case, to bear witness to the event.'

'As thee wishes.'

'Speaking of events . . .' Maelgwn spied Tiernan and Ione as they came strolling in through the outer-bailey portcullis with their arms wrapped round each other, appearing lost in their own little world.

'Well I never.' Calin gave half a laugh.

'We shall have to start calling thee Eros soon,' Maelgwn said as he nudged Tory affectionately for another good deed well done.

'I had nothing to do with it.'

'That be what thee said about Calin and Katren, and look how they ended up,' Maelgwn joked.

'Shh . . .' Tory didn't want Calin becoming wise to the conspiracy.

'I know thee all drew me in, thyself, Katren and my mother,' Calin admitted. 'But as thou had already promised to train me the perfect wife, I thought it would be downright rude to ignore such a gift.'

'Sure, sure . . .' Tory and Maelgwn made sport of his tale.

'Good morning, Majesties.' Tiernan and Ione finally reached them.

'So it would seem,' Maelgwn teased, while Calin whistled and cheered.

'We were just heading to the beach for kata, art thou coming, *Sensei*?' Tiernan inquired.

'Aye.' Calin jumped to his feet, to second the notion. 'Please, it be my last day.'

Tory looked at Maelgwn who nodded with a smile.

'Alright!' Calin cried as he took off towards the beach after Tiernan and Ione, the King and Tory not far behind.

PART THREE

REALITY

21

SECRETS FROM
THE STONES

The month leading up to the summer solstice flew by. The new recruits had begun their training, the school in the village was opened, and Tory helped Maelgwn prepare for his journey into the future.

Taliesin had remained at the court to lend a hand, and Tory was delighted to be able to spend more time with him. She often tried to quiz him about what he knew of her journey home and why it was so important that Maelgwn came too. The Merlin was unable to answer her questions, however, as the situation she would return to in the future was sure to have changed.

Taliesin didn't want to influence any decisions Tory might make by discussing some of the possible outcomes of her journey. The only thing the Merlin would say was that he was quite sure Tory would make contact with him.

'I was not so experienced then as I am at this point in my evolution,' he warned her. 'You will find my insight lacking a tad. But be patient, for I shall make sense of it all eventually.'

'Make sense of what, Taliesin?'

'What you tell me.'

'Which will be?'

'What's important.'

Riddles, that's all Tory ever got from him. 'Don't you have any advice for me at all?'

'Yes, I have,' he answered, becoming more focused. 'Stay in tune with yourself, Tory, and use your new-found abilities of second sight and truth saying. As you know, the forces of evil run rampant across the earth in your time and they are in a more sophisticated form than ever before. So stay alert to those around you, and beware of whom you take into your confidence.'

Tory was alarmed by his warning. But when she tried to question him further, the Merlin maintained that he had no real reason for the caution. He advised her to pay heed to his words and learn to trust in the universal scheme of things.

This was easy for him to say, she thought. Taliesin had been trusting and using creation for eons, while Tory was a mere novice at this immortality thing. It was rare that she felt physical pain anymore, or tired, and the elements certainly didn't bother her. She had no need to worry about hurting herself, or what she ate.

Which left her free to ponder the answers to the secrets of the ages.

The High Merlin explained that Tory's first encounter with the divine, at her wedding, had set her apart as one of the Chosen by enhancing her second sight. This enabled her to see the truth in others and future events. Tory's episode at Arwystli, however, had empowered her to such a level of awareness that she could not only see the future, she could change it.

This level of awareness was the plane of thought where most negative thinking had been eliminated. It was made up of two regions: the first was the region of abstract thought, where plans and ideas form the blueprints for earth life. The second was where these thoughts became concrete. Here, will was one's strongest form of expression.

'So basically,' the Merlin concluded, 'you have to understand, or rather believe, that whatever you want to happen, will . . . as it always has. You know all this, Tory, it is the very nature of personal reality. Just put your beliefs into action.'

Following Taliesin's advice Tory resolved to visualise a wonderful homecoming. To test her new abilities granted from the powers that be, she convinced herself beyond any doubt that her parents would be waiting for her at the stones when she arrived home. She couldn't imagine how this would ever come to pass, but then these details were a problem for the universe to sort out.

Those members of the court of Aberffraw who were to be present at the stones on summer solstice were invited by King Brockwell to stay at Arwystli, as it was much closer to the site. The party could easily reach the 'King's Men' stones by midnight, when the astrological conditions were forecast to be correct for the time travel. Brockwell had invited all the masters, even Vortipor and Cara made the trip up from Dyfed to be present. Tory couldn't see what the fuss was about, however, as they would only be gone an hour.

On the morning they were to leave, Taliesin provided Maelgwn with a change of clothes for the trip: jeans, a shirt, a jumper and trekking boots. Tory whistled in approval when she saw him in his modern attire. 'I cannot take thee back to the twentieth century looking like that!'

'Why not? Be something amiss?' Maelgwn already felt awkward in the restrictive clothing.

'Nay, but thou dost appear most tempting. The modern women will find thee way too delectable, I fear.'

'Thee need have no fear,' Maelgwn said, as he took hold of her. 'If any other woman sought my favour, thou art well aware I would have to decline.'

'Am I?'

'Of course, I probably wouldn't understand her proposition.' Maelgwn copped a hit for his wit.

'Thee would understand well enough. Women art not backward in coming forward where I am from.'

'Oh really?' He laughed. 'I never would have guessed.'

The party reached the stones with plenty of time to spare. They set up camp, ate and drank their fill, then sat around reminiscing about that extraordinary day one year ago when Tory and Maelgwn had first met.

Tory had one photo left in her camera and asked Taliesin to take a photo of all the masters together. She'd wanted the High Merlin in the picture, but he regretted to inform her that he would just ruin the exposure.

Midnight approached, so Tory dragged her belongings into the ring of stones. She bid everyone goodbye in turn, asking them what they would like her to bring back for them from the future. She had become a mite teary eyed by the time she reached Brockwell, and his request set her tears flowing.

'Just thy good self.' He embraced her.

'I shall see thee in an hour.' She smiled to console him as they parted. Yet with the thought that she would not see Calin for a whole year in her time, she had to turn back to hug him again. 'I will miss thee, Bro.'

'Then let me come.'

Tory saw Katren's shocked expression at the suggestion and so advised, 'Nay Calin, thy home be here, for now. I shall see thee soon, I promise.'

The Merlin moved to escort Tory to the middle of the circle, where Maelgwn awaited her. 'Just make it back to this place one year from tonight and I shall take care of the rest. Tory, I would ask that thee note any changes in the twentieth-century Britain you are about to encounter, compared to the twentieth-century Britain you left behind, no matter how small or insignificant the difference might seem.'

'I will.'

'The Goddess will guide and protect thee both.' He embraced them, showering the couple with his calming energies.

'See you in the twentieth century, dude,' Tory called after him, giving Taliesin the thumbs-up.

At his station behind the King's stone, the Merlin focused himself, uttering an incantation under his breath. He raised his arms and floated upwards until he was suspended over the huge stone. A loud thunderclap sounded and all eyes looked at a turbulent storm cloud erupting in the otherwise clear night sky. A charge of lightning shot from it to meet with Taliesin's extended palms, and flowed into his body in a steady current.

'What's he doing?' Tory was distressed, watching as the great force surged through his being. Maelgwn pulled her close to him and the mist began to rise, spreading around them as it twisted its way towards the raging storm cloud above.

'He's creating a circuit,' Tory answered herself in a whisper, astounded by the spectacle. Hollywood was never this good, she decided.

The masters watched the centre of the circle until the light, generated from the mist, became too intense. The haze spiralled up into the cloud, like a tornado being sucked up from the earth, and left the circle void of its occupants. Thereupon, the large cloud seemed to vanish into the heavens. Those who bore witness to the phenomenon were left gaping in its wake, and made themselves comfortable to await the final outcome; the next hour was going to be a long one.

Tory woke to find herself curled up in Maelgwn's embrace, the morning sun streaming down upon them. She had trouble raising her head, feeling as groggy as she had after her first experience of time travel. Eventually, she freed herself from Maelgwn's grasp, knelt up and looked around. But she was rather disillusioned by what she saw. 'It didn't work, shit!' Tory stared at the stones that stood in their original form, just as she'd left them in 520 AD. 'Where the hell are we now, then?'

Maelgwn sat up. 'What be that noise?'

Tory listened a moment. 'What noise?'

Maelgwn stood to focus on the sound, and pointed to the sky.

Tory gazed up and jumped to her feet, excited. 'Power lines. Maelgwn, I am home!' She overwhelmed him with a hug.

The King's attention was then diverted by another foreign sound, as he heard a car approach and pull up on the road opposite the stones. 'Plane?' he guessed.

'Nay, planes travel through the sky. That be a car.'

Maelgwn drew his brow as this made no sense. Why not call this a plane, when it moves across it?

'We had best get moving.' Tory quickly collected her bags, not wanting to explain to some custodian of the site what they were doing there. *So much for the powers that be! Looks like I'll have to find my parents on my own.*

Maelgwn threw on the backpack and followed her as she set off through the fields. Tory considered that walking along the road might overawe Maelgwn, so they would stay in the fields until he became accustomed to the different noises. She decided they should first see if they couldn't find her elusive Aunt Rose, so she pulled out her old road map.

'Tory?'

A voice from her past resounded through her brain and she stopped dead in her tracks. No, that's impossible, it couldn't be! she resolved as she turned back to view the stones.

'Tory, it is you!'

'Brian!' Tory dropped everything and ran to him.

'Tory.' He caught her as she flung herself into his embrace. 'Where the hell have you been! I thought I was coming here to pay my respects to your memory, and here you are!'

'I don't believe it!' They laughed, elated, echoing each other's mind.

I promise I shall try not to die on thee next time round. Tory grinned broadly as she recalled Brockwell's pledge. She was so blown away to see Brian she could barely speak, and she turned to her mystified father. 'Dad,' she cried, and ran to his awaiting arms.

'Child, you had us so worried.'

'I missed thee so.' She used the old tongue, backing up to hold him at arm's length. 'And I have so much to tell thee.'

'Where hast thou been this past year?' Renford implored her. 'When we found the hire car and no trace of thee, we . . .' He shuddered to think of what he'd suspected. 'Let's just say we feared for thy safety.'

Maelgwn, who had walked back to them, dropped the luggage on the ground. 'Calin, Myrddin, what art thou doing here?'

'What!' Tory smiled as she corrected his mistake. 'No, no, no. This be my brother, Brian, remember the photo? And this be my father, Professor Renford Alexander,' she announced with pride. 'Brian, Dad, I'd like you to meet Maelgwn of Gwynedd, my husband.'

Her father's pipe dropped from his mouth. 'Tory, this be no time for thy fairytales. Dost thou want thy poor father to have a heart attack?'

'Tory, I swear to thee, this be Myrddin,' Maelgwn insisted, looking at her father. 'I would know thee anywhere, High Merlin.'

'Whoa there,' Brian said. 'Tory, are you telling me you're married to this huge dude here?'

'Yes.'

'Awesome.' He shook Maelgwn's hand with a dumbfounded look on his face. 'Hey, bro.'

Tory then turned to her father, playfully placing her hands on her hips. 'And I am not spinning one of my tales. He be exactly who I claim, and I can prove it.'

'I am honoured to meet thee, sir, again.' Maelgwn held out his hand in greeting. Myrddin had been his favourite of Taliesin's long list of esteemed colleagues, and the King felt sure this was he.

The professor, noting Maelgwn's fluent use of the ancient tongue, gripped hold of his new son-in-law's hand with his own. 'Spirits preserve us! The honour be all mine, son. Welcome to the family.' He began to chuckle; whoever this tall, dark man turned out to be, Renford was more than happy to make his acquaintance. 'Well, we had best get thee both back to your aunt's, we can speak in more comfort there.' The professor escorted Maelgwn to the car, making polite conversation in the King's own language.

'It's so good to see you.' Brian took up Tory's saxophone case in one hand and put his other arm over her shoulder.

'Ditto.' She smiled. *Strike one up for the powers that be*.

Brian drove a large four-wheel drive these days, which surprised Tory. 'What happened to the bike?' she said.

'Wrapped it round a tree,' he confessed, tossing her luggage in the back. 'You live and learn.'

'If one is as lucky as it seems you are,' Tory said with a grin, considering that he had had at least two narrow escapes from death.

Maelgwn was more exhilarated by the car ride than Vortipor had been when he had first experienced flight. The noise blasting from the cassette deck didn't escape his attention though, as his frown clearly indicated.

'Terrible, I know,' Tory's father agreed. 'It be music, supposedly.'

'Metallica,' Brian explained, getting into it.

Maelgwn listened carefully, trying to appreciate it.

'I think Albinoni is more his pace,' Tory informed them, laughing at Maelgwn's bemused expression.

'Nay, this hast a certain quality.' Maelgwn didn't want to insult anyone. 'It be . . . powerful.' He smiled at his new kin, who appeared so familiar; this was Brockwell alright, no doubt about it. Maelgwn was amazed at the technology of the vehicle and asked Brian questions about how the car was driven.

'I could teach thee, if you like,' Brian suggested, drifting from language to language.

'That would be wonderful.'

'No, you say *awesome*,' Brian corrected him. 'That would be *awesome*, get it?'

'Awesome,' Maelgwn repeated with a smile.

Oh brother! Tory rolled her eyes. Please Goddess, don't let him turn into a twentieth-century yobbo.

Once they reached Aunt Rose's lovely thatched cottage, on a farm in Oxfordshire, Maelgwn and Tory received another rude shock.

'Lady Gladys!' they both exclaimed, as she came running down the garden path to greet them.

'Dear child! I knew it, what did I say?' she asked her brother as she reached Tory and hugged her niece fiercely.

'Tory, this be thy Aunt Rose,' her father said, explaining that Rose fancied herself as a bit of a psychic.

'Your father thinks such things are nonsense,' her aunt said, as if to imply that he was the one who was potty, not her. 'I told him you would return but, of course, he wouldn't believe me. This must be your Otherworld companion, no doubt?' Rose turned to Maelgwn, who stole her heart as he took up her hand and kissed it.

'Lady, Maelgwn of Gwynedd, at thy service.'

'My husband,' Tory clarified.

'Delighted,' Aunt Rose said coyly, though she'd barely understood a word Maelgwn said. 'The spirits have had much to say about you two.' She led them towards the house, thumping her brother on the way past. 'I told you she got married.'

Brian laughed as he pulled the bags out of the car. 'Well, it would seem the women in our family aren't as looney as you thought, hey Dad?'

The professor was quite perplexed. 'I must confess, a wee dram would be mighty friendly at this stage, Brian.'

Aunt Rose put on a delicious lunch of wondrous foods in Maelgwn's honour: pies, fresh bread and salads, followed by Devonshire tea.

Tory told them of her journey to the Dark Age, and Maelgwn expanded on the story here and there. She also produced the instant photographs she'd taken that confirmed elements of her adventure.

'Hey, that's me!' Brian spotted Calin in several of the shots.

'Indeed, Calin Brockwell, King of Powys and Duke of Penmon in Gwynedd. He is also Maelgwn's Champion and one of the bravest warriors I've ever met. He just got married.' Tory pointed out Katren to him.

'Wow, what a babe.'

'And look Renford, there's me.' Rose pointed to Lady Gladys in Tory's wedding photo. 'My, I do look nice, don't I? And I must say, you look rather lovely yourself, my dear.' She winked at Tory.

With the aid of a magnifying glass, the professor carefully scrutinised the photo of the seat of Gwynedd at Aberffraw and the picture Tory had taken of the ruins at Llyn Cerrig Bach. 'What are these blurry patches?' he asked.

Tory leant over his shoulder. 'Oh, they're ghosts.'

'Get outta town. Let me see,' Brian demanded.

'Well Tory, I certainly have no explanation for all this,' her father confessed, pouring himself another drink.

'Where's Mum?' As soon as she asked, Tory knew something was wrong when everyone's expression changed. 'What? Has something happened to her?'

'No.' Brian sounded as if he wished something had.

'Your mother and I have separated, child. She's currently on tour in America somewhere.'

'With her new composer boyfriend, who's half her age,' Brian added with spite.

'Brian, please,' his father urged, as he was not making it any easier on his sister.

'Well, she should know all of it,' Brian protested.

'We are in the process of a divorce, Tory. I am sorry.'

Maelgwn placed a hand on Tory's shoulder and she patted it to assure him she was fine. 'Don't be.' She kissed her father. 'I know what Mother is like, and so I suppose it's probably for the best.' Tory came round her father's chair to take a seat on his lap. 'Are you alright?'

'Quite blissful, thank you. I much prefer living in Britain.'

This house in Oxfordshire belonged to his sister Rose who had no children of her own and her husband had died many years ago. So she was delighted to have her brother and Brian living there.

Tory and her father walked off lunch in the garden. She took the opportunity to ask him about the perfectly preserved ring of stones she'd seen this morning, as this was the first major change Tory had noticed in Britain since her arrival.

'What do you mean?' Renford was puzzled. 'We Britons have always taken pride in preserving our ancient sites.'

Tory found his response very confusing as this would mean that the land ownership in Britain had changed from the last time she was in the twentieth century. The ring of stones was in Oxfordshire which, according to history in the modern reality Tory had been born into, belonged to the Saxons who would in time become the English people.

Therefore, by Tory's reckoning, Wales must reach way beyond the borders of what had once been known as Prydyn.

'The Saxon raiders that ravaged Britain during the Dark Ages never managed to gain supremacy over the allegiance set in place by the Dragon and his allies,' Renford explained to her.

If this was true, then most of Scotland, Ireland and Prydyn had never fallen into the hands of raiders, and much more of their native culture must have been preserved, Tory mused on the quiet. These lands had therefore maintained their own identity, separate governments and individual beliefs, as their people had never been forced by the English to give them up.

Tory was very pleased to learn this; Taliesin, as always, had been right in thinking the pact would serve the native Britons well. She could hardly wait to start delving into the history books to find out what else had changed. Tory guessed that the way history had unfolded in this reality explained the fine condition of the stones. The absence of war and the greater respect for the native culture in Britain had managed to preserve them this time round.

Later that evening, while Tory and Brian were beating each other up in a sparring match in the garden, Tory's father showed Maelgwn his library, which had been carefully transported from Australia.

'Well I can certainly see where this year will be best spent, Professor.' Maelgwn's attention was drawn to a parchment written in the ancient text that was lying on the desk. 'This be about me.' He read the ancient tongue, understanding it perfectly.

> I saw Maelgwn on a great journey
> his life spent in preparation.
> Plans hidden within plans,
> he knew naught of the Goddess' intent
> The Otherworld sped him on his quest
> to awaken their sleeping prophet.
> The fate of the Mother Country,
> held within a single memory.

'Indeed. I have seen these words before, they be part of a dialogue claimed to have passed between Taliesin and Myrddin. Can thee tell me anything of the origin of this particular copy?' Renford asked.

Maelgwn held the tattered parchment in his hand to inspect it more closely. 'It be Taliesin's penmanship. A poem of which I know not. Where did thee find this?'

'An archaeologist working at a dig at Lynn Cerrig Bach found it and asked me to look into it for him. Art thou sure of its writer?' The professor restrained his excitement as he awaited the reply. 'It was Taliesin Pen Beirdd?'

'Aye, I would know his script anywhere. I have certainly read enough of it.'

'I knew it. I don't know how I knew it, but I knew it!'

Maelgwn was pleased to have made him so cheery, but he couldn't understand the professor's doubt. 'But surely thee recognises Taliesin's hand, Myrddin?'

'Why doth thou think me to be this old wizard, Maelgwn?' He had seen the photos of Calin and Lady Gladys, who were clearly recognisable as Brian and Rose. Was it any more unlikely then that he might have lived in another life and time? But as Myrddin, the High Merlin of the druids? Although this was very flattering, Renford thought it rather unlikely.

Maelgwn did his best to be tactful, seeing how ill at ease the comment had made the professor. 'Why, thou art his very image, save quite a bit of hair and thy attire. But as well as this, I have been considering Taliesin's story of thy origins and what became of thee, and it seems to make sense that I should find thee here.'

Renford took a seat, waving for Maelgwn to do the same. 'Please, tell me the story of Myrddin's origins.'

'Surely as a historian thou art aware of the story of Myrddin?'

'Believe me, Maelgwn, I have read many theories, so varied and outrageous that I would dearly love to hear thy version of it.'

Maelgwn drank the shot of liquor, and gasped for air. 'Whoa, good mead.'

'Whisky, mother's milk.' Renford grinned, pouring him another as he awaited the tale.

Maelgwn accepted the refill, deciding to take this one a little slower, and leant back in the comfortable armchair. 'According to Taliesin, Myrddin was begotten by an incubus. His mother was of the Middle Kingdoms, but his father was of the Otherworld. He was bequeathed by the sorcerers of Vortigern, the archtraitor and one-time overlord of Britain, to appease the spirits. The leader had fled his allies, the Saxons, and while Vortigern attempted to build a fortress to keep them and the might and anger of Britain at bay, all his building materials kept vanishing. Vortigern's wizards told him he must find a fatherless boy whom they could slay and sprinkle his blood on the foundations at the site. After an extensive search, Myrddin was brought forth to be sacrificed, having no earthly father at least. Although only a boy, Myrddin outwitted them all. He explained the real reason for the disappearances was due to a subterranean pool on the building site that housed two dragons.'

'"Dragons" meaning?' Renford queried, quite sure there was no such thing as a dragon.

Maelgwn recalled Tory mentioning that very few beasts of this type still existed in this time, so he explained. 'Big, burly, fire-breathing, and quite often airborne creatures of the Otherworld.'

'I see.' Renford quickly poured another shot. 'Do go on.'

'Vortigern had the pool drained, and as predicted two dragons emerged. One was white, and Myrddin told the leader that it represented the Saxons and Vortigern himself. The other dragon was red and personified our ancestors, the Britons, led by Aurelius Ambrosius and my grandfather. The dragons did battle and despite the white dragon seeming at first the more powerful, the red dragon recovered and drove the other one back. Thus Myrddin foretold the downfall of Vortigern and the Saxons, and the coming to power of Ambrosius and the native Britons. The boy was imprisoned by Vortigern for his prophecy, but was rescued by Ambrosius when he conquered Vortigern as predicted. Myrddin then remained in the service of Ambrosius for many years.'

'So what became of him after that? Some say he was trapped by an enchantress in a tree, others claim he went mad.' Renford quoted from the depths of his memory:

> After the Battle of Arthuret
> he led a secret life,
> concealing himself amid the trees
> of the great wood, like a hermit.
> There he remained for an eternity
> with no memory of his former life or kin,
> living wild with the beasts of the earth
> until the time of the gathering,
> when his senses would be restored.

Maelgwn sat forward in his chair, wide-eyed at the professor's words, feeling this confirmed his suspicions even more. 'This could be applied to what Taliesin claims became of thee. For Taliesin was sent, by the Goddess, back to the Old Land, to learn the secrets of the ages from the Old Ones.'

'Do you mean Atlantis?' Renford asked.

'Aye, Tory hast referred to it thus,' Maelgwn recalled. 'After he'd studied the old ways, Taliesin returned to Britain, twenty years before I was even born. He sought out Myrddin and found him trapped in a tree, only not by a beautiful enchantress but by an evil sorceress named Mahaud. She had disguised herself as an alluring wood nymph to fool the Merlin into teaching her his craft, which he did. Mahaud then used this knowledge to imprison him. After breaking the enchantment, Taliesin instructed Myrddin in the greater mysteries for a time and together they devised a scheme to save Britain.'

'Did he tell thee what they planned?' The professor was becoming very interested now as something deep inside him seemed to stir, sending cold shivers down his spine.

Maelgwn chuckled. 'The thing about Taliesin be that he never tells anyone anything, outright. He said they went opposite ways through time and that when he and Myrddin were reunited, the Chosen Ones would rise and Britain would be redeemed.' Maelgwn reached over and took up the parchment he'd read earlier. ''Twas this that got me thinking though, for I know Taliesin's writings art housed where no amount of digging would uncover them. Thus, I do not think thou hast acquired this by accident.'

'I was beginning to think the same thing myself.' Renford had turned white.

'If Taliesin stayed in my time to tutor my mother and then myself, does it not make sense, therefore, that Myrddin came forward to tutor and guide Tory?'

'Aye, perhaps.'

'Then thy poem of Myrddin's plight makes some sense. If one considers that the "wood" spoken of refers to life itself, and if Taliesin knew that thou had lost all memory of thy origins, thy kindred, and thy pact with him, then perhaps he sent this remnant of thy conversation to jog thy memory.'

'And thy good self also, let us not forget.' Renford had reserved judgement on whether or not this man was who he claimed to be. He was either a brilliant impostor, or the genuine article; very few people spoke Brythanic with such ease.

'That would answer Tory's question as to why it was so important that I come with her,' Maelgwn thought aloud.

'I note thee speaks of Myrddin in hearsay only, how be it then that thou recognises him in me?'

'The truth may seem strange, sir, still it be all I have to offer.'

'Please Maelgwn, I will not doubt thy word. In fact, there be very little I will doubt after this day.'

Maelgwn nodded in agreement. 'In my youth, Taliesin enlightened me to many different states of being, so that I might learn the wisdom through my own incarnations, past and future,' he explained. 'In short, I met Myrddin in a dream state in the Otherworld, where no time exists. Myrddin could assume several different guises. There was the face of the Merlin, which was vaguely recognisable as thee. The appearance of a simple apple tree was one of his favourites, until the incident involving Mahaud. But in his mortal form,' Maelgwn sat forward, 'I swear, he looked just like thee.'

Tory and Brian had worn each other out. Tory was envious of her brother who had achieved another Dan grade in her absence and, coincidentally, had started tutoring others in his skills since moving to Britain.

'Funny, hey, that we both ended up doing the same thing?' Tory said as they took a seat on the back step, peeling off their protective layers and sculling down bottles of water.

'Yeah, only your pupils changed the course of history. I wish I'd seen one tenth of the action you and Maelgwn have.'

Tory was amused. 'Spoken like a true Brockwell.'

'So, what's the story with this guy, was he really me?'

'For sure, Taliesin said we emanated from the same soul mind. All of us: you, me, Maelgwn, Taliesin, Dad, Aunt Rose, and god knows who else. We are all twin souls who incarnate together over many lifetimes and are constantly drawn to each other as we are so compatible.' Tory began to laugh, tickled by a memory.

'What?' Brian urged, hating to be left out of the joke.

Tory had to catch her breath before explaining. 'You actually tried to take advantage of me.' She cracked up again.

'Get-outta here!' Brian sprang from his seat. 'No way man, he wasn't me then.'

'Relax, I told you then you'd feel this way.' She squirted him with her water bottle. Brian would have got her back but his was already empty.

Tory went quiet for a moment as Brian shook off the attack and resumed his seat. 'Do you remember the championships just after we'd reached Dan grade?'

'Oh, cruel!' He reacted as if he was mortally wounded by the memory.

'What?'

'What!' He echoed her innocent air. 'You're talking about the year you broke my leg, two days before we competed, and then went on to victory without me, yeah?'

'I guess so,' Tory concluded with a smile, relieved that she didn't have to reveal his previous fate.

'So what about it?'

'Oh nothing. How is Master Teo these days?'

'I haven't seen him since we moved. He and I had a bit of a falling out, I'm afraid.'

Tory couldn't understand this, as they'd been the best of friends before Brian's death. 'What about?'

Brian stood, hesitant to answer. 'I kind of blamed him for your disappearance ... if he hadn't made the situation so tense for you, you never would have left. I know you said Teo wasn't the reason, but I thought he was.'

In a strange way Brian was right; Teo would eventually evolve into Taliesin and he was the catalyst behind her trip back to the Dark Age.

'Why, what other explanation did I give for going?'

'I don't know, you wanted to find yourself, or some shit like that.' As Brian calmed a little he had to laugh at the notion. 'You obviously did, huh? I should have gone with you.'

Tory raised her eyebrows. 'Well, you certainly would have found yourself!'

Tory woke at dawn the next day. She left Maelgwn in bed, still sleeping. A year in the future would be a well earned holiday from royal life for the King, time out from the chaos to do what he pleased for a change.

Tory wandered down to the kitchen, still half asleep.

'I want one,' Brian whinged, when he saw her master's attire, displaying the Dragon on the back.

She hadn't even heard him enter. 'No problem. I have friends in high places.' Tory gulped down some juice.

Brian watched her; she'd changed somehow, but not on the outside. Although she looked healthier and happier than he'd ever seen her, no matter how she tried to act the rough and tumble, outspoken rebel she'd been before she left, his sister had acquired a certain quiet wisdom. 'So you're really a queen, hey?'

'Yeah. And you're really a king. Let's train.' Tory brushed off his admiration, she wanted to forget all those airs and graces.

'I was just asking.' Brian heard the annoyance in her voice.

'Brian, I don't mean to be blunt, but I really need to forget all that for a while and just be me, Tory Alexander. One gets so tired of being adored all the time.' She held her hand to her head in a dramatic pose.

'I'm sure.' Brian pushed her out the door.

When Maelgwn stirred to find that Tory was already up, he wandered downstairs to the back garden where he beheld a most idyllic scene. In harmony with the misty countryside, streaked by early morning sunshine, Tory and Brian practised kata. They appeared perfectly in tune with each other and all around them.

He sat down and watched, realising how alike Tory and her brother truly were: the way they moved, how they spoke and appeared. Brian's hair, half as long and just as fair as his sister's, was pulled tightly off his face into a ponytail that hung down his back, as Tory's did. It was strange having this older, sharper version of Calin around. It was also a little offputting to have to share so much of Tory's attentions with him. The pair had scarce been out of each other's sight since he and Tory arrived.

'Hey bro.' Brian startled him out of a daze. 'You on holiday or something?' He beckoned Maelgwn to join them.

As Maelgwn wandered over, Tory announced with excitement, 'Thou shalt have to get used to taking orders from Calin for a change. Brian has agreed to take over thy training for a while, and mine.'

Maelgwn was pleased, well aware of Brian's skill and status. 'Awesome, dude!' the King said and gave him a high-five.

Tory rolled her eyes melodramatically. 'How quickly they learn.'

'You bet, babe.' Brian appeared pleased with himself, assuring his brother-in-law, 'Thou art going to reach Dan grade by the time I get through with thee.'

Brian was making a good living out of teaching his skills in Britain and had many promising students. The martial arts had been a part of British culture and heritage since the Dark Ages, akin to the Asian cultures of Tory's past reality. This was one of those mysterious coincidences that had the modern historians puzzled; how had these skills developed concurrently in two different civilisations that supposedly didn't come into contact with one another until a much later date?

Tory began to wonder if other time travellers had been the cause of similar mysteries that had puzzled her as a student. Local folklore told of a great War Goddess who brought the fighting skills to Britain from the Otherworld. The fact that Tory had come from the future must have been overlooked, misinterpreted, or purposefully never recorded, and so another misconception had occurred.

Who could say if the similarities in language, ritual and beliefs of vastly removed tribes in her past reality hadn't been caused by others like herself? Still, as Taliesin had learnt his craft from the Atlanteans, she supposed that the credit for the similarities did ultimately fall to them. Without their insight and skill her quest through time and space, whatever that truly was, would never have been possible. Perhaps the gods of Ancient Greek and Roman mythology were still sitting back in Atlantis, or Olympus, moulding future history. If so, then the like of Taliesin, Maelgwn and herself were just pawns in a game that the gods were constantly striving to complete.

It took the King all of a week to settle into twentieth-century life.

Maelgwn had no fear of the technology around him, as he had come into contact with most of it before through Taliesin. He was even surprised a few times by electrical items that didn't have all the functions he expected, as some of Taliesin's appliances were even more advanced. Modern inventions that he hadn't seen before, like the different forms of transport, he had been told about. Still, he didn't much like all the noise they made or how they polluted the air, and he had certainly lost all enthusiasm for learning to drive. Aunt Rose had a couple of horses which had belonged to her husband, so Maelgwn happily took charge of grooming and exercising them, and he rode to most places. He loved staying at the farm and was happy not to venture far from it as everything he desired of the modern world was right there. Brian and Renford had built a large shed for a gymnasium, where Brian held his classes. Maelgwn trained with the rest of Brian's students, and had additional lessons after hours when his brother-in-law could give him extra attention. All the great literature the King could possibly desire was to be found in Renford's library, and Maelgwn liked to help Rose and Renford out around the house in return for their hospitality.

Tory and Brian took Maelgwn on a day trip to see the sights of London, which was not at all as the King expected. He explained he'd never actually visited the city, as it was in Mercia — Saxon country — though he had fought quite near there once or twice. The museum fascinated him most of all. After spending the morning

514

there, the three of them wandered around the city for hours. Some things Maelgwn found inspiring, some wondrous, and other so-called achievements he considered just plain sad. By the end of the day, the noise and the pollution were beginning to take their toll. So the three of them decided to escape reality for a while and took solace in the cinema watching the latest Spielberg flick, which Maelgwn absolutely adored.

After this little adventure, however, the King was none too keen to leave his tranquil nook in the country; the various noises of the city made his head ache as they put all his senses on overload. From a young age, Maelgwn had been trained to hunt and track, and thus his ears and mind were constantly alerted to every little sound. He liked the quaint country towns though, and was becoming something of a regular at the local pub, where he, Brian and Tory often went to play pool.

For these reasons, Tory wasn't surprised when Maelgwn declined a trip to Gwynedd. Brian was driving their father to Mon to return the parchment, offer his professional analysis, and collect his fee. Maelgwn explained that he was happy to remember his home as he knew it, and Renford agreed with his reasoning. The professor had seen a photo of the valley as it had existed in Maelgwn's time and felt it would certainly break the King's heart to see Llyn Cerrig Bach in its present state of upheaval.

In a sweet gesture, Aunt Rose decided to go along for the weekend trip. So Tory and Maelgwn had some time alone together to celebrate their first wedding anniversary.

22

DISSOLUTION

Renford had spoken to the archaeologist who was in charge of the dig at Llyn Cerrig Bach, Professor Miles Thurlow, and had obtained permission to inspect the pieces they'd uncovered at the site, none of which dated beyond 60 AD. This was why the parchment had been such a curious find; apart from the fact that it hadn't disintegrated over the centuries, it dated to a much later period around 500 AD, Maelgwn's time. This was one of the reasons that Maelgwn's little anecdote regarding Myrddin had made such an impact on Renford. The mysterious disappearance of his daughter had prompted the professor to take an interest in the sacred sites of Britain that had been used by his ancestors to some unknown end. This kind of phantasmic research was completely against his professional ethics, and so Renford had kept his study of the sites and the cosmology behind them to himself.

Originally he'd sought only to find a possible explanation for Tory's disappearance.

After her hire car was found abandoned on the roadside, police had questioned the locals who all claimed to have seen a great light emanating from the King's Men stones the same night Tory had vanished there. As Renford was well aware that Myrddin had been one of the greatest curators of the sacred mysteries, he had to wonder if this was the real reason he'd taken to the study of the megaliths far more ardently than expected.

Surely not, Renford assured himself, as they sped along the road. Still, he was interested to see what the dig at Llyn Cerrig Bach had turned up.

After dropping Aunt Rose at the hotel, Brian drove Renford to the site. Brian followed his father to the office, not the slightest bit interested in what was going on. He had also seen the photo of the valley as it had once been, and considered the upheaval around him a crying shame.

Renford introduced himself to the woman at reception, advising her of his appointment to see Professor Thurlow. Brian eyed her over, and thought about trying to chat her up, until he noticed her wedding ring.

She was most apologetic, explaining that the professor had been called away early this morning and she didn't know how long he might be detained. He had, however, left the professor's payment with her and arranged for his partner, Professor Paradis, to show Renford around.

When Professor Paradis met them at the office, Brian was pleased to see that he was accompanied by the most delectable looking woman he'd ever seen. 'I should hang out with you more often,' he said quietly to his father, as they watched them approach. She was introduced to them as Professor Paradis' daughter, Naomi, and she wasn't wearing a wedding band. As they were escorted to the main dig, Brian couldn't take his eyes off her; he was racking his brain to think of where he'd seen this woman before.

When Naomi politely excused herself to get back to her work, Brian left his father to converse with Professor Paradis and followed her. 'So, what do you do here?'

'I doubt very much that my work would be of any interest to you.' She sounded less accommodating now, but her French accent was driving him out of his mind.

'To the contrary,' Brian assured her, before delivering an intelligent insight into the valley's history in fluent Brythanic.

She tipped her head to him to acknowledge her mistake. 'Perhaps it might after all. Follow me.'

To the ends of the earth, Brian thought, admiring her form.

'So, Mr Alexander, what kind of work do you do?'

'Well, Ms Paradis.' He ever so nicely made a mockery of her formal tone. 'I'm a triple black belt. I teach Tae-kwon-do and kick boxing in Oxfordshire.'

She was impressed but tried very hard not to show it. 'Funny, I've always wanted to learn, but, of course, I never get the time.' Naomi led him into the restoration room, where the finds were being cleaned and housed.

Here he saw one of the goddess statues from the temple and a wave of recognition rushed over him. This was accompanied by a clear memory of ripping away vines to reveal the shapely carving.

As Brian was so obviously stunned by the find, Naomi commented, 'She is beautiful, isn't she?'

'Aye, I've seen her before,' he uttered, as he viewed the statue more closely.

'That is impossible I'm afraid, as she only came out of the ground a few days ago. She hasn't even been photographed yet.'

The vision hung with Brian like a screen between himself and reality. 'There are more of them.'

'How do you know?'

'I remember them, from when I was young, I think.'

Naomi began to laugh, convinced that he was pulling her leg. 'Very funny.'

'I'm serious,' Brian insisted. 'I have a memory like an elephant and I distinctly remember this statue and eight or nine others just like her in a circle.'

She stopped laughing when she saw that he was sincere. 'But my father estimates that this statue has been lost underground for at least five hundred years.'

'He must be mistaken. I'm sure I remember her.'

Naomi shook her head slowly. 'Father is never wrong. But should we find any others, I will be sure and let you know.' With this she moved to the desk to resume her work.

Renford had been left to study the site alone for a time as his guide had been called to the phone. He wandered

519

away from the action to have a puff on his pipe without offending anyone. Finding a large rock in the shade of a couple of huge trees, he sat down and began to chug away on his pipe.

He hadn't been settled but a couple of minutes when he heard someone whispering close by. The professor looked around, but seeing no one, decided he was imagining things. A few moments later the whispering began again, only louder. The professor felt cold shivers pass over him as he recalled his daughter's comment regarding the ghosts in her photograph of Llyn Cerrig Bach. He strained his ears a moment to hear if he could make out what the whispers were saying, but they stopped again, and he heard naught but the sounds of the work site. 'Don't be so ridiculous. You don't even believe in ghosts,' he mumbled to himself.

With his words, the utterances intensified. They were garbled at first, but gradually grew louder until a word was finally audible. *Myrddin*.

Professor Paradis was alarmed to see his esteemed colleague running as fast as he was able back towards him. 'What is it, Professor? Is there something wrong?'

'No,' Renford assured him, as white as a sheet. 'I was just startled by a snake. I'll be fine.'

When Renford had calmed down, he viewed the pieces in the restoration room. Then he collected Brian and thanked Professor Paradis and his daughter for their time.

'I left my number on your desk,' Brian told Naomi. 'So when you find those other statues, you can let me know.'

Professor Paradis looked at his daughter curiously as their guests departed. 'What other statues?'

'God knows.' She shrugged, heading back to the site. 'Pay him no mind, father. I shan't.'

Renford said nothing of his experience to anyone, and had no intention of mentioning it until Brian came to see him that night.

'I want to talk to you about something, got a minute?' Brian said as he stuck his head in his father's room.

'Of course. What is it?'

Brian was a little backward in coming forward. 'I had a kind of . . . mystic experience today.'

Renford chuckled. 'Brian, I assure you, an erection is not a mystical experience and no, I do not have Professor Paradis' home phone number.' His father went back to the book he was reading.

'Dad, I'm not talking about that. It's that statue they dug up.'

'What about it?' Renford was still only half with him.

'Have you ever taken me there before? Llyn Cerrig Bach I mean, when I was a child perhaps?'

'No. You stayed in Australia with your mother most of the time. Why do you ask?'

'Then it must have something to do with that Brockwell guy,' Brian thought out loud. 'Thanks Dad.' He moved to leave.

'Hold on a second. Would you mind telling me what this is all about?'

'Don't worry. You don't believe in all that shit, anyway.'

'It would seem I'm up to my neck in "that shit", as you so eloquently put it,' Renford confessed, peering over his reading glasses.

'Why, did something weird happen to you at the site today?'

'You might say that. But first, tell me about your statue, I'm most interested.' Renford propped himself up in his bed to pour a whisky.

Brian grabbed himself a shot glass and sat down. 'Well, I remember seeing that statue when it was still standing, alongside others like it. But Naomi told me that they've been buried for hundreds of years. How would you explain that?'

His father just shook his head.

'I figure it must have something to do with King Brockwell. I mean, he was there, right? So what if I am remembering one of my memories from when I was him?' Brian cringed in retrospect. 'Shit, I'm starting to sound like Aunt Rose.' He drank the shot his father had poured for him. 'So, what say you, Professor? Do you think there might be something in all this? Or is the mystery that surrounds one's life on earth only here to mess with your head, until you die or go insane trying to figure it out?'

Renford shrugged and answered, 'I'm not the one to ask, son. I think my mental faculties have finally taken their leave.'

'Don't be ridiculous, Dad, what would make you say that?'

'I believe I ran into a couple of Tory's ghosts today, and it would seem Maelgwn isn't the only one who calls me by the name of Myrddin.'

'That's right, Maelgwn called you that the day we met. What do you make of it?'

'After today, well?' Renford gave a shrug. 'But you must swear not to mention this to anyone. Especially not your Aunt Rose, I'd never hear the end of it.'

'Sure, but what are you going to do?'

Renford was bemused. 'What else can I do, but find out as much as I can about Myrddin and see if anything gels, as with you and the statue.'

The fact that his son had had a psychic experience scared Renford; first Rose, then Tory, and now Brian. His wife had certainly never shown any sign of clairvoyance, and as his sister had perceived Tory's situation after her disappearance it was clear that these abilities unquestionably ran in his side of the family.

On Sunday morning, Maelgwn rose, leaving Tory to snooze for a change. They'd been making the most of having the place to themselves, and so hadn't had much sleep.

We could just stay here, settle down, have a family. If we never return to all the responsibility, war and politics of my time, would history really miss us? Maelgwn smiled at his dream. Unfortunately he knew he was predestined to return home to become this great king everyone kept predicting he'd be, and Taliesin would surely hunt them down before long if they failed to join him again in the past.

Maelgwn was heading to the kitchen to make a pot of tea when he was distracted by a knock at the front door. Upon answering it, he was confronted by a man who appeared not much older than himself and whose nationality was unfamiliar to him. His reddish skin was much darker than Maelgwn's, and the man's size and build were similar to Brian's. His eyes were very dark, almost black, as was his hair, which was braided into a long plait that fell all the way down his back. The man stood out as a warrior, unlike most of the men the King had met here, so Maelgwn figured him to be one of Brian's students.

'Is Brian home?' The visitor appeared just as stunned by the sight of Maelgwn's huge presence in the doorway.

'No, sorry. But Tory be.'

'Tory!' the man cried, aghast. 'May I see her please?'

He made it sound as if he had every right to speak with her, so Maelgwn inquired, 'Who are you, sir?'

The man smiled broadly. 'Tell her Teo is here.'

'Her *sensei*?' Maelgwn remembered the name.

'The same,' Teo confirmed, appearing a little curious. 'And who might you be?'

'Maelgwn, Tory's husband.' He held out his hand in greeting.

'What?' He pushed Maelgwn aside and stormed down the entrance hall calling out, 'Tory!'

It took but seconds for her to appear at the top of the stairway, having recognised Teo's voice the first time he'd cried out her name. 'Teo, what are you doing here? Brian said —'

'Your husband!' He pointed a finger in Maelgwn's direction. 'You got married?'

'Well, yeah. I thought you'd be happy for me.' Tory was confused. She had only ever known Teo to be calm, gentle and full of reason, but the man before her seemed to be a completely different person. They'd had a brief affair, so what? It had been his decision to end it, so why all the drama? Unless, of course, their story had also unfolded differently this time round.

'Happy for you!' He gripped his brow with both hands. 'Could I speak with you a minute please ... *alone.*'

'Of course.' She beckoned him towards her father's library, then looked to Maelgwn with a shrug. The King appeared irked as he folded his arms. 'Please Maelgwn, I shall explain later. I promise.' She ventured a kiss before heading to the library, scratching her head. *As soon as I find out what's going on, myself.*

Just as she closed the library door, Teo was upon her. He spun her around, backing her up to the door, his lips and body pressed hard against her own.

What in hell's name? Tory jabbed him in both kidneys before thrusting him away from her. 'Have you taken leave of your senses, I just got through telling you I am married!'

'I lost my mind, alright, and my best friend. Over you!' he appealed in anger. 'To discover that you were off getting married to some ... giant! Tory, how could you do this to me?'

'What is all this guilt shit, Teo! Don't try to lay that on me, my friend, 'cause I am over it! For starters, Brian has told me that he realises his mistake and has every intention of apologising. Secondly, you were the one who decided you couldn't teach and sleep with me at the same time, not me! And thirdly, I would have let you all know what had happened to me, if I'd been able to.'

'So where were you then? Where were you that you couldn't pick up a phone or post a letter at least, huh?'

Good question, Tory thought, and she wasn't sure if she should confide in Teo in his current mood. *But surely Taliesin wasn't referring to himself when he warned me to beware of who I took into my confidence.* Still, something inside told her to be careful. 'I had a bad fall and suffered amnesia for a time,' Tory explained without too much of a pause, so it sounded quite believable.

'So that's how you ended up married to someone else.' Teo's tone became more intimate as he again tried to approach her.

'No, Teo. Let's get this straight right now. I married Maelgwn because I love him, understand?'

Tory withdrew from his grasp, yet he was not swayed. 'I don't believe you, Tory. You've just forgotten.'

'I forget nothing.' She stopped and held him at arm's length. 'For heaven's sake, when we split up you said if I found somebody else, so be it.'

'But I didn't mean it!' He took hold of her hand and held it to his heart. 'We had something special, didn't we? I just presumed that in the end . . .'

'I know you did. But you made all your own choices, Teo, as did I.' She slid her hand out of his grasp and placed it on his shoulder. He appeared dazed and hurt, but he had calmed down since she'd made contact with him. 'I can't say I'm sorry, Teo, when I'm not. I have just had the best year of my life. I had no way of knowing what you were going through,' she added quickly to appease the anger that was again rising in him. 'If it's any consolation, when my memory finally started to return, I did miss you. Brian tried to contact you, but nobody seemed to know where you were.'

Teo nodded, his head bowed low, and unexpectedly he collapsed into tears. This caught Tory off guard; she had never seen him cry before.

'I don't know what's happening to me, Tory.' He sounded scared.

'What do you mean?'

'I don't know, I'm not myself, am I?' He raised his head and stared deep into her eyes. 'Don't you think I've changed?'

Tory's heart sank and her stomach churned. Indeed he had, he was so negative, so angry. 'You've been in torment, Teo. But you don't have to feel that way anymore. Things will sort themselves out now, you'll see.' She gave him a hug.

Teo had no real kin and had been on his own all his life. His childhood hadn't been so good, but his interest in the martial arts had saved him.

'I've lost you, though.' He pulled himself together, and Tory wiped the tears from his face.

'No you haven't, I'm right here. You just can't shag me anymore.' This got half a laugh out of him.

'But that was the best part.' He invited a punch and received one. 'Ouch, I meant to mention that before, your strikes have improved.'

527

'You'd better believe it.'

Teo stayed for a cup of tea then left peacefully. He apologised to Maelgwn for his rudeness, but Tory knew he did this more as a good show for her benefit than because he was truly sorry. Teo said he would return to see Brian in the next day or so and asked Tory to give her brother his regards.

'He has a darkness about him,' Maelgwn said as they watched Teo drive off.

'I noticed that, too. But Teo's been through much worse than this little trauma, and he will get over it, given time.'

They returned inside where Maelgwn sat Tory down at the kitchen table. 'He was thy lover, was he not?' he asked in a very civil manner, not jealous as he'd been in the past.

'Aye, Maelgwn, he was.' The confession saddened her. They had never spoken about her past, or his, still it was bound to come up sometime. 'The first and last, before thee. I was going to say something about him, but when thee never asked, I guess I put it off. I was afraid thee would be disappointed that the Goddess had not sent thee a virgin. And never in a million years did I think that the two of thee would meet, or I would have told thee sooner, I swear!'

'Tory, calm down. I am not angry with thee, nor disappointed. In my experience, there be no great thrill in taking a virgin to thy bed. I would have wed thee if thou had known a million lovers before me.'

'Really?' Tory sprang to her feet and hugged him. 'I do love thee, Maelgwn of Gwynedd.'

'And I love thee, Tory Alexander.' He held her face in his hands and kissed it.

'So what about thee? "In my experience" thee said just now. How much experience is that exactly?'

Maelgwn's smile was broad, his cheeks flushed. 'Well I was in the monastery for some time, as thou art aware.'

'And how about before and after that . . . hmm?'

As Maelgwn seemed to be having a bit of trouble answering, Tory thought she'd give him a hand. 'At what age did thee lose thy virginity then?'

'Five and ten.'

'Five and ten!'

'That be late, Brockwell was only two and ten when he lost his.'

'I'd believe it. So who was she?'

'Why, I do not know.'

'I was referring to *thy* first love, Maelgwn, not Brockwell's.'

'Oh I see. I do not know that either.'

'Thee must have been there, Maelgwn. How could her identity escape thee?'

'Well, it was the feast of Beltaine, and King Catulus was giving a huge celebration as I had rid his kingdom of the dragon. He was into masquerades at the time, so we all wore masks. Yet I have to confess, I am fairly sure it was his daughter.'

'And?'

'And what?' He laughed.

'And so how many others have there been?'

'None, that I have felt enough for to even recognise.' He raised Tory and seated her on the table

529

before him. 'Now let us forget my conquests a moment, I have need to ask thee something.' He paused to look her in the eye, suddenly serious. 'Dost thou still love him, Tory?'

She smiled at his concern. 'I believe I did once, though thinking back, it may have been more curiosity and lust. But, he be a dear friend, always was. Please do not judge him from what thee saw of him today, Teo be a good and learned soul really.'

Maelgwn wasn't so sure and he felt awkward speaking his mind; he didn't want to seem as if he were condemning her friend. 'Hast thou told him anything of thy journey?'

'Nay, I said I fell and got amnesia. But I did intend to tell him the truth.'

'I'd rather thee did not and I cannot really explain why, only that I wish it. Please Tory, if thee would do this for me, I would be most grateful.'

As the request seemed so important to him, she agreed.

Six weeks later, Tory discovered that she was pregnant. She had conceived at exactly the same time as she had the year before. The child was due just before summer solstice, which meant that she could give birth in the safety of a hospital. Tory just hoped the baby was on time.

Maelgwn was ecstatic and wasn't prepared to accept that any problems might arise. This was fate as he saw it, and best of all, his wife and unborn child were completely safe. In this time nobody knew, or would even care that Tory carried the heir to the throne of Gwynedd. This was the perfect sanctuary, as Taliesin had obviously foreseen, and it proved to be yet another reason why the Merlin had insisted that Maelgwn accompany Tory to the twentieth century.

When the rest of the family were told the news they were overjoyed. Tory had assumed that Brian would tease her about becoming fat and so forth. But when he didn't she finally realised that he was not a child anymore, he had matured just as she had. In fact, Brian was rather excited at the prospect of becoming an uncle and his delight equalled that of their father, who was more than ready to become a grandfather. Tory laughed as she watched Maelgwn's enthusiasm wane when Brian explained that in this day and age, the father was expected to attend the birth.

'Maelgwn hast studied medicine, thus I expect the whole process shall interest him greatly. Be that not right my love?' Tory added to his discomfort.

'Don't let her trick you, bro,' Brian advised. 'She just wants thee close so that when the pain gets really bad, thee will be within striking distance.'

'Now stop confusing the poor lad.' Renford had seen his children's routine before; Brian and Tory often ganged up on others in this way. 'I was present at the birth of these two and I assure you, Maelgwn, I would not trade that experience for all the knowledge of the Ancients.'

Tory and Brian appeared quite touched.

'Indeed, I have not known a single day as joyous since.' Renford chuckled as the expression on his children's faces changed, and they both grabbed for the closest cushion to throw at him.

It was a stormy winter's day and everyone decided to stay indoors. A fire was blazing in the lounge and the whole family sat around, doing little more than drinking tea, eating and reading.

Tory was reading out and translating a book on childbirth to Maelgwn, while Renford silently read a book on Myrddin that was hidden by the cover of the latest spy novel. Aunt Rose had started knitting baby's clothes already and was finishing off a bonnet in blue, as she and Maelgwn both insisted the child would be a boy.

Brian was the only one who seemed disgruntled by the peace and quiet, and when Rose noticed she called him over. 'Show me your hands, Brian.'

'Cool, are you going to read them?' He had been wanting her to do this ever since he'd discovered she could read palms.

Rose usually steered away from reading the fortunes of those she knew, afraid of seeing something tragic, but today the mood took her. She studied her nephew's palms carefully and then gasped, nearly scaring Brian out of his wits.

'What? What is it?' Brian asked her, ignoring the phone that had started to ring in the hall.

'Why thou art about to fall madly in love, my boy.'

'Really. How do you know?' Brian frowned, as the ringing was starting to bother him, and nobody else seemed to hear it. 'Isn't anyone going to get that?'

'Yes, you are,' Tory said. 'It will be for you, anyway.'

'Hold that thought.' Brian made for the phone and answered it with an air of annoyance. 'Hello? Who? Naomi! Yeah, I remember you.' He sounded pleased, closing the door to speak with her.

All eyes looked to Rose, rather amazed.

Even Renford had to laugh, knowing who the woman on the other end of the phone was. 'You're good, Rose, I have to say.'

Rose and Tory were rather rocked by his statement, not that the professor noticed as he'd gone straight back to his book.

'Read mine, Aunt.' Tory approached Rose holding out her hands before her.

Rose sat staring at Tory's hands for some time and finally looked at her niece, completely stumped. 'I can see nothing. The lines on both your hands are exactly the same, child. Usually right is past, left is future, so this would indicate that for you, time has simply stood still!' her aunt joked, unable to explain it.

Of course, I should have known. Tory had nearly forgotten about her immortality, though her new state of being had made her pregnancy noticably more comfortable this time round. Her morning sickness was practically non-existent and she certainly wouldn't have to worry about dying in childbirth or the scars it might leave. 'Must have something to do with the time travel,' Tory put forward as a feasible excuse.

Brian returned, appearing as white as a ghost. 'They found another statue, Dad.'

Renford removed his glasses as he looked to his son. 'Oh dear.'

Tory asked what he meant, and so it was confession time.

She suggested that perhaps Brian recalled seeing the statues in her photos, bringing them out again for him to look over. But once she'd sorted through them, she realised she had only photographed one of the statues.

'Then how did I know there was more than one? You didn't mention it.'

This was true and Tory confirmed that his guess that there were eight or nine statues was exactly right; it had to be a past-life experience.

'They would represent the nine muses who warmed and guarded the sacred cauldron. They each bequeathed one of the nine metaphysical laws,' Renford informed them.

'How knowledgeable of you, father.' Tory was surprised at the information he stored in the recesses of his mind. But in truth, Renford had just been reading about them in his concealed copy of the book on Myrddin.

Brian snatched up one of the other photos. 'The babe! Of course, that's where I've seen her before.'

'Seen who?' Tory inquired.

'The babe in the photo, she's Naomi. I knew I'd seen her before.'

Tory and Maelgwn both laughed at the news.

'What's so funny? It's the truth!'

'Then you're in big trouble, bro.'

'Aye, she be a spirited creature to say the very least,' Maelgwn agreed.

'Well, she's invited me up there for the weekend,' he boasted, not at all worried about their comments.

534

'That is purely so she can quiz you about the statues. I'll stake my life on it,' Tory teased.

'If she wants to know bad enough, I just might get laid,' Brian scoffed. 'So, if you will all excuse me, I'm off to pack.'

'If Professor Paradis has you locked up, I'm not coming to bail you out,' Renford warned his son as he left the room.

'Fear not Dad, no woman can resist me.'

Tory and Maelgwn were reduced to laughter again.

'That's what he thought last time,' Tory said wryly.

When Rose left the room to make supper, Renford seized the opportunity to confide in his daughter and her husband. He told them his own strange story regarding the visit to Llyn Cerrig Bach, and of the whispering voices he'd heard.

Tory explained that she too had heard the voices, however their message to her, if any, had not been audible. Her words proved to Renford that he was not going mad, but this didn't really make him feel better. If anything, he felt worse, as he couldn't write the experience off to senility.

'It may not have been ghosts,' Maelgwn suggested. 'It could have been the trees.'

'The trees!' the professor repeated, sounding even more horrified.

'Aye. As a shaman, Myrddin had a great understanding and communication with all forms of life, especially trees.'

Renford knew his son-in-law's comment to be in accord with what he'd read of the Merlin. This was the one thing about Myrddin that Renford could identify with; he did love his native woodland.

Renford resolved to spend more time in the countryside becoming attuned to nature once the warmer weather returned. Until then he would study all the sites associated with the Merlin, like Dinas Emrys. This was where the story of the boy Myrddin and Vortigern had unfolded. Myrddin reportedly lay sleeping in a cave at this site, with the Thirteen Treasures of Britain. It was said he awaited a particular person, a youth with blue eyes and golden hair. When this youth approached the cave, a bell would ring. A black dog with yellow eyes would appear and lead the youth to the spot where the cave would be revealed to him. Apparently all false seekers who pursued the treasure were turned from the quest by storms or sinister omens.

After patching things up between them, Brian and Teo had taken to hanging out together as they did before Tory's disappearance. Yet the friendship Tory once shared with Teo hadn't been the same since he'd learned of her pregnancy. Words seldom passed between Teo and Maelgwn. They were both learned men of high spiritual awareness and she had hoped they might get over it. Judging from the way they'd been avoiding each other, however, she supposed not.

Fortunately Teo was not hanging around as much as he might have, as Brian had become infatuated with Naomi who lived halfway across the country on Anglesey. Brian made the trip up through the snow covered countryside nearly every weekend to visit her and help out at the site.

By the end of winter Tory looked like a beach ball, yet wore her bundle very well. The extra weight didn't bother her in the least. She was still practising kata to the best of her capability and steered away from the more strenuous exercises. She was much more accepting of her pregnancy this time, and soothed the child in her swollen belly with soft ambient music every day. The tragic loss of her last child still haunted her, so she made damn sure this child knew that it was wanted and well loved.

Maelgwn was surprised at how much he enjoyed helping Tory prepare for the coming of their babe, and attending birthing classes with her had been a real education for him. He was not at all afraid of being present at the birth anymore, feeling himself well prepared for the event.

As the months rushed by them, Maelgwn's reluctance to leave the twentieth century intensified. Sure the air was more polluted here, modern Britain was crowded, chaotic and noisy, but the amount of information that was at his disposal was phenomenal. The evening television news was an education in itself. He imagined he could spend his whole life studying and not even make a hole in the amount of material that was available. There were texts on subjects he had never even heard of: scientific theories and technologies, countries and cultures, the list was endless. He did not miss his kingdom and his position at all — were it not for his loyal subjects, the King felt he would never return.

The baby's due date came and went and Tory was beginning to despair, afraid she'd created a delay by her very fear of it. She wished now that she'd maintained the same mind as Maelgwn who believed that nothing would go wrong. Instead, the household was thrown into an uproar come the stroke of midnight that marked the eve of summer solstice, leaving Tory but twenty-four hours to have the child, recover, and make it to the stones.

While she was rushed to the hospital, a million thoughts raced through her mind. *I haven't run into Taliesin here, as he said I might. Perhaps this child was the only real reason I had to return here, and if so, then surely the birth shall be over in no time.*

Her illusion of a quick and easy birth was shattered when eighteen hours later she found herself still sweating it out. 'Maelgwn, thee must return without me.'

'Nay, my love, I am staying right here.' He kissed her hand that gripped his so tightly.

'Gwynedd cannot afford to lose thee,' she reasoned with him, so exhausted she could barely speak.

'And I cannot afford to lose thee.' Maelgwn tightened his grip.

'Thee will not. Taliesin said his younger self was to be found *here*, in the twentieth century. Therefore, I can seek him out and instruct him to prepare for this instance. So in many years from now, after he has travelled to the Old Land and returned to Gwynedd to rewrite history by taking me back there, he will know that I have been detained in labour and devise a means for my return. Before we left, Taliesin hinted that a situation might arise causing me to seek him out, and I am guessing that he knew this would happen all along. Which, of course, he must, as this is all in his distant past.'

'But what if he dost not? Nay Tory, I shall not risk it.'

'Listen to me, Taliesin said I sought him out and told him of my destiny, remember?' Tory finally recalled the conversation with Taliesin that had been eluding her for hours. 'If I never seek him, then how shall he know? It was meant to happen this way, Maelgwn, I am sure of it. I shall join thee in the past in but a few hours.' Yet Tory knew that in her reality she faced a whole year without him, and what if she proved wrong in her presumption? *I shall find a way back, no matter what.*

Maelgwn bowed his head, disappointed that he would miss the first year of his child's life and even the chance to glimpse his babe before departing. 'I will not leave the two of thee here unprotected.'

'Maelgwn, besides my own skills, I have Brian and Teo.'

'Nay! Swear to me, Tory, that thee will not let Teo near our child.'

Tory was alarmed by the malice he still held towards Teo, but she nodded faintly. 'I promise.'

'Or near thee,' Maelgwn added in a much softer tone.

'Beholden to thee alone until death do us part, that be what I vowed, Maelgwn.' She held his face; the pain in her heart was more overwhelming than that which emanated through her body. 'Fear not, I will find thee.'

Although the staff in attendance could not understand the language the couple were speaking, they were all close to tears as they witnessed the lovers' parting kiss.

Maelgwn said his farewells to his kin in the waiting room. It wasn't easy to leave the quiet family life, the like of which the King knew he would never see again. Renford, in particular, was sorry to see him go, and although he understood that his son-in-law was obliged to do so, there was a tear in his eye as he hugged the huge King. 'May God speed thee, son.'

'And may the Goddess protect thee, Professor, until next we meet.' As Renford appeared doubtful, Maelgwn threw his arms wide to add, 'Anything be possible.'

Brian drove Maelgwn to the stones in silence. He didn't know what he could say that might ease the torment his friend was going through.

It was very close to midnight by the time they arrived, and Maelgwn was a bundle of nerves. He hadn't felt so torn in all his days; it still wasn't too late for him to change his mind and stay with her.

'Maelgwn, I know you are worried, but you must realise by now that I would never let anything happen to Tory or your child. So please, consider the fate of Britain first,' Brian said, as it was his task to see that the King returned.

'I am tired of putting my country first, why must it always come before me!'

A crack of thunder startled them both and they looked up to witness the storm cloud unfolding overhead.

'Holy shit!' Brian began to back out of the circle. No sooner had he cleared it than a bolt of lightning shot from the clouds and struck the King's Stone, causing the mist to rise.

'Brian, swear to me that thee shall see my wife and child safely here next summer solstice.'

'I swear it to thee, Maelgwn,' Brian announced. The mist became too bright for him to see the King anymore. 'I shall miss thee, bro.'

Maelgwn bowed to him. The Prince watched as his brother-in-law became obscured by the haze, then a shape began to emerge from within the trunk of the tree behind Brian. A familiar face took form — blazing red in colour, it stood out in the darkness. The sound of sinister laughter reached the King's ears, yet Brian appeared totally unaware of it.

No! It was too late to turn back. 'Brian, be —' Maelgwn tried to yell out a warning but the haze was sucked up into the sky, the King's body and soul along with it.

'Where be Tory? Maelgwn, wake up, please!'

The King's eyes opened to see Brockwell and his other knights hovering over him.

'Where be Tory?' Brockwell repeated.

'Give him room.' Taliesin pushed the knights aside and knelt beside the King.

When the Merlin was within range, Maelgwn clutched him tightly by his robe. 'Did she find thee?'

'Aye, that she did. Rest assured, all be going to plan.' Taliesin patted the King's shoulder.

Maelgwn breathed a sigh of relief then became tense again. 'Did thee know Mahaud was in the future with her?' The King sat upright to get his bearings and pointed. 'She emerged from that tree and made herself known to me, just as it was too late to turn back.'

The Merlin recognised it to be an elder tree, which in the sacred alphabet of the tree calendar was called Ruis. This was akin to the thirteenth month of the year, which was attributed to the Dark Queen of fate and the inevitable. *Cute, Mahaud.*

Taliesin frowned and answered, 'Nay, Maelgwn, this be unexpected and unfortunate. The Goddess used her powers to assist Myrddin to suppress his great knowledge for a time, in the hope of preventing the witch from finding him. Did thee find Myrddin?'

'Aye, but as thou hast said, he remembers naught.' Maelgwn was frantic. 'Send me back, I must protect Tory and our child.'

'Child!' All present looked at their King amazed; he'd only been gone an hour.

'Tory hast given birth?' Katren was eager to hear how she fared.

'Aye.' Everything had happened so quickly that Maelgwn hadn't really had time to consider that he was, most likely, a father by now.

'I am impressed.' Calin helped Maelgwn to his feet. 'Congratulations.'

'So was it a boy or a girl?' Katren asked.

'Why, I do not know.' Maelgwn was immediately saddened by the thought of missing the birth. ''Twas a boy, I think.'

'Indeed! A strong, healthy boy and he enters this world as we speak,' Taliesin announced, raising everyone's spirits.

But Maelgwn's attention wasn't distracted for long. 'Taliesin, I have to warn them.'

'Please everyone, calm down. I cannot send thee back, the channel hast passed until the next hour.' The Merlin wasn't even sure he could raise the energy to do it then, as he was already exhausted from completing the feat twice in as many hours. 'Myrddin will find himself.'

'And what if he dost not? There must be a way I can speak to Tory.'

'Rest a moment,' Taliesin advised him. 'There be one thing we might try.'

23

WHERE IS HOME?

Maelgwn and Aunt Rose's prediction proved to be right. After twenty-four hours in labour, Tory gave birth to a boy whom she named Rhun. He was in perfect health and of a fair size, weighing in at seven pounds. Rhun had his father's colouring, and masses of dark hair already covered his tiny head. Tory and her family fell madly in love with him at once.

Brian returned to the hospital by morning, shaken by what he'd seen. Still, he could confidently tell Tory that Maelgwn had returned, if not without much procrastination. Brian held his little nephew in his arms and told Tory of his vow to Maelgwn and how determined he was to keep it.

'He also insisted I keep Teo away from Rhun,' she informed her brother.

Brian wasn't at all surprised to hear this, knowing all too well how the two felt about each other. For months he had listened to Teo going on about what he believed was Tory's betrayal of him. Although he was Brian's best friend, there was nothing Teo could say about Maelgwn that could tarnish the respect Brian felt for the King. 'Well, Teo doesn't know who your father truly is,' Brian said to the babe he held. 'Nor does he know of the part your parents have to play in history. So if the Dragon wants Teo kept away from you, we shall just have to oblige him, won't we?'

'Do you think he's changed? Teo, I mean. You know him better than anyone,' Tory asked.

'Well, he claims you hurt him badly,' Brian began. 'But such melodrama isn't like Teo at all. Even if your marriage had hurt him, the Teo I used to know would have been happy for you. I mean, what happened to "our friendship is the most important thing"?'

'That's exactly what I thought.' Tory didn't know what to make of it. 'So when am I going to meet this girl of yours?' Tory gently took her child, smiling at him in adoration.

'This weekend. I invited her down to see the baby. Typical woman, she went all gooey on me, she loves kids apparently. I thought it was a good excuse to get her away from her father and the dig for more than five minutes.'

'You've spent just about every weekend this winter up at the dig, and you still haven't nailed her in all that time?' Tory pretended to be horrified.

'Of course I have.'

But Tory knew Katren better than that. 'Liar.'

'Alright, I didn't. Something about her keeps bringing out the gentleman in me,' he explained, taking up Rhun's tiny hands. 'But this weekend is going to be different, because this little guy is going to get Naomi's maternal juices flowing for me. Aren't you mate?'

Tory chuckled; Brian was a lot smarter than Brockwell. 'You just might be right there.'

Tory and Rhun went home sooner than expected. The doctors had been so amazed by the speed of her recovery that Tory thought she'd better leave before they started asking questions.

Rhun was proving to be exceptionally resilient as well. The nurses in the maternity ward were sad to see him go as he was such a placid, happy baby, who was calm even amongst the other screaming babies in their care.

Within a few days of their arrival home, Tory began to notice how Rhun's moods reflected her own. Whenever she started to miss Maelgwn, no matter how far she was from the baby, Rhun inevitably started to cry. This was added incentive to put her love to the back of her mind and concentrate on finding the elusive Taliesin. This was going to prove a challenge, as Tory knew the dig on Mon had yet to uncover the temple altar. She wasn't too keen to tell them about it either, as they would surely want to cart it off to a museum somewhere. Most likely this would render the relic useless and close yet another doorway to the Otherworld forever. In any case, Tory decided it was about time she went up and had a snoop around the site herself. Naomi was expected tomorrow, so Tory would ask her permission. Perhaps the spirits at the site could tell her of Taliesin's whereabouts.

Naomi still hadn't arrived by late Saturday afternoon, and Brian began to worry that something might have happened to her. He appealed to Rose to ask her spirits if they knew anything. She explained that they could see no immediate tragedy, but they did indicate a surprise.

'Well, I hope it's of a hot and sweaty nature,' Brian remarked, as the sound of a car coming down the drive sent him racing out the front door.

Brian was surprised to see a large black Mercedes four-wheel drive, with black tinted windows. This was not Naomi's car, nor her father's, but it was a beauty.

Naomi sprang out of the passenger seat and wrapped her arms around him. 'Sorry I'm so late, Miles held me up.'

'Miles who?' Brian became immediately jealous.

'Thurlow, my father's partner. He arrived back from the Azores a couple of days ago, and when he heard I was coming down to Professor Alexander's place he offered to drive me. I hope you don't mind?'

'Mind, why should I mind?' Brian tried to sound pleased that they again had a chaperone.

The professor jumped out and shook Brian's hand. 'Sorry to intrude like this, but I needed to speak with your father about the implications of his analysis.' Miles noted Brian appeared somewhat overwhelmed. 'Is there something wrong?'

Although Professor Thurlow was not as large as Maelgwn, and appeared perhaps a few years older, if it weren't for the glasses and the ponytail they could be one and the same. *This is going to be a surprise alright!* 'Sorry, Professor, you just look a lot like my sister's husband, a hell of a lot!'

'Tory!' Brian bolted down the hall and into the lounge. 'I think you'd better prepare yourself for a shock.'

'Do you want to be more specific?' Tory marked her place in the book she was reading and looked up at him.

'Professor Thurlow is here to see Dad,' he explained, gaining his father's attention also. 'But he looks more like Maelgwn to me.'

'Ha-ha.' Tory went back to her reading.

'Hello?' Naomi called from the front door.

Brian, becoming flustered, disappeared again to retrieve Naomi. He guided her and her companion through to the lounge.

Tory didn't look up immediately as she wanted to finish the sentence she was reading.

'Tory,' her father urged.

She raised her eyes and nearly had a stroke. *By the Goddess!*

Miles held out his hand to greet her. 'Miles Thurlow, pleased to meet you.'

He smiled and Tory's heart leapt into her throat. 'How do you do.' After quickly shaking his hand, she greeted Naomi and then excused herself on the premise that she had to check on the baby.

She raced to the solace of her room and closed the door behind her. 'Holy shit!' she exclaimed, horrified by the connotations of his presence here. 'Please God let me be mistaken about this.' Maelgwn had been gone less than a week and she missed him like crazy already. Rhun sensed his mother's dismay and started to cry.

'Hush now!' She took Rhun in her arms to comfort him. 'It was just a bit of a scare, that's all. We're okay.' She comforted the baby, rocking him to and fro.

Hearing the child's cries and knowing that Tory must also be upset, Brian knocked and entered. 'I tried to warn you.'

'I know, thanks.'

As she didn't seem to want to talk about it, Brian edged around the subject. 'Well then, are you going to bring Rhun downstairs so he can go to work on my girlfriend, or what?'

Tory smiled faintly. Something told her she should keep the child out of Miles' sight, herself too for that matter. 'I'll tell you what, you bring Naomi up here to see him and I'll go and work out for a while, okay?'

'Alright!' He landed a big kiss on her cheek. 'Good call.'

'Just take good care —'

'Tory? It goes without saying. Don't worry about a thing.' He handed Tory her towel as he guided her out the door. 'Do me another favour, send Naomi up on your way past.'

Renford found it difficult to answer all of Professor Thurlow's questions. He was put off by the fact that he looked so much like his son-in-law, yet he lacked Maelgwn's broad-minded understanding.

'So why has the parchment not perished by now?' Miles queried.

'I have no answer for that. Yet I can assure you, it's not a fake. I had it concisely dated.'

Miles didn't appear satisfied or completely convinced, as he mulled over Renford's answer. 'I also wanted to ask about your son's knowledge of the statues. Do you know anything about that?'

Renford was again hesitant to reply. 'I am a seeker of facts myself, Miles, but some things, I've come to realise, defy explanation. Brian claims he remembers seeing them standing, which has led most in this family to believe it was a past-life memory. For, as you know, the relics have been buried for several centuries.'

Renford poured them a whisky, and Miles thought perhaps the professor had already had one too many. But then the whole family seemed a bit strange; what did it take to get a straight, logical answer around here?

Dinner that evening proved rather interesting. Brian had obviously had his way with Naomi as they were all smiles for each other. Thus with romance in the air, Tory sat as far away from Miles as possible. She'd convinced herself that she was not the slightest bit interested in getting to know him, and resolved to avoid him if she could. Tory would have taken dinner in her room but her family wouldn't hear of it.

To Miles, Tory seemed the sanest of the clan, and her beauty hadn't escaped his attention either. This led him to wonder where and who the father of her child was, and Naomi conveniently inquired for him.

'Is your husband not here?' Brian had told her that his sister and her husband were staying at the house, yet there was no place set for him.

'He has been called away on business, I'm afraid.'

'What kind of work does he do?' Miles asked.

'He works for the government,' Tory responded without so much as a second's thought, astounding those in the room who knew the truth with her quick retort.

'Really, in what field?'

'That, Professor Thurlow, is on a need-to-know basis and you don't need to know. In truth, where he goes and what he does is a mystery to me most of the time.'

'What, are you saying he's secret service?' Miles smiled, half disbelieving her.

Tory merely shrugged in response, turning her attention to the wonderful meal before her, and Miles was again left to ponder what it was they were all hiding.

As soon as dessert was finished, Renford bade them all goodnight. Tory and Naomi helped Rose in the kitchen, leaving Miles to question Brian about the statues.

'Look, I'm not saying I saw them in a past life. All I'm saying is that I recollect seeing them covered in vines. When that was exactly, I don't claim to know, I just remember I was young, say six or seven at the time.'

'And you can't tell me anymore about the site, you don't remember anything else?'

'Sorry.' Brian shook his head. 'Tory's the one you should be asking, she's the expert on Llyn Cerrig Bach.'

Miles seemed very interested to hear this. 'Why is that?'

Brian suddenly realised he'd almost put his foot in it. 'Well, she's the real psychic of the family.' He then laughed, which led Miles to wonder if he was joking.

Tory and Naomi returned with a fresh pot of coffee, and Brian pulled a large joint from his pocket.

'Anybody interested?' He looked up to catch Naomi's reaction and was surprised to find it quite agreeable.

'I have been known to indulge.' She sat down beside him.

'I don't think I should, Brian, with the baby and all, besides I'm kind of tired.' Tory tried to graciously decline.

'Oh come on, Tory, you piker. One joint isn't going to hurt. We haven't got blasted together in ages,' Brian appealed.

Tory rolled her eyes, twisting her arm up behind her back. 'Okay.' She took her seat again.

Brian then looked at Miles, who laughed at the suggestion. 'I haven't smoked grass since the seventies, Brian.'

'Then you can have a flashback,' Brian insisted, lighting up and passing the joint to the professor.

'Really I . . .' Miles observed the joint smoking away before his eyes. 'Well, perhaps just a small toke.' Maybe if he played along, someone might open up and start talking sense.

As soon as Naomi got the giggles, Brian carted her

away to his room. Tory, not wanting to be left alone with Miles, rose to leave also.

'I wonder if I might talk with you a moment?' Miles reached out to take hold of her hand as she moved past him.

'What about?' She shrank from his touch.

'Sorry.' He'd obviously made her feel ill at ease and couldn't figure out why he'd reached for her in the first place; he was normally much more reserved. 'I just wanted to ask you about Llyn Cerrig Bach. I spoke to Brian about it earlier and he suggested I talk to you. He claimed you were psychic, but I wasn't sure if I should take him seriously or not.'

Thanks a lot bro! Tory could just imagine how a truthful response would grab Miles. 'I take it you don't believe in that sort of thing, Professor?'

He looked up at her, wondering what was causing her obvious dislike of him. 'Tory, you can call me Miles.'

'I think "Professor" suits you better.' Tory kept her distance, almost as if she were afraid of him.

'Have you got something against me because I look like your husband?'

Tory was alarmed. 'Who told you that?'

'Brian,' they both announced at once. Brilliant, Tory thought, with a shake of her head.

'Look Tory, whatever the problem is, I'm truly sorry. I just want to know if there is anything else you can tell me about the site, that's all.'

Tory looked at him blankly, knowing damn well he wasn't going to take anything she said seriously. 'Professor, I could tell you a thing or two about the temple in the valley, but I can't give you a logical explanation for how I know what I do.'

Miles was getting a bit fed up with these incoherent answers. 'That's what Brian said. What do you mean exactly? Were you there in a past life too?'

His tone was extremely patronising in Tory's opinion, thus hers became equally so. 'No, actually I wandered into the Otherworld and the fairies took me back to the year five hundred, so I could have a look around for myself.' She smiled at him ever so sweetly.

Miles tried to calm himself, not wanting to seem rude. 'Alright, I apologise. Please, just tell me, do you claim to be psychic or not?'

'I don't claim to be anything. I am, however, chosen,' Tory answered, using 'Taliesin tactics', in the hope he'd get frustrated and give up.

'Chosen for what?'

'Whatever.' She shrugged. 'Look, I don't have all the answers, Professor. If I did I'd be in seventh heaven. However,' Tory was struck by a thought. 'I will say this, you haven't found the site's greatest treasure.' Tory smiled at her own brilliance; she would get them to unearth the gateway for her.

'How do you know?' Miles was exhausted with the conversation and wondered why he'd even bothered asking; she was only going to serve him another riddle.

'Professor, let's pretend for a moment that you're not a sceptic. Then you would ask, what is it?' Tory lightened up a little. He'd obviously never even considered the possibility of the greater mysteries, and so would find it hard to accept the suggestion of psychic ability unless she could prove it.

'Alright. What is it?' Miles slouched back in his chair to finish his cold cup of coffee.

'Dig in the centre of the circle of nine and there you will find a large stone altar that bears the Celtic cross.' Miles sat forward in his seat, more interested, but Tory continued before he could start asking questions. 'However, you must not remove the tablet from where it is unearthed, until I have seen it, agreed?'

'Why?'

'Agreed?' Tory was adamant. 'If I cannot trust you, Professor, I shall tell you naught. And believe me, you know little of the toys with which you play.'

Miles was awestruck, as Tory's entire presence appeared to change. She seemed larger somehow, more powerful. 'I agree. If we find it, I will call you at once.'

'*When* you find it, Professor. If you are always so afraid to commit yourself, I'm surprised you have ever obtained anything you sought,' Tory said in jest.

'No offence, but my sources are usually a little bit more concrete.'

'No offence to you, but they are usually the vaguest kind of reference, being entirely derived from nothing more than physical understanding.'

Miles laughed at the way their conversation was progressing. 'Is this where we start talking about life, the universe and everything?' He decided it was the grass causing the peculiar feeling he had in his stomach, and the illusion that Tory seemed to glow like an angel. *Yeah, I'm stoned alright.*

'No, this is where I bid you a goodnight, sir.' Tory made her way to the door. 'And don't forget, you promised.'

Come Sunday morning, Tory decided to make herself scarce to avoid answering any more of Professor Thurlow's questions, at least until he'd found the altar and was more accepting of her abilities. She had also felt the need for some fresh air, so she packed a picnic lunch, a rug, the baby's things, and a couple of good books in her backpack and, with Rhun resting comfortably in a pouch against her chest, she made her way across the fields.

It was a fine day and a cool soft breeze was blowing. As Tory walked along relishing the great outdoors, she thought about Miles Thurlow and wondered how he could possibly be a future incarnation of Maelgwn. Her husband was certainly more broad-minded than the professor, and unquestionably more developed physically. Perhaps when a soul incarnated, its progression didn't necessarily develop akin to that of human civilisation. From what she could surmise this theory was certainly true of Taliesin; he'd been Teo in the twentieth century long before he'd become Gwion Bach in the fifth.

Tory ambled on with no real destination in mind but when she came to the King's Men stones, she figured it was as good a place as any to settle in the shade of a tree and read. She found it comforting to consider that Maelgwn was in this very spot awaiting their return home, and in a sense she felt closer to him here.

Tory got lost in the silent bliss of a book for some time, before she became aware of footsteps. She looked up to see Teo, who appeared as if he'd just been to hell and back. *How on earth?*

'I thought I might find you here,' Teo explained with a smile.

Odd, Tory thought, when I didn't even realise I was coming here myself.

'Hey, you look great!' He took a seat beside her and planted a kiss on her cheek.

'Well thank you, kind sir. I wish I could say the same. What happened to you?'

'Saturday night.' He flopped back onto the large rug, his shirt falling open to expose his smooth, bronzed, muscular torso.

'Do you end up in this state every weekend?' Tory didn't mean to sound condescending, but it was rather disheartening to see her former *sensei* in such a decrepit state.

He laughed. 'Every weekend? Every night more like,' he explained, holding his head that clearly pained him. 'It's got to stop, I know.'

'Then just don't do it! Self-inflicted, no mercy.'

'I know, I know.' Teo sat back up, not looking at Tory. 'But I'm finding it hard to get back on track, and I'm in no way blaming you for that,' he said before she could get the wrong impression. 'The simple truth of it is, I just can't seem to get you out of my system.' He turned his dark eyes to Tory to catch her reaction.

'I don't know what I can do,' Tory said, wishing she could somehow take the memories back; she couldn't stand to see him so dispirited. But when he leaned across to kiss her, Tory stood up quickly. 'Damn it, Teo.'

He held his palms up, motioning his surrender. 'I'm sorry.'

'No you're not,' Tory insisted, hands on hips.

'You're right. I'm not,' he grinned, trying to make light of it.

'If you think I'm going to be dipping and dodging your advances the whole time Maelgwn's away, you've got another think coming, mate. I could certainly whip your arse in its present state, so don't push me!'

'I can't help myself,' he replied, looking defenceless.

'In that case, I can't see you anymore.' Tory crouched down and began to pack up.

Teo reached out and clutched her right wrist tightly. 'No, Tory. I'm truly sorry, I am.'

Tory wrenched her arm away from him, far from convinced.

'Even when we weren't lovers, I used to flirt with you. I'm just having trouble adjusting to this no affection bit, but I'll try. I will.'

His plea seemed heartfelt and even a little fearful. Tory realised she couldn't abandon Teo just because he was going through a rough time, for which she had been the catalyst. 'I want to stand by you, Teo, because you are my good friend, and I love you. But you always make it so damn difficult for me.'

'I know I do,' he admitted. 'Please, couldn't we just start over? I'll act like a long-lost brother, if you would regard me as such again. I really miss the three of us, Tory. I miss being part of the family. I guess the reason I was so pissed off at Maelgwn was because he'd taken my place.'

'How can you say that?' Tory sounded hurt. 'You were, are, and always will be, an integral part of my life. And not just this life, I'm talking forever!' She wandered a little way from him, as a tear escaped her eye; she missed Taliesin, too. 'You really have no idea.'

Teo was surprised by this. He hadn't seen Tory so upset since the day they'd decided to stop seeing each other, and he stood to calm her. 'Tory? I didn't mean —'

Tory turned abruptly and grabbed hold of his shirt. 'I want the real you back! I know that sweet, wise and understanding guy I loved is in there somewhere, and I want to see him, I miss him.' She let go, having expended her frustration.

'From now on, I promise. Just one more chance.'

'Alright,' she decided after much procrastination, and Rhun at once began to cry. This struck Tory as unusual as she almost always sensed when Rhun wanted something, long before he'd have to cry for it.

When she settled her child easily and found he wanted nothing bar her attention, she decided she should be very wary where Teo was concerned. But as the afternoon sky was fast clouding over, she took him up on the offer of a lift home and kept her suspicions to herself.

Over the next couple of months, Brian, Tory and Teo spent much time together focusing on their art, each with their own objective. Brian had students approaching grading, including Tory. Teo, having given up his vice, had been invited by the family to take up residence in the gym, as he practically lived there anyway. They had offered him a room in the house but he had insisted that the spare room in the gym was fine. Tory thought it was important for Teo to feel part of the family again if he was to overcome the negativity that seemed to overshadow his every thought.

A few weeks of country life and the constant familiar company of the Alexander clan made Teo feel a new man. Able to maintain his focus with greater ease, Teo was happy assisting Tory in her preparation for the next Dan grade and he seemed almost back to his old self. At times he abused his privilege as her teacher, but it was usually in jest and no more than any other male might have done. Tory didn't find Teo's flirting to be seriously offensive and had started to relax in his company, every so often spying a glimpse of Taliesin's brilliance in him. However, he chose to ignore Rhun most of the time, just as he had Maelgwn. This unfortunately seemed to indicate that the malice Teo felt for her husband was still very much alive, and though Teo never spoke of his feelings for her anymore, Tory knew they still underlay everything he did.

24

THE VISIT

On the day marking her second wedding anniversary, Tory finally heard from Miles about the altar. He apologised for taking so long to contact her, explaining he'd been tied up with other projects.

'You didn't take me seriously, did you Professor?' Tory saw straight through him, even with a telephone line between them.

'No, I didn't, regrettably. Yet, as fate would have it, we've stumbled upon your altar anyway. And it's just as you described,' he was excited to confirm.

'Indeed,' Tory said, not in the least surprised. 'You haven't moved it?'

'No.' He sounded amused by the notion. 'I think we'll need more equipment.'

'Please Miles, promise you won't touch it until I get there.'

'That was the deal,' he confirmed, a smile reflecting in his voice; he was glad for an excuse to see her again.

'Good. I'll catch a ride up with Brian tomorrow.'

Just one problem; Brian was planning a dirty weekend, and so Naomi was driving down to visit him instead.

'Now what am I going to do,' she wondered, as she didn't want to be left alone with Miles for any length of time.

'Well you can still borrow my car. It will do you good to get away for the weekend.' Brian totally misconstrued her woes. 'Between Naomi and Aunt Rose, I'm sure Rhun will be well cared for.'

'It's not that.'

'You fancy him, don't you, Tory? You think he's Maelgwn.'

'I don't know what I think. Though the professor looks a lot like Maelgwn, they don't seem the same in other respects. You hang around at the site all the time, haven't you gotten to know him at all?'

'Well, to tell you the truth, Naomi and I haven't been spending as much time at the dig of late,' Brian was pleased to say. 'And Thurlow travels a lot, he never seems to be there. Look, if he bothers you so much, you could always take Teo with you,' he suggested, tongue in cheek.

'Yes, I can just imagine how they would take to each other.'

'I don't see what you're so worried about, if Thurlow gets out of line just hit him.' Brian dangled his car keys before her eyes, and Tory grabbed hold of them to stop the annoying noise he was making. 'So why are you going up there, anyhow?'

'I just want to have a look around. I'll let you know if I discover anything of interest.'

Tory reached Llyn Cerrig Bach that afternoon. There was very little resemblance between the valley she drove through and the one she remembered, and although the road to the dig ran the same course as the old dirt track, much of the fairy wood had unfortunately disappeared.

She was pleased Maelgwn hadn't visited Gwynedd during his stay; she had taken a detour to see the remains of the citadel at Degannwy and found nothing but the mound on which it had been built. Where the great house at Aberffraw had once stood on Anglesey, as home to the Kings of Gwynedd for generations, there was but one small cottage on a vast expanse of land overlooking the ocean. To see both his estates completely obliterated would surely have rattled Maelgwn — it bothered her and she'd fully expected to find them thus.

Miles had been impatiently awaiting Tory's arrival all day. This wasn't at all like him, as he was usually too absorbed in what had been going on in the world centuries ago to worry about anybody or anything in the present. Yet today he had the concentration span of a two year old. He couldn't stop his attention from drifting to the entrance to the carpark, all the while praying that Tory hadn't changed her mind.

She's married, he reminded himself as he spotted Brian's car and so left his office to greet Tory. 'How do I look?' he asked his secretary, Amanda, as he passed through the reception area.

'As windswept and handsome as always. Why?'

'No reason,' Miles replied. 'Remind me to give you a raise.'

Professor Paradis opened his office door, and emerged reading a report that was falling to pieces in his hand. 'Was that Miles I just heard come through here?'

'I think so, he must be ill.' Amanda sounded quite serious. 'He's all . . . playful.'

'Playful. Miles?' Paradis sounded rather sceptical.

'Well, he just gave me a raise for saying he looked nice.'

'What?' Paradis moved to the door to see if Miles was still about, and spied him speaking with Tory. 'Uh-huh, well there's your answer right there.' He chuckled as Amanda hurried over to take a look for herself. 'Must be Renford's daughter. Apparently this psychic thing runs in the family. She told Miles about the altar months ago.'

'Wow! Just like Brian.' Amanda took another look to see Miles and Tory heading for the office. 'Quick, they're coming.' She hustled Paradis back to the desk and she sat down, sporting an innocent look, just as Miles entered with his guest.

'Wait till you see it, it's just beautiful.' Miles was truly excited by the significant find.

Tory just shook her head with a smile. 'I've already seen it, Professor. I keep telling you.'

Miles opened his office door and invited Tory in. 'Could we get some tea, Amanda? Thanks.' He closed the door.

Paradis stared at his partner's office in disbelief; it was not like Miles to skip an introduction. Professor Thurlow was notorious for being preoccupied with his work, but never so with a woman. Paradis shook his head finally. 'It's a pity she's married.'

After Amanda had brought in the tea and left the room Miles said, 'I'll show you, as soon as you finish your cuppa.'

'No, I need to see it when nobody else is around, like tonight,' Tory stated very matter-of-factly. 'Can you arrange that?'

'Not tonight, no. There are others who want to see it. But perhaps tomorrow night, as it's Sunday, it's a safer bet.' That worked out well, he thought, Tory would have to stay overnight.

Tory just nodded, accepting the delay as she sipped her tea.

'May I ask why you have to see it alone?'

Tory placed the cup on the table and smiled. 'No, that wasn't part of the deal.' She stood up, tossing the strap of her bag over her shoulder. 'Do you know of a good hotel around here?'

'I do, in fact.' He paused. 'My place. It's on the island, it's quiet.'

'It sounds way too nice for a happily married woman like myself. I'm afraid a hotel will have to suffice.'

'I wouldn't hear of it. I was your guest in Oxfordshire.'

'You were my father's guest,' Tory said, smiling at his persistence as she headed for the door; his grin was starting to get to her. 'I'm sure there must be a nice hotel around here somewhere.'

'There isn't.' Miles leant on the door to block her escape. 'They're all terrible.' His dark eyes met hers.

'Look Professor, I'm *married*.'

'I know,' he stressed, taking a few paces away from the door. 'I just want to spend some time in your company. I find you . . . interesting.'

'I realise this, and that's why I'm not going to sit around all night while you make a mockery of everything I say.'

'But I think you're for real.'

'Well there's a breakthrough.' Tory clapped her hands together with a laugh.

'Why are you being so hard on me? You don't know me.'

'Oh, yes I do. You're exactly like my father aged, what . . . thirty-seven?'

'Thirty-five,' he corrected her, catching her drift.

'Whatever. But even Dad's wising up in his old age,' she said.

'Wising up to what?'

'The greater mysteries.'

Miles stared at her then asked, 'What is this hunk of rock we've dug up?'

'It's an altar.' Tory wondered why he'd asked when she'd already told him.

'Right. An altar that even a crane can't lift.' Miles folded his arms.

'You tried to move it? You shit, Miles!' Tory whacked his shoulder. 'You specifically promised me you wouldn't.' Her eyes became stormy, as did the weather. Miles was silent in the wake of his betrayal, and Tory gave him a shove to wake him up. 'You could have destroyed it, don't you realise.' She calmed down to a degree, knowing that anger wasn't going to help the situation any. 'This isn't just some ancient stone you've dug up, it is a sacred site. You can't take off with part of it.'

'Apparently not.' He frowned. 'And now that you've told me what it isn't, could you kindly tell me what it is?'

'I don't see why I should tell you anything.'

'Well, perhaps the reason I don't understand is because you never explain whatever it is you're talking about,' he said, throwing his arms in the air, exasperated. 'Every time I have a conversation with you, I just end up with this labyrinth of answers that I can't even recall the questions to. For instance, what did you mean when you said that I had no idea of the toys with which I played? Were you referring to the stone?'

'Don't be ridiculous, Professor. That's only a piece of rock, what could it possibly do?' Tory said sarcastically.

'Okay, I deserved that. But if you'd just give me a straight answer, I promise I'll believe it.'

Miles appealed to Tory in a way that reminded her of Maelgwn, and it was just as hard to resist him. 'I'll show you tomorrow night, and I can guarantee you won't want to move it anywhere. So, I suggest you look into restoration.'

'Restoration! You can't be serious?' There was little profit to be had in restoration, and in this case it would require a huge initial outlay. 'I'm not in the restoration business, I'm afraid.'

'Look, I'm just trying to save you some time.'

Miles shook his head, as he fell into his seat and observed her for a moment. 'You are the most peculiar person I have ever met.'

'Peculiar is good,' Tory decided.

'Please allow me to cook you dinner. I'm a great cook.' She looked as if she was about to decline again, and Miles held a hand over his heart. 'You'll be perfectly safe, I promise.'

Tory knew he was trouble, but there was nothing to be gained by running away from it. 'Then, I accept.'

Naomi reached the house at Oxfordshire about five hours after Tory's departure. The altar was foremost in her mind and the news of it threw Brian into a state of panic.

That's why Tory's so interested all of a sudden, Brian surmised. She'll tell me if she discovers anything of interest . . . no way! I'm tired of missing out on all the action.

'Brian, what's wrong?'

'Nothing,' he answered, pulling on his jacket as he stood. 'We have to get up there.'

'What! But I just drove all the way down here.'

'Shit!' Brian wasn't paying the slightest attention to Naomi's grievances. 'Tory's got my car, you'll have to drive.'

'But what about our weekend together? I've been looking forward to it all week.'

'We'll still be together.' Brian helped her to get moving, pulling her gently but impatiently from her chair. 'And that's the most important thing, right?'

'I suppose so,' Naomi growled. 'At least tell me why?'

'I just have a premonition, I have to find Tory. Will you help me, please?'

Naomi sighed; how could she possibly say no to such a rueful face.

Tory left Brian's car in the enclosure at the site and Miles drove them back to his place. Tory hadn't given any thought to where he might live, until the car pulled into the long dirt driveway. It was the cottage on the point at Aberffraw where the house of Cunedda had once stood. She hit herself on the head for not guessing. 'You live here?'

'Yes. What's wrong with that?'

'Nothing.' Tory began to laugh.

'What's so funny?'

'Nothing, really.' Tory caught her breath. 'I love this place, and it just seems a coincidence that you own it.' She tried to cover up what she was really thinking as he certainly wouldn't believe the truth without proof.

'All the way down to the water,' Miles said with pride.

As soon as Tory climbed out of the car she romped off across the property like a woman possessed, laughing and exclaiming with delight. She didn't care what Miles made of this behaviour, the call of the familiar consumed her as she ran towards the beach. 'I'm home . . . yes!'

The clouds rumbled as lightning flashed across the sky, yet Tory wasn't swayed from her course; the storm's pending fury only added to her release. She discovered that something of the house at Aberffraw did remain — the stairs that led to the beach. Tory stopped still, astounded by the sight of a familiar landmark. She and Calin had argued in this very spot. 'Ha!' she shrugged, running down to the beach.

'Tory, it's going to pour any minute,' Miles called from the bottom of the stairs.

'I don't care!' she cried out, but didn't stop running.

'You'll catch your death,' he insisted, not prepared to follow her further.

'No, I most certainly won't.'

'Well where do you think you're going, exactly?'

Tory laughed. 'Exploring, wanna come?'

Miles was exasperated; she did pick the strangest times to do things, and this wasn't really what he'd planned for this evening. 'Then who would cook dinner?'

Tory merely shrugged and flashed him a cheeky smile, then continued on her way.

'Damn it!' Miles couldn't figure out if he was annoyed because Tory had run off on him, or because he hadn't followed her. She was a real wild child alright, being in her company was like the magical mystery tour. But she was fascinating, for she lived in a world so much more wondrous than his own. Her world was more like the relics he dug up from the ground, the remnants of the fabled Old Ones.

He watched her disappear along the beach; she would surely return once it began to rain.

By the time Brian and Naomi arrived, the dig was practically deserted. Brian found his car at the site, but nobody there could tell him where his sister had gone.

'Great!' He gave his tyre a boot.

'What's so important?' Naomi asked, becoming annoyed. 'If you don't tell me, Brian, I'm not going to pursue this little adventure any further, and remember, I've got the car keys.'

Brian took hold of Naomi, figuring he'd get around her with a bit of charm. 'When you get all riled up like that . . . I gotta tell ya, that accent just makes me crazy.'

Naomi laughed. 'So what are you going to do about it?'

Good question.

Tory had to return to the car sooner or later, and it wouldn't be the first time he'd slept on a back seat.

The rain came, as did nightfall, and Tory still hadn't returned. As he'd finished cooking dinner, Miles grabbed a torch to go after her.

He opened the back door and was startled to see her looking like a drowned rat on his doorstep. 'Where the hell have you been?'

Tory only smiled as she pulled a chunk of rock and metal from behind her back and placed it in Miles' hands.

'What is this?'

'A little more credibility for me, another perplexing mystery for you.'

Upon closer inspection he discovered that it was an iron helmet, or part thereof, that looked like it had been embedded in the rock for some time. His smile grew suddenly. 'Where did you get this?'

Tory pulled off her wet jumper. 'In a cave down by the beach. Your beach,' she stressed.

The professor was speechless; he'd explored nearly every corner of the world in search of antiquities, but he never thought that he'd find them in his own backyard. 'I grew up here and there's no cave down by the beach.'

'Oh yes there is. At low tide there used to be a cave leading up inside the cliff face. Unfortunately it's now permanently underwater, so I had to go swimming. Could you direct me to your bathroom?' she asked as she was dripping all over his kitchen floor.

'You went swimming? In this! Below a rock face, in near darkness! Tory, are you mad?'

Tory knew the cave was there, alright. She may have been heavily sedated when Cadogan carried her through it, but she remembered. The temptation to investigate the remnants of Aberffraw had been too great. In the water she had felt battered and confused, panicking as the waves pounded her under. Finally, she was forced to let go and stop breathing, only to discover there was no need. Not far down the cliff face she found the underwater cavern and was thrust by the sea up inside it. Afterwards, when Tory had made it back to the beach, her body healed itself as before, so now she was just a bit shaken and cold.

'One more question,' Miles asked as he showed her to the bathroom. 'How could you see anything in there?'

She pulled Brian's car keys from the pocket of her jeans, holding up a mini torch. 'It's waterproof, there's a Swiss Army knife on it too.' She tossed them to Miles and grabbed her bag. 'Hey, nice place you've got here, Professor.'

Miles stared at her intently. 'How come your clothes are all tattered and yet there's not a mark on you?'

Tory just smiled, waving a finger at him. 'You've used up your twenty questions for this hour, now I'm going to take a bath, if I may.' She looked to the large, footed tub with relish.

'Of course.' He examined the dripping wet chunk of rock in his hand. How could Tory be married when she was the perfect woman for him? He might not understand her at all, but how nice it would be to have a lifetime to figure her out. Her husband was fortunate indeed. Miles only hoped that he realised it, for if he were married to such a woman, he would certainly not be leaving her on her own.

Tory came out from the bathroom to find dinner on the table, and they ate in relative silence for a while.

'This is very good.' Tory gave her compliments to the chef, whose thoughts seemed elsewhere.

'So what's he like, this husband of yours?' Miles suddenly emerged from his daze. 'Brian said I look a lot like him.'

'Quite.' Tory took up her wine. 'But you're very different in other respects.'

'How so?'

'You don't think alike, or have anything in common, as far as I can tell.'

'But surely, some of our physical features are different?' Miles reached for the remote control and aimed it at the stereo.

'Well, he's of a bigger frame than you, though you're probably about the same height.' Tory observed Miles closely, trying to define the other differences, and shrugged. 'You're a bit older ...' The music began to play, and Miles' choice rocked Tory to her foundations. 'Albinoni.'

'He is one of my very favourite composers.' Miles put down the remote to get back to his dinner. 'Some say this is the saddest piece of music ever written, but I find it rather beautiful and uplifting.'

Tory smiled in agreement, absolutely speechless, her heart pounding in her chest.

'So then, are you ready to tell me about your little discovery?' He referred to the helmet. 'And I am warning you now, I won't believe you found it by accident.'

'I don't know what I can tell you, Professor. I just know things about certain places, certain people.'

'Well, you have my fullest attention,' Miles encouraged her to continue.

'I am wary about saying any more as I fear that you shall sell off the treasures left here by your ancestors, just as you intend to sell that altar to the highest bidder.'

Miles was a little stunned by the remark. 'How did you find out about that?'

'If restoration is not a possibility, Professor, it doesn't take a genius to figure it out,' she reasoned. 'Can I ask why you got into archaeology?'

'Because I enjoy digging up the facts . . . you know, those little details you seem to forget all about.'

'And what about the truth? You'll never learn the truth about the treasures you find, because you can't see beyond their surface value. How do you put a price on the greater mysteries of the ages, Professor?' Tory paused, angry at herself for losing her cool.

'Who are you, really?' He sat back in his chair, intrigued.

'I think it's time I went to bed, where shall I sleep?'

As she sounded exhausted, Miles stopped his inquisition and gestured towards his bedroom.

'The couch will be fine.'

'I'll take the couch,' Miles insisted. 'I sleep on it more often than the bed anyway.' The house did have a spare room once, but it had long since been turned into an office, cum library. 'You don't have to turn in so early. If I promise not to hound you with any more questions?'

Tory shook her head as she collected her bag. 'I am truly too tired, Miles, or I would love to. We can talk tomorrow. Goodnight.'

Brian's hunger woke him early. It was so snug underneath Naomi and all the blankets, towels and clothes that lived in the back of his car, that he was very reluctant to move anywhere just yet. The sun was barely up and as it was a Sunday, no one would arrive at the site for hours. With this revelation Brian decided to rouse Naomi, and he became so engrossed in the exercise that neither of them heard a car arriving.

Professor Paradis approached the steamed-up vehicle to hear the sound of his daughter's voice coming from within. The car windows were fogged over so he knocked. 'Naomi, are you in there?' he asked, sounding very calm though a little surprised.

'Holy shit, it's my father,' Naomi whispered, thrown immediately into a panic as she searched through all the layers on top of her for her clothes. 'Yes,' she answered, mildly comforted that the windows were frosted over.

'Well, what are you doing sleeping in the carpark, child?' Paradis had to wonder, amused by her dismay. 'She does have a bedroom at home you know, Brian, and you are both quite welcome to occupy it when on Mon.' The professor laughed. He knew Naomi was not a child anymore, and since his wife had died he was just thankful to have his daughter still around to care for him in his old age. Her love life was her own business.

Naomi relaxed a little. 'It was rather late when we got here.' She pulled on her jeans, battling with Brian to do so. 'We were looking for Brian's sister. You wouldn't happen to know where she is?' She slapped Brian away from her so she could finish dressing.

'Why I believe she stayed at Miles' place,' her father informed them.

'What!' Brian was spurred into action, ripping on his jeans. 'Do you know where he lives?'

Naomi nodded.

'Then let's go.' Brian, still half naked, burst out the back doors to greet the professor, pulling on the rest of his clothes.

Naomi couldn't believe him at times. Still, she had to admit his body did warrant exhibition. As she finished tying her laces and climbed out of Brian's car, her father commented, 'Your standards seem to have waned of late.'

Brian, realising the old professor was having a dig at him, slapped a hand down on Paradis' shoulder and said, 'Disproving the age-old theory that quality is more important than quantity.' Brian served him a wink, ducking very quickly towards Naomi's car before she killed him.

'Just promise me you won't marry him.' Paradis pretended to be concerned for her.

'Come on Dad, I know how you treasure the thought of having five or six little ones just like him running around your feet in a few years.'

Paradis appeared to be wounded, holding a hand to his chest. 'No more please, my weak heart.'

Naomi smiled and kissed her father's cheek. 'Later, Dad.'

'Heaven forbid, you're even starting to speak like him.' His daughter just laughed as she ran off to the car. It was wonderful to see her so happy and, as far as sons-in-law went, he could do much worse than Brian Alexander.

Miles was awake when Tory raised herself for kata at dawn the next morning. He had managed to sleep for a few hours during the night, yet even then his mind had been plagued by images of her. Such an erotic dream, he recalled, and so vivid! He could still feel her dress of shimmery white, still smell the lushness of the wood where he'd lain down beside her.

He watched Tory creep through the early morning shadows of the cottage towards the back door, and he held his silence, wondering where on earth she was off to now. As soon as the door had closed, Miles quickly ran to watch her from the kitchen window; she was heading for the beach.

Brian and Naomi arrived at Miles' place to find the house empty.

'Brian, they're not here,' Naomi said, to stop him from pounding the front door down.

'Well, the car's here,' Brian roared. 'He'd better not be up to anything with my sister.'

Naomi was not bothered by his mood. 'Well maybe they're down on the beach.'

'Good call.' Brian's spirits lifted as he headed off to check.

He found Miles seated at the top of the stairs. Tory was further off along the beach, watching the ocean as she practised her art.

'I had no idea Tory was into martial arts.' Miles looked up at Brian as he came to a stop alongside him. 'I knew you were, of course. But Tory?' Miles shrugged, astonished.

'A triple black belt, my friend. You obviously didn't try anything, then.' Brian patted the professor's shoulder. 'Good man, now I don't have to kill you,' Brian said, jogging off down the stairs to speak with his sister.

Miles watched them closely. Tory seemed to have a strong objection to whatever Brian was telling her, and Brian seemed to be doing a lot of pleading.

'Hi.' Naomi took a seat beside Miles. 'Sorry if we're interrupting anything.'

'Not at all,' Miles assured her, sounding rather disheartened about the whole thing. 'What brings you two here?'

'I have no idea. You know what they're like,' Naomi said, looking down at Brian and Tory, and really meaning their whole family.

'I'm beginning to.' *And what I wouldn't give to know their secret.* 'You want some breakfast?'

'I do,' Naomi sighed.

Brian and Tory followed them back to the house sometime later. Brian was quietly exploding with excitement, as he'd managed to persuade his sister to let him accompany her to see the High Merlin. They'd spent much time discussing how they could manage this without Miles and Naomi realising what was going on.

Later that day, Tory accompanied Miles to the top of the cliff at the end of the beach to point out where the underwater cavern was to be found.

'I didn't go all the way in, you'll need a chainsaw to get through some of it, but the passage used to lead to the west tower and to the dungeons of the Royal House of Aberffraw.'

'But how can you be so sure the remains are of that particular castle? It was only ever mentioned in mythology, after all.'

Tory, who'd already started to head back to the house, rolled her eyes. 'I just am, okay?'

'Was it a past-life thing?'

Tory hated the way Miles spoke about anything he didn't understand, he made it all sound so ludicrous and puerile. She stopped and looked back at him, too annoyed to even comment.

'Look I'm sorry, Tory.' Miles didn't want her to get mad at him again. 'But nothing you say ever makes any sense.'

'Why does everything have to make sense?' Tory was tired of having to argue with those of rational logic. 'Just face it Miles, life's not logical.' She strode off and Miles followed.

'Tory please . . . I just want you to tell me the truth. Is that so much to ask?'

'Yes it is, as a matter of fact. I've given you everything you need to find the truth out for yourself, just like the altar. If you'd just put two and two together, you could figure out what the site at Llyn Cerrig Bach is all about.'

Tory considered that the nine statues should have been a large enough hint. Surely it was obvious that the statues represented the nine muses who guarded the cauldron, all he had to do was study the local mythology. The cauldron was also commonly referred to in druidic script as the Chair, the Honey Isle or Avalon. Thus, was it not as plain as the nose on his face that the site was considered by the ancients to be a doorway to the Otherworld?

'The mysteries of this planet exist so you can solve them for yourself, Miles, not so I can solve them for you. For heaven's sake, just open your mind. Anything is possible, until proven otherwise.'

Miles looked very perplexed and he said nothing for a while. 'I have a confession to make,' he announced finally. 'I had a dream about you last night.'

The hair on the back of Tory's neck stood on end, and her eyes opened wide at his words. 'Describe it to me.'

He grinned. 'I don't think I should somehow.'

Oh shit! Tory raised a hand to her mouth. 'Just tell me where it took place then?'

'Well, actually ...' Miles scratched his head, seeming a little embarrassed about it now. 'In a wood.'

Tory jumped into the air, slapping her hands together. 'It is you!' she announced excitedly, taking hold of Miles by the shoulders and giving him a hug.

'What do you mean?' Miles was happy to learn he'd said something right, yet he hadn't a clue what that was.

'You can't make a mockery of my psychic episodes anymore my friend, because you've just had one.' She laughed at his look of despair. 'That's the past you saw.'

'I hate to be a stickler for convention, but you could never prove that.'

'I was there, wasn't I?' Tory challenged him.

'Alright then, what were you wearing?'

Tory began to back up, a large smile growing on her face. 'A dress made of a mysterious white shimmery fabric that sparkled the colours of the rainbow. Of a sort of seventeenth-century, nymphish design, I recall.' Tory giggled at his bewilderment, and bounded back towards the house.

'It's psychological ambush, she's trying to drive me mad!' Miles concluded, in a daze. *How could she have seen a dream?* Perhaps Tory had more psychic ability than he'd given her credit for.

They all drove out to the site that evening and waited around for Professor Paradis, the last person on the site to leave. Brian tried very subtly to persuade Naomi to wait for him back at her place, but she wasn't about to leave him before she had to. So the four of them watched from the office window as Paradis drove out the gate.

'Okay, now what?' Miles was dying to know what this was all about.

'Shut off all the power on the site and wait here,' Tory instructed, grabbing her bag and heading for the door. 'Brian.' She beckoned for him to follow.

Miles protested. 'Hold on a minute, you said —'

'I know.' Tory cut him off. 'But I have to check it out for myself first. No offence, but you're like a walking negative charge. So please, just shut off the power as I ask and we'll get this show on the road, okay?'

'What about me?' Naomi moved to follow Brian.

'I'll be back in a second.' He kissed her then darted off after his sister.

Naomi folded her arms, irked that he would rather spend time with Tory when he saw her every day of the week. 'Who does she think she is, anyway? Just taking over like this?'

'Unfortunately, I promised. And I do sort of owe her a favour or two,' Miles explained, shutting off the power.

'Wow, you can sound like a real bitch when you want to.' Brian congratulated Tory on her performance as they made their way down into the dig.

'You liked that?' Tory was rather pleased with it herself. 'Question is, did they buy it?'

The lights went out.

'Guess so.' They both laughed as they paused for their eyes to adjust to the darkness. The waxing moon was nearly full, and after a moment they could see their way by the beautiful blue light it cast over the site.

Tory approached the large hole in the ground where the altar stone lay, avoiding the other pits from whence the statues had been raised. She wanted to cry at the sight of the pillage, as the energy was so much weaker now. She slid down the earth bank, coming to land on the stone. 'I hope this still works, or I'm in deep shit.'

'Check it out!' Brian admired the rock he landed on. 'I kind of recognise this.'

'No doubt,' Tory assured him. 'Let's see if anybody's home, shall we?' Tory took a deep breath and prayed to the Goddess that the Merlin heard her. 'Taliesin! In the name of the Dragon, I seek an urgent audience with thee,' she cried out into the night sky.

After a couple of minutes, when nothing had happened, Brian cocked an eye. 'Are you sure about this?'

Tory was looking a bit doubtful herself. Taliesin hadn't met her yet, so it was no use announcing herself. Still, there was another whom he might answer. She gave Brian a pat on the shoulder for assurance, and readied herself for a second attempt. 'Taliesin Pen Beirdd, my name be Sorcha Lawhir, wife of King Caswallon of Gwynedd and messenger of the Goddess. I ask thy counsel in her stead and in the name of the Dragon that guards this island,' she yelled with zeal as the light began to burst forth from the ground beneath their feet.

Miles was back at his desk, going over some data on his computer when Naomi entered with two mugs of coffee.

'Thanks.' Miles glanced up to find her staring out the window behind him, and he turned quickly to see what had her so mystified. A huge expanse of light emanated from the location of the altar. 'God damn you, Tory!' He made for the site as fast as he could with Naomi following close behind.

They reached the excavation in time to see the last of the glowing mist retracting into the stone. Then all was dark and still as before, and there was no trace of Tory or Brian.

'It's some sort of doorway, Miles.' Naomi freaked, she'd never witnessed anything like it.

'That's impossible, Naomi, people don't just disappear. I'm sure we'll find them around here somewhere.'

'No Miles, you're wrong. This place is even marked as sacred. It's something beyond our understanding and we shouldn't be messing with it.'

Miles stared down at the cross that taunted him with guilt for ever daring to try to move it. Was that why he'd been denied passage to wherever it led?

'You bastard, Brian, you'd better be coming back,' Naomi yelled into the pit.

'Don't worry. Tory left her son behind, she won't be long.'

'But if she has no idea what she's doing?'

'She knows.'

After dinner on Sunday night, Renford went upstairs to fetch the book he was reading from his bedside. As he passed Tory's room, he was surprised to find Teo creeping around. The professor could have sworn he'd just heard Teo in the kitchen, but he quietly ducked to one side of the doorway to see what he was up to.

Teo approached the cot where Rhun lay sleeping and watched the babe a moment, a smile crossing his face. He reached down to touch the child and a flash, like blue lightning, lashed out from the dragon medallion that hung above the child's bed. Before he left, Maelgwn had given Tory his medallion and asked her to hang it over their baby's bassinet to protect him. The impact of the energy force had obviously hurt Teo, and it cast him halfway across the room, yet he maintained his silence as he recovered from the shock of it. A moment later he bounced back up, appearing most annoyed. He held the palms of his hands out towards the child and his fingertips began to glow like hot coals.

That was enough for Renford, he quickly and quietly crept to the stairs then thumped his way back down the hall to the doorway. He barged into the room to find nobody but the sleeping child. The professor searched all the possible hiding places, but to no avail. All the windows were shut and he hadn't taken his eyes from the door. Now he really thought he was losing his marbles! He took up the sleeping child, resolving to watch him until Tory returned. He fetched his book and returned downstairs to the kitchen to get a cup of tea.

There, once again, he encountered Teo, wiping up dishes as Rose washed them. This confirmed what Renford had thought all along. 'Did you just go upstairs for any reason?' he asked; if Teo lied, Rose would certainly correct him.

'No.' Teo seemed surprised by the question.

Renford looked at Rose, who shrugged. 'We've both been in here since dinner.'

The professor wasn't so sure of what he'd seen, as any possible explanation for it escaped him. He'd never had any reason to distrust Teo, but he would keep Rhun close in any case.

When they appeared at the Merlin's hideaway, Tory attempted to set straight Taliesin's initial confusion. He knew she wasn't Sorcha, though he commented on the resemblance. She had every intention of introducing herself properly, but Taliesin interrupted her.

'You are Tory Alexander, who I gather, was once Sorcha Lawhir . . . a sad, sad loss for Gwynedd and indeed all of Britain.' He shook his head. 'And Brian, my it's good to see you.' The Merlin shook his hand.

'How do you know me, we haven't met before?'

'I seem to recall I was your *sensei* once.' Taliesin struggled to recollect when exactly. 'I've been doing a lot of past-life regression lately, I could have my lifetimes mixed up.'

'What?' Brian looked at Tory, who urged him not to worry about it.

Tory dispensed with the formalities, preparing the Merlin for her tale. 'This may sound a little strange — you told me yourself that you wouldn't understand it all at first — but I promise, you will.'

She recounted the story of her plight, informing the Merlin about the role he had played in it. Yet she omitted the part about the immortality potion he'd given her, as it was up to the gods to inform Taliesin of this, in accordance with what the Merlin had already told her. Moreover, Brian was present and Tory wanted no one to know her secret. As she spoke, she noticed that where once Taliesin's abode was enormous, it now only comprised one chamber. Although it still housed many beautiful antiques, the room no longer contained anything dating beyond the period of 2000 BC–1994 AD, as this represented the span of Taliesin's life so far.

'Keridwen said I must learn the sacred mysteries on my own. This is my cursed punishment.' Taliesin was so despondent, not himself at all.

'Well, you told me that you'd grown so disheartened with the state of Britain that you besought Keridwen to teach you the proper use of your knowledge, so that you might instigate the plan I have spoken of and change the fate of this land altogether! Now the Goddess will not agree, but she will compromise in the end and send you back through time to learn the greater mysteries from the Old Ones in Atlantis.'

'Atlantis! How grand, I tire so of the modern world.' Taliesin sounded excited by the prospect. 'And I actually did all this, already?'

'Aye.' Tory was pleased that he was looking more eager.

'Splendid! I should summon Keridwen at once.'

'Wait a minute.' Tory took hold of his arm. 'You must not forget the reason why I'm here.' She made sure she regained his full attention. 'You have to remember that I don't return with Maelgwn to the Dark Age as planned. I'm stuck here in the twentieth century, as I have already explained. You must remember, therefore, that when you calculate the first return, you also have to consider my return the following hour, or none of this will ever come to pass.'

'What?'

'Look, I don't need you to understand this right now, I just need you to promise that when the time comes, you'll remember what I've said.'

'I shall remember, gracious lady.' He took up her hand and kissed it.

Brian thought this was rather gross; he still saw Taliesin in the image of an old man, as had Brockwell. 'So, how do we get out of here?'

'The same way you came in,' Taliesin answered, motioning to the stone in the middle of the room.

'Oh yes, I nearly forgot to warn you.' Tory frowned, anxious. 'People upstairs are trying to remove your altar stone from its resting place.'

Taliesin laughed away her fears. 'Good luck to them, nobody else has managed it. And even if they do move it, the stone shall only return by the next morn.'

Tory smiled at this, as he led her to the stone.

'Hey, Taliesin,' Brian turned to them, already in position. 'You wouldn't happen to know where Myrddin is hiding out, would you?' Brian wondered if Taliesin could shed some light on their father's dilemma.

'Why no, I haven't seen him since the battle of Arthuret,' the Merlin replied.

Of course, Tory realised, if Taliesin has not yet returned to Atlantis, then he has not yet learnt the secrets of time travel. So he had yet to return to fourth-century Britain to free Myrddin from the tree, and hatch the scheme that would change the course of Britain.

'Fear not great lady, I look forward to embarking on this quest, and I shall leave as soon as I can persuade Keridwen.' Tory took her place next to Brian, and Taliesin bowed to her in parting. 'I will see you in the past, Tory Alexander.'

'And I look forward to seeing you, sir, in the future.' She gave him the thumbs-up, turning her attention to Brian as the mist began to rise. 'When we get back, I have to get out of there quickly. I don't want to have to answer any questions.'

'You got it,' Brian assured her, grabbing hold of her hands.

Miles had just started to doze off when a blinding light burst forth from the cross, and the mist began to rise before his eyes. It felt like the apocalypse as he watched Brian and Tory emerge from the haze, unscathed.

'Brian!' Naomi jumped on him. 'Don't ever do that again, not without telling me.'

'I have no intention of doing that again, period.'

Miles stood, arms folded, as Tory made her way past him in silence. 'Thanks for telling me.'

'Why Professor, I showed you, didn't I? In case you haven't worked it out yet, it's a doorway.'

'To where?' he demanded.

'You find out,' she said, picking up her pace.

'I gotta go.' Brian pulled himself away from Naomi. 'But I'll call you tomorrow.' He crossed his heart and blew her a kiss as he ran to catch his sister up.

'Brian!' She wanted to tell him not to bother, but she couldn't; the thought of never seeing him again was too horrible. 'I love you.'

'Right back at ya.' Brian's voice echoed through the darkness.

Tory had reached the car by the time Miles caught her up. As she unlocked the door and opened it, he slammed it closed. 'You know I've got no chance of working it out without you.'

'Well, maybe next life.' She opened the door and he again slammed it closed.

'Damn it, don't leave.'

'Come on, Miles. You wouldn't even have called me if you'd been able to move the bloody thing. No one gets the chance to lie to me twice.'

'Absolutely correct.' Brian came to stand between them, urging Miles back. 'Don't make me kill you now, when you've been doing so well.' He held Miles at bay while Tory got into the car.

'Brian, you don't understand.'

'Oh, yes I do.' Brian jumped in the car, starting up the engine. 'Better than you do, I'd say.' He winked, backing the car up at racing speed and taking off into the night.

'Why does everyone know more about me than I do!'

'So what do you make of it now?' Naomi joined Miles in the carpark.

'I don't know,' he answered, annoyed by the question. 'I need time to think.' He headed for his car, turning back as he walked. 'Sorry, Naomi. Goodnight.'

'It has been,' Naomi decided, as she headed for her car to drive home to bed.

25

AWAKENINGS

Tory and Brian arrived home from Llyn Cerrig Bach in the early hours of the following morning to find their aunt sitting in the kitchen, near scared out of her wits.

As Tory made them all tea, Rose told them of a nightmare she'd had. 'A horrid old woman, a witch I think, was standing in the middle of my kitchen, laughing at me. It felt as if my entire body was being restrained by her. It was awful!'

From Rose's description of her assailant, Tory feared it was Mahaud. Although, as she sat in the kitchen with her family, she couldn't sense the presence of the evil crone. Tory assured her aunt that the wicked witch could never exist in such a harmonious environment, and hoped that Maelgwn had been correct when he'd told her thus.

Weeks passed and still Tory refused to take Miles Thurlow's calls. He'd tried writing to her but she wouldn't even open the letters, let alone read them.

Tory kept up her training, practised her saxophone, and submerged herself in her history studies. Though she had achieved her third Dan grade and found Taliesin, there was still close to nine months remaining before the summer solstice. She'd thought that she would welcome some time to herself, yet within a week, she was bored and hankering for a quest of some kind. Rhun was no trouble, and although Tory loved spending time with him, she craved an intellectual challenge. Since the night of her aunt's dream, she'd also been thinking about finding a place of her own. She feared that if Mahaud was in the twentieth century, it was Gwynedd's heir she was seeking. Tory considered she could do something really novel and get a job of some kind. But then again, if she was living alone this would prove difficult with a young child. She was mulling on this notion when her father came into her room.

'Tory please, Professor Thurlow is on the phone.'

'I'm not here,' Tory said, remaining engrossed in her study.

Renford frowned at her childish retort. 'Yes, yes, but he asked me to give you the message that he's in the restoration business, and he urgently needs to speak with you about it.'

Tory turned to her father, considering whether or not she should take the call. Renford was relieved when she followed him to the phone.

'Alright, what's the story?' Tory said flatly.

'Thank God, I was about to jump in the car! I've got to hand it to you, Tory, you really know how to hold a grudge,' he replied, his tone warm and friendly.

'Well, you really know how to piss me off, Professor. Speak now or forever hold your peace.'

'Okay, please, just don't hang up. I've been calling because, after investigating the possibility of restoring this site of yours, I have a few investors who might be interested in getting the funding under way. But . . .' he paused before posing his problem. 'I have a feeling they will respond with more enthusiasm to a sales pitch coming from you.'

'So who are they, perverts or psychics?'

Miles laughed, he liked her humour. 'Druids, in fact. It would seem that in the order are some of the richest and most highly placed men in Britain these days.'

That's not surprising, Tory thought.

'One of them called me when he read about the site, and asked if we were considering the possibility of restoring it.'

'You, of course, lied and said you were.'

'Indeed.' Miles feared that he would never live long enough for Tory to allow him to forget his misdemeanour. 'But the trouble is, we didn't exactly see eye to eye. I think if anybody's going to sell them on this project, it will be you. So, when can you get here?'

'Wait a minute, are you hiring me?'

'I am, we can discuss the details when you arrive. The druids have asked to view the altar and the statues on the weekend, and we need some time to get a strategy together before then. So your presence is required yesterday.'

'I need some time to think about this.'

'What's there to think about?'

'I'll call you in the morning, I promise.' She hung up before he could argue.

This would get Rhun away from the house, which would make her feel much safer. Ever since Maelgwn's departure she had sensed something watching her. The job Miles offered her was too tempting to resist, yet she had to consider her own emotions. She was pretty clear about how she felt. Although Miles was Maelgwn, deep down inside her, Tory knew that Miles didn't possess the qualities that she most adored in her husband. The way she saw it, this was some kind of test. The powers that be were making it a little difficult, in her opinion, but there must be a reason why such an opportunity had been thrown her way. After all, it had originally been her idea to restore the site, why shouldn't she have a hand in its resurrection? Not that she hadn't already.

After a very restless night for both herself and Rhun, Tory decided she would take the challenge. She would make sure that she was earning enough money to get her own place, support herself and get a nanny. If this couldn't be arranged she would decline, as she wouldn't stay with Miles again. She could foresee the long hours she would be putting in with him on this, and it was going to be hard enough to keep him at bay without living with him to boot! If their relationship remained on a professional level this was exactly the kind of project she'd been waiting for, and it was certainly a cause she believed in.

Tory announced her immediate departure to her family at breakfast that morning. Teo wasn't there as he was sleeping off a hangover from a party the night before. Brian pleaded his friend's case on his behalf, telling them that the celebration was in honour of an old friend and so Teo had been obliged to go.

Tory hadn't been spending as much time in Teo's company since grading, but he seemed to be powering along quite well on his own. She feared that, in her absence, Teo's decadent binges might start all over again. So, as much as Tory hated to sound like a mother, she asked Brian to keep an eye on him.

He understood well enough and urged her not to worry. 'You just keep your eye on Thurlow,' he warned, before telling her to pack her things and he'd drive her up to Mon.

Her father was thrilled by her involvement in the project. Rose asked Tory to keep in touch and swore that she'd contact her if her spirits had any word from Maelgwn.

When Tory arrived at the site's reception desk, baggage, baby, and all, Amanda didn't quite know what to think.

'Tory!' Miles surfaced from his office to greet her. 'Thank god you're here.'

'Professor.' Brian followed Tory in carrying her saxophone case.

'And you're here too.' Miles didn't sound as thrilled to see him.

'Not for long, I'm afraid. I've got a class to teach tonight.' He dropped the luggage and winked at the girl behind the desk. 'Hey Amanda, looking mighty good, babe.'

'Why Brian, you're looking rather fine yourself. Thank you so much for noticing.' She graced Brian with a smile.

'Well, we should really start work.' Miles was eager to get Tory alone, or at least away from her brother.

'Actually Miles, I only dropped in to tell you I'm here. I thought I should hire a car and find somewhere to live.' Tory knew he wouldn't be game enough to suggest she stay at his place while Brian was standing there.

'Then I'll give you a hand,' he said. 'The quicker we get you settled, the quicker we can get started, right?'

Satisfied that all was to his liking, Brian left. Miles offered Tory some tea before they began all their running around, and she was thankful for a moment to rest.

No sooner did Miles have Tory in the privacy of his office, than he changed his tune. 'Tory, I really think you should consider staying at my place, just until the weekend.'

'No way, Miles. No offence, but we will drive each other nuts.'

'Look, think about it a second. If you find a place of your own today, you'll have to find a nanny and who knows what else. We don't have the time to spare. If we work on the proposal at my place, the long hours won't tax you so much as there's no travel time, and the baby can be with you while you work. Then, after we secure the interest of the investors on the weekend, we'll be able to relax a bit and I'll do whatever I can to help you get settled elsewhere. Please Tory, I really need your fullest attention right now.'

'You've obviously given this some thought.' Tory really didn't want to admit that what he said made perfect sense. 'Alright, but just till the weekend, promise?'

'I do.' Miles was pleased with the outcome. He then turned to the baby basket on his coffee table. 'Wow, he looks just like me.'

Tory smiled. 'He takes after his father.'

Miles ventured so far as to touch Rhun's little hands, and was rather happy to be given a huge smile in response. 'What's his name?'

'Rhun.' Tory almost cringed as she said it, hoping he didn't ask why on earth she'd chosen such an Old World name.

'That's a very traditional name,' Miles remarked, thinking nothing more of it.

Tory restrained her amusement. 'His father's from a very traditional family.'

The decision to start work on the proposal first thing the following day was unanimous. Miles cooked up a feast, after which they sat and talked by the fire for hours. Tory was surprised to find that Miles' whole manner had changed since their last meeting. He'd stopped plaguing her with questions, content just to be in her company. This was a worry for Tory as Miles was much more like Maelgwn now, and several times during the course of the evening she forgot herself and nearly mistook him for her husband.

Although Miles was making a distinct effort not to annoy his guest, when they finished off a glass of port before bed he chanced one question. 'I know you'll probably get angry at me, but there's something I have to ask.'

'Where did I take Brian that night?' Tory guessed his mind but she wasn't upset by it, in fact she was rather impressed that he hadn't asked earlier.

'Yes.' Miles felt a bit disappointed to be so predictable.

'Surely you have worked out where it leads by this time, Miles. Just out of curiosity, where do you think we went?'

Miles hesitated, then realised that in all probability nothing he could surmise would sound as ridiculous as the truth. 'Well, the statues seem to indicate a doorway to . . . the Otherworld?'

Tory applauded his conclusion. 'Very good . . . and correct, too.'

Miles half frowned, half smiled. 'And what business did you have there?'

'I had to meet someone.'

'Anyone I might know?'

'You wouldn't believe me if I told you.' Tory stood up to go to bed.

'Try me.'

'Taliesin Pen Beirdd.'

'You're right, I don't believe you. But still, I would be interested to know, did you have any reason to seek *him*, in particular?'

599

'I had to deliver a message.'

'From whom?'

'Himself.' She flashed a smile and waved goodnight.

As agreed, Tory and Miles began work early the next day. Though there was a mountain of figures, estimates, and documents to be compiled, the task proved to be easier than they'd first imagined. Tory had the vision where Miles had know-how, and they were surprised at how easily the proposal fell together; the days simply flew by.

For Tory it seemed like working with Maelgwn again, and she found herself daring to trust Miles once more. He was wonderful with Rhun, and Tory half suspected that Rhun instinctively sensed his father in this man. Although she was pleased they got along so well, she would be relieved to find a place of her own before they got too attached to each other.

Through living with Tory and Rhun, Miles discovered a cosy kind of family bliss he'd never known or even considered before. He loved the sound of the saxophone wafting through the house in the late afternoon as he cooked dinner. He loved rising at sunrise and minding Rhun as he watched Tory practise kata on the beach. Once again, he'd begun to wonder about this husband of hers. Tory never mentioned him, only that she was to meet up with him in June the following year. Miles wanted to tell Tory how he felt about her, but he'd decided to refrain from saying anything until their conference with the wise and wealthy of Britain was over.

* * *

The meeting went extremely well, far better than Miles could have hoped. Tory's manner and repartee was nothing short of spellbinding, and exhibited all the knowledge of someone three times her age. The druids, who were primarily scholars and businessmen, were impressed by her presentation and, in the end, were eager to get involved.

In appreciation for a job well done, Miles insisted on taking her out to dinner. As he'd already arranged for Amanda to mind Rhun for the evening, Tory agreed to the plan.

They celebrated their triumph with champagne by candlelight, and Tory's defences dropped to an all-time low. Miles held his glass up to her and proposed a toast, 'To the modern miracle, Tory Alexander, whose presence and insight have been a godsend to this project. And though words are inadequate, I want to express how much I appreciate all your hard work.'

'Well you haven't seen my fee yet, Professor, but you're welcome. It's been a pleasure.' Tory clinked her glass against his and had a sip. 'Your performance today was quite outstanding too, Miles. I have to admit, I was fairly impressed.'

He nodded with a grin, graciously accepting the compliment. 'Well I had a remarkable tutor.'

Though Miles had been the perfect gentleman all week, he was definitely seeming a bit fresh at this moment. Tory considered this might be a good time to bring up her living arrangements. 'You haven't forgotten we're finding me a house on Monday morning?'

Miles became mildly disgruntled by the notion. 'It hasn't been so awful, has it? And my place is certainly convenient for you and Rhun.'

'I know it is, but that's the whole point.' She reached out and placed her hand on his. 'I don't want to make a convenience of you. It's not fair and it's not right.'

'I don't mind.' He placed his free hand on top of hers.

'I know you don't, not now. But come time for us to leave, you shall not be of the same mind, Miles. It's going to be hard enough as it is.'

'Well this is a cosy little scene.' Brian made his disapproval felt as he seated himself at the table.

'I'm so sorry, Miles,' Naomi said as she caught Brian up. 'He saw you from the street.'

'That's quite alright, Naomi.' Miles leaned back in his chair, clearly put out by the intrusion. 'We have nothing to hide.'

'I thought you weren't going to stay at his place?' Brian's accusing eyes rested on his sister.

Tory sat back, folding her arms, irked that Brian saw fit to check up on her. 'Hi Brian, so nice to see you.'

'Tory.' Brian leaned over and grabbed hold of her arm, so as to hiss quietly in her ear. 'You're a married woman, and despite how much he may look like him, the professor here is not your husband.'

'Really?' Tory reclaimed her arm, and in a very dry tone said, 'I never would have guessed.'

'Look Brian, this is not what you think.' Miles attempted to defuse the situation. 'There's absolutely nothing going on.'

'Damn right, nor will there be.' Brian stood, ready to throw his weight around.

'Brian, please! *Sit down*.' Tory gave him a very cool glare, but Brian didn't comply. 'Look, I want a place of my own, but in all honesty I haven't had time to find one. I had to prepare for the conference today, which, by the way, was very successful, thanks so much for asking.'

'You can stay at Naomi's place, there's plenty of room there.'

'Brian, I really don't think this is any of your business.' Naomi tried to urge him to leave with her.

'I promised him you'd be there, Tory, and I meant it.' Brian's glare was intense.

'When I need your help, I will ask for it.'

'Brian, please, can we just leave,' Naomi begged him.

'He's not Maelgwn,' Brian stressed again as he was leaving.

Miles looked at Tory who was very perplexed after her brother's little outburst. 'Your husband's name is Maelgwn?'

Tory nodded. 'That's how Rhun got his name. It's a kind of family tradition.'

'Let me guess,' Miles lightened the mood a little. 'Your husband's father's name was Caswallon.'

'You got it.' Tory tried to regain her cheery mood, but with little success.

'Come on, we'll fetch Rhun and go back to the house.'

Though she thought his suggestion was sweet, Tory realised that Brian was right; she could easily fall for

Miles if she didn't make herself more distant from him, and fast.

Her feeling of foreboding grew; was it wrong to have befriended this man, knowing their attraction to each other was inevitable? When they returned to the cottage, Tory told Miles she wanted to take a bath and go to bed.

Damn you Brian! Miles couldn't see Tory allowing such an intimate situation to arise between them again. He dreamt of her every night now, and the impression of urgency and love these dreams left him with grew stronger and stronger each time. The images varied but in his dreams Tory hardly ever appeared to be of the modern world. This was quite alarming, with her whole family running round claiming to have had past-life experiences. Did Tory's mystic ways rub off on everyone who came in contact with her?

When Tory came in from kata the next morning, Miles announced that he planned to go into the office. He didn't say why he was going into the site on a Sunday morning, but he needed to take a look at the piece of parchment that was in the safe in his office. The night before he had dreamt not about Tory but about a huge room of books, written in the same hand as the parchment they'd found at the site. He also recalled seeing an old, old man.

'Remember how I taught thee, concentrate,' the old man had instructed him with zeal. 'For thou art there with her now. The soul is everlasting, thou art part of one and the same whole. Reach out.'

'What does your friend Taliesin look like?' Miles asked, as he buttered some toast.

Tory gave him a peculiar expression. 'Taliesin looks different to different people. But to most men, he appears old and wise. Why?'

'No reason.' Waves of goose bumps came over him, and he made greater haste to get to the office. As Miles drove, he wondered about the mysterious parchment. Perhaps it held an explanation of the old man's directive.

Tory phoned Naomi to ask her to pick them up while Miles was out. It would be easier this way, she thought, as she wouldn't have to argue with him about the move.

When Naomi got the call, she was more than happy to help. Brian hadn't enjoyed setting his sister straight and had been brooding over their harsh exchange of words all night.

'You can stop pining now, that was Tory,' Naomi was pleased to inform Brian as he looked such a sorry sight, moping over a bowl of cereal. 'Miles has gone out to the site for the morning, so Tory asked if we could pick her and Rhun up before he gets back.'

Brian's spirits lifted with the news, but not in the way Naomi expected. 'You do that then.' He kissed her as he rose and pulled on his jacket.

'Why, where are you going?' She was bothered by his mood, as he grabbed his car keys and headed for the door.

'To see Thurlow.'

Brian drove into the site and was pleased to see Miles' car already in the carpark. He made his way to the office and found the professor behind his desk, seemingly lost in his thoughts as he gazed out the window. The piece of parchment was in his hand, and Brian's father's report was spread out before him.

'I need to speak with you, Professor.'

Miles turned with a start, appearing overwhelmed to see him. 'Brian! Praise the Goddess, thou art here. Where am I?'

'Maelgwn?' Brian recognised his brother-in-law's voice, but he could hardly believe that it was coming from Miles.

'Aye.' The King appeared somewhat disturbed by his dilemma.

'Get outta town, how did thee get in there?' Brian peered into the man's eyes. 'And where be Miles, then?'

Maelgwn took hold of him and gave him a shake. 'Brian, I have to see Tory. I do not know how long I can remain focused. It hast been a long, long time since I attempted something like this.'

'Awesome.' Brian was so amazed that he had trouble thinking straight. 'The phone,' he suggested, grabbing it and dialling Miles' home phone number.

When his sister answered, Brian instructed, 'Stay there, don't move until I get there.' He hung up, proud to be of service to the Dragon. 'Come on, my car is outside.'

Brian sped them towards Aberffraw, considering as he drove that this morning hadn't turned out at all as he'd planned. His objective had been to get the professor away from his sister, and here he was driving him to see her. 'So you are Miles after all?'

'Aye, he be my twentieth-century embodiment.' Maelgwn looked down at himself. 'I could certainly use a bit of building up.'

'So where is Miles?'

'I expect he be in here too, but only I have conscious command.'

'For how long?'

'Well, that depends on how long I can concentrate,' Maelgwn said.

'Wow!' Brian was utterly mind-blown.

'I'm not as practised at mind control as I once was.' Maelgwn regretted his lack of discipline. 'How fares Tory and our babe?'

'Good, great in fact! Your son is excellent value, Maelgwn. He even got me laid!'

Maelgwn was amused to hear this. 'Naomi?'

'Scoop, ay?' Brian gave him a wink, becoming more serious. 'This guy, Miles, he has his eye on Tory.'

Maelgwn gave half a laugh. 'Somehow, Brian, I do not find that at all surprising. What dost Tory think of him?'

'Not much at first, but lately they seem to be getting along better.' Brian couldn't work out what to make of the relationship now. 'Does that bother you?'

'I do not know,' Maelgwn answered, then became quiet as he contemplated the question, but his deliberation was cut short when Brian pulled into the driveway of the cottage.

'Could it be that I still own this place?' Maelgwn asked, recognising the landscape. 'After all this time.' He climbed out of the car and wandered in circles for a moment.

'This way old son.' Brian steered Maelgwn towards the front door. 'She's in here.'

When Tory saw Brian come through the door with Miles, she nearly had a fit. 'Thanks a lot bro.' Tory thought it must look wonderful to the professor, her sitting there all packed up and ready to leave.

'We have a surprise.' Brian turned to Maelgwn, who stood speechless staring at his beautiful slender wife with their child in her arms. Brian gave him a shove to wake him up, yet Maelgwn was still hesitant to speak. The King's eyes darted across to Naomi. Brian became aware of the problem, so he grabbed hold of her and quickly escorted her towards the door.

'Tory, it be me,' Maelgwn ventured in a whisper.

Tory knew her husband's sweet resounding voice at once, and her eyes closed with relief. *Thank you.*

'What's going on now?' Naomi asked Brian, as she watched Miles and Tory come together for a fevered kiss. 'What's wrong with Miles' voice?'

'I've been giving him lessons,' Brian explained, picking Naomi up and carrying her out of the room.

After a long embrace, Maelgwn turned to the baby. 'Oh Tory, he be so fine!'

She gently placed Rhun in Maelgwn's arms and the look of pride on his face said it all. 'There's not a thing wrong with him, he's as strong as an ox,' she said.

'I can see that.' Maelgwn held out the child to admire his form.

Tory gazed at Maelgwn, ever astounded at the scope of his abilities. 'How hast thou managed this?'

Maelgwn remembered his task suddenly, holding Rhun closer to himself. 'That not be a concern at present. First I must warn thee, I have seen Mahaud here. The night I left she was waiting at the stones.'

His claim brought to her mind Rose's dream. 'Well I have seen no sign of her, though I think Rose dreamt she saw her in the kitchen back in Oxfordshire. That's one of the reasons I moved here.'

'A wise move too, this be fairy country. If Mahaud dared to set foot here her powers would be considerably weakened.' Maelgwn kissed the top of his son's head, relieved to find them both safe and well.

'How long art thou here?' Tory's tone became more intimate.

'I cannot say . . . perhaps a day, perhaps less. So thee must listen to me carefully.'

Maelgwn rekindled her knowledge of the nine metaphysical laws, so that she might better be able to physically defend herself against Mahaud. These laws, revealed by the nine muses of the cauldron, were the Law of Rebound, the Law of Challenge, the Law of Equalities, the Law of Summons, the Law of Polarities, the Law of Abundance, the Law of Balance, the Law of Cause and Effect, and the Law of Three Requests.

He said Taliesin had suggested that Tory try to make contact with the fairy folk to seek their assistance and protection. Apparently the elementals that occupied this land were more than familiar with the crone, for they had withstood her evil intent throughout the centuries to maintain a free reign here, and indeed, throughout most of Britain. The nine laws applied to dealing with the nature kingdoms also, especially the Law of Summons. It was, therefore, doubly important for Tory to know the laws by heart. The Merlin was quite sure his mother's kin would come to the party, but only if they were specifically invited. Maelgwn then passed on Taliesin's advice as to how she might win the trust and favour of the folk.

This instruction was sheer heaven to Tory, for it was the kind of knowledge she'd craved, and missed since leaving the Dark Age.

Maelgwn also confirmed her father's true identity. He conveyed Taliesin's claim that Mahaud had been the reason Myrddin had shed his great knowledge for a time, and with the assistance of the Goddess, he'd disguised his form so that he would not even know himself. Taliesin, Keridwen and Myrddin deemed this to be a necessary precaution to avoid detection by the negative forces that constantly worked against them. When the time came to put their divine plan into action, Myrddin would seek out his true self. So, with Mahaud at large waiting to corrupt anyone who showed enough negative potential, Maelgwn urged Tory to warn her father, as the evil witch had tricked him before.

The King decided it would be best for Tory and Rhun to stay here at Aberffraw, for this was the land and burial place of his great ancestors. All of them were here, and Maelgwn felt they would surely be keeping guard over Gwynedd's heir.

Tory hated to question his wish but she felt that this arrangement was not really fair on Miles.

'Tory, I promise that he will understand so much more now, thou shalt not have to lie anymore.'

'Maelgwn . . .!' Tory took a seat on his lap. 'Thou art missing the point. I am driving the poor man out of his mind, not to mention thy visions of me plaguing his sleep.'

'Sorry, I could not help it. I had to focus on thy image to find thee, and in my fondest memories thou art always naked, or becoming thus.' He sounded rather casual about the whole thing, until his hold over Miles began to weaken. 'I was not to know Miles was perceiving the all of it.'

'Maelgwn, what be wrong?' Tory held his head firmly between her hands. 'Please, not yet, I am not ready to let thee go.' As Tory became distressed, so did Rhun. 'Maelgwn?' The tears began to stream down her face as the lids of his eyes closed, and his head became a heavy weight in her hand. 'I miss thee.' She held his unconscious form until her weeping had ceased.

Brian was at the front door within the hour. He was funny like that, he always seemed to sense when Tory needed him. From the state he found her in, he presumed that Maelgwn had left.

'How did Miles react?' Brian asked.

'He's still passed out,' she told him meekly. 'What am I going to say to him, Brian?'

Her brother didn't see a problem. 'Tell him I punched him out at his office and he must have dreamt the whole thing. That explains why he's missed a whole day.'

'I cannot lie to him.' Tory had never had to lie in her life, she'd just stretched the truth a bit here and there. 'Lying is for cowards who are too afraid to face the truth.'

Brian shrugged as he came to sit beside her and began to stoke the fire.

'Brian, where's Naomi?'

'She's not talking to me.' He wasn't angry, just sad and resigned.

'She started asking questions you couldn't answer?'

Brian nodded. He wanted to keep their secret, yet it was becoming increasingly difficult with all that had gone on in the past few months. 'She said if I don't trust her by now I never will. But I do, Tory.'

She took a deep breath. Naomi was part of all this now but Tory was not sure if she was ready for it. 'Call her up, get her over here,' she resolved with a smile. 'No, on second thoughts, I'll do it.'

'You're the best.' Brian hugged her, as she reached for the phone.

Tory had long since disappeared with Naomi along the beach when Miles finally emerged from the depths of his slumber to find Brian making coffee in his kitchen.

Brian saw him slouched in the doorway of the bedroom and moved quickly to help him to a seat. 'How's it going, Professor?'

'As well as could be expected.' Miles was shaking, though he was neither cold nor fearful. It was pure awareness that made him tremble, and it passed over him in waves, alerting all his senses.

'Do you remember much?' Brian thought he'd try to calm the way for Tory, if he could.

'I have seen ...' Miles held his head with both hands; he remembered so much he didn't know where to start. 'Where is Tory?' he panicked, thinking that she may have left.

'She's on the beach, clearing up a few things with Naomi for me. They'll be back presently, I hope.' He walked into the kitchen to get the professor some coffee. 'But if there's something on your mind, feel free to ask. I know most of what Tory knows.'

In the depths of Maelgwn's memory, Miles recalled seeing Brian as the dark warlord of the past. 'I know thee. I mean, you, Brian, or is it Brockwell?'

Brian nearly dropped the cup in his hand. 'Oh shit.'

Tory and Naomi had walked all the way to the cliff top that overlooked the ocean, and sat watching the waves crashing against the rocks below. Naomi stared at the photos of Katren and Brockwell, appearing at a loss for words.

'Are you okay?'

'Oh yes,' Naomi confirmed in earnest. 'This explains so many things, it's as if I have been released from death, somehow.' She beamed with happiness. 'I always knew there was more to this life, and now I find I was right. I am grateful that you confided in me. I was too

613

harsh on Brian, I should have known he would have told me, if he could.'

'Make no mistake, Naomi, Brian loves you. Always has, always will.'

Naomi was touched. 'I had you all wrong. I won't be so quick to judge in future.'

'Tory!' Brian came racing towards them. 'He's awake.'

'How much does he remember?' Tory got to her feet as he reached them.

'Well, he called me Brockwell.'

Tory entered the house with her heart in her mouth. 'How are you?'

'Feeling more myself now, thanks.' He smiled.

'I'm so sorry, Miles.'

'Please don't apologise. You were right, even if you had confided in me, I wouldn't have believed you . . . not in a million years. I have learnt much these past few days, about a great many things.' Miles shook his head, unable to believe that after so many years of study and travel, one could still be naive to the ways of the world.

Tory sat down opposite him, finding comfort in his resolve.

'That's some man you're married to, talk about a lateral thinker! After being granted a glimpse of my past, I'm not surprised that you've been frustrated with me.'

Tory noticed him trembling and pulled a large blanket from the back of the lounge to place around his shoulders. 'Miles, I'm not entirely convinced that it was your past.'

'But the time period I saw couldn't have been later than . . .'

'Sixth century.'

'So that is the past, no?'

Tory smiled and shook her head. 'No. Time is an illusion, you won't still be running your life around a clock when you're dead, Miles. Your soul mind could choose to go anywhere, backwards, forwards or sideways — as in another dimension or an alternative reality. That would depend on what you were ready to conceive of and that which you needed to learn. I have already passed through all these different realms. I was born in the 1960s, but in a world far removed from this one . . . more polluted, with more prejudices, wars, hatred and greed than at present. I know I am not mistaken about this, as in the reality I originally stemmed from, Brian died four years ago.'

Miles shook with another burst of awareness. He could almost feel his brain expanding to absorb all the possibilities. 'You are a phenomenon.'

Tory shook her head modestly. 'I had very little to do with it.'

Miles wasn't referring to her travels, but to what she'd accomplished through them. He had seen her hailed as a queen and a goddess, a *sensei* and a warrior, a teacher and an adviser to kings — the same kings who had indeed changed the course of British history. Maelgwn was right. I understand why you must return, and I would be honoured to have you and Rhun stay with me under the protection of this house and our forefathers until that time.'

'Miles, that's a lovely thing to say. Still it is I who art beholden.' She crouched down before him and took his hands. 'Thank you so much for understanding, but it's close to eight months till summer solstice, so you'd better think about this a while.'

He slowly shook his head, very calmly. 'There is no question, not with that witch on the loose. You are staying here, even if I have to move out.'

'Well then.' Tory warmed to a smile. 'We'll see how we go.'

Tory called her father in Oxfordshire, as Maelgwn had suggested, and passed on the message from Taliesin regarding Mahaud. Renford confessed that since she'd moved to Mon, he'd visited many of the sites that had been associated with Myrddin and had felt and seen nothing that would lead him to believe that he was who Maelgwn claimed.

'Even Dinas Emrys?' Tory asked.

'Even there.'

Tory couldn't understand this at all. She insisted that her father must stop harbouring doubts and asked that he keep looking, as she knew Taliesin was never wrong.

Life was very tranquil at the cottage in Aberffraw until one afternoon, late in December, when Teo showed up to pay Tory a visit. They'd spoken a couple of times on the phone since she'd left Oxfordshire, but he hadn't mentioned driving up to Mon.

'Teo, what a surprise!' She met him in the garden, a little startled by his presence.

'Hey sunshine.' He climbed out of the car. 'It was getting a bit chilly down home, so I thought I'd pay you a visit.'

He was in a wonderful mood as he walked up to meet her, until he spied Miles standing in the doorway with Rhun. Teo came to a halt, his mood changing immediately. 'I thought you'd gone away somewhere on business?'

Miles didn't know this guy very well, but he recalled Maelgwn hadn't liked him much and in his arms Rhun became disgruntled at the sight of him. 'What difference does it make?'

'Miles.' Tory cautioned him to stay out of it; this was none of his business.

'Hey, what gives?' Teo realised this wasn't Tory's husband at all, but someone who looked very much like him. 'Are you living with this guy?'

'We're working together.'

Teo backed up, seeming disillusioned with her. 'Yeah right,' he shook his head and headed back to the car.

'Thanks so much for the benefit of the doubt. Think what you will then.'

'If it's all so innocent, why didn't you tell me?' Teo chose to pursue the argument, as he usually did, and Tory didn't appreciate his tone of voice.

'I don't have to answer to you.'

'Damn right, I'm history.'

After taking a moment to get over her pride, Tory went after him. 'Are you going back to Oxfordshire?'

'What do you care?' He slammed the car door as the engine roared to life. 'Friends don't hide things from each other.' He glared into her eyes for a moment, and Tory was startled as his pupils flashed red.

'No, Teo wait. Please!' she cried as the car tore off down the drive.

'Wow, what an arsehole.' Miles came out to join her.

'We've got to find him. I think I know where Mahaud has been hiding out.'

26

TYLWYTH TEG

Their search proved fruitless. Tory called Brian at home to warn the family to keep an eye out for Teo. But she wasn't sure what to advise them to do if they did meet up with him, beyond trying to act completely normal.

Her father phoned her straight back to tell her about what he'd seen in her room when she was at Llyn Cerrig Bach that first time. He and Rose had just spoken, each about their experience that night. Between what Renford had witnessed and Rose's nightmare, they had managed to piece together how the events they witnessed may have unfolded. Renford was sorry he hadn't mentioned the occurrence sooner, but he'd convinced himself it must have been his imagination playing tricks on him.

Tory had been right in saying that the witch couldn't survive in the harmonious environment of the house, that's why Teo chose to stay in the gym. This latest case of possession also explained why Teo was so much more himself when he was in frequent contact with her family. Tory supposed that her own disappearance, and Brian blaming him for it, might have been so traumatic that it created sufficient negativity around Teo for the witch to attach herself to him. Now Mahaud had only to feed Teo's negativity with any mixture from her select menu of deadly emotions: hate, fear, jealousy, greed, pride, excess, lust, and the like. This sustained her until such time as Teo was evil enough to generate the right amount of negative energy to manifest her own wicked form. Teo was a mighty powerful soul and Tory didn't like to think what could eventuate if Mahaud fully possessed such a warrior.

This was what Teo meant when he'd said he wasn't himself. He had repeatedly asked Tory to help him, but she hadn't understood what kind of help he needed. She could see now why he was always touching her. Tory thought back to the day Teo had learnt of her return. During the course of their confrontation, as long as she'd been touching him he'd remained calm; the conflict of energy within him must have been what caused him to cry.

Rose also brought to Tory's attention the fact that Teo had chosen to visit the cottage at Mon on the last day of the thirteenth month, by the old calendar. *The Nameless Day*. The thought sent shivers down Tory's spine. This was the time of the year when the Dark Queen, in her destructive aspect, was most powerful. Tory thanked the Goddess now that Miles had been present, or she surely would have invited Teo inside.

This, no doubt, would have sealed her son's fate. The power of the enchanted land where she was living to dispel evil would not apply if she invited an evil presence onto it.

I have to be smarter than this, I should have known! Tory scolded herself, considering it was high time she sought professional help.

She'd been mulling over Maelgwn's instruction in regard to contacting the elementals of the Middle Kingdoms, or the Tylwyth Teg as he called them. She'd brought herself up to scratch on the nine laws, and now felt as ready as she would ever be to form such an alliance.

Although the devas of the Otherworld were as varied as the more physical species of life on earth, they had four main groupings belonging to one or more of the four elements that constitute all physical matter.

Salamanders were fire fairies that would appear to the naked eye as nothing more than the bright little sparks dancing around above a camp fire. They could be found in a soft burning candle flame, swaying before your eyes, relaxing your mind and your mood. But they could also manifest as a huge, raging monster, mercilessly laying waste to everything in its path. As Tory had grown up in Australia, she had come face to face with this element in the native bushland many times. Although the destruction did seem harsh, fire was simply part of nature's replenishing process. She'd been told that fire, being the first element of creation, was also the least accommodating to humans. The Salamanders personified courage, creativity, valour, and loyalty — the traits most lacking in modern society. If one didn't grasp these traits, it would be dangerous to seek Salamanders. Still, Taliesin had predicted that Tory should fare well with them.

Sylphs, the devas of the air, were the second element of creation. They concerned themselves mostly with learning and the intellect, adaptability and travel, and anything to do with speed or thought. These elementals are commonly found floating about in the mists of Britain. In addition, they are the howling demons who couple with the other elements to incite storms of dirt, fire and water. Tory had always been an ardent student, and with all the travelling she'd been doing lately, she figured she and this element had a bit in common.

The third element of creation was water, and its race was known as the Ondines. Tory believed she may have brushed with this clan on the night of her swim, as something had certainly been guiding her through the dark watery depths. These water devas concerned themselves mainly with emotions, one's understanding, receptivity and sympathy.

The Gnomes of the Earth represented the fourth element of creation. Tory had been born under the sign of Taurus, and as an Earth sign she showed the traits of practicality, conversation, thrift, and abundance.

She had been advised that the key to communicating with any life form was to first win its favour and trust. The best way to do this was simply to offer something that the particular elemental might fancy or need, and then introduce yourself. What on earth would an element desire, Tory wondered. Maelgwn hadn't worked with the fairy kingdoms much, although his mother had. He had advised Tory that the task of an elemental, besides its care of Mother Earth, was to try to obtain its four-fold nature. That is, the understanding of the other three elemental groups aside from that to which it already belonged. This was one of the few areas in which fairies found the human race could actually be of assistance to them, as people were made up of all four elements. Therefore, Tory considered at great length what she might offer the differing clans, to help them better understand the traits of the others.

One evening, when Tory found she had the house to herself, she impatiently waited until dusk to perform the rites. Sunrise or sunset was the best time to attempt to communicate with the folk. Tory had chosen sunset because in Wiccan belief, this was the time for truth finding rather than new beginnings, as sunrise would suggest. So as the sun sank low in the sky, Tory headed to the beach bearing her gifts and enough wood to make a fire on the sand.

Rhun was comfortably resting in his pouch against her chest, taking a great interest in what his mother was doing. So much so that Tory was forced to turn him round, so that he might have a better view and stop his squirming.

Tory stood with the ocean to her west, as this was the water element's associated direction. The fire was blazing to the south, while a mound of sand to her north represented the earth. She had borrowed a sword that usually hung on the wall of Miles' living room, and she stuck it into the sand pointing east; in the sacred tarot and ritual of the druids, the air was represented and summoned by a sword.

As she'd been advised to always address the elements in the order of their creation, Tory turned to face the fire and stated in the old tongue, 'My name be Tory Alexander, Queen of Gwynedd, and messenger of the Goddess. Denizens of the Otherworld, I come before thee now, seeking thy wise counsel and protection.'

Tory turned to each symbol and direction in turn.

> *Come to my aid ye of Fire,*
> *the fire that first gave me life.*
> *Hear my plea, ye of Air,*
> *the breath of life that set me free.*
> *I seek thy comfort ye of Water,*
> *purge me and bring me clarity.*
> *Be my support ye of Earth,*
> *the mother that has always nurtured me.*

Rhun began to chuckle with delight, his arms outstretched as his eyes darted about in wonder; Tory was curious to know what he saw that she could not.

She approached each symbol bearing the gift she wished to bestow, again in order of their creation. To the Fire she gave her pocket encyclopaedia, explaining that perhaps it might better understand the air's great thirst for knowledge. She moved to the sword and tossed a tissue to the wind. This tissue held tears she'd shed when pining for her love. Tory expressed that she hoped the Sylphs might better grasp the emotional depths of water. Tory then wandered to the water's edge and sprinkled it with fresh rose petals, so that the Ondines might experience some of the earth's sweet pleasures. And lastly, in the mound of sand, Tory buried a handwritten copy of the small verse she'd used to request the presence of the elementals, as it was as close as she'd come to Fire's creative talents of late. She'd wrapped inside the paper one of her rings, some Australian coins, and a few other little trinkets she thought they might like. Gnomes were very predisposed towards material possessions, and relished unusual bits and pieces made of any sort of metal, especially gold. She then returned to the centre of the circle and stated her woes in regard to Mahaud.

Afterwards, Tory thanked the elementals in turn for listening. She requested politely that if any of them thought or heard of anything that might help to guard her child from the crone, to please let her know. She then bid them all good tidings and a goodnight.

With her task completed she kicked sand on the fire to put it out, stamped the sandy mound down hard, and retrieved the sword, bowing to the ocean. She then wandered back to the house with Rhun, basking in the light of a beautiful moon. Although nothing miraculous had happened to prove she'd made contact with the occupants of the deva kingdoms, within herself, Tory felt closer to the divine, that unexplainable force from whence all life stems.

The next day Tory rose before sunrise as usual, to feed and change Rhun before kata. Miles was up and about also and, after making himself a cup of tea, he took Rhun to escort Tory down to the beach.

It was a beautiful morning, not cold at all. The dim sky was perfectly clear, as was the air. After Tory had kissed Rhun and continued on her way, Miles sat down with the baby on the stairs. This ritual had been the same every morning since the snow melted. Yet this day, for reasons unknown, Rhun began to cry as he watched his mother depart.

Miles didn't know what to do. This had never happened before. 'Tory,' he called her back. 'Are you upset about something?'

'No,' she assured him as she jogged back up the stairs to see what the problem was, whereupon Rhun calmed down and was as sweet as pie. Tory shrugged, a little baffled, then turned to leave them once more, but before she'd reached the bottom step, Rhun began crying again. So Miles decided to follow Tory down to the beach, and Rhun seemed quite content to sit in Miles' lap and watch.

Tory hadn't been at her exercise but five minutes when a mist came rolling in over the water. As it enveloped them, they were astonished to find that the haze gave host to hundreds of tiny balls of light.

'Unbelievable,' Miles said as the child in his arms began squealing with elation, openly reflecting his mother's mind.

'They must have liked our offerings, hey?' Tory acknowledged Rhun's excitement.

'Tory.' Miles' face turned as pale as a sheet.

She turned to see what had him scared him so, and at first glimpse Tory thought his horror was due to naught but a horse. Yet, as the animal came closer, she noticed the horn on its forehead. 'What do I do?' Tory said to Miles; she wasn't good with animals.

'You're asking me?' Miles could barely speak, let alone think. 'Just don't touch it. According to fairytales, they can only be touched by a virgin.' He grinned.

Tory took a few hesitant steps towards the beautiful white beast before bowing to it. To her surprise the animal stopped and bowed to her also. Then, to discredit Miles' claim, the unicorn came forward to place its snout under Tory's hand and gave her a soft nudge.

'I could be wrong, of course,' Miles said, admitting he stood corrected.

Like me, thou art eternally virtuous, Tory was informed by a sweet and somewhat mischievous male voice. 'Who are you?' she asked as she stroked the animal's nose gently.

A messenger.

'And what be thy message?' Tory smiled, delighted they were understanding each other so well.

Miles was confused; Tory appeared to be having a conversation with the animal, yet all he could hear was the singing of a choir — the voices more beautiful than anything he'd ever heard.

The adverse presence that plagues thee hast gone into hiding and shall remain thus until both thy homes are within thy sight. She desires to keep thee here, but it be not safe for thy babe. The child must return.

The animal began to back away, the mist thickening in its wake.

'What are you saying, that I do not go? I must!' Tory pleaded. 'Taliesin has left for Atlantis, and I have no way of contacting him if I am delayed again.'

627

The long road home be no longer. The mist consumed the beast completely.

'Wait,' Tory pursued it. 'I don't think I understand.' Tory came to a standstill when she realised her chase was useless. *I don't want to understand. Please don't let anything go wrong, I couldn't bear another year here alone.*

Time proved the unicorn right; no one saw or heard from Teo, not even Brian. Tory worried for his safety, as Mahaud would be feeding his lesser desires to increase her power.

Tory had more or less left the project at Llyn Cerrig Bach since her job there was done. She'd been spending all the money she'd earnt on necessities to take back with her and gifts for all the friends she so dearly missed, the largest of which was a Spanish guitar for Selwyn. Tory just hoped all the excess baggage she was carting wouldn't be too much of a strain on poor Taliesin.

Days before Tory was due to depart, her father and Aunt Rose made the trip up to Mon. Tory had told them of the Otherworld warning, thus none of them were prepared to take Rhun from the protection of the property at Aberffraw until the last minute.

Brian, who had classes to teach, said he would meet Tory at the stones to say goodbye. They'd spent a lot of time together of late, and neither one wanted to stretch out their farewell. Her brother was presently of two minds; he didn't want Tory to leave but he couldn't go back with her either, as Naomi was now pregnant with their child and so his life was here.

Miles, too, would prove hard to leave behind, Tory

thought. His support and company had been nothing short of a godsend to her. Yes, she was in love with him, and she hoped that when her time with Maelgwn had come to an end she would somehow be able to find Miles again.

In the early hours of the eve of the summer solstice, Miles was wrapped up in a blanket on his lounge still wide awake. Tory would soon leave him, and his heart wouldn't let him rest. It was near daybreak when he heard weeping coming from his room, and he walked quietly over to find the door open. Moonlight streamed in through the window onto Tory who was propped up on her pillows, her head in her hands.

'Are you alright?' he asked in a whisper, fearing he would wake the child.

'Damn it,' Tory cursed upon seeing him in the doorway. 'I didn't want to wake you.'

'Who can sleep?' he joked, leaning against the doorframe to support his weary head.

'You've been so good to us, Miles. It's not fair the way things worked out.'

'Oh I don't know, it's not really so bad. The project is coming along nicely, I've got this new head space to explore, and I even had a family for a while.'

Tory's heart split in two, as she knew how hard it was for him to refrain from saying what he really felt. 'If I wasn't married I would stay, really I would. Perhaps someday . . .'

Tory stopped abruptly and Miles moved closer. 'Go on.'

'Forget it.' Tory had a mental flash of Miles still waiting around for her when he was sixty and her never showing. She couldn't make him a promise she wasn't sure she could keep.

'Tory.' Miles knew she was edging around something. 'I love you.' He sat down and took hold of her. 'If there is any way you can foresee that we can be together in this life, I want you to tell me.'

'I love you too,' she admitted, softly. 'I can promise I'll try to find my way back here, Miles, but the cosmos works in strange ways, so you must not wait for me.' She gave a heavy sigh. 'I'm going to miss you, Professor.' The tears began to flow again down her cheeks. 'I just don't know where I'm supposed to be anymore. No matter where I am, I will always miss someone else, somewhere else.' She raised her eyes to look at him.

'That's the story of my life.' Miles placed his arm around her. 'But from what I can gather, we shall be together at some point. So we'll just look forward to then, shall we?'

Tory nodded with a sniffle.

'Alright then.' He let go of her to take up his blanket. 'I'll see you at breakfast.'

'Goodnight, and thanks again, for everything.'

'Anytime.'

She lay down to sleep, but her anxiety made a mockery of her attempt. *This time tomorrow I shall be with him, and nothing will go wrong*, she told herself. Yet all the while in the back of her mind, the Otherworld prophecy played on her fears.

* * *

Brian had finished his last class for the day and decided to take a shower while he awaited Naomi's arrival. They planned to eat dinner somewhere then meet up with everyone at the stones later. Tory and the others had planned not to arrive at the site until a half an hour before midnight, to minimise the danger.

By the time Brian was dressed Naomi still wasn't there, so he presumed she was just running late, as usual. Glancing out his bedroom window, he spied her car and, to his horror, Teo's as well.

This sent him rocketing downstairs, and outside to investigate. Brian found no trace of either of them, though the engines of both cars were still warm. *If he touches her, his life won't be worth living.* Brian crept around the side of the house to the gym. As he peeked his head around the corner he was startled by Teo, waiting for him. The laughter that echoed from his friend chilled Brian to the bone.

Teo looked and smelt awful, sick even. His features appeared more hardened than before, dark rings circled his eyes and his whole body exuded perspiration. When his laughter ceased, Teo's mere breathing was a worry as it loudly resounded with the growling presence of a beast — like a lion but more human.

'What's happening, bro?' Brian thought he'd best handle this calmly.

Teo smiled, the pupils of his eyes burning red. He motioned Brian to follow him down to the gym, then disappeared into thin air.

631

'Oh shit!' Brian looked about him, then back to the gym where his friend reappeared. Teo opened the door and vanished into a red haze that appeared to emanate from inside, closing the door behind him with a laugh.

'Naomi!' Brian tore to the door. After battling to open it, he was overwhelmed by the abomination he found seething within.

The gym floor dropped away into a bottomless fiery pit that was crawling with life forms so hideous and vile smelling, that Brian gagged on the first whiff of their putrid existence. Evil spirits joined to form a whirlwind of red gases which girded the centre of the room. Here Naomi was huddled, terrified by the hellish abyss surrounding her. She didn't dare raise her head as the archfiends in the whirlwind lunged at her to frighten her back into retreat.

Holy Mother! Brian gasped; he'd taught a class in here not an hour before.

Teo appeared again on the island in the centre where Naomi was stranded. He took hold of a clump of her hair, dragging the sobbing girl to her feet.

'Teo, you son-of-a-bitch, I know you're in there somewhere. Don't you hurt her.' Brian was at a loss for what to do.

'Oh, we don't want to hurt her.' The creature that was Teo put his arms around Naomi. 'We like her.' He licked her cheek.

'Brian!' Naomi struggled to get away from Teo's restraint, she was going to be sick.

'And,' Teo added, passing a hand over her belly and raising his eyebrows.

'What do you want?' Brian snarled, as if he had to ask.

'We want *Tory of Gwynedd*.' Teo's own voice was now completely drowned out by the other. It gargled and snarled so loudly that Naomi passed out from shock. 'Bring her back to us. And be sure she brings the child with her, or thee shall pay with the life of thy own!' The force of the words blew Brian back from the doorway and the door slammed closed.

He sprang to his feet, but the door handle burnt the flesh of his hands and Brian was forced to let go. Although the evil voice that stemmed from Teo sounded male, Brian knew well enough who it was. 'The bitch must pay!' He kicked the door, melting the toe of his shoe.

They were doing splendidly, Tory thought, arriving at the stones with only fifteen minutes to spare. But when Brian met her with his news, Tory was frustrated to admit that the Otherworld had been right; she was not going anywhere, just yet.

She was no longer afraid of facing Mahaud, now she was just plain angry. 'What does it take! All I want is for my husband, myself, and our child to be together in the one place, at the one time. Really! Am I asking too much!' Tory shouted at the heavens. She asked for a pen and paper to quickly write a note, which she tied around Rhun's waist so it would not go astray.

'Be brave little one, thy father awaits thee at the other end.' Tory lay Maelgwn's medallion across Rhun for protection and kissed him goodbye, for who knows how long. Still, she remained calm and accepting so as not to unduly upset him.

As Brian witnessed his sister leave her child's basket in the middle of the circle, he became alarmed. 'She said you had to bring Rhun.'

'And the folk said he had to go back to his father.' Tory was not in any mood to be reckoned with. 'Don't worry, I have a plan.'

'Tory! You weren't there, you didn't see'

'You wouldn't believe what I've seen!' she roared. 'And I'm telling you, if you march in there unprepared she's going to fry us all.'

'Listen to her, Brian, she's right.' Miles knew from Maelgwn's recollections of the instance to which Tory referred.

'What are you going to do, child?' Renford wished he could help but he wasn't very knowledgeable about such things.

'We're going to find your bloody memory . . .'

A cloud appeared in the night sky, and lightning flashed down to make contact with the King's Stone.

Tory could feel Rhun's fear and he began to cry. She wished with all her heart that she could run to his comfort, and into the comfort of Maelgwn's arms, yet somehow she remained still as the mist ascended into the heavens, her child along with it. 'Myrddin is my only way back now.'

The basket containing Rhun materialised in the Dark Age, along with all Tory's gifts. But everyone at the stones became disgruntled when, once again, their *sensei* did not show.

'Be this in thy plan, also?' Maelgwn angrily quizzed Taliesin, as he approached the manifestation to claim his son.

The Merlin didn't have to answer, the look of horror on his face said it all.

The King held his child, who had grown so since their last meeting, and read out aloud the note he carried.

> *Major problem hast erupted. Mahaud.*
> *Could use thy help, if thee can lend it.*
> *I am seeking Myrddin. WAIT FOR ME.*
> *Love thee, miss thee, Tory.*

'Maelgwn, you must concentrate right now. Every second thee wastes, be hours, days passing,' Taliesin urged, somewhat bewildered by this unforeseen development.

'Well, am I not there too!' Brockwell pointed out, stepping forward. 'I am not afraid of the witch, we've met before.'

'True,' Taliesin considered his plea, motioning the King to the spot before him. 'But Maelgwn hast been taught certain techniques that enhance his soul's mobility and allow him to concentrate for extended lengths of time.'

'But with thy help, High Merlin,' Brockwell insisted. 'Please, can I not try?'

'No harm in that, I suppose.' Taliesin ushered him to a seat beside Maelgwn.

Maelgwn passed the child to Katren. 'I want my Queen back before this night hast passed,' he announced to Taliesin in warning.

The Merlin was weary from incanting and was running a tad short on patience. 'Then let us get on with it.' He placed one hand on Brockwell's forehead, the other on Maelgwn's. 'Close thy eyes now, and be at peace.'

Miles drove all night and the party reached Dinas Emrys by dawn. As they climbed out of the car and stretched, Tory woke her father who'd slept most of the way.

Upon finding himself at the site, Renford was convinced they would only be disappointed by pursuing the legend of Myrddin's cave here. 'Tory, my sweet, didn't I tell you I have already sought out this area to no avail?'

'But the legend required a blond-haired, blue-eyed youth,' Tory said as she waved Brian over. 'Does it not make sense that your son would be the key?'

'I'm not a youth!'

'Compared to Myrddin,' Tory threw an arm around Brian's shoulder, 'you're a baby. Let's go.' She gave him a slap on the back and headed off towards the mountain.

Aunt Rose, although she would loved to have gone, settled back in the car. Poor Renford, however, was obliged to make the hike.

'Come on, Dad,' Brian urged him along, as Miles gave him a hand.

Tory led them round the base of the mountain, and Miles drew her attention to the mist rolling in. They all stopped in their tracks as the haze rolled over the landscape and surrounded them. There were no lights this time, but as the legend stated, there were bells — sweet, resounding bells — that filled the senses with a lovely feeling of peace.

'I think we might be onto something,' Renford said, though he didn't sound too keen, especially when he heard the growling.

From the mist emerged a large, black, wolf-like dog, its eyes blazing yellow, its upper lip raised to expose its huge, white fangs.

'Easy boy.' Miles attempted to calm the animal but it only snarled louder, forcing him to back up before it took off his hand. 'Jesus Tory, are you sure about this?'

'Allow me.' Brian came forward to try his luck.

As soon as it caught sight of Brian, the dog humbled itself. It began to whimper as it approached him, as if apologising for mistaking him.

'Hey boy.' Brian absolutely loved dogs, so he rumbled and patted the animal affectionately. 'I think he likes me, hey?' He then looked at the dog rather curiously and asked, 'Did you say something?' He paused for confirmation. 'Yeah, we are as a matter of fact.'

The dog took off in front of him.

'Okay.' Brian stood to follow the animal, presuming everyone else had heard their conversation. 'Well come on, you heard the dog.' He rolled his eyes and disappeared into the mist.

'Oh dear,' was all Renford could say as he obliged.

'I just love your style of archaeology,' Miles commented to Tory as they fell in behind the others.

The dog led them to a stone wall in the cliff face at the base of the mountain, and instead of stopping before it as expected, the animal disappeared into the stone obstruction. Brian reached out to the rock face before him, passing his hand through it. 'Whoa, way cool!' He motioned everyone in behind him as he penetrated beyond.

'I don't believe it.' Renford paused halfway, unwilling to face his destiny. So Tory and Miles grabbed hold of him on their way through.

The cave was torch lit. Brian followed his guide down a long, stone passageway that led to a door with no handle. Brian tried to push it open but without success. 'Damn, now what?'

Tory shook her head; how thick he was at times. She took up his right hand and placed it on a silver plate embedded in the wall, and the door simply disappeared. 'Indiana Jones you ain't, mate,' she commented, wandering in to take a look at their findings.

'What is it all?' Brian asked as he followed her.

'Nobody touch anything,' Tory warned them. 'Amongst this lovely little collection of antiquities be the Thirteen Treasures of Britain.' She recognised Dyrnwyn (White Hilt), the sword of Rhydderch, mounted on the wall.

'I thought you said Taliesin had the Thirteen Treasures.' Brian was confused.

'He has. I presume he picked them up at a later date.' Tory was drawn to a large obstruction that was covered with a glittering golden cloth. She cast the cover aside to reveal a strange silver chariot. The disc-shaped vehicle could have been mistaken for a space-age motor-scooter, but Tory knew well enough what it was and she squealed with excitement.

'What is it?' Brian couldn't imagine.

'This be my ride home,' Tory answered as she circled it, running her fingers over its frame. 'Behold the Chariot of Arianrod, it is saïd to take one quickly to the place of one's desire.'

'Hold on a minute, this looks like it's from the future,' Brian protested.

'But it isn't. It's more likely to have Atlantean origins. What do you think, Miles?' Tory turned to seek his opinion.

'That's an interesting theory.' Miles gazed fondly at Tory a moment, before they were all startled by a movement overhead.

An owl came swooping out of the shadows to take a seat on a perch next to Renford. *It's about time!*

'Pardon?' Renford looked at the bird.

That thee showed thyself.

Renford turned to the others. 'Did you hear that, the owl spoke. Didn't it?'

Though they had heard naught, all three nodded in the hope that Renford would pursue the conversation.

Oh brother! We had best get thee back to normal Myrddin, one cannot bear to see thee living in such ignorance.

'I beg thy pardon?' Renford was insulted.

Then, I forgive thee. The bird vexed him further. *See that chalice over there?*

Renford turn and spied an old goblet. 'Yes.'

It be thy Holy Grail, Myrddin, where thee bade the Goddess to store thy knowledge. Go and drink from it. It is

639

high time thee freed thyself from the menial existence thou hast been forced to lead.

Renford didn't know if he was suited to being a Merlin. 'Art thou sure thou hast the right man?'

One would wonder, I know, but I would recognise thee anywhere, old friend, trust me.

Renford looked at his daughter for support, as he ever so slowly approached the piece in question.

'It's alright, Dad, really.' Tory urged her father to do whatever the hell was being asked of him.

Everyone held their breath as Renford reached out and took possession of the Grail. 'Shouldn't we put something in it first?'

As Renford moved to turn the seemingly empty goblet upside down, Tory recalled how Taliesin had acquired his knowledge from a single droplet. 'No Dad, the droplet, catch it.'

Renford watched the drop fall from the rim of the chalice, and holding out his hand he chanced a catch that was successful. As the liquid splashed against his skin, Renford fell to his knees in much pain.

'Dad!' Brian moved to his aid but Tory held him by her side.

'Stay back,' she whispered. 'He'll be fine.'

Brian wasn't so sure he agreed with his sister's diagnosis, for a brilliant white light shot out through his father's eyes, nose, mouth and ears, forcing them all to turn away a second.

When they heard Renford's hysterical laughter, which seemed to have an added depth of lunacy about it, the three dared to look up.

'The sleeper awakens!' Myrddin announced, raising his arms into the air.

Tory didn't recognise her father at first, the man before them was so much younger and had so much more hair!

Brian freaked. 'Tory! Where is Dad?'

Taller and more slender than Renford, Myrddin had long, jet-black hair that fell about him in wisps. A patch of white hair sprang from both his temples, making him appear all the more wise and weird. His face and features were more gaunt than before. His eyebrows were bushy, his beard and moustache trimmed and neat. Two streaks of white hair sprang from the corners of his mouth and ran through his beard to meet very neatly at a point below his chin, forming a perfect 'V' in amongst the black. The Merlin wore a long robe of dark blue, girdled at the waist, and a mantle about his shoulders. But his eyes were her father's.

Tory had inherited these same green eyes, where Brian's baby blues had been passed on from their mother. 'This is he,' Tory, wonderstruck, concluded upon closer inspection. *It is true then, I am the daughter of Myrddin.*

'Indeed, Taliesin is never wrong,' the Merlin confirmed. 'Speaking of which, we have to save him.'

'No, it's Naomi we have to save,' Brian told him.

'And Teo,' Tory added.

'Well, I was close.' He winked at Tory, before looking to the owl. 'Tobias, old friend.' He wandered over to have a chat.

'Now I have seen everything.' Miles was looking rather pale.

'How are we ever going to explain this to Mum?' Brian whispered to Tory.

'We don't explain anything to anyone. For I am . . .' Myrddin looked at Brian, transforming himself back to Renford's form, 'our secret.' He chuckled. 'Fear not my lad, Mahaud will pay.'

27

THE RETURNING

M yrddin declared that they needed to draw Mahaud further into Gwynedd and away from the borders of the old Saxon country in Oxfordshire, so the party headed to the cottage at Aberffraw. Rose and Renford had been having a lovely discussion on the way there. Renford had returned to the car with the others a much changed man, and had apologised to his sister for his profound ignorance of her abilities all these years. He vowed from now on that she would find him far more open-minded.

Brian drove this time as, unlike Miles, he was having no trouble keeping his eyes open; he was worried sick about Naomi.

Tory placed a hand on his shoulder. 'The hell you saw was just an illusion, Brian, designed to appeal to your greatest fears.'

Brian showed her the burn marks on his hand. 'I this an illusion, Tory?'

'In a way, yes. It is just the result of a clash o polarities, which you lost, because Mahaud's will wa more focused and therefore stronger than yours.'

Myrddin sat forward in his seat to verify Tory' claim. 'Mahaud is what is known as a Mental elemental she feeds off negative thought patterns. She has mad mental and mystical psychism her forte, so as soon a you display a negative emotion or have a negativ thought, you are granting her control over th conscious, then subconscious or subliminal level of you mind. If she obtains a firm hold, as with Teo, she can pollute your superconscious and universal mind as well.'

As Brian still looked a little confused, Tory outline the situation. 'Mahaud would have overawed you with her horrors, vexed you to the point where you lost you temper, and then bypassed your conscious to you subconscious to suggest that the door would burn yo when you touched it. As you believed that she was th greater force, you accepted the notion instead o rejecting it.'

'But how am I to reject a notion, if I don't ever know of its existence, that's not fair.'

'Exactly,' Myrddin stated with conviction. 'Mahaud represents all that is unfair, unwise and impure, so believe nothing she presents to you. Trust you instincts, stay positive, and know your own mind. Ther nothing can harm you.'

Brian pulled into the driveway at the cottage bringing the car to an abrupt halt. 'Are you telling me that I could've just walked over to Teo and reclaimed Naomi from him, there and then?'

'If thy belief had been strong enough, yes.'

'Shit!' Brian thumped the steering wheel.

'Hey Brian, you wanted action,' Tory reminded him as he opened his door in a huff.

Myrddin nodded in agreement as he climbed out of the car after Rose, stretching and exclaiming rather loudly, 'Ah, Aberffraw!' He wandered around the grounds of the cottage. 'This will do just fine. There be a transverse of energies here that should serve our purpose nicely.'

'A ley crossing, you mean?' Tory inquired.

'Indeed.' He walked off to the lawn behind the cottage, rather excited.

Tory turned her attention from the Merlin to Miles who was still sleeping in the back seat of the car, and noticed he was shaking. 'What's wrong?'

'Die witch!' he cried, becoming agitated.

'Miles,' Tory shook him, 'wake up.'

'Huh!' He sat up, eyes parted wide and full of fear. 'Tory!' He grabbed her and held her tight. 'I saw your body fall on the stone ground in a great pool of blood. I saw a bat, I saw a necklet.'

'Waistlet,' Tory corrected, stroking his hair to pacify him. 'Fear not, it was my past you saw.'

'And you survived?' Miles sat back, unable to shake the feeling of dread and loss he felt. He vaguely recalled seeing this vision before when Maelgwn had been speaking to Tory of the crone, but it hadn't affected him then as it did now.

645

'I did.' She smiled. 'I have to go check what my father's up to, will you be okay?'

When Miles nodded, she kissed his cheek and made off around the back of the house.

Tory caught up with her father. He'd stopped in the middle of the grassy flat and was concentrating on seeking the point where the energy grid crossed.

'Pardon my ignorance,' Tory said to him. 'But weren't such doorways usually land-marked by the Ancients?'

'Do you recall a large sundial?'

'Yes, in the courtyard.'

'It would have been located about here, wouldn't you say?' Myrddin sized up a location before him.

'Aye, that's about right.' Though everyone else saw him as Renford, Tory chose to see her father as he truly was. She found it comforting to see him so young and virile. Myrddin, holding his palms together and his arms outstretched, pointed his fingers towards the ground. With a deep breath, he lunged forward and spread his arms. As he did so, the earth before them piled aside into a tidy mound around the sundial's perimeter.

'By the Goddess, Renford.' Aunt Rose was aghast. 'You have come a long way.'

'Thank you, dear lady.' He bowed. ''Twas nothing really.'

'That was just great. Wait till Miles gets a load of this,' Tory squeezed her father's arm, before taking off to fetch Miles. 'I'm so excited to have you back!'

'Well, I'm so pleased to be here,' he exclaimed.

Tory just laughed; he was so different, kind of mad, yet all-knowing. Now she knew at least two other souls who were in the same predicament as her, as Myrddin and Taliesin were also everlasting. Perhaps there are more of us, Tory considered, as she rounded the cottage to find Miles and Brian sprawled out on the ground.

Brian was just sitting up when Tory ran to his aid. 'What happened? Are you alright?'

'Great!' He stood up and jumped about. 'I made it here before Maelgwn did. See, he still be out cold.' He staggered about, a little woozy.

'Brockwell!' Tory nearly fell over. 'What art thou doing here?'

'I have come to fight Mahaud.' He reached for his sword and was confused when he found it missing. 'They said I couldn't do it, but I be here alright.' He looked over at the car rather cautiously.

Miles stirred and Tory knelt down to help him. 'And who are we at the moment?'

Upon seeing her, he pulled her down close and kissed her.

'That had better be you, Maelgwn,' Tory threatened.

'Aye.' He smiled broadly, propping himself up onto his elbows. 'Now, tell me why thou hast chosen to stay here to confront Mahaud, when she surely would have followed thee back?'

'Because she holds Katren hostage.' Tory used the name Katren instead of Naomi so Maelgwn would understand who she meant, totally forgetting how Brockwell would react.

'What! How?'

'Calm, Calin. I do not mean thy wife. Her name be Naomi, she be my brother's lady. But as thou art Brian Katren be Naomi, understand?'

'Aye . . .' Brockwell thought but a second, 'then we must save her.'

'Well, Myrddin be around the back working on that right now. Thou should go and let him know of thy arrival.' Tory gave him a slap on the shoulder and headed him off in the right direction. She considered i was rather good that Brockwell would be filling in fo her brother through all this, as Brockwell wasn't a personally involved and would not be as easily distracted by Mahaud's tricks.

'Come on.' Tory helped Maelgwn to his feet. 'The house be much more comfortable.'

As they walked, Maelgwn was very quiet. They paused to unlock the door and he touched Tory's chin turning her around to look him in the eye. 'Be Miles part of the reason thee wanted to stay?'

'Nay.'

Maelgwn followed her inside, silently closing the door behind them. 'Thee told him thee loved him, Tory Be that true?'

So it works the other way round; Maelgwn also recall Miles' thoughts and memories. 'Of course I do, I love thee!' Tory was burning up and her heart began to pound in her chest. 'But I haven't so much as kissed him, Maelgwn. In fact, he never even tried!'

'I know.' He held his palms up to her, motioning he to calm down. 'What I be trying to say be that, if thee wishes to stay here in the future with me, I understand for 'twas most probably the way it was meant to be in the first place.' Maelgwn had to say it, though he'd fought through every syllable.

'Goddamn it, Maelgwn!' Tory sounded annoyed with him as she grabbed hold of the collar of his shirt. 'How many times do I have to tell thee! I love thee! I wed thee! I even had thy child, which, by the way, I would not have endured for another living soul.' She took a deep breath, and was forced to a smile when Maelgwn relaxed. 'Yet, still thee can doubt it. I am coming back! I already have the means, I found the Chariot of Arianrod.'

'Truly?' Maelgwn couldn't believe it. 'That be the only one of the Thirteen Treasures which Taliesin doth not possess. He never did find it.'

'Then that confirms my return. He hast been unable to find it because I am to bring the chariot back to him when I return. That be why it was not with the other twelve Treasures when Taliesin found them. How could it be, when I will have taken it back already? Time be very deceiving, indeed.'

'Taliesin will be beside himself if this be the case, as the chariot would simplify his life greatly.'

'I do not mean to interrupt.' Myrddin walked right through the wall of the cottage. 'But I need to use thy phone.'

'Myrddin, thou hast found thyself at last.' Maelgwn was very pleased to meet him face-to-face.

'Thanks to thee, Maelgwn, old son. How art thou, and how fare all in the Gwynedd of old?'

'Very well indeed,' the King replied.

'Yet I be sure it would be even more so if we could get thy lovely Queen back to thee. So if it pleases thee, the phone?'

Tory pointed to it, a little surprised, but asked naught of his intent.

He dialled a number. 'Stay very quiet,' Myrddin instructed them before turning back to the phone. 'Teo! What are you doing there?'

The Merlin spoke with Tory's voice, and she was so shocked she nearly forgot his instruction and laughed out loud.

'I do realise that, yes. I'm not going now,' the Merlin informed Teo. 'It's a very long story, is Brian there?' He paused. 'No, I've been looking for him all night, and Naomi. Have you seen them?' He paused again, appearing rather amused. 'Teo, is there something wrong? You were acting a little strange last time we met.' His tone became more inviting. 'No, I forgive you, you should just take better care of yourself.' He suppressed a laugh. 'Well if you do see Brian, tell him I've got a couple of problems that I really need to discuss with him. Tell him to call me urgently.' He waited for the next query. 'Oh, Miles got called away to some island off the coast of Africa, and I can't find Dad or Aunt Rose anywhere.' He winked at Tory. 'Look, I can't talk, the baby's crying.' Myrddin pointed to a distant corner of the room and the sound of a child crying resounded for all to hear. 'I'm still at the cottage, so he can call me here. Thanks Teo. Bye.'

Tory and Maelgwn shook their heads, amazed by the man's brilliance.

'She suspects a trap,' the Merlin informed them with a smile. 'Thus she shall certainly bring the girl as a hostage.'

'I believed it,' Maelgwn assured him.

Myrddin shrugged. 'Whether she did or not, she will come. So we must prepare. Tory, grab your saxophone. There be a little tune I wish to teach thee.'

Tory moved to do so at once, although she thought his timing rather inappropriate. 'Haven't we got more important things to do right now?'

The Merlin smiled. 'This tune be known to some as the Pan call.'

'I'll be right back.' Tory hastened to fetch the instrument.

Myrddin explained that each elemental had an appropriate musical note, which resonated to its correct frequency: Fire – C, Air – E-flat, Water – G, Earth – F. These four notes, when played in the right sequence and key, comprised the Pan call. But Myrddin warned her that the forces of Pan should never be summoned unless truly required, for Pan's energies were known to be highly stimulating and if not used once invoked, could cause complete havoc. The true power of the Pan ray was that of healing, especially in cases of fever. The only way to destroy Mahaud was to charge her with as much positive energy and love as they could summon, for this was poisonous to the evil crone.

Evening found them all well briefed by the Merlin. No matter what took place, it was imperative that they all maintain a positive view; anger and fear were the air

Mahaud breathed. Myrddin cast an etheric shield around his novices. He explained that the invisible shield of white light would block out harmful thoughts from any earthlings, or earth-bound entities from the etheric world. It was a kind of sealing of one's aura, preventing the witch from detecting their presence before they wished to make themselves known.

Once they had Mahaud surrounded, the Law of Rebound (a greater force will always rebound a lesser power) would come into play; there would be no escape for the evil crone this time. But their success depended upon maintaining a focused and positive outlook as a combined power. If they could sustain this unity, any negative force Mahaud projected at them would rebound back on herself as positive energy.

The evil witch would be taking a great risk venturing so far into fairy country. But the idea of Tory and her child left alone and defenceless would be far too attractive for the witch to resist. The moon was waning, which would work very much in their favour, as practitioners of magic knew this was the time of the month for endings, undoings, eliminating and separating. In addition, Mahaud still hadn't an inkling of Myrddin's involvement, which put them at a very definite advantage.

The stage was set and all lay waiting in the shadows for the crone to make herself present.

Rose, Brockwell, Maelgwn and Myrddin were all armed with one of the four implements, by means of which they could each summon an element. The Merlin had brought this personal collection from amongst the antiquities in his cave. These were the tools he used when performing such rites. The choice of who would be best to summon each element was decided by their individual birth signs.

Maelgwn was a Leo and thus a fire sign, so he was sent to hide in the south, armed with a large rod, because in the old rituals of the druids, fire was summoned by the rod and was represented by the similar symbol of wands in the sacred tarot.

Aunt Rose, a Pisces and therefore of water, hid in the west, holding a chalice that represented the cups of the tarot.

Brian was a Taurean, like Tory, but Brockwell had been born under the sign of Aquarius. So, belonging to the element of air, he headed east with White Hilt, the Sword of Rhydderch, on the proviso he did not use it for anything but the summons.

Myrddin, having strong associations with the Earth, awaited the confrontation to the north. He had in his possession a sanctified stone of crystal, which was represented by the pentacles in the tarot.

Tory stood in the middle of the sundial, holding her saxophone and a doll wrapped in a blanket. Myrddin had cast a spell on the bundle so that when the witch saw it, she would believe it to be the real heir of Gwynedd. The circumference of the sundial performed the same function as the 'casting of a circle' in Wiccan practice. This was to protect and harness one's own power, which in Tory's case was positive. At the stations of north, south, east and west, a torch burned brightly to acknowledge the four elements and the four winds. Once inside this circle, Mahaud could be contained and she could not call upon any other dark forces to assist her in her struggle. The trick was to entice her to step into the fairy ring, and this was Tory's task.

As they heard the sound of a car tearing into the driveway Myrddin bethought them all. *Now whatever happens, do not reveal thyself until Tory hast Mahaud in the circle. Save the evil crone eluding us again.*

Teo stormed down the hill dragging Naomi along with him. He clenched the back of her neck and her hands were bound behind her back. 'What trickery is this?' he hissed upon viewing the set-up.

Teo and Naomi walked straight past Brockwell, who was hiding in the east near the house. Upon seeing Naomi, Brockwell was tempted to do her captor in there and then. Tory, however, had insisted that Teo must not be harmed; they must draw the crone out.

'This be merely a precaution to protect myself, Mahaud. I want Teo and Naomi back please,' Tory requested politely.

Teo laughed. 'Nothing can protect you,' he told her, his voice so deep and husky it was nearly inaudible. 'Give me the child.'

'But if you are so powerful you can take it, surely?' The doll in her arms was heard to cry — a nice touch on the Merlin's part. This seemed to make Mahaud all the more anxious to get hold of the baby.

'Foolish child. Do you think me an amateur?' Teo became angry, pacing to and fro with Naomi in tow. 'Place the child outside the circle and I shall cast forth this whimpering mass.' He shook his hostage like she was a rag doll.

'Please Tory!' Naomi begged her.

The girl was hysterical, not that she could blame her, yet Tory demanded calmly, 'But what of Teo?'

The beast erupted into laughter again. 'He's not talking to you.'

'Why, he knows I love him. I miss you, Teo.' She looked straight into his burning eyes.

Teo let loose a long growl, indicating that there was a struggle going on within him. Naomi screamed also, as the volume of his protest was overwhelming.

It works! Tory surprised herself, not that she'd ever doubted it. 'Teo, listen to me.'

'No, he's not interested,' the beast snapped at her. 'Place the child outside the circle, or she's toast.' Teo raised his fingertips to Naomi and they began to redden.

'Alright!' Tory gave in. She moved to the perimeter and kissed the doll in her arms, before raising her tearful eyes to view the crone. 'I'll place the child outside and back away, and you let Naomi walk.' Tory set down the bundle and then backed away with caution, watching the crone carefully to make sure she complied.

Teo thrust Naomi on ahead of him and she ran to the safety of the circle into Tory's awaiting arms.

Mahaud snatched up the bundle, most impressed with herself, only the Merlin had designed the spell to wear off upon her touch. The beast's holler of aggravation rocked the very pillars of hell. The doll ignited into flames and the witch cast it aside. 'Now you die!' Teo turned his ravaged sights to Tory.

'Teo wouldn't hurt me,' Tory said, and she seated Naomi on the ground in the centre and approached the

655

edge of the circle again. 'Who be the least afraid, Mahaud? Shall I meet you on your ground, or you on mine?'

'Teo hates you!' The witch snarled, avoiding her challenge.

'Does not.' Tory played along.

'Why didn't you help me, Tory?' Teo's own voice returned for a second, and the evil fell from his face. He appeared exhausted as the evil again came over him, and the beast that was Mahaud laughed to mock her adversary's pain.

'Teo is a far stronger soul than you, Mahaud. I still believe he can beat you. You're no threat to our friendship.' Tory confidently stepped outside the circle and took a stand. 'I am not afraid of the likes of you.'

Teo approached her and to ensure he had her full attention, he pulled her chin up so she had to look into his eyes. 'You should be.'

A cold, sharp knife punctured her skin and bore into her stomach, then Teo twised the weapon up to her ribs to ensure the strike was fatal. The afflicted area went numb, it was as if she was just a spectator and someone else had been wounded. She felt her blood gushing from her body, and for a moment reality became a total blur.

Naomi screamed. Maelgwn and Brockwell, despite specific instructions to the contrary, divulged their presence as they came screaming towards the crone.

'Stop where thou art!' Tory demanded their restraint and her tone was so sharp that both men halted at once. She lifted her head to view Teo's expressionless face as she withdrew his blade from her body. 'I know it wasn't you, Teo.' She placed a hand on his shoulder and crouched over as if she were going to die, yet her wound was already healing. Tory looked back up to him, her eyes filled with compassion as she grabbed him by the pressure points in his neck and squeezed as hard as she could muster. 'Nice try, Mahaud, but not good enough.'

When Teo's body began to lose power, the beast roared in protest as he shrank down to the ground.

'Sorry Teo.' Tory shut out the bloodcurdling screams, dragging his motionless body into the circle. 'Get out, quickly,' Tory urged Naomi.

Teo began to lose consciousness, his eyes still ablaze, then a red and black haze slowly escaped through his eyes, nose, mouth and ears.

Maelgwn was left totally bewildered by the scene he'd just witnessed. Still, as the crone began to materialise before him, he put it to the back of his mind and stepped forward to execute his role. He pointed the rod towards the circle, and when engaged it took on a strange glow. 'I am Maelgwn, King of Gwynedd, and I hold thee Mahaud in this sacred ring by the power of fire, by all that is creative, brave, and strong.'

'I am Brockwell, King of Powys, and I hold thee Mahaud in this sacred ring by the power of air, all that is knowledgeable, free and of speed.'

Naomi was rather surprised to hear Brian address himself thus. He looked mighty fine, nevertheless, as he pressed the button on the hilt of his sword and a laser beam of red extended from it, which he aimed towards their foe.

Rose came forth from her hiding place. She held out her chalice, which was illuminated from within, toward the sundial. 'I am Rose, confidant to the spirits of the Otherworld. I hold thee Mahaud in this sacred circle by the power of water, by all that be feeling, understanding, and sympathetic.'

With this, Teo seemed to have excreted all the poisonous gases from his body, and Tory dragged his comatosed form back out of the circle and well clear of it.

Myrddin emerged from his cover, his crystal ablaze. 'I am Myrddin, High Merlin of the Druids, second only to Taliesin. I hold thee Mahaud in this sacred circle by the power of earth, the great mother of all that be productive, nourishing and balanced in this world. Thou art constrained by the four elements of creation and are bound by life itself to comply.'

Mahaud's body, still lacking enough density to be totally solid, took the form of a beautiful maid — the maid to whom Myrddin had once lost his heart. 'And where hast thou been hiding thyself my love, in a tree perhaps?' She laughed, rather sweetly.

'I forgive thee, Mahaud. I bear thee no malice,' he stated very sincerely. 'In fact, thou taught me an invaluable lesson.'

'Stop it!' she shrilled, annoyed that she hadn't vexed him. Mahaud again changed form into a hideous beast with seven heads, snarling and breathing fire, but not even the flames seemed to be able to extend beyond the circle.

The Merlin grinned at this as he quietly began to recite a healing incantation.

The seven heads of the beast took on human faces, one of which was the wicked crone's. The creature's tail began to lash out violently, as all seven heads screamed and cursed in pain. Then it began to emit the foulest odour, worse than the smell of death — more like that of the already decomposed. 'Thou art a fool, Myrddin! Thy betrayal was *so* easy,' the witch taunted him.

Yet the Merlin remained focused on his purpose, because with every attempt to vex him the witch grew a little weaker. Maelgwn, Rose and Brockwell had joined the Merlin in his verse.

Mahaud was obviously having no luck with Myrddin, so she turned her eyes to Maelgwn. 'Thy wife never told thee of her immortality, did she, Dragon?' The witch laughed; she didn't miss a trick.

Maelgwn struggled to concentrate on his words of peace, love and healing, though her tone was so cutting it was hard to ignore.

'She longs for the arms of another.'

Tory confronted the witch on his behalf. 'Our love be eternal, Mahaud. One should not offer views on matters thou could not possibly understand.'

'I understand everything!' she roared, feeling Maelgwn's faith strengthen.

'Then why are you like this?' Tory tried to reason with the old witch, for she truly couldn't fathom why one would choose to be hurtful, it seemed so useless and unnecessary, illogical even. 'You could be beautiful.'

Mahaud roared with laughter, weakened by Tory's concern. 'And thee could be a whore hound to the satanic forces, just look into my eyes, little girl.' The witch stuck out her long tongue and started wriggling it around in an attempt to disgust her.

This was not the prettiest of sights really, and the odour was becoming insufferable. Yet Tory kept her humour. 'Quite frankly, my husband be proving enough of a handful at this time.'

'Well, he's had so much practice. Hast thou any idea how many lovers he had before thee?' The witch turned an eye to catch Maelgwn's reaction, and she felt him again straining to concentrate. 'Did he tell thee about his more debauched activities in Cornwall?' She swung back round to vex him, the groans from the other heads turning into mocking laughter.

Tory blasted out the note of F on her saxophone. Then G, C and by the last note of E-flat, Tory had Mahaud's full attention.

The witch swore and cursed in protest, yet Tory paid her no heed. She repeated the sequence over and over, as the other four intensified their efforts. The crone was in pain, so she changed her form continuously from one vile manifestation to the next in an attempt to thwart the tranquillity they sought to create.

But she was too late. A green mist rose out of the ground all around them. A million tiny lights encompassed the circle, gracing it with their lustre, and the voices of fairy folk sang to the tune that Tory played.

The witch was so weakened by the enchantment that she was obliged to resume her true form, which was nothing more than a dark mist. This was quickly swept away by the swirling beams of light, the witch's evil noise and odour along with it.

Those left in her wake wondered at the spectacle surrounding them. The healing energy that emanated from the etheric matter was so exhilarating it made them tremble, and the scent of spring flowers filled the air.

The Merlin thanked all the elements in turn, the others echoing his appreciation, before he dismissed them and the mist dispersed.

'Brian!' Naomi went racing over to Brockwell, smothering him in kisses. 'Is she gone?'

'Pardon?' Brockwell asked in the old tongue, not understanding a word she'd said.

'What? Speak English, darling,' she said, thinking that he was teasing her.

Brockwell frowned. There must be an easier way of communicating, he thought, resolving, with a shrug, to kiss her.

'Is it over?' Rose asked Myrddin.

The Merlin raised his eyebrows. 'Until such time as humankind hast perfected itself, we shall never see the back of these low-grade beings, I am sad to say. Though Mahaud, as we know her, hast definitely been neutralised.' Myrddin gave Rose a hug of assurance as he escorted her to the house. 'So you can add another to your long list of talents, sister.'

Tory approached Maelgwn and they held each other for some time. It was he who pulled away first, looking to the bloodstained tear in her shirt. He caressed her skin, soft and smooth underneath. 'How, Tory?'

'Taliesin,' she confessed. 'I should have died at Arwystli, but he gave me an immortality potion of the ancients. I found out later.' Tory looked up at him.

'Be there anything else thou hast failed to tell me?' He remained very calm.

'In regard to what?' Tory asked in her sweetest manner.

'Everything, Tory, I want to know everything about thee.'

'Well, be that not the whole idea behind being wed? So we can spend the rest of our lives getting to know each other.'

'But it would suddenly seem that we can expect thy life to be considerably longer than mine.' Maelgwn's voice became more tense, though he tried hard to remain civil.

'Maelgwn, this be exactly why I failed to tell thee. Would thee rather I had died, perhaps?' The events of the past few days piled on top of her and within a second Tory was in tears.

'Nay, of course not.' He took hold of her and squeezed her. 'I would prefer thee had confided in me,' he explained in a softer tone. 'I know I give thee just cause to doubt me at times.'

'Nay, Maelgwn, I never doubted thee.'

'Well, whatever the case may have been, from now on, no more secrets, agreed?'

'Aye.' Tory's crying subsided and she wiped the tears from her face. 'So art thou going to tell me all about thy debauched activities after thee fled thy father's kingdom for Cornwall?'

Maelgwn didn't seem too keen. 'Thou dost not want to know about that.'

'Aye, I do, I want to know everything about thee,' she mimicked him, but Maelgwn was conveniently distracted.

He appeared concerned as he watched something going on beyond Tory in the distance.

'What be wrong?'

'Dost thou think we should tell Naomi that this be Brockwell, not Brian, before he rapes her?'

Tory looked at the pair and laughed. 'Indeed, Brian won't be at all amused.'

Teo woke the next day remembering little of his life since Brian had left Australia, over two years ago. He didn't even know how he'd managed to get to Britain. Brian and Miles had also regained control of themselves by morning. So Brian was there to greet Teo and apologise to him for accusing him; he'd never imagined it would cause such grief.

Teo was so stoked to see both Brian and Tory that he could bear them no ill will. He wanted to hear all about what had transpired while he'd been out of it, so everyone kept him entertained for the rest of that day with their many tales of the weird and wonderful.

Miles still kept a close eye on Teo, but this was not necessary. Teo was his own person again, his beaming expression was evidence of this. As expected, he was a little sad to hear of Tory's marriage. However, he accepted it was his own fault, as he should never have let her go in the first place.

Tory decided to stay with her family for a few more days, as with the chariot she could cheat time a bit. Now that her secret was out in the open, her kin had faith that she would return to them and were not as reluctant to let her go.

The entire clan made the trip to Dinas Emrys, and even Aunt Rose managed the hike to the cave. They were not met by a beast or bells this time, for Myrddin knew his way through the mists well enough. He stopped to speak with particular trees along the way. Tory had half expected that her father would accompany her back to the Dark Age, considering Taliesin's prophecy.

'Oh good heavens, no,' he exclaimed as they entered the cave. 'Although I would dearly love to see my old friend, I have much to do before that time. Our reunion will come in due course and, dear daughter, I do believe you'll be there to witness it,' he announced with a wink of encouragement.

Tory hugged everyone in turn, her father, Aunt Rose, Naomi and Teo, who she thought was not going to let her go at all.

'I have just got you back and now you're leaving me again.'

'*I am coming back*,' she repeated for the fiftieth time.

Brian encouraged his friend to let go, applying a little pressure in the right place, and then took hold of Tory himself. 'Make the world a better place,' he whispered, a lump forming in his throat.

'I'll be back before you know it and we'll work on it together,' she resolved, refusing to get upset.

Brian nodded then took a step back so that Miles might have a moment.

Miles didn't say anything, he just threw his arms out wide in his own endearing fashion and Tory melted into them.

'Words cannot express, Professor, so I will not even try,' she sniffled, releasing him and stepping away. 'I'll be back.' She turned and stepped into the chariot, not sure what to expect. 'Now, how do I drive this thing?'

'As you are familiar with where you are going, just the thought of your destination should be enough,' Myrddin instructed. 'Send Taliesin my highest regards. Tell him all goes splendidly, and to take good care of my treasure until next we meet.'

'I shall.' Tory had one last look at them all. She released a deep sigh as she closed her eyes and her thoughts turned to Maelgwn and Rhun, to the masters and the stones. She concentrated harder, believing nothing had happened, when the cheers of a familiar crowd reached her ears, and Tory opened her eyes to find that she had at last made it home.

Maelgwn lifted her out of the chariot and, after a long kiss, set her down on the ground.

'Sorry to have kept thee all waiting around like this, the twentieth century be hell!'

From the garbled sound of thirteen excited people all talking at her at once came a 'Here, here!' from Brockwell. 'Although the women art mighty fine.'

Katren kicked Brockwell for his observation, as she had her arms full with Rhun.

'But not as fine as here, of course,' he quickly appeased his wife.

Katren handed Tory her child. 'He be sovereign, Tory, in every sense of the word.'

'I know.' Tory smiled, pleased to see her dear friend. 'He takes after his father.' Tory turned to her husband, but the fond exchange was disturbed by Taliesin's incessant chuckling.

'Alright, old man?' Maelgwn asked. 'Doth thou wish to share thy amusement with the rest of us?'

Taliesin, who was so hysterical and exhausted that he could barely move, had somehow managed to drag his near useless carcass into the chariot. 'I shall see thee all back at Aberffraw.' He contained his amusement as he closed his eyes to concentrate. 'In a couple of thousand years.' He burst into laughter once more and vanished without a trace.

'I told thee he would be pleased,' Maelgwn said.

'Come Majesty, tell us everything,' Ione urged her, the others echoing the request. 'We have several hours till sunrise.'

Come first light, they broke camp. Although sorry to part, the masters were all eager to get home to their own estates, kingdoms and kin.

'See thee all in Arwystli on Lughnasa,' Vortipor declared, as he and Cara took their leave to the south-west, towards Dyfed.

'Indeed,' Brockwell confirmed, then turned to Maelgwn. 'Art thou quite sure we cannot tempt thee all to a feast tonight?'

'Any night but tonight, friend.' Maelgwn helped Tory up onto his horse. Rhun was nestled in his pouch, fast asleep for the moment.

'Lughnasa, then,' Brockwell said with a wave, and rode off towards Powys in the west with Katren close behind.

'Ready to go home?' Maelgwn asked.

'Yesterday.' Tory beamed, still unable to believe they were really going home.

So the King led the rest of their band once around the stones, then away to the north-west towards the sweet fairy lands of Gwynedd.

Within moments of Tory vanishing, the spirits of everyone in the cave waned considerably.

'Oh, come on,' Myrddin encouraged them all. 'It's not the end of the world.'

'Yeah, but it's the end of living in Tory's world,' Brian grumbled as he left the room of treasures to trudge back down the stone entrance hall from the chamber. Teo and Miles followed him out, not much happier about the state of affairs.

'Oh ye of little faith.' The Merlin rolled his eyes, as he and Rose fell in behind Naomi.

Both Brian and Miles had their eyes to the ground as they passed through the rock face into the bright daylight.

'No way!' Teo exclaimed, thumping the other two in the shoulder, and they looked up to discover a woman who, judging from her appearance, they could only assume was a goddess.

She was of sturdy build and wore a large sword on her hip. Her attire had a distinctly tribal feel, though it was of pure white. Her long, golden hair fell in thousands of tiny braids, weighted at the ends with ornate silver beads. There was a band of gold around her crown and her waist, and she wore matching silver bands around her upper arms.

'Did you miss me?'

> My name be Tory Alexander
> and my memory burns eternal.
> I have been a traveller
> through the Otherworld,
> through time, reality and dimension,
> I have known no bound.
>
> I have been with the Dragon
> in his lair at Aberffraw.
> I know the strength of his roar,
> the sweet passion of his fire.
> Proud are his people
> and brave are his warriors.
> The Goddess shall evermore sing thy
> praises, Maelgwn of Gwynedd,
> great King among Britons.
>
> I have sought the greater mysteries
> from the wisest of souls.
> Myrddin and Taliesin
> know my plight.
> How wondrous their teachings,
> how widespread their journeys.

Oh for their reunion,
and the sweet purification
of the mother country.
I have seen the mist rising on the land,
I hear the four winds,
seek the four elements,
I follow the phases of the moon and stars.
Messenger and warrior of the Goddess,
I have felt Pan's healing ray,
sent on the aroma of a thousand flowers,
and a million tiny beings of light.

As sure as my name be Tory Alexander,
my quest shall always lead me
in search of the greater truths,
that have been forever lost
in the Dark Age.

BIBLIOGRAPHY

Alcock, Leslie, *Arthur's Britain*, Penguin, London, 1973.

Ashe, Geoffrey, *The Landscape of King Arthur*, Webb & Bower, London, 1987.

Bede, *Ecclesiastical History of the English People*, Penguin, London, 1990.

Berresford Ellis, Peter, *Dictionary of Celtic Mythology*, Constable & Co, London, 1992.

Bletzer, June G, *Encyclopaedic Psychic Dictionary*, Donning Co, Virginia, 1986.

Chadwick, Nora K, *Celtic Britain*, Newcastle Publishing Co, California, 1989.

Coghlam, Ronan, *An Illustrated Encylopaedia of Arthurian Legends*, Element Books, Dorset, 1993.

Devereux, Paul, *Earth Lights Revelation*, Blandford Press, London, 1989.

Devereux, Paul, *Places of Power*, Blandford Press, London, 1990.

Frederic, Louis, *Dictionary of the Martial Arts*, Athlone Press, France, 1991.

Hope, Murry, *Practical Celtic Magic*, Aquarian, London, 1987. *See section on* The Nine Metaphysical Laws.

Maclean, Fitzroy, *A Concise History of Scotland*, Thames & Hudson, London, 1970.

Matthews, Caitlin, *Mabon and the Mysteries of Britain*, Penguin Arkana, London, 1987.

Matthews, C and J, *The Little Book of Celtic Wisdom*, Emement Inc., London, 1993.

Matthews, John, *The Song of Taliesin*, Aquarian, London, 1991.

Matthews, John, *Taliesin*, Aquarian, London, 1991.

Matthews, John, *A Celtic Reader*, Aquarian, London, 1991.

Geoffrey of Monmouth, *The History of the Kings of Britain*, Penguin Classics, London, 1966.

Nennius, *Historia Brittonum*, British American Books, California. [undated]

Roberts, Anthony, *Atlantean Traditions in Ancient Britain*, Rider & Co, London, 1977.

Somerset Fry, P, *Castles of the British Isles*, David & Charles, London, 1990.

Stewart, R J, *The Way of Merlin*, Aquarian, London, 1991.

REFERENCES

The author gratefully acknowledges the use of the following quotations.

The extract from *The Primary Chief Bard* in Part One, page 114 and the *The Chair of Ceridwen* in Part Two, at the top of page 308, are both taken from *Taliesin: Shamanism and the Bardic Mysteries in Britain and Ireland* by John Matthews and are reproduced with the kind permission of The Aquarian Press, HarperCollins*Publishers*, London.

The extract from *Artorius* by John Heath-Stubbs in Part One, page 115 and the extract from *The Chair of Taliesin* in Part Two, page 239, are both taken from *Practical Celtic Magic* by Murry Hope and are reproduced with the kind permission of The Aquarian Press, HarperCollins*Publishers*, London.